The Last Silk Dress

Every   cite-
ment. "   usan
Chilma   remember

They   their
husban   well
with th

"Wel   olph,
"and I   has
time to   can
do, sew

"I w
"I'll
I cou   oom
swam   nnie
standing

"Cor
"Yes   face
toward   true
daughte   ired
sweetly.

You   g inside her   roud
to have   deah
young g

WITHDRAWN

REDWOOD

LIBRARY

Gift of
Cassie Helms

I faced Connie across the room while they all applauded.

Other Bantam Starfire Books you will enjoy

THE SOLID GOLD KID by Norma Fox Mazer and Harry Maze
THE GIRL IN THE BOX by Ouida Sebestyen
WAITING FOR THE RAIN by Sheila Gordon
MORE THAN MEETS THE EYE by Jeanne Betancourt
SAVING LENNY by Margaret Willey
CHEAPER BY THE DOZEN by Frank B. Gilbreth, Jr.,
    and Ernestine Gilbreth Carey
FAREWELL TO MANZANAR by Jeanne Wakatsuki Houston
    and James D. Houston
HEARTS DIVIDED by Cheryl Zach
WINDS OF BETRAYAL by Cheryl Zach

The
Last Silk Dress

ANN RINALDI

BANTAM BOOKS
NEW YORK • TORONTO • LONDON • SYDNEY • AUCKLAND

RL5, IL age 12 and up

*This edition contains the complete text
of the original hardcover edition.*
NOT ONE WORD HAS BEEN OMITTED.

THE LAST SILK DRESS
*A Bantam Book / published by arrangement with
Holiday House, Inc.*

PRINTING HISTORY
Holiday House edition published April 1988
Bantam edition / March 1990

*The Starfire logo is a registered trademark of Bantam Books, a
division of Bantam Doubleday Dell Publishing Group, Inc.
Registered in U.S. Patent and Trademark Office and elsewhere.*

*All rights reserved.
Copyright © 1988 by Ann Rinaldi.
Cover art copyright © 1990 by Lisa Falkenstern.
Library of Congress Catalog Card Number: 87-25128.
No part of this book may be reproduced or transmitted
in any form or by any means, electronic or mechanical,
including photocopying, recording, or by any information
storage and retrieval system, without permission in writing from
the publisher.
For information address: Holiday House, Inc.,
425 Madison Avenue, New York, NY 10017*

*If you purchased this book without a cover you should be aware that this book is stolen
property. It was reported as "unsold and destroyed" to the publisher and neither the
author nor the publisher has received any payment for this "stripped book."*

ISBN 0-553-28315-4

Published simultaneously in the United States and Canada

*Bantam Books are published by Bantam Books, a division of Bantam Doubleday Dell
Publishing Group, Inc. Its trademark, consisting of the words "Bantam Books" and the
portrayal of a rooster, is Registered in U.S. Patent and Trademark Office and in other
countries. Marca Registrada. Bantam Books, 1540 Broadway, New York, New York 10036.*

PRINTED IN THE UNITED STATES OF AMERICA

OPM   10 9 8 7

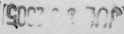

For my son, Ron,
the Military Historian
*(once again for you,
because you are such
an inspiration)*

Contents

AUTHOR'S NOTE   xi

PROLOGUE   1

PART ONE: July 21, 1861   17

PART TWO: January 20, 1862   99

PART THREE: April 5, 1862   163

PART FOUR: June 20, 1862   231

BIBLIOGRAPHY   326

ACKNOWLEDGMENTS   329

. . . The Federals had been using balloons in examining our positions, and we watched with envious eyes their beautiful observations as they floated high up in the air, well out of range of our guns. While we were longing for the balloons that poverty denied us, a genius arose for the occasion and suggested that we send out and gather silk dresses in the Confederacy and make a balloon. It was done, and we soon had a great patch-work ship of many varied hues which was ready for use in the Seven Days' campaign (June 25–July 1, 1862).

We had no gas except in Richmond, and it was the custom to inflate the balloon there, tie it securely to an engine, and run it down the York River Railroad to any point at which we desired to send it up. One day it was on a steamer down on the James River, when the tide went out and left the vessel and balloon high and dry on a bar. The Federals gathered it in, and with it the last silk dress in the Confederacy. This capture was the meanest trick of the war and one that I have never yet forgiven.

—General James Longstreet
Confederate States of America

Author's Note

The letter from Confederate General James Longstreet on the previous page captured my imagination and gave me the idea for this book. I was intrigued by the thought of the women of the Confederacy giving up their last silk dresses for an observation balloon. However, once I started doing research to determine exactly where this happened, the letters from historians all said the same thing: the "silk dress balloon," the subject of Longstreet's letter, was a myth.

How could that be? Why would Longstreet write such a letter? I started doing more research. Reports of Southern observation balloons appeared in the Northern press as early as July 1861, but these were discounted and chalked up to Confederate accounts of those who saw the Northern balloons of Professor Thaddeus Lowe, the famous balloonist for the Union army.

Tom D. Crouch, in his book *The Eagle Aloft, Two Centuries of the Balloon in America,* tells us that the Confederate commanders P. G. T. Beauregard and Joe E. Johnston did have a balloon at their disposal by the end of the summer of 1861. But the origin of this first Southern balloon "remains a mystery."

In his very comprehensive book, Crouch also tells us that the earliest Southern balloon was "a small unmanned signal craft sent aloft from the positions ringing Washington in July, 1861" and another one, this time manned, was "seen rising from Confederate fortifications on Munson's Hill on Sept. 4, 1861."

All these accounts are sketchy. My point is—if some

balloons were a mystery to researchers, why not the silk dress balloon, too?

Crouch states that "by mid April, 1861, the Confederates had their own makeshift balloon but it caused more amusement than fear in Union camps." Crouch cites the best known Confederate balloon as "the silk dress balloon," and describes it as "the patchwork affair that was to become the central element of Southern folklore."

It seems that this cherished story had its roots in that same letter by General Longstreet, published in *Century* magazine in 1886. Crouch and others claim that the truth behind the legend of the silk dress balloon is that it was constructed by Captain Langedon Cheeves in Savannah, Georgia, at Chatham Armory during the spring of 1862. He had bought quantities of multicolored ladies' dress silk in Savannah and Charleston.

It is said that the balloon was used in the Battle of the Seven Days. It was transported down the James on the ship *Teaser* and captured on July 4, 1862, by the Yankees. Many accounts of the Confederate balloon that was stolen from the deck of the *Teaser* by the Yankees do not mention that this is the balloon Cheeves made. Many accounts just say "a Confederate balloon."

It is also stated that a second silk dress balloon was constructed in the Savannah-Charleston area in the summer of 1862. Records do not document the fate of this balloon, Crouch tells us. "Some reports say it was blown loose by a high wind and captured by Union troops and some say it was lost during the Union siege of Charleston in 1863."

I did learn that the war records in the Confederate capital of Richmond were burned when Richmond was taken by the Yankees. Who knows what accounts and stories were lost forever to history?

Then was General Longstreet's letter a piece of fic-

tion? And if so, why did he write it? I decided that if it
was fiction I would take the tale one step further and
create a story of how such a silk dress balloon might
have come into being. I selected Richmond as my
setting because Civil War buffs suggested that if the silk
dresses *were* collected for a balloon, it would have been
there.

My setting, therefore, is painstakingly researched, as
is everything else that happens of historical note in the
time frame of the story: the way the citizens of town
gathered at the Spotswood Hotel to hear news of the
Battle of Manassas (or, as the North referred to it, Bull
Run); the existence of gambling houses in Richmond;
martial law presided over by General John Henry Winder;
the manner in which the wounded were brought into
town after the battles and cared for by the women; the
hospitals that sprung up on every corner. The account of
how the ladies made thirty thousand sandbags in the
basement of St. Paul's is factual, and most of the ladies
mentioned, with the exception of Susan and Connie and
Mrs. Turnstable, actually lived in Richmond at the time.

The burial of former president John Tyler and the way
the Confederate cabinet argued over what flag to put on
his casket is factual, as is General Winder's price-fixing
in town and the way the people left church and brought
food to the soldiers passing through on the trains. The
incident in which the Washington Artillery of New
Orleans comes to Susan's house to salute her for making their flag is based on a similar incident from the
book *Heroines of Dixie, Spring of High Hopes*, edited
by Katharine M. Jones, in which Constance Cary writes
of such an honor being bestowed upon her by the
Washington Artillery of New Orleans.

The account given by Timothy Tobias Collier of his
experiences as an artist for *Harper's Weekly*, when he is
accosted by the Vigilance Committee, is based on a

similar account in *Civil War Times Illustrated,* August 1967—"As the Civil War Artist Saw Himself" by Frederic Ray.

The details about the Confederate "ironsides," the *Virginia,* are factual, as is the arrival of General "Jeb" Stuart's cavalry in Richmond on the day Susan and her mother meet Lucien in the lawyer's office.

Against the dramatic background of war, in which a weary city tried to stay alive and its people bravely carried on, I wove my fictional story of Susan, her brother Lucien and the events that befell them.

Susan and all her family, Connie and Kenneth, Timothy Tobias Collier, Sarah and Nate, Fanny, the girls at Miss Lulie's, Detective Simkins and Tom McPherson are all fictional characters. Mrs. Harrold, who lived next door to the Chilmarks, really did "take in privates." Mrs. Wigfall really did exist, although I have used her and her husband for my own purposes in the book, as I did Lieutenant Hotchkiss (who was on General Stonewall Jackson's staff) and Mayor Joseph Mayo.

I write this to clarify how I played my fictional story against a factual background. But the one question remains: Was there really a silk dress balloon? I like to think there was; that General Longstreet wrote the truth in his letter. After all, the war records in Richmond *were* destroyed by the Confederacy before the town was taken. And even the historians tell us that the origins of one or two Southern balloons "remain a mystery."

It was only one step further in my mind, after I researched the fascinating and colorful town of Richmond, to imagine . . . if the ladies of the Confederacy really did give their last silk dresses to make a balloon which was, in the end, stolen by the Yankees . . . it might have happened like this. . . .

PROLOGUE

Whenever I think of my father, which is very often, I remember the day of the riot at Tredegar Iron Works. And I think of the way he got hit with the rock and how his face bled. That is the memory that will always come to my mind first, I suppose, when I think of my father.

For me that was the moment the war started. Oh, I didn't know it then. I was at Tredegar for an outing that bright, warm thirteenth of April 1861. Fort Sumter had been fired upon the day before, and my father had come home for his noon meal and said that Mr. Anderson, who owned part of Tredegar, was organizing a demonstration. And I'd begged to be allowed to go back with him. So he took me.

It was only to be a parade, after all, but I can close my eyes and in a moment hear the ugly chanting of the mob as it came down the street. It was supposed to be an orderly procession, but the people were already loudly disorganized. They were singing the "Marseillaise." It was an angry singing and the crowd lunged forward as if borne on hundreds of caterpillar legs.

I was on a wooden platform that had been hastily erected in front of Tredegar with Mr. Anderson; my father, who was his chief engineer; and a reporter from the *Richmond Dispatch*. The very platform seemed to tremble as the mob approached, waving its fists and singing and yelling.

"Gentlemen." Mr. Anderson held up his hand.

"Ladies," for there were some amongst them who were pretending to be ladies, too.

"Secession!" they were yelling. "We want secession!" They made a chant of it, and it echoed off the buildings of Tredegar. For a full three minutes they chanted as Mr. Anderson held up both arms to quiet them.

"You shall have secession! I have been to the capitol to see the governor! He informed me of his determination to support the Union, but . . ."

They booed loudly. They hissed.

"You've got to quiet them, Joe," I heard my father say to Mr. Anderson. "They're getting ugly."

Again Mr. Anderson held up both arms. "If you will just listen to me."

"We're not listening to any speeches," a man from the middle of the mob yelled. "We've waited long enough. The Confederacy is being formed! We want to be part of it!"

A lusty cheer rose from the mob's midst. In the distance a cannon fired, echoing off the Tredegar buildings. Someone threw a rock which skidded across the platform.

"Susan," my father yelled to me, "go inside."

But I stood rooted to the spot.

"On to the capitol!" someone yelled. And the cry was taken up like a banner. The crowd surged forward, bumping against the platform, which shook under me. In the next moment some of the people were rushing across it, and now it trembled and creaked under their weight. I was pushed backward against the front of the building. And for a moment I thought, *I am going to be crushed. I am going to be trampled to death.*

"Watch out, little girl!" someone yelled in my ear. My bonnet strings were pulled roughly and the bonnet yanked off my head. Someone else gave me a push, and I landed against the brick wall of the building.

"Susan!" I could hear my father but I could not see him. I held my breath and flattened myself against the building while the frenzied souls rushed by.

"Let's have order," I heard Mr. Anderson yelling. "We've got to keep it orderly!"

"Susan!" I heard my father again. I closed my eyes. I heard a rip and looked down to see my dress torn near the hem. *I am going to be killed,* I thought. I remember thinking it was all a mistake. I wasn't supposed to be killed today. I only came with my father to see a parade.

"The flag!" someone was yelling. "Tear it down!"

Incredibly, a man was climbing the stonework of the building right over me. His boot got a foothold just above my head, slipped and jammed down on my shoulder. I cried out in pain and gripped my shoulder, but I could not move because of the onslaught of bodies still rushing past.

"Susan! Stay there, Susan! Don't move!" I saw my father's face in the crowd. He was trying to push toward me, but he couldn't get through. It was like a nightmare, suddenly, one of those dreams from which you wake and find it was too real.

"The Stars and Bars!" the crowd was yelling. "Raise the Stars and Bars!"

The crowd slowed in its mad stampede to mill about and look up as the Stars and Bars, the new flag of the Confederacy, was raised above the front doors of Tredegar Iron Works. I took advantage of the lull to push through to my father. I felt his warm strong hand in mine, saw the tears in his eyes as he too looked up to see the Stars and Bars floating in the fine April breeze.

The crowd cheered lustily. Hats were flung in the air. And the Stars and Stripes hurtled gently to the ground.

It landed a few feet away from us on the platform. And then it happened.

My father released my hand and went over to pick up the Stars and Stripes. And as he did, the rock hit him. I saw him get up with the flag under his arm, saw him reel from the blow, saw the rock hit the platform and then watched in horror as the blood trickled from the side of his face.

"Daddy!" I screamed.

"On to the capitol!" The mob took up the chant again. Desperately, in spite of the pain in my shoulder, I fought my way through to my father, who was standing there getting pushed as the crowd hurried past.

"Daddy, are you all right?"

"Of course, Susan," he said. He put his hand to the side of his face, took it away, saw the blood and smiled. "Well," he said, "I believe I'm the first casualty in Richmond, of the war."

"Come on, Daddy." I grabbed his hand and pushed hard. I fought my way through the press of bodies. It was like swimming against the waves as I'd done when I'd been in Charleston while visiting my mama's family. I heard my dress rip again. Someone stepped on my foot. I held my breath and plunged through, holding my father's hand. I felt his strong arm around my shoulder as we made our way toward the front doors of Tredegar. Then, miraculously, my father got the doors open, and we were inside.

"Are you all right, Susan?"

"I'm fine, Daddy. A bit mussed, that's all. What about you?"

He had taken out his handkerchief and was patting the side of his face. "I'll be all right. It's just a scratch."

"It's more than a scratch! Look how you're bleeding."

"It's nothing. Come along. Let's go upstairs to my office. We'll wait this thing out."

Upstairs in his office he held the handkerchief to his face. "I never should have brought you. I told Joe it might turn out like this. He wanted to cause excitement among the people, he said. Well, he's got all the excitement he can handle now."

"Daddy, I'm worried about you. Look at your face."

"It's nothing, Susan!" He walked to the window and stood gazing out on the crowd below. I followed him. When I looked to see if the bleeding had stopped, I saw unchecked tears on his face.

"You're crying, Daddy."

"Am I?" He turned from the window and brushed the tears aside. The flag was still bundled under one arm. "I suppose I am." He hugged me, and I caught the familiar fragrance of his tobacco—Wedding Cake it was called—all mixed in with the smell of the soap he used. He stood in the center of the room, smiling at me. "Your mother will disown me for bringing you here today."

That's what he was worried about. Mama. That's what he always worried about. "She doesn't have to know what happened," I said.

His smile deepened. "Just look at yourself, Susan."

I nodded, looking down at my torn dress. "I hate this dress anyway. Mama makes me dress too childish. I'm glad it's torn."

"You look fine to me."

"Well, I'm not. I'm more grown up than she lets me look. I . . ."

He was smiling at me knowingly. "Don't be in such a rush to grow up, Susan," he said. "I don't think your mother could accept that right now. It only means she's getting older."

"Well, it isn't fair that I have to dress so childishly, Daddy. Connie doesn't have the shape I have and her mama doesn't dress her like this."

"I understand," he said gravely, "but I'd like you to stay my little girl a little while longer."

He could always win me over like that. "I'll sneak in the back way when I get home. Rhody will sew the dress for me. And Mama will never know what happened."

"I doubt that. Your mother, Susan, has the news gathering abilities of the best reporter in this city. She'll hear what happened. Depend on it. I saw that big ape out there who hit you with his boot as he climbed the wall to hoist the flag. Did he hurt you?" He reached out and touched my shoulder and I winced. "Move your arm," he directed.

I flexed it in a circular motion.

"Nothing broken," he mused, "but you'd better have a hot bath when you get home. Well," he sighed, "they've done it now. We'll have secession all right. Richmonders have waited long enough for it." He went to his desk, took out a bottle of brandy and poured some into a glass. He drank the brandy, set the glass down, then went to shut the windows, sealing out the world.

He still had the flag under his arm.

"Don't you want to do something with that flag, Daddy?" I asked.

He looked down, remembering it then. "The flag, yes."

I could tell it meant a lot to him. But that didn't surprise me. He had gone to West Point, but had always hated the army after he'd graduated and served in it. He said he wasn't aggressive enough for command. But he had a belief in Country. These past months, whenever talk of secession had come up, he'd fallen strangely silent.

I went to him. "Let's fold the flag," I said.

He nodded, and we did so. "Now, what shall I do with it?" he wondered aloud. "I suppose we won't be needing it around here for a while." We looked at each other, and he went to his desk, pulled out a drawer and put the flag in it.

"We may never need it around here again, hey, Susan?" He smiled at me, and I was reminded of how I loved the way his eyes crinkled at the corners, the way his hair was going gray where it fluffed around his ears. My father was a good-looking man with an intelligent light in his eyes that drew people toward him. At forty-eight the lines in his face were friendly, not bitter. I knew his every expression, his every mood, for he was my whole world.

The reason for that was simple. I was his only child left at home. And my mama was crazy. Oh, not stark raving crazy, but walking-around-capable-of-holding-her-own crazy. She had been that way for as long as I could remember. And everyone knew it.

"And how is your mama today?" people would inquire of me. Oh, she is just fine, I would say. And they would smile. Poor little girl, that's what they thought of me. The fine ladies of Richmond whispered about Mama behind her back, even while they made halfhearted attempts to put up with her. "Crazy," they would say. "Puts on airs because she comes from that fine plantation near Charleston where her daddy owned over a hundred nigras. Well, a lot of good it all did her when she took that trip down there with that beautiful daughter of hers, and the child caught the yellow fever and died. Went against her husband's wishes going down there like that. Good thing he didn't let her take the boy or she'd have lost him too.''

Many of the ladies in Richmond remembered my sister Isabel, who had died at the age of four, before I was born. Isabel, the beautiful golden-haired daughter of Mama's. The one I could never live up to.

"I want to talk to you, Susan.''

I pulled myself to attention. Daddy was having another brandy, sitting behind his desk. "Sit down,'' he said.

He looked so serious, I sat. Outside, the recently made Tredegar cannon boomed, reverberating against the windows.

"If a man raises his hand against the Constitution of the United States, he is not a reliable man, Susan,'' he said. "And he will not be a reliable man for any other government. Do you understand?''

I did not, but I lied and said yes. I wanted to understand his anguish because I knew that whatever was bothering him today was important to him.

"There is strength in union, Susan. We were a band of brothers before this. Now we are just a band.''

Cannon boomed again. "I'm confusing you,'' he said.

I smiled at him.

"It's all right. These are confusing times. And I never put my feelings about this secession business into words for you before. We're leaving the Union, Susan. Virginia is leaving the Union. What you've heard is that it's a revolution like we had back in 1776.''

"Isn't it?''

"I don't know, Susan. I don't know what it is. I may never know. All I am sure of is that it's wrong to break up the Union. And I haven't figured out yet how I shall tear off parts of myself and say this part is for America and this part is for Virginia.''

He looked so sad that I wished Fort Sumter had never been fired upon by the South. I wished the whole thing had never started.

"In January," he recited quietly, "cannonballs cast for both North and South lay side by side on the floor of Tredegar foundries. I saw them with my own eyes." He patted the side of his face with the handkerchief. The gash had stopped bleeding, but the area around it was getting swollen and ugly. "Anderson and his partners knew war was coming. But they needed every dollar they could scrape up to get out of financial difficulties. They found a way of breaking off pieces of themselves, you see."

I started to speak but thought better of it.

"What do you think that crowd out there would do if they knew about our Northern customers here at Tredegar, Susan?"

"I think they'd storm the building," I said.

He smiled. "Right. But war makes good business, Susan. It will bring in a lot of money. Still, I shouldn't be burdening you with this. You're just a child."

"I'm fourteen and I understand," I said.

"I know you do. You always were intelligent. Too bad you weren't born a boy. You deserve to go to the university. Are you still running off from your mother and hiding in your brother's room and reading his books?"

I blushed. "Who told you that, Daddy?"

"Rhody. Don't worry. Your secret is safe with me. We have to confide in each other these days." He sighed. "Speaking of your brother, which I seldom if ever do, I've been thinking of him more and more these days. War comes and a man thinks of his son."

I waited. I held my breath. Rarely, if ever, did he speak to me of Lucien.

"Your brother is an abolitionist. He doesn't believe in slavery. Did I ever tell you that, Susan?"

"You never told me anything about him, Daddy."

He nodded gravely. "Do you remember anything about him at all?"

I chose my words carefully. "When he used to come home from college he was nice to me. He brought me things. He used to . . . put me up in front of him on his horse and take me for rides."

He raised his eyes to look at me. "What else?"

But he knew. And he was waiting for me to say it. "You had an awful fight with him. I remember you shouting at each other. A long time ago, when I was about seven. And then he left."

"Yes," he mused, "he left." He sighed deeply, and when he spoke his voice was raspy. "He's still in Richmond, you know."

"Yes, Daddy, I know. All the ladies in Mama's circle gossip about him and the unforgivable things he does to make a living."

He smiled sadly. "I don't think he's as notorious as all that, Susan. The ladies your mama is trying to impress would gossip about anything."

"Have you seen him, Daddy?"

"Only once in seven years. A mistake." He nodded sadly. "I shouldn't have tried to see him. It went badly. I made a lot of mistakes with your brother. I'm not proud of them. If . . . things had been different I would have him here now to discuss my views with. Not that you aren't doing fine. Yes, just fine." He poured himself another brandy.

"Daddy, are you sure you're all right?"

"I'm as all right as a man can be just having seen the flag of his country torn down. Look, I'm going to confide in you. I expect you'll keep my confidence."

"Of course, Daddy."

A band struck up outside, and we listened for a moment to the bright and sassy music. Then he went on. "A good portion of my money is in banks in Liverpool, England. I think we're on a fool's errand here in the South with this war, Susan. My heart is with the Union. But this is the only time you'll hear me say it. When we walk out of this office today, I am a true Southerner. Does that seem hypocritical to you?"

"You could never be hypocritical, Daddy."

He smiled. "I shall continue to work for the Confederacy through my job here. I owe Mr. Anderson for his faith in me. I owe Virginia. And I owe your mother, who is a staunch Confederate. Life has broken her heart too many times. I will not add to her heartache. But in the practical matters of money, I'm betting on the North. That way my family won't be bankrupt when this is over."

I nodded. My father had always been a shrewd businessman so this meant little to me.

"One more thing, Susan. I've been watching you. You love the Cause, don't you?"

I blushed. "I just wish Mama would let me do more for it, that's all."

"You want to please her." He sighed. "I know the feeling. I'm sorry for the way your mother is, Susan. I know it's difficult for you. You've taken the brunt of it with her. She can't help the way she is. The three children she lost, the trouble with Lucien..." He waved off those thoughts. "And she never did like living here in Richmond. Perhaps I shouldn't have brought her this far north. They never quite accepted her here. And there have been"—he blushed somewhat—"other difficulties in our marriage which I cannot discuss with you. I know it seems to you that she just won't be pleased sometimes. Give her time. With the war coming I'm sure you'll be drawn closer together. Now there is something else." He cleared his throat.

"Yes, Daddy?"

"I know that in the months to come, you'll have questions. About the war. You say you love the Cause. Right now to you it's parades and bright music and parties and speeches and songs. But it's more than that. Much more. Our life is going to change, Susan. I know that in the months to come you'll have questions about the war if you're any daughter of mine. I don't know if I'll be here to answer them for you."

"You mean you're going away again?" I felt a sense of alarm. "You've traveled so much for Mr. Anderson. Just in this past year you went North. And in November you went to Harpers Ferry. And in February to Charleston!"

"I had to go North to the armories to get patterns and drawings for muskets, Susan. Before the Republicans took over the War Department in Washington. I did the same thing in Harpers Ferry. And in February I had to confer with Governor Pickens in Charleston about the ammunition needs of the Southern batteries. I must go where my job sends me. That's why I'm talking to you like this. Because I know you're bright and you'll have questions about the war. And when that time comes I want you to do what you think, in your heart, is right."

We looked at each other. What was he saying? "Yes, Daddy," I said.

"Listen to me carefully, Susan. If this time ever comes—and you'll know it when it does—do what you think is right. Even if it hurts those around you. Those you love. That is the most difficult thing we must ever learn to do. Do you understand what I am saying, Susan?"

"I think so, Daddy."

"Remember that I told you this. When your brother left, it was because of something I did to please your mother. We can't do things to please others, Susan. Not if we don't think what we are doing is right. Now, do you understand?"

"Yes, Daddy," I breathed.

"Susan, don't cry."

"I can't help it. I don't like seeing you like this."

"I know. But promise me you'll remember what I told you here today."

"I promise, Daddy."

"Good." He got up. "Look, some people have started to light torches for the orderly procession to the capitol. Hear that? The church bells are ringing."

I went to stand beside him at the window, and we listened to Richmond's bells and watched an orderly crowd assemble. Afterward we went downstairs to our carriage. On the way home he told me stories about when he was at West Point. He knew I loved those stories. I had heard them dozens of times, as other children had heard fairy tales.

Whenever I remember my father, I think of how he was that day at Tredegar Iron Works, the day after the war started when he got hit with the rock picking up the American flag. The day he told me to do what I thought in my heart was right, when the time came that I must do it. Even though it hurt those I loved. That, I think, is how I shall always remember him.

PART ONE

July 21, 1861

Chapter One

My mother wanted to see me.

Rhody stood in the doorway of the parlor where I was doing my sewing and made her announcement with as much resignation as if she were telling me that the Yankees were marching into Richmond.

"Your mama say now, Miz Susan."

"I'll be there, Rhody."

I made some final stitches in the buttonhole of the shirt I was sewing for the army. I was not good at buttonholes. I knew that. My stitches were hopelessly uneven but I didn't care. Oh, I didn't mind sewing for the army but it would have been so much nicer if Mama had let me join one of the many sewing circles that had sprung up in town. My friend Connie belonged to one, and she said the chatter and gossip flew as fast as the ladies' needles. But of course that was what Mama was trying to keep me away from. The gossip. Especially now that the war had started and the Confederate army had its forces assembled around Richmond. Because feelings were running high and many of the ladies of Richmond were making remarks about my brother Lucien, who had refused to join the army.

Something crashed at the end of the house where the kitchen was, and I heard Mama scolding Wilium, Rhody's twelve-year-old son.

"You call this LETTUCE? The trouble with you is that you wouldn't know anything decent if you saw it!"

"No, ma'am," came Wilium's reply. "I mean yes, ma'am. I gots the best they had."

"The best they had went to the Spotswood Hotel. To Varina Davis's table."

"Yes, ma'am. Who dat Varina Davis?"

"You know who she is! She's the wife of the president of the Confederacy. And look at this asparagus! It isn't fit for pigs! I could have sent a pig out, and he wouldn't have settled for this!"

I saw Rhody raise her chin as the outburst went on, increasing in intensity. I knew how she must be hurting. Wilium was none too bright. Some people said he was half-witted. But I knew him better than that. I knew he only appeared to be half-witted when it served his own purposes, but that at times he displayed a brain as good as the next person and that with some schooling he would have been absolutely smart.

Wilium was all Rhody had, and she loved him. Her husband died two years after Wilium was born, of old injuries inflicted by his master. She used to have Sallie, her sister Lettie's daughter. I am told Lettie, five years younger than Rhody, had been a tall, honey-colored raving beauty in our household. She'd run off right after Sallie was born. Rhody had raised Sallie like her own. But then one day Sallie ran away too. It was around the same time that my brother Lucien left, but I didn't dare ask my father about that. For a long time nobody talked about Sallie. And then a few years ago the letters started coming from her in Philadelphia. Two a year they came, addressed to Rhody.

"Up North, Rhody, they call old Abraham Lincoln's wife a hellcat," I said.

"What's dat got to do with the fact that your mama's waitin'?"

"All the ladies in Mama's circle take great pleasure

knowing that the president they have up North has a hellcat for a wife, Rhody.''

She stood there, arms folded across her bosom. "Do they now?" She knew what was coming. Her eyes narrowed.

"Yes. And you know something else? Some of them say my mama's a hellcat too."

"You don't be talkin' dat way 'bout your mama now. No matter what the fine ladies of Richmond say. She's still your mama."

"I know, Rhody." I flushed under her accusing gaze. "But I just wish she could be a little nicer sometimes. Doesn't it seem to you, Rhody, that she's getting into her rages more and more often these days?"

She eyed me impassively. "Seems to me you oughta get up offa dat chair before she brings her rage in here."

"Just let me finish this old buttonhole."

She scowled, peering down at my work. "Those stitches is uneven."

"I don't care."

"You'll care if'n your mama sees 'em."

I stitched vehemently. "At fourteen, Rhody, a girl ought to be allowed to do more for the Cause than sit alone in the parlor every morning and stitch buttonholes, what with war brewing all around and nobody knowing when the Yankees will get to Richmond."

"Ain't no Yankees comin' to Richmond far as I kin see."

"A girl should at least be allowed to attend one of the sewing circles. Mama and Mrs. Harrold next door go every day."

"Your mama has good reason for not wantin' you to go."

"She has not! I wasn't even allowed to go to the station when the citizens of Richmond brought food to the soldiers when the trains came through. I'm not allowed to do anything. I might as well be dead.''

"You gonna be if'n you don't come along this minute."

"All right, I'm coming!"

The windows in the room were open because the temperature was climbing. It would reach ninety before the day was over. From the street outside I heard a lot of commotion. "What's going on, Rhody?"

We lived at Court End, a usually quiet and always elegant section of town. But now the street was alive with noise and people. "Rhody, what is it?" I ran to the window, but she blocked my view with her ample body, after closing the inner panels of lace curtain behind her.

"Miz Susan, I don't wanna deal wif your mama if'n you don't get yourself in that kitchen right now. My Wilium's takin' the brunt of it.''

"Wilium doesn't mind. He's a dear and he's used to her.''

"That may be so. But she don't get no better when she's ignored.''

"Why are there so many people in the street?''

"Cause o' the battle.''

"You mean they've started? At Manassas? Is there news?''

"Couldn't wait to start, it 'pears to me. Couldn't wait to start killin'.''

"Rhody, you know why. I explained it to you. We had to keep Manassas Gap open so the railroad could continue running east and west. Why, everyone's been on pins and needles trying to figure out whether the Federals would attack at Harpers Ferry or at Richmond. What have you heard, Rhody?''

She shrugged. "I hear at the market dat they be fightin' at that Manassas place since six this mornin'. I hear that people be congregatin' at the Spotswood to get news of the wounded.''

"Then I must go.''

"You ain't goin' nowhere.''

"I have to! Constance's brother is at Manassas. Why Kenneth was practically a beau of mine. You know how many dances he escorted me to. And Connie is my best friend. Won't you tell Mama you can't find me?''

"You ain't goin' to no hotel, Miz Susan. Your mama told you don't go out alone. The streets ain't what they used to be in this town with all those strange soldiers and pickpockets and pernicious characters hangin' round.''

"All the soldiers are at Manassas, Rhody. That's how much you know!''

"I knows you'll be in trouble if'n you go outta this house.''

Across the Persian carpet we eyed each other. "You know how I go out, Rhody. So you know it'll be all right.''

She shook her head vehemently. "No, no, uh-uh, no. What you do is bad, Miz Susan. And I can't let you do it. You got nobody out there fightin' that you gotta run off to the Spotswood.''

She was right about that. I didn't. My father was at the Gosport Navy Yard in Norfolk, working on the raised hulk of the Yankee ship *Merrimack*. The Yankees had set fire to the ship when the Confederates took over the Norfolk Navy Yard in April. At the end of June my father had left for Norfolk to help turn the *Merrimack* into a great fighting ship for the Confederacy. They were rechristening it the *Virginia*.

Oh, I was proud of the work he was doing but I missed him dearly. He was the only one who could stand between me and my mother's wrath, which asserted itself whenever things didn't go right in her world. I

was tired of him being away from home, leaving me
with Mama's tirades.

"Rhody, I just can't face Mama today and that's it."
I stamped my foot. "Make some excuse for me."

I heard footsteps in the hall. Mama! I looked around
the parlor desperately. At the other end were three
ceiling-to-floor windows that formed a half circle, jut-
ting out over the garden. To go out, all one had to do
was raise the bottom sash. I ran to Rhody, hugged her
and dashed across the room. I raised the bottom sash of
the middle window and disappeared into the July sunlight.

From the corner of my eye as I ran, I saw a flash of
lilac gown. I heard a shrill voice float out on the
summer air.

"I'm late already for my sewing circle, Rhody!
Rhody, there you are! Didn't you hear me talking to
you? Where is she? Rhody, if you're covering up for her
again! Where is that little Yankee brat?"

It was simple enough to get back into the house
again, and I slipped up the servants' stairway. Persian
carpets muffled my footsteps in the second-story hall.
Then I ran up more steps to the third floor. The
doorknob of the room at the end of the passage turned
easily, and I went in.

It was dark, but I was accustomed to that. The velvet
curtains were drawn against the July sunshine and only
a slim slant of light cut across the dimness. I plopped
myself in the middle of the bed, dwarfed by the huge
carved headboard, and surveyed the room. Dust moats
floated in the air in the beam of sunshine. In the corner,
books and maps were piled on the desk. I was familiar
with them all. Books lined the wall shelves also. I sat
on the bed, my heart pounding, smiling in satisfaction
as I heard my mother's voice, dimly, far below.

It was hot in here, stifling. I got up and opened the windows, pushing aside the velvet curtains. There, that was a lot better. I knew the room so well, I did not need light. This was where I hid whenever I wanted to get away from my mother's rages. I felt at home in the familiar mustiness.

This was Lucien's room.

My strange brother, whom I knew only from the contents of the room. The many books on history, mathematics, science and law, the maps of the James and York rivers, with his initials L.D.C.—Lucien Dobson Chilmark—in the corners. He had drawn all the maps and marked the little coves and inlets where the fishing and hunting and trapping were best.

I knew he had done a lot of fishing and hunting as a boy as well as the obligatory riding and shooting that were done by every Southern gentleman. The books were all from the University of Virginia Military School, where he'd gone to college.

What I knew about him came from two sources—the half-understood contents of this musty room, and Mama's reports about what the ladies of Richmond were saying about him these days.

He lives in Rocketts, they said, around by the wharves, doing shameful things to make a living. I heard Mama tell Rhody that he was disgracing himself and all of us because he was not a true son of the Confederacy, fighting the war.

One day Mama came home from her sewing circle to say someone had told her Lucien was making money by selling food in Richmond marketplaces at inflated prices. He hunted ducks and fished for oysters and terrapin "to fill the stomachs of the congressional and military folk who have surged into our city, placing a strain on our resources," Mama moaned.

But the best time was when she told Rhody, in an absolute frenzy, that Lucien had been seen in a brothel in town, that he probably owned part of it.

"What's a brothel?" I asked Rhody.

"You never mind now, it ain't nuthin' good," was all Rhody would say. So I asked Connie, who knows such things because she is so close to Kenneth. And I found out that it's like the house on Cary Street, the place with the huge mahogany door with the brass knocker. Connie and I were walking by one day and the door opened and we saw the madam wearing an ornate dress with a genuine emerald necklace. In the middle of the day!

That's what a brothel is. A place where loose women give their favors to men for money. What had Lucien been doing there? I didn't dare imagine. Did he really own part of the place? And he an abolitionist, too! He was steadily growing in fascination for me. And I was starting to feel a sense of kinship with him, if only for one reason.

My mama hated him more than she hated me.

But enough time wasting! I closed the door of the room and went to the cherry highboy. Inside I knew where the items were that I was after—the old trousers, the shirt and the waistcoat. Expertly, for I had done this before, I unbuckled the belt of my dress, undid the many buttons on the bodice, and slipped out of it. Next I took off my petticoats, then I stepped into the trousers. They must have been worn by Lucien when he was a boyish sixteen, because I could make them fit by tying the belt of my dress around the waist.

I was narrow in the waist, which was a matter of pride with me. So many of the girls I went to Miss Pegram's with were chunky. And others had to stuff handkerchiefs in their bosom to make their dresses fit properly. I didn't have to do that. Mama, in one of her kinder moments, admitted that my face had what she called "a substantial beauty." My hair was shoulder length, dark, curly and shining, but I knew Mama would have liked me better if I were blond, like the adored Isabel had been. For that reason I always felt as if I could never measure up to her expectations. Was that why she refused to acknowledge that I had a good shape? Or was it because, as Daddy said, she couldn't bear the fact that I was growing up since it meant she was getting older?

Well, I couldn't help that. I was growing up. Mama couldn't deny it much longer. Rhody had told me I had well-rounded shoulders and that my bosom "wuz jus' right for a girl your age." And that by the time I was sixteen the boys would be "buzzin' round like bees at a barbecue."

I don't know what Mama was worried about anyway. I could never compete with her. She was blond and slender with perfect skin and a well-proportioned body. The men had buzzed around her all her life, like bees around a barbecue.

I put on the old shirt of Lucien's. Then the waistcoat. The shirt was loose enough to conceal the fact that I wasn't a boy. I reached for the familiar pair of old boots. They fit well with copies of the *Richmond Dispatch* stuffed in the toes. I preferred to use the *Dispatch*, which had advocated secession after many soul-searching editorials. When I couldn't get that I used the *Enquirer.* That's the Democratic Bible in town and Mama loves it. She won't allow the *Examiner* in the house. It's a secessionist paper, all right, but it criticizes everything President Jefferson Davis does.

Then I pulled the band off my head and stuffed my shoulder-length hair up under an old soft slouch gray hat. The disguise served me well. I felt comfortable in it.

The house was quiet. I went back down the servants'

stairway where I stood listening. No sound came from the kitchen. From the front of the house I heard Rhody carrying on a one-way conversation with herself. I mustn't let her see me. She would try to keep me from going out like this. Nervously I fingered the cuff of the shirt where the initials L.D.C. were embroidered in blue. Mama must have left for her sewing circle. I crept through the empty kitchen where pots of food were simmering on the stove. Mama was entertaining the Wigfalls for supper. I grabbed an apple from the table and went out the back door and through the kitchen garden, where I passed a stunned Wilium.

"Damn!" he said.

"You tell, Wilium, you dare tell and . . . and I'll let Rhody know you were out in the streets with the Cats the other day!"

Cats was the name for the gangs of boys who roamed Richmond's streets. Wilium nodded solemnly, his eyes wide with amazement. Could I trust him? I didn't know. But it was too late now. I ran into the street.

Chapter Two

I had to walk two blocks west and five south to get to the Spotswood, but I didn't mind. I munched my apple as I walked, knowing I was just a blur of gray in the busy city. I was like any one of the males hurrying to and fro without uniform or arms, but with a definite sense of purpose.

In boy's clothing I was free. I was too young to be in uniform, and since no one would recognize me as Susan

Dobson Chilmark, I was not a target for taunts because my brother was not quite the flower of Southern manhood he was supposed to be, fighting for the Cause. So far Mama had managed to protect me from those insults but I couldn't stay shut up in the house forever. So I had started going out in Lucien's clothes after my father left in June.

I'd had some fine adventures, wearing them. I'd been to market to hear the gossip, I'd been to the Kanawha Canal bank where freight and passenger boats left for as far west as Lynchburg, and one fine day I'd even walked to the Confederate Navy Yard in Rocketts. And I'd looked at the faces of the men around the docks, wondering which one of them was Lucien. The total sense of freedom I got from wearing the clothes elated me. Rhody had been right, however. Richmond had changed when it became the Confederate capital in May. Women didn't walk alone on the streets anymore.

There was a time when Connie and I could wander about at will; we'd go for hair ribbons to Anderson, Green and Haws on Main Street or to Adie and Grey's Apothecary for headache powders for Mama. Then we'd stop to browse amongst the books at J. W. Randolph's. Or go to Pizzini's for ice cream. But now Richmond was a great camp. The trains brought Southern men in all kinds of uniforms, there were training camps all over the city, and many of the troops were lawless. The soldiers, be they Georgians in butternut or Alabamians in blue, thought that wearing uniforms entitled them to say anything they wanted to a pretty girl.

No doubt this was what Mama had in mind, too, when she forbade me to go out. But she wouldn't say it. Nor would she admit she didn't want me exposed to gossip or insults. Instead she called me a Yankee brat.

She insulted me, saying I was atrocious at sewing and in general, disorganized, undisciplined and impossible.

The street in front of the Spotswood was mobbed with people of every description. I made my way through the crowd onto the verandah that ran the length of the five-story hotel and slipped through the front doors. The lobby was ablaze with lights, even in mid-day. For a moment I was blinded by the scene—the crowds of people milling about, the smoke-filled air, the waiters in fancy getups rushing to and fro with trays of drinks from the famous Spotswood Bar, the confusion and the noise.

Almost immediately I spied a group of ladies whose menfolk were fighting at Manassas. Among them were Connie and her mother, Mrs. Turnstable. I couldn't approach them. I couldn't make myself visible to anyone. The way I was dressed, like a street urchin, I'd be thrown right out. So I hid behind an ornate pillar and whispered to attract Connie's attention. It took several tries, but she turned and saw me.

Her eyes widened. Connie knew of my dressing in boy's clothing. She was never adventurous enough to try such a thing herself, but I knew she secretly admired me for it.

"What?" She edged away from her mother and whispered it.

"Meet me in the alcove behind the stairway."

She nodded and I darted off. The alcove was away from the mainstream of activity, near the kitchen in back. In a few minutes Connie appeared.

"Have you taken leave of your senses, coming here like this? If anyone sees you, you'll be in real trouble."

"I had to come and find out. Is Kenneth safe?"

"We don't know yet. It's too soon. But it's so awful!

Mama's almost out of her head. Oh, Susan, I can't bear the idea of Kenneth being out there!''

I couldn't either. When I thought of dear Kenneth with his laughing blue eyes, the smile that lit up his whole being, and the way he'd been part beau and part brother to me, I wanted to die. "Why do you think I'm here, Connie?" I said.

"Mama says we'll stay until the last list of wounded comes in by telegraph. Manassas is only twenty-five miles south of Washington, Susan, and we should have word soon. Oh, Susan, what are we going to do? There's such a pall over everything!''

I hugged her. Connie was not one for palls. Her round, cherubic face was usually anticipating the next party, the next bit of mischief. But it looked years older today. "I'll stay here with you," I offered.

"You can't. If anyone saw you, and your mother found out you were dressed like a boy, you'd be in real trouble. But it isn't only that, Susan, it's something else. And I don't know how to tell you."

"What?"

"Mama says we can't be friends anymore."

I stared at her in disbelief. "Why?"

She lowered her head. "Because Kenneth is out there fighting and your brother... isn't.''

"But my father..." And then I stopped. Daddy's letters said we were not to divulge the nature of his work. "My father's off working for the Cause," I said. "I can't tell you how, but he is."

"I believe you, Susan. But my mama wouldn't care about that. She says if I'm seen with you, she'll punish me."

"Well, if you were any kind of friend, Connie Turnstable, you wouldn't care. My mama is always punishing me for one thing or another."

"I want to be friends, Susan." She raised her troubled gray eyes to me. "And I want you to still consider me one. We'll just have to avoid being seen together for a while. Until Mama relents. Even in school."

We both went to the fashionable Miss Pegram's, and while summer did not mean full classes, we still had dancing and music three days a week. "We can pass notes in school!" I said excitedly. "And meet in secret! Like in a novel!"

She shook her head. "I don't think we ought. I can't go against Mama."

"You're a little ninny, Connie! You always were!"

She gasped. Her face went white.

"Friends are loyal to each other," I said, "especially in bad times. That's what friends are for!"

"Susan, you have my undying devotion!"

"Ninny," I hissed. "Kenneth would scold you good if he knew you were saying such things to me. I have your undying devotion until it displeases your mama."

"Constance! Constance, where are you?" I ducked back into the shadows as I heard her mother coming down the hallway. "Constance, who are you talking to?"

"No one, Mama. I'm coming. I thought I saw someone I knew, but I was mistaken." She turned, gave me one last beseeching look and ran off.

No one, indeed! I felt the tears gather in my eyes. If Kenneth lived through Manassas he'd kill Connie for what she'd just done to me. I knew that. Why he'd be the first to . . . oh, I couldn't bear it. Numbly I made my way along the fringes of the lobby. All around me people were greeting each other, asking for news of the battle. There was a loud cheer as someone on the landing made an announcement. Something about the "Confederacy" and its "generals" and its "army."

Next thing I knew I was out on the verandah, being jostled and pushed. As I stood there a clear, crisp voice came from over my shoulder.

"Here, boy." I was handed a coin. "Go fetch me a newspaper. Hurry back, there's a good fellow."

I took the coin and obeyed. Dodging carriages, I crossed the street, gave the coin to the newsboy selling the *Richmond Dispatch,* took the paper and went back to the hotel. I stood there in a daze. All I could think of was Connie. We had been the dearest of friends ever since I started at Miss Pegram's three years ago. She and I and sometimes Kenneth had had so many adventures together. Why, just last year we had come to this very hotel to see the Prince of Wales when he'd visited Richmond.

We'd taken tea in the tearoom and had been in the lobby when the handsome prince came down the curving stairs. Just as he got to us, he dropped his silk handkerchief. Connie was the one who stooped to pick it up. Then, stepping forward, she curtsied and offered it back to him. He took it, pressed it to his lips, then bowed, kissed her hand and gave the handkerchief back to her in front of everyone. He asked her her name, and she even introduced Kenneth and me to him. She still had the handkerchief, too. It was her most prized possession.

"Ho, boy! You have my paper?"

I turned and looked up dumbly at the man. He was tall and cut a good figure in his gray suit, designed in the style of the day. His face was deeply bronzed, and except for a trim mustache, he was beardless. His brown eyes smiled down at me. "My paper," he said.

"Yes, sir." I handed it to him.

"Thank you." He held out a coin. I was just about to

take it when he scowled, grabbed my wrist and clutched it fiercely. "Where did you get this shirt, boy?"

I was too startled at first to understand the question. Then I tried to pull away but couldn't. "It's mine. I don't know what you mean, sir. Please let me go."

But he wouldn't. Roughly he was pulling me to the end of the verandah, out of earshot of the crowd. He paused, still gripping my wrist. "I said, where did you get this shirt, boy?"

"It's mine! And I'll thank you to unhand me."

He laughed. "Fancy language for a street rat. You look like one of the confounded dogs that are plaguing this city since the dogcatchers are otherwise employed." Then his face grew even angrier. "Yours, is it? And whose house did you break into to steal it? You little ruffian. I want the truth from you, and I'll have it now."

"I don't know what you mean, sir. Please let me go!" A stab of fear went through me. Mama had warned me not to go out. Now even in my boy's disguise I was not safe. I started to tremble.

"I'll let you go, you little ragamuffin. After I thrash you! After you tell me the truth!" And he pulled me along with him, calling out to hail a carriage. It must have been his carriage, for he addressed the driver by name. "I've got a real catch here, Nate. With all the thievery that's been going on these days, I'm going to make this one pay."

Perceiving that he was about to pull me into the carriage, I fought with every ounce of strength in me. I kicked and lashed out with my free hand. I looked around desperately for help. Any one of the people within sight would have come to my aid had they known I was Susan Dobson Chilmark, daughter of Hugh Chilmark. But who would believe it was me under my disguise?

I kicked again, catching the man in the shins. "Ow! You'll pay for that!" He grasped me roughly, covered my mouth with one hand and with the other arm around my waist, lifted me effortlessly into the carriage, closing the door behind us.

The carriage started to move. I screamed again, despite his hand over my mouth. My heart was beating wildly, and I felt faint. It was dim in there. The curtains were closed, and I could smell tobacco and whiskey, all the masculine smells I remembered from my father.

"I'm going to take my hand away from your mouth," he said. "If you scream, you'll have more to scream about, I promise. My place has been robbed twice in the last month, and I'll have no mercy with the likes of you. I want the truth. If I think you're lying, I'll thrash you soundly. You hear?"

I nodded. He took his hand away, turned me to face him on the seat and held each of my wrists firmly. "Now talk."

I could not believe this was happening to me. My head was swimming, and I couldn't think. We were going at a fast clip over Richmond's streets, and through a crack in the curtains I glimpsed buildings and people flashing by. I had to get out of here! I was in mortal danger. Oh, why hadn't I listened to Mama and Rhody! I saw the man's firm jawline, the desperate look about the eyes, and I knew I was in very real trouble.

"The shirt is mine." I tried to sound brave.

I saw the slap coming as he released me, and dodged it. I had Mama to thank for my quickness. I'd dodged enough of her slaps over the years. I rolled away from him on the floor, but he reached out, grabbed my arm and pulled me toward him.

"I warned you, boy. No wonder the mayor has you little ruffians switched. Very well, then." He raised his arm but I fought and kicked. Then I felt his two strong hands on me, and he pulled me up over his lap and proceeded to thrash me.

I'd been hit by Mama before, but never like this. His hand came down on me again and again, like hot irons on my legs, my thighs, my bottom, until I screamed, "Please, sir, don't hit me anymore. I'll tell you!"

He released me. I fell to the floor. I pulled away from him, sobbing and trembling. I leaned against the opposite seat. He was bending over, nursing his hand and glaring.

"Well?"

"The shirt is . . . my brother's."

His eyes blazed with renewed anger, and he reached for me again. *He's going to kill me,* I thought. *The man is mad, surely, and he's going to kill me. And I am telling him the truth!*

He grabbed me by the shoulders this time and pulled me up so that I was kneeling on the floor in front of him. "You're lying, boy."

"I'm not," I sobbed.

"What's his name, this brother of yours?"

"Lucien." I hiccupped. "Lucien Dobson Chilmark."

"God's teeth, you haven't had enough? You want more? Must I take you home and use a buggy whip on you? Lucien Chilmark has no brother. I am Lucien Chilmark."

I remember nothing else at all except going limp and mercifully passing out.

Chapter Three

The first thing I saw when I awoke was a ceiling with a faded painting on it of some country I did not recognize, but that definitely was not America. I hurt. For a moment I could not think why because my mind was half shut down, like the furnaces at Tredegar Iron Works on a holiday. And then I remembered what had happened to me, and my mind exploded with fear, like a blast of hot bright air. I whimpered.

There was a rustling of material, and I looked up at the most beautiful woman I had ever seen. Her hair was the color of corn silk. Her eyes were violet blue, and she was wearing a dress of the most luscious peach silk that followed the lines of her body, making her look like a freshly iced cake.

"She's coming out of it, Lucien," she said. She was holding a cold compress on my head. My hat was gone, and I became frightened, realizing that my hair was spread out on a pillow, exposing my identity. I started to raise my head, but couldn't.

"Easy," she said in a low, musical voice. I was covered with a light blanket, and as my mind began to focus, I took in my surroundings.

It was a man's room. The walls were paneled in deep rich wood, and wooden shutters on the inside closed off the daylight. In the corner, where gaslight glowed softly against crimson draperies and gold-framed hunting scenes, there was an ornate desk.

Behind it sat Lucien Dobson Chilmark. My brother.

I closed my eyes and moaned, because I still hurt from the thrashing he had given me. And as I remembered the terrible ride in the carriage, his anger, my fear at being trapped with such a furious and threatening man, I whimpered again.

"Would you like some tea, dear?" the woman asked.

Tea, yes. My mouth was parched. I looked at her. "What's your name?"

"Fanny."

"I love your dress."

"She's a girl, all right," Lucien Dobson Chilmark said from across the room.

"Yes, I'd love some tea," I told her.

She left the room to get it. I lay propped against a pillow, staring at him. His coat was off. He was wearing a fine white shirt and silk cravat, and his waistcoat was molded to his body. I noticed that he was a trim, yet well-built man, tall, with good shoulders. A decanter sat next to him on the desk. He was smoking a cheroot and playing cards. The smoke curled up around his head.

In the glow of gaslight I could not quite believe he was real. I had always fancied meeting him someday, but I had pictured him coming to the front door of our house to take me for a carriage ride. All those years of imagining what he was like, of studying the contents of his room, and here he sat across from me.

He looked very dashing, to be sure. But I could not, by any stretching of the imagination, connect him with the brother who owned the books and maps in that room.

I gave another little whimper of self-pity. He threw a card down on the desk and got up, walking toward me.

I clenched my fists under the blanket. He was handsome, and he walked gracefully, with the easy movements of a self-confident man. There was a determined calm about him, and he had a straight, dramatic nose. The mustache was trim and his hair was thick and dark brown and curly. And he had the deepest and saddest brown eyes I had ever seen.

"Are you all right?" He looked down at me.

I picked some fuzz off the blanket. "Yes."

He nodded. He seemed about to say something else, but moved away and then turned and stopped a few feet away. "Well," he said, "what are you looking at?"

"You."

"And? What do you see?"

"I see a cruel man who would beat a woman."

The muscle in his jaw twitched, and I knew I had hurt him. "I . . ." He shook his head and walked back to me. "I have never struck a woman in my life."

"You did today."

"Did I know you weren't a thieving boy? Did you tell me?"

I shook my head no.

"I gave you enough warning. And if you run around in that getup you're asking for anything that befalls you. I knew Charlotte wasn't exactly the cream of Southern motherhood. God's teeth, I knew that. Does she know you're running around in that outfit?"

"No." I don't know why I answered him truthfully, but something in his gaze and his demeanor compelled honesty.

He grunted. "I see she hasn't improved with the years, has she? She's just as crazy as she always was. Running around raising cain about the wrong things and never seeing the truth right in front of her eyes. Am I right?"

I could not answer. My eyes filled with tears. He saw the tears and a gloom settled over him. "Look here, I'm sorry. I'm sorry if I . . . hurt you."

I sniffled, wiped my face with my hand and nodded.

He turned and went back to his desk. I took small notice of the fact that he called our mother Charlotte. It seemed natural coming from him. And then Fanny came in with the tea, and I sat up and took it gratefully. After a few minutes I felt better.

"Is this a brothel?" I asked Fanny.

Lucien threw back his head and laughed. But Fanny only smiled. "No, dear, it isn't."

Lucien was wiping his eyes. "How do you know about such places?"

"I just know," I said primly. "My friend Connie told me. I overheard Mama tell Rhody that someone said you owned part of one."

"They're saying that about me, are they? What else are they saying?"

I sipped my tea and refused to answer.

"This is a gambling house," he explained. "It's respectable and a lot of political and military people in town come here. A great many of these places have sprung up in Richmond. I'm in partnership with someone else. I'm a man who believes in taking advantage of opportunity."

"Is that why you're selling goods to Richmond markets at inflated prices when people can't afford to pay such prices these days?"

He never flinched. "Dear," he said to Fanny in a very moderate voice, "leave us, will you? I'd like to be alone with my sister."

With a rustling of her beautiful peach silk dress, Fanny got up. She smiled down at me and smoothed back my thick hair, which was in disarray around my forehead. "You'll be all right," she said softly. And then she leaned over to adjust the blanket. "His bark," she whispered, "is worse than his bite."

I nodded and looked up at her gratefully. "I love the color of your hair," I said impulsively.

"Well now, honey, you've got nothing to apologize for with those thick curly locks of your own."

I shook my head. "My mama's hair is about the color of yours. And Isabel had hair that was almost golden, too."

"Who's Isabel?" she inquired politely.

"She was my sister. She's dead."

"Oh, yes," she said. Then she walked over to Lucien, who was still playing cards at his desk. She stood behind his chair, put her arms around his shoulders and kissed the side of his face. He got up. "Have Nate bring the carriage around."

"It's early afternoon. I can walk."

"Not today. Not in this town. Feelings are running too high. Please." He was tender with her, and the look in his eyes bespoke concern and love.

"Oh, all right." She kissed his face again and left. Slowly he brought a chair over to the settee and sat down.

He lit a fresh cheroot, scowling as the smoke drifted past his eyes, and for a moment he just sat and looked at me. I struggled to a sitting position. I wanted to look him in the eyes and not be lying down when he spoke to me.

"Is Fanny your mistress?" I asked.

His eyes narrowed. "Somehow I sense you would be disappointed if I said no. Am I correct?"

I nodded yes. He ran his thumb along his chin. "How old are you?"

"Fourteen."

"Ah, yes, girls of fourteen conjure up all sorts of romantic notions, as I recall."

"Well, is she?"

"Yes."

"She's very beautiful. And she's much too nice for you."

I had meant to hurt, but he smiled. "Thank you. And

you're probably right. What's this business about the hair?''

"What?" I stared at him.

"No, don't tell me," he said, "let me guess. You feel you can never quite live up to Isabel, the golden princess. Am I right?''

How did he know? I stared at him. But of course! Isabel had been only three years younger than he.

He smiled sadly. "Isabel and I were playmates," he said quietly. "Have you forgotten? She was always Charlotte's favorite. Lucky for me, or I probably would have been dragged along on that fateful trip to Charleston, too."

I nodded.

"Let me tell you something," he said sternly. "Isabel was very pretty. But, as Fanny told you before, you have very beautiful hair. And now that I look at the rest of you . . ." His eyes raked over me quickly and he sighed and shook his head. "Your face is . . . very attractive."

I held my breath. "Is that all?"

He looked at me without blinking. "Is what all?" he said.

"Don't I have a good figure? Can't you tell I'm not a boy if you really look at me?" I let the light blanket fall from my shoulders and I straightened up on the settee, stuffing the boy's shirt into my trousers.

His face was expressionless. He cleared his throat. "I don't know why I didn't notice you were a girl before. Even in those clothes. Very stupid of me."

I smiled. "Rhody says that by the time I'm sixteen the boys will be buzzing round like bees at a barbecue."

He studied the end of his cheroot. "No one could have put it better. Now that we have that cleared up, can you tell me what you were doing at the Spotswood today?"

"Waiting for news of the battle."

"Why the boy's clothes?"

"I often go out in them."

"Why?"

"Mama won't let me go out of the house. I wear your clothes so I won't be recognized. And so I'll be safe on the streets."

"You weren't very safe today."

"True. But I was doing fine in them until I met you."

"Are you telling me that Charlotte keeps you prisoner?"

"No, I'm not saying that."

"What are you saying, then?"

It occurred to me that I did not have to answer to him, that I owed him nothing. Until I looked into his face. And then I knew better.

"I go out with Rhody, when she has time. Or with Mama to church, or to the shops. I go for dancing and music to Miss Pegram's. But I'm not allowed to go to the station with food when the soldiers come through. Neither am I allowed to join a sewing circle like all the other girls. I sew for the army alone at home every day. Mama just doesn't want me out and about."

"Why not?"

I shrugged. But he was shrewd. He knew. "People are saying things about me, because I haven't joined up. Is that it?"

I nodded, not looking at him.

"Have the remarks become that bad, then?"

"Mama says so. I haven't heard any."

"I don't suppose I'm helping Charlotte socially by my actions. Somehow that doesn't quite devastate me the way it should. But I'd forgotten that I'm also hurting you."

"I don't mind. All that bothers me is that I want to prove I'm a real Confederate and I can do things for the Cause. But Mama won't let me try."

He fell silent. Were his eyes just a bit sadder? "She is still quite mad, I see. She always was. You know that, don't you?"

I nodded. "Can you tell me why?"

"Haven't people told you?"

"I know some of it."

"How much?"

"I know about Isabel. And the two infants she lost after Isabel died. And that she was never happy here in Richmond and never quite fit in. Is there more?"

He nodded.

"Would you tell me?"

"No. There's no reason to. You'll not get any more out of me. You know enough to realize that you have to put up with Charlotte. I don't envy you, but she'll toughen you up for life. She can't hurt you if you don't let her."

I nodded, grateful for his advice.

"Now tell me why you're so intent on helping the Cause."

I looked at him as if he were demented. "One might as well ask why the sun comes up each morning," I said.

"I've wondered about that, too, the mess the world is in today."

"Are you poking fun at me?"

"No," he said solemnly. "I never poke fun at people's beliefs. I'd very much like to hear your reasons."

I took a deep breath. "Once, when I spent the night at my friend Connie's, we went to the campgrounds at Howard's Grove. The soldiers are all so brave. They'd left their homes to come to Richmond and defend the Confederacy. And you know how Patrick Henry said 'Give me liberty, or give me death,' during the Revolutionary War?"

He lowered his eyes and smiled wryly. "I've heard tell of it."

"Well, everyone says what we're doing is no different than what the rebels did in 1776. We're not allowing the North to push us around and tell us how to live. Isn't that what Patrick Henry meant when he said give me liberty, or give me death?"

"Somehow I don't exactly think so, Susan."

"But everyone says..."

He got up abruptly. "Everyone says! They're fools, all of them!"

He was angry. I gasped. "How can you say that? Why, our soldiers are out there fighting right now. And maybe dying."

"I'm saying it. The Cause stinks." He carried his chair back across the room. "The South has turned lunatic. It has too many long-winded orators who got carried away with themselves and now everyone has to pay for their words. The system is evil and corrupt and they're defending it."

He turned to look at me. "Has our father never taken you to Davis and Dupree's here in Richmond?"

"What's that?"

"A slave auction."

I stared at him as if he were mad. "Daddy would never take me there. Why, I don't think he's ever been there himself."

"Oh, he's been there, all right. Where do you think he got Rhody and her husband and her sister Lettie? He's protected you, shielded your sensibilities. Most Southern men do that with their womenfolk. Our father bought the three of them, although he got more than he bargained for with Lettie. If I had my way, I'd take you there. Let you see for yourself."

"Nobody ever told me that," I said quietly.

"Of course not. Rhody is like a benevolent aunt to you. Wilium is like a court jester. But they all come from somewhere. Ask yourself where. Slavery is evil, Susan, and Southerners have talked themselves into believing it's good. They eat their lies for breakfast and serve them, warmed over, for supper. They've created an aristocracy that rivals the one England had when your precious rebels broke away from it in 1776."

He was walking back and forth, in and out of the shadows created by the gaslight. I said nothing. He went on. "And the North is superior in men, munitions and supplies. We have less than half the people they have, less than half the railroad mileage and less than one-third the bank capital. To say nothing of our miserable manufacturing output."

"That isn't true!" I argued. "Five railroads serve Richmond!"

"Richmond is only a small part of the South. And our politicians were crazy to make it the capital of the Confederacy. It's too close to Washington."

"Well, that may be so. But we rank thirteenth in manufacturing. We have nine hundred sixty-four merchants. And they've established a direct line of shipping between us and Liverpool, England!"

He raised his eyebrows. "And we have no navy," he enunciated slowly. "Someone's been educating you. You haven't learned all that at Miss Pegram's."

"I've read all your books. And I read the newspapers every day. And as for us having no navy, well, Daddy's working to change that."

"I was wondering when you would mention him. Where is he?"

"He's in Norfolk working on the *Virginia* to make it into a fine fighting ship. He writes that the walls are made of pitch pine and oak two feet thick. On top of that, they're putting iron."

"Tredegar iron, I take it."

"Of course. Why not?"

"They've got slaves working at Tredegar. Joe Anderson found a way to cut labor costs."

"Daddy said a lot of men left for the military. And the Irishers went back North when the war started."

"Anderson had slaves working for him a long time before that."

"Well, I don't see why that should detract from what Daddy is doing," I said impatiently. "He's even put some of his own money into the *Virginia*. That's how much he believes in it."

Lucien's smile was wry. "I see he's still trying to make certain things up to Charlotte."

"Why do you say that?" I snapped. "Can't you just believe he's doing his patriotic duty?"

He laughed. "Hugh Chilmark? The West Point graduate? Feeling a patriotic duty for the South? Come on, Susan, you know him better than that. I've seen my father only once these last seven years, but I know one thing. I'd bet my half of this gambling house that he isn't for secession."

I lowered my eyes and said nothing.

"Hugh Chilmark cared little for politics, Susan," he said more gently now. "I take after him in that respect. What he cares for is his country, his job with Tredegar, his place here in Richmond and pleasing Charlotte."

"He cares for me," I said.

His eyes softened. "I'm glad you and he get on."

"I love him dearly." My chin trembled as I said it.

We were both silent for a minute. "I still think he's doing what he's doing to make some things up to Charlotte," he insisted.

"What things?"

His eyes smiled for the first time. "No, you don't, Susan Dobson Chilmark. You won't get certain information out of me. What you don't know about our lovely family, I pray you never find out.''

"And that's why you won't fight, I suppose. Because you're angry with our family.''

"No,'' he said calmly. "I am very much a Southerner, Susan. But I refuse to fight for a Cause that is corrupt. So I fish and hunt on the rivers and yes, I sell the food at inflated prices. I didn't create the inflation. It's the only way, besides this place, that I can make a living.''

"You were sent to college,'' I accused.

"I was sent to military college. I was supposed to go to West Point, but I didn't make it in. So I went to college here. Which means, since I want no part of the military, that I have no way to make a living. But when this war is over I hope to come out of it with money. To help rebuild the South. I hope to be one of the right-thinking men to have a part in that.''

"I think you are mean to say such things about the South,'' I said petulantly.

He seated himself in the chair behind his desk. "I never asked you to like me,'' he said simply. "I never asked you to run around in my clothes so I would haul you out of a crowd for questioning. Our meeting today was purely accidental.''

"Are you sorry we met?'' I had to know.

"No, but I'll bet you are.'' He leaned back in his chair, and his eyes twinkled mischievously. "I'd be willing to bet it's the first time in your life anyone ever took a hand to you.''

I twisted a corner of the blanket in my lap. If only he knew all the times Mama hit me! My silence was long and painful, and he mistook it for resentment and cleared his throat awkwardly. "I shall give you dinner in a while and take you home. I don't want you to seek me out again unless you are desperate and have nowhere else to turn. Does *that* answer your question?''

It did, but not the way I wanted. For, in spite of everything, he intrigued me. And I found I wanted the approval, if not the friendship, of this strange, troubled brother of mine. I sensed there was more to him, something worthwhile behind the brittle exterior.

I sipped the remainder of my tea, which was cold by now. "Why can't I see you again?" I said.

"Because of what I am. Because of my reputation. It wouldn't be good for you."

I set my cup down. "Am I to believe you care about what's good for me?"

"You can believe whatever you wish. It's no business of mine what you believe. But I want you to stop running around the streets in boy's clothing, especially if it's mine."

"Do you want to know what I think?"

"No, but it's clear you're going to tell me. So go ahead."

"I think you're not as much of a bear as you pretend to be. I think you're covering up a lot of feelings by pretending to be so gruff and stern."

He gave me a stony stare. "You're a very bright girl, Susan," he said. "I appreciate your intelligence. I'm not one of those Southern men who thinks women should only discuss embroidery and childbirth. But even with men like me there is a limit."

Fortunately Nate came in just then with dinner on a huge silver tray. He spread a white cloth on a round table in the corner and started setting the dishes and silverware down. He poured the wine. The fragrance of the food nearly drove me to distraction.

Lucien pulled out a chair. "Come and eat," he beckoned.

"I don't want your overpriced food."

He laughed. "It's part of the house buffet. Good customers eat for nothing."

"I am not a customer in your gambling house."

He sat down and opened a white linen napkin. "Too bad. Nate's an excellent cook."

Nate smiled and left.

"I thought you were an abolitionist," I said.

"We still enjoy a good meal now and then, just the same as anybody else."

"What's Nate?"

He gave me a questioning look, then grinned. "Oh. Nate is an employed body servant. I pay him well for his services." He started to eat. "I'll have him take you home later."

"But I thought you were going to take me home!" I got up off the settee, the blanket falling to the floor around my feet.

He smiled. "Does it matter if I do or not?"

"Of course it does. Nate won't understand why he can't take me to the front door of Mama's house. And you do."

He took a forkful of fish. "Do I?"

"Why, of course you do, Lucien." I approached the table. "If Mama sees me dressed like this she'll whip me."

"You should have thought of that before you put those clothes on."

"Please, Lucien. You don't understand what she's like when she's angry."

He took a sip of wine. "Ah, but I do, I lived there once, remember?" He set the glass down. "So she hits you, does she?"

I flushed. Across the expanse of white tablecloth he leveled a knowing gaze at me. "I thought it was something like that. Before . . . when I said no one had ever laid a hand on you, I expected a saucy answer and got only a suspicious silence instead. Does she make a habit of it?''

I shrugged. ''Just take me home today, please, Lucien. That way I can sneak in the back door. Why, if you like, I could even hide you in the stable and send Rhody out to see you. Wouldn't you like to see Rhody again?''

He wasn't to be put off. ''What does our beloved father have to say about this? It's my guess that he either doesn't know or doesn't have the courage to stand up to her.''

I raised my chin defiantly. ''He doesn't know,'' I said firmly. All right, so now I admitted Mama hit me, but I had to protect Daddy.

He reached for a roll and buttered it. ''And she's got you too scared to tell him. Am I right?''

I raised my eyes to look at him beseechingly.

He set his knife down. ''See Rhody? I might like that. And here I thought you'd be glad to get out of this place and never see me again after the way I treated you today.''

''You haven't frightened me,'' I said. ''I'm very tough. Like you said before—Mama did that to me.''

''Well, that makes two of us she's done it to, then,'' he said. ''All right, I'll take you home, you little beggar. Now come over here and eat some of my overpriced food. You look as if you need it.''

Chapter Four

Lucien took me home. Nate drove the carriage, and I sat across from my brother inside. He asked me some questions about Rhody and Wilium, told me I could have the books in his room if I wanted them, and then there was a lull in the conversation.

"Why did you leave home?" I couldn't help it. I had to ask.

He had been looking out the window. The gaze he fastened on me when he turned was almost as severe as it had been earlier in the day, when we'd first met.

"What?" he asked. "Did Father tell you?"

"That you and he argued and you left because of something he did to please Mama."

He grunted. "He's honest, anyway."

"What did you argue about?"

"Lettie's daughter, Sallie."

"Why?"

"Sallie was very intelligent. And she was . . . well, she could pass for white. She was also very beautiful. Father gave her papers and freed her. He sent her North."

"But I thought . . . I mean if you're an abolitionist, why wouldn't you approve of that?"

"Because I loved her."

I heard the intake of my own breath. "You loved her?"

"Yes."

"Did you . . . have an affair with her? Is that why they sent her North?"

"Really, Susan, have you no delicacy?" But he smiled. "An affair would have been forgiven. Half the men in the South have nigra mistresses. Love was something else. It could not be forgiven."

I fell silent, contemplating.

"She was two years younger than I was. We played together, she and Isabel and I. Charlotte tolerated her as a playmate for Isabel. Then, when Isabel died, Charlotte couldn't stand to have her around anymore. But Rhody loved her, so father kept her. As we got older, I taught her to read."

I was wide-eyed with amazement. No nigra in our house or in the houses of anyone I knew in Richmond could read or write.

"I went away to college," his voice came sparingly, "and on visits home I began to realize how beautiful she was. I fell in love with her. When I was home from college one time she was in my room reading one of my books. Charlotte caught her. There was a horrible scene. There was always a fear of slave uprisings in the low country where Charlotte came from, and she was terrified of a nigra being able to read. I went downstairs to enlist Father's help while Charlotte was upstairs, slapping Sallie around."

He paused. "You see why I assumed, so easily, that she hits you. She did that with Sally quite a bit. Look, maybe I shouldn't be telling you this."

"Oh, don't stop now," I begged. "Please. I won't tell anyone. I promise."

He smiled. "Very well. I went down to ask Father to stop Charlotte. Father and I got along pretty well, except where Charlotte was concerned. She was the bone of contention between us. When she wanted me punished or my allowance or my privileges taken away, he did it. He never went against her wishes. It was something I always resented. Anyway, he wouldn't go upstairs and defend Sallie, even though he liked her. And he wouldn't let me do it either. He said I'd done enough damage by teaching her to read, that I'd gone against their beliefs. He was very angry with me over that. I wanted to tell him I loved Sallie, but I didn't do it."

"Why?"

He laughed bitterly. "I thought it would make things
worse for Sallie. That's what I tell myself on good
days. On bad days I admit that I just didn't have the
courage to stand up to our parents. Today, when I met
you, I was having one of my bad days."

I nodded.

"So, instead, I lashed out at him for his old-South
traditions and philosophies. I gave him an intellectual
argument. I gave him my abolitionist talk. Nigras are
people. Look how fond he was of Sallie. She was part
of the family. She was intelligent. What was wrong with
teaching her to read? How could he be so hypocritical?
He said he wouldn't hear another word of it, and I
slammed out of the house. I went out drinking. I got
home in the small hours of the morning. When I awoke
late the next day, I felt as if there were ten devils behind
my eyeballs fighting to get loose. And I went downstairs to find that Sallie was gone. Father had shipped
her North. Charlotte insisted upon it, he said."

So now I knew what Daddy had been trying to tell
me that day at Tredegar, what he'd done to Lucien
because Mama had insisted on it.

"I was so furious. I argued with him again. I told
him that for once he ought to stand up to his wife.
He . . . struck me across the face. And then I told him
that I loved Sallie. Do you understand? I told him after
she was gone."

"Would it have made any difference if you'd told him
the night before?"

"Probably not. But it would have made a difference
to Sallie." He fell silent.

"I think that's the saddest story I ever heard," I said.
"And I know Daddy feels bad about it, Lucien. He
never told me what really happened, but he did say

once, before he left, that he felt bad about something he'd done to you."

He grunted. "A lot of good that does anybody. He wouldn't even tell me, at the time, where he'd sent Sallie. We had more angry words . . . terrible words . . . and he said things that caused a permanent rift between us. I left home and college. I was almost through with my studies anyway."

"But you're in touch with Sallie now," I said. "I know, because she tells Rhody in her letters. I read those letters to Rhody. And write back the replies."

He nodded. "A few years ago, when she wrote to me, we started corresponding."

"Why didn't you go North to see her?"

"I couldn't do that," he scowled. "No, no, it was out of the question. It was better I leave her be. She has a life of her own in Philadelphia, teaching."

He would tell me no more. We rode in silence. He retreated into his gloom.

"Do you know Mama calls me a Yankee brat whenever she's mad at me, Lucien?"

He turned to stare at me, coming out of his reverie. "No, I didn't, Susan, I'm sorry."

"Why do you suppose she calls me that?"

He smiled. "Father told me you were conceived in Saratoga when we summered there one year. That could be why. It's her way of hurting you."

"Well, that doesn't make me a Yankee."

The carriage was nearing our house, and he rapped on the window to tell Nate to park it a block away. Then we walked, and I took him to the stable behind the house.

I squinted up at him through the slants of sunlight that came through the cracks in the stable wall. "I'm glad we met today, Lucien. My friend Connie has a brother, and she talks about him all the time."

He looked embarrassed. "Well, don't go talking about me. To anyone. You hear?"

I nodded yes, solemnly. Then he reached into his pocket, pulled out a paper and stuffed it into my hand. "Here. This is my address. I live at Thirty-nine Elm Street at Rocketts Landing. It isn't a fancy neighborhood, and I only want to see you if it's important. Or I'll be angry. And you know what I'm like when I'm angry." He grinned. "I'm a little bit like Charlotte."

"Thank you, Lucien."

He reached into his pocket again. This time he stuffed money into my hand. "For a carriage, if you need me. And don't let me see you in those clothes again, either."

"Can I ask one more question?"

He sighed. "Go ahead."

"Do you put your money in banks in England?"

"My money is in U.S. Government bonds. Why do you ask?"

"No reason. Can I kiss you, Lucien? Would that be all right?"

He took off his hat and ran his hand through his curly brown hair. He shrugged nonchalantly, but I saw two spots of color rise to his cheeks. "I suppose so," he said.

"Well, you have to lean down. You're awfully tall, you know."

He did so. I put my arms around his shoulders and kissed his face. "You smell like Daddy. Tobacco and soap and whiskey," I said. "Especially whiskey."

"Get inside," he ordered gruffly, "before you get into trouble."

"All right. You stay here, and I'll send Rhody out." I walked into the sunlight, and when I turned back he was standing there in the dimness of the stable, holding his hat in his hand. His face was soft, looking at me, as if he had found something he had lost a very long time ago. And just remembered what it was.

Chapter Five

Mr. Wigfall, the former U.S. senator from Texas, and his wife, Charlotte, were two of Mama's favorite people. Senator Wigfall now served in the Confederate Congress. He usually talked politics with Mama, but tonight the talk was of nothing but the battle.

No one really knew anything about the results of the battle yet, of course. The Wigfalls' comments were based only on rumor. I was so worn out from my day's adventures that I could barely keep track of the conversation. Yet, I was still interested. I was worried about Kenneth. I was hurting over what Connie had said to me, and still smarting from what Lucien had done to me, even while the idea of him, and his words, were spinning around in my brain.

"I doubt anyone will sleep in this town tonight," Mama was saying. "Thank heaven it's cooled down. Susan, deah, do eat. You haven't touched a bite yet."

Mama was in one of her good moods tonight. All her anger with me from the morning had melted away as if from the midday heat. She had even complimented me on the way I looked in my blue muslin dress. It had been an offhanded compliment, to be sure, but when she had said, "Susan, I do believe you will become a real lady yet," I had positively glowed, even while I knew the dress was much too childish.

Mama could throw crumbs of compliments like that at me and feed my soul for a whole day. Of course, she could afford to. She was beautiful and confident. She had married my father at seventeen—only three years older than I was now! She had given birth to Lucien at eighteen and, in spite of having had four other children afterward, her figure, at forty-four, was lush and perfect. She was tall and aristocratic-looking. The lines in her face were few and her dazzling smile showed perfect white teeth. Tonight she absolutely glowed in her lavender silk gown, with the ivory lace outlining the full bosom that rose above the low neckline.

She smiled at Senator Wigfall. "I do wish we could heah some news of the battle."

Whenever Mama wanted to impress someone, she reverted to her thick South Carolina accent. She did it whenever she was plotting to be nasty, too.

"They say," she went on, "that every weary-looking man walking through town is being stopped and questioned. I do hope it isn't unpatriotic of me to have this dinner party tonight. Do you think so, Senator?"

The way the senator was eating, he wouldn't have considered it unpatriotic if Abraham Lincoln himself had supplied the food. "My deah Mrs. Chilmark . . ."

"Call me Charlotte. Do."

"My deah Charlotte. You know you have me confused here. I don't know which of you two beautiful Charlottes to pay attention to first."

His own wife, also named Charlotte, was a small-boned, delicate, dark beauty, who said little and smiled frequently. Like most of the other women who knew Mama, she was aware of her mercurial moods. She knew about her temper tantrums, and I think she did not trust the gushing happiness Mama was displaying tonight.

"My deah Charlotte." Senator Wigfall turned to Mama. "You could never be unpatriotic. And I'd much rather be in your charming presence than down in Mechanics Hall where the entire cabinet is fidgeting and pacing. President Davis is still at the front, and the telegraph has brought only fragmentary dispatches. It is much more pleasant heah."

I could barely wait for the meal to be over. Mama had ordered ice cream from Pizzini's, the Italian confectioner's in Richmond, and my mouth watered for it. I knew I was going to have to play the piano for our guests and I wanted to do so and get it over with so I could go to my room. I needed to sort out my thoughts which were flapping in front of my eyes like the fluttering lace curtains in the room.

But before anything else could happen, Charlotte Wigfall had to display her flag, the Texas state flag. She did so immediately after supper.

She spread it across the carpet. The shimmering silk reflected the gaslight as the flag lay in all its red, white and blue beauty.

"I can't believe you made it yourself, Charlotte," Mama said.

"It was indeed a labor of love," Mrs. Wigfall said shyly.

Senator Wigfall puffed up with pride. "President Davis is going to present it personally to the First Texas Regiment after the battle," he said.

The flag was made in three sections, with a vertical blue bar at one end on which was a single white star. A red and white bar streamed horizontally out from the blue. "I made it from three of my best silk dresses," Mrs. Wigfall said.

The idea of using one's precious silk dresses for such

a thing appealed to my finest senses. "But silk is so hard to come by," I said.

"Isn't that what makes it more precious?" she asked.

"It certainly is lovely," Mama murmured.

We gazed at it as it lay in repose on the carpet. The sight of it brought tears to my eyes. "I would so love to make a flag like that," I said impulsively. "Oh, Mama, couldn't I?"

"Now, Susan, don't be silly. I can't permit you to work on good silk when you aren't that proficient at sewing."

"I could teach her," Mrs. Wigfall offered. "You know, Charlotte, Susan is about the only young girl in our group of friends who doesn't belong to a circle to sew for the army."

"Susan sews for the army every day at home," Mama said firmly.

"But, Charlotte, it isn't the same." Mrs. Wigfall lowered her voice to a conspiratorial whisper. "You know there is a definite patriotic fervor when the women get together to sew. I understand your reasons for keeping Susan away from certain women who are wont to be unkind to her because of your... particular circumstances. Nevertheless, it doesn't look right that Susan shouldn't be taking part in some patriotic activity."

"Oh deah, I suppose you are right." Mama fanned herself furiously, and I could see how the wheels inside her head were turning, even behind her languid gaze. And I knew what she was thinking. Senator and Mrs. Wigfall were socially prominent people who had befriended her in spite of the vicious remarks circulating about Lucien. It would never do for her not to comply with Charlotte Wigfall's suggestion.

"But do you have the time to devote to teaching Susan to work with silk?" Mama asked. "You know her sewing is absolutely abominable."

I seethed with anger. My sewing wasn't that bad! Why did Mama demean me so?

Mrs. Wigfall put an arm around me, sensing my discomfort. "Why, Charlotte, you don't give me very much credit as a teacher! You know I taught my own girls, Louly and Fanny. And there wasn't anyone more dense about French buttonholes than they were!"

"All right," Mama agreed.

"Wonderful!" Mrs. Wigfall clapped her hands like a pleased child. "We can start as soon as possible. I'll send a note around when I'm ready. Susan can come to our suite at the Spotswood. And I'll be sure to let everyone know she is working on sewing flags for the Cause! Won't it be nice?" She turned to her husband.

"You are a generous woman to share your daughter with my wife, Mrs. Chilmark," Senator Wigfall said solemnly. "She misses Louly and Fanny, who are temporarily way up there in Massachusetts with their grandmother. And as you know, Halsey is at the University of Virginia, but may soon be in the army. Susan will be a comfort to my wife, and I appreciate that."

Mama positively glowed. "I'd be happy to share Susan," she simpered. "She is such a deah child. Do play the piano now, Susan, darling. Show the Wigfalls how beautifully you've learned to play 'The Bonnie Blue Flag.'"

Mama came into my room the next morning when the dark was slashing against the windows in pelting rain. She stood at the foot of my bed, a white-robed figure, an apparition from a dream.

"A great battle has been fought," she whispered. "Our General Joe Johnston led the left wing of the army and our General Beauregard the right. There are dead and dying all over the field. The Lynchburg

Regiment was cut to pieces. One hundred and twenty in
General Wade Hampton's Legion were wounded.''

I sat up in bed wondering if Mama were sleepwalk-
ing. She did that occasionally at night. Fortunately,
Daddy had always been home to guide her back to bed.
But she was not. She was fully awake.

"We beat the Yankees. Word came late last night.
Judah Benjamin, the secretary of war, burst into Mechanics Hall. He had memorized the text of the telegram sent
to Mrs. Davis. 'Night has closed on a hard fought field,' it
said. 'Our forces have won a glorious victory.' ''

She closed her eyes and clutched the bedpost. "Thy
right hand, O Lord, is become glorious in power; Thy
right hand, O Lord, hath dashed in pieces the enemy.''

Her eyes gleamed with malice. "First reports say that
congressmen and gentlemen and ladies came from Washington to picnic and watch the battle. That's the kind of
people they are up North. I could have told everyone
what kind of people they are. I know them. I know how
despicable they can be.''

It was in moments like this that I suspected that my
mother was more than half mad.

"What can I do, Mama?''

"Do?'' She looked at me. "You can get on your
knees and thank the Lord for our victory. Come, Susan,
get out of bed and on your knees and pray with me.''

I got out of bed. She knelt down right in the middle
of my room, and I knelt next to her as she started
reciting psalms. Some of them I knew. We belonged to
the Second Presbyterian Church on North Fifth Street,
and I was not particularly religious. But I prayed with
her, and as I did I could feel her body trembling in the
half-light of morning, next to mine.

It frightened me. I wished my father were home. He
would know how to handle Mama now. I didn't. When

she finished praying she got to her feet. "Go back to sleep," she ordered. "The weather is beastly. I will see you at breakfast."

All that day it poured rain. The rain disturbed the workings of the wires so that for almost twenty-four hours we were without another word from the Battle of Manassas. I came down to breakfast to find Mama bright and cheerful in her blue poplin breakfast dress.

"Good morning, Mama."

She smiled serenely at me. "Your father has written. He sends his love and hopes you are doing well with your music and dancing."

"Is he coming home soon?" Was it possible that the scene in my room earlier this morning had never happened? That I had dreamed it?

"No. He says it doesn't look as if they will be finished with the ship by November, as planned, even though everyone is working seven days a week. He can't get away for a while yet. He writes that the engines were defective to begin with and that weeks under water practically ruined them."

"He'll be so tired, poor Daddy."

She compressed her lips. "Well, at least one man in this family is doing his part for the Confederacy. Susan, what time did Wilium bring you home from your visit to the Withers' yesterday?"

I stared at her dumbly. "It was past two, Mama."

"Oh. I must have been napping. Poor dear, so young to lose a babe. Well, I'm glad you could be of some use to her. She's a dear friend of Mrs. Davis, you know. Did she like the soup Rhody sent over?"

"Oh yes, Mama, she was so appreciative." I knew Anita Withers's baby had been sick. Rhody must have sent the soup over with Wilium and lied about my accompanying him, only Rhody had forgotten to tell me where I was supposed to have been yesterday. But it was all right. I was safe. Anita Withers would be too distraught to know who had visited her.

"I don't like you missing your dancing and music lessons, Susan, but Miss Pegram sent a note saying she would be closed for the next few days because of the battle." She sighed. "The wounded have started coming to town already. I expect the trains will be bringing more in. Mayor Joseph Mayo has called a meeting at Capitol Square this morning to make arrangements for their care. My sewing circle ladies and I will attend."

Rhody appeared in the doorway. "The Richmond Citizens' Committee is here, ma'am, to solicit rooms for the wounded."

"Put them in the front parlor, Rhody. I'll be there in a moment."

"I hear the trains be comin' in at the station soon with the first load of wounded. I may take Wilium and go to see if I can help."

"Very well, Rhody, but I'll be needing you later on."

"I be here, ma'am."

"Mama, could I go to the station with them, please?"

"Absolutely not, Susan."

"But I could help."

"Susan, there will be women there whose husbands and sons and brothers will be horribly wounded. Everyone knows your brother is shirking his duty."

"But if they saw me at the station willing to help!"

"Don't you understand!" she snapped. "There are terrible things being said about your brother! I can bear them! I must! But I will not have you subjected to the taunts of the women at the station today. Some of them will not be rational."

Her words lashed me from across the room, silencing

me and making me tremble. But in spite of her anger, I felt a hope rising in me. Was it possible she was really only attempting to shield me from the cruel gossip? A faint stirring of joy beat in my breast. Was it possible she loved me, after all? I could bear almost anything if I thought that.

But in the next instant all hope failed. "A true Southern daughter, Susan, is sweet-tempered and submissive and gracious at all times. You only show your Yankee tendencies when you behave otherwise."

Tears gathered in my eyes. "But I'm not a Yankee, Mama."

She got up from the table. "I must go to my meeting. I expect to find you home when I return. Someone must be here to take messages when Rhody is away at the station."

She left me trembling and confused. Certainly she must love me somewhat if she wanted to protect me from the women at the station. But why did she act so hateful about it? Tears of self-pity welled in my eyes and throat. What had I done to deserve such treatment from my own mother? Oh, if only Daddy were home. But the thought of him made me put my head down on the table and cry.

Chapter Six

I was kept busy answering the door. First it was a boy with Rhody's order from the market, then a member of the Citizens' Committee delivering fresh bandages. One message was for me! It was a note from Charlotte

Wigfall, saying she would be ready to receive me in her suite at the Spotswood in two days.

"There is a great need for small renditions of the Stars and Bars," she wrote. "We can start you on that."

The Stars and Bars! The new flag of the Confederacy! The note cheered me and when Mama came in at two, cross because Rhody was not there to fuss over her, I had cold duck and fresh fruit laid out in the kitchen for her. I had made fresh biscuits and a new pot of coffee.

She came in soaking wet. "Has the whole town gone mad? I hear it's a carnival at the station. Half the city is there. They say it's ghastly." She stood in front of the stove in the kitchen, smoothing her dress as if by straightening her appearance, she would right the world again. "On the ride home I passed all manner of vehicles carrying the wounded. They'll be coming here soon. Yes, I'll eat now. Good of you to have fresh coffee and food for me, Susan. I'm starved."

I glowed at the praise and sat down at the kitchen table with her. Rain pattered against the windows, and it was downright cozy in the kitchen. Mama was tired but exuberant from her meeting. She chatted about the plans being made for the wounded, and I listened. In a few minutes Rhody came in the back door with Wilium.

"I never, in all my born days, saw such doin's as I saw at the station," Rhody said. She tied an apron on and set to work cleaning the fish that had come from the market. "The good Lord musta been lookin' elsewhere, that's what I told myself when I saw those poor boys moanin' and cryin' for water and for their mamas. We stayed long as we could, then figured we'd be needed back here."

"You figured right," Mama said.

Wilium was wide-eyed with some remembered horror. "I saw one lady throw herself on one of them dyin' boys. They had to carry her off. She was covered with blood and actin' crazy."

"Go get yourself cleaned up." Rhody handed him an old towel, and he went outside to wash.

"Our forces have won a glorious victory," Mama said dreamily.

"Then maybe it shudda been a little less glorious," Rhody mumbled.

At that moment there was a knocking on our front door as if someone were intent on making a hole with the brass knocker. I followed Mama and Rhody into the large foyer.

It was still raining. Rivulets of water poured down our street. A wagon was stopped out front, laden with wounded. The driver, disheveled, rain-soaked and miserable, got down, took off his beat-up hat and approached our steps. "Ma'am, they told me this was one of the houses that would take in wounded." He pulled a raggedy list from his pocket. "This is Chilmark, isn't it?"

"You have the right place." Mama stood there, holding her cloak over her, surveying the dirty heap of bodies in the wagon. Behind her I stared, openmouthed. One could not help but hear the groans of the poor boys who lay on the rude straw of the mud-splattered wagon.

"Who is in the wagon?" Mama asked.

"Wounded, ma'am." The young driver said the word with special emphasis as if my mother were dim-witted.

Mama drew herself up imperiously. "I am aware of that. Who are they?"

"North Carolina boys, ma'am."

"Are there any officers?"

"No, ma'am. Privates mostly."

"I only take officers," my mother said.

I stood stunned. My mouth fell open. I could not believe what I had just heard. I met the young driver's eyes, but he did not seem surprised. Perhaps he had seen too much over the last twenty-four hours for anything in life ever to surprise him again. He opened his mouth to speak, thought better of it and turned away.

"Mama!" I whispered urgently.

She gave me a withering look. "Perhaps," she called after the driver, "you will direct the next wagon of officers to me."

"I'll be sure to do that, ma'am," he said with infinite patience.

"But, Mama..." I tugged at her sleeve.

"Go into the house, Susan," she ordered. "Rhody, take her inside."

"Come along, Miz Susan." Rhody reached out for my arm, but I pulled away.

"Do you know if there are any wounded officers coming in this direction?" Mama was calling after him. "I was down on the list for officers."

"They all look the same to me when they're bleedin', ma'am," the driver said. He started to climb back into his wagon.

"Mama, please, you can't turn those soldiers away. Don't let him drive off! Mama..."

She whirled, her eyes blazing, and slapped me. Full force she slapped me on the side of my face. "How dare you tell me what I can and cannot do! Go into the house this instant!"

At that moment a clear, crisp voice came through the rain from the house next door. "Give me the privates."

Reeling from the blow of Mama's hand, I wiped the tears from my face and saw Mrs. Thomasia Christian Winston Harrold, our next-door neighbor, standing on her front steps in the rain. The wagon driver, who had witnessed our little drama but who had known better than to say anything, took off his beaten hat and got down from his vehicle again. He walked around to the front where he could look up at Mrs. Harrold, who was a widow with two children. His eyes, dull with fatigue and disenchantment with the human race, surveyed her calmly while he stood in the downpour.

"You sure, ma'am?"

"I'm sure. My name is Mrs. Harrold. I'm on your list. I have room for three."

"Bless you, ma'am," the driver said. And he proceeded to move the wagon forward to her house.

As he did so, Mrs. Harrold smiled sweetly over at Mama.

"You understand," Mama called to her, "that I was assigned officers by the Richmond Citizens' Committee. I didn't want there to be any mix-up."

"I understand, Charlotte," Mrs. Harrold said sweetly, but she had seen Mama slap me, and Mama knew it. And Mama also knew that Thomasia Harrold was held in high esteem by the influential ladies of Richmond, the very ladies whose good graces she was always trying to work herself into. To make an impression on them, Mama had often sent me to help Mrs. Harrold with little Jennie's piano lessons or to read to her young brother. And she always made sure the right people were aware of her kindnesses to the young widow.

Now Mama stood there in the rain, clutching her cloak around her, watching the driver pull his wagon to Mrs. Harrold's front steps. And I knew she was figuring a way to get out of her predicament.

"Perhaps, Thomasia," she called, "Susan can help you. I'd be glad to send her over this afternoon, when she gets some dry clothes on."

The wagon driver had one wounded man on his feet

and was supporting him, bringing him up the steps. He was bleeding badly. Mrs. Harrold was reaching out to aid him as he stumbled, half-carried by the driver. "That would be wonderful, Charlotte. It's so good of you," Mrs. Harrold called back without looking. "I certainly can use all the help I can get."

Inside the foyer, Mama threw her wet cloak at Rhody and stood glaring at me. "Don't you ever, ever give me an argument in front of anyone like that again. Do you hear me?"

"Yes, Mama."

"You've embarrassed me. You've made a fool out of me in front of Mrs. Harrold and that driver! She saw me slap you, and she'll tell everyone now. I hope you're happy. Of course, she didn't hear you sass me. In her mind you're an innocent little darling. Little does she, or anyone, know what a trial you are to me, with your constant arguing, your sneaking off and your impertinence! I'd think you'd behave better, with your father away and wounded coming to my house today! I ought to send Rhody for that switch in the kitchen and use it on you before you go over there."

The switch was her final threat over me. She kept it behind the kitchen door. On several occasions she had attempted to use it. Fortunately, I had been too fast for her every time, so that when she finally caught up with me she was so winded and hysterical that she flailed wildly and uselessly at me.

But it still held a terror for me. Sometimes in my dreams at night I saw her coming after me with it. "No, Mama, please," I said. "I'm sorry."

She was breathing heavily with rage. "Go and get into dry clothes and take yourself next door. Be of some use to that woman. And remember, this house was commissioned to take in only officers. You tell her that if she asks. And if I find you told her any different, you'll be sorry.''

The only household help Mrs. Harrold had was Mifri, a young nigra woman whose real name was Mary Frances. She had been christened Mifri by the Harrold children—Jennie, who was nine, and Robert, now six— when they had been babies. I found Mifri in the kitchen scurrying around in a frenzy. ''Chicken soup! They wants chicken soup!''

''Who, Mifri?''

''One of them wounded soldier boys. Won't have anythin' but. The ways they speak, can't hardly understand them, but Mrs. Harrold, she say one asked for chicken soup.''

I watched her stir the contents of the pot on the stove. ''You here to help?''

''Yes,'' I said.

''Chicken soup of all things. Everybody knows how dear chickens are in this town.''

It was true. Ever since the New Orleans Zouaves had arrived on the seventh of June, every henhouse in Richmond had been robbed. Rumor had it that the Zouaves had been recruited from the jails of New Orleans. They wore red caps and bright blue jackets, red Turkish-style trousers, white leggings and black boots. Everyone in Richmond despised them.

''They so sick, those boys,'' Mifri was saying. ''One gone and got hisself shot in the face. A minié ball passed right through his jaw. The Missus is up there right now, pickin' teeth outta his mouth. Make the soup, she says. We only have half a dozen chickens left. Only thing I doan have is parsley. And everybody knows you can't make good chicken soup without parsley.''

''We have parsley in our kitchen garden. Want me to get some?''

"In this rain?"

"I don't mind."

"Oh, wouldn't that be fine now, honey."

It took me only a few minutes to pick the parsley and help Mifri sprinkle it into the soup. Then she led me upstairs. Mrs. Harrold wouldn't let me into the room where the soldier lay who had had the minié ball pass through his jaw. I could hear his moans as I stood in the hallway.

When Mrs. Harrold came out of the room, she instructed me, in a calm voice, to see to the second young man in the room at the end of the hall. She explained that the third young soldier was sleeping.

"Ma'am, do you have any hog meat or hominy?"

The soldier assigned to me sat up in bed, swathed in bandages, for the wound was in his shoulder. He looked to be very young, no more than seventeen, and he had a freckled face, lank blond hair falling over his brow and pale blue eyes.

"Miss, could I have some hog meat or hominy?"

"Mifri is making some nice chicken soup," I said.

He nodded solemnly and surveyed me with his quiet, feverish gaze. "What place is this?"

"It's the home of Mrs. Harrold. She took in you and two other soldiers earlier today. Do you feel very poorly?"

"I'm tolerable, miss. I know who you are."

I stared at him. He was really in a delirium if he thought he knew me.

"You're the little girl from next door. The wagon we were in stopped there. I remember now. It was rainin' and the woman at the door said she only took in officers. You told her it wuz wrong, and she slapped you."

I blushed. "We don't need to talk about that now."

"I saw you stand up to her. I wuz in the wagon, half outta my mind with pain, but I saw you. I wanna thank you fer that, miss. Who are you?"

"My name is Susan Dobson Chilmark. Is there anything I can do for you now?"

"You kin come in here so's I kin get a better look at you."

I stepped into the room and went to the side of his bed. "It's some hog meat and hominy I'm wantin', not chicken soup. You got any hominy in this house?"

"I'm not sure."

"Are the two friends they brought me in with dead?"

I was shocked at the calm of his words. "No. Mrs. Harrold is caring for them."

"We druv the Yankees back. We did, didn't we? We druv 'em back."

"Yes, you did. It was a glorious victory. All the town is celebrating and taking in the wounded. Might I get your chicken soup now?"

"Yes, miss. You might do that."

"You're a pretty little thing, aren't you?"

I blushed as I stood there with the tray.

"How old are you?"

"I'm old enough to see that you eat and get some nourishment."

Instead of responding to that he got a faraway look in his eyes. "It's been three godforsaken weeks since I had myself any decent hog meat or hominy. Or even a boiled sweet purtater."

"Well, you'll have something good if you eat this."

He pulled himself up against the pillows and smoothed his lank hair. Very solemnly, he took a piece of tobacco out of his mouth and set it on the table beside his bed.

Then he nodded at me, which I assumed meant he was
ready to eat.

I gave him the bowl. I knew how important eating
was to his recovery and I knew, too, even before I
handed him the bowl, that he was not going to eat its
contents. He was frowning at the steamy fragrance. But
he thanked me politely. Then he took the first spoonful
and put it in his mouth.

I held my breath. He gulped one spoonful of soup
and shook his head, handing the bowl back to me.

"What's wrong?" I said dismally.

"My mama's soup warn't like that. I might take
some if it warn't for them seaweeds afloatin' around in
it."

"Seaweeds?" I couldn't believe my ears.

"All that green stuff." He gestured to the bowl, and
looking down, I saw the parsley from our kitchen
garden. "Oh, but that's parsley! It's good for you!"

"Much obliged, miss. But them's seaweeds. I been
to the sea in North Kaalina, and I know what that is.
We don't eat no seaweeds in our soup."

"What will you eat, then?"

"Well, since you ain't got no hog meat or hominy or
sweet purtater in this house, I think I might just starve.
But look here, you bein' such a pretty little thing, I hate
to make you cry. You got any sour soup?"

"What's *that?*"

He shook his head wearily. "You folks got a fine
fancy house here and I'm much obliged to you fer all
your fussin', but you don't know about sour soup?"

"No," I said miserably.

"Why it's buttermilk, Miss. You jus' set some on the
stove and let it bile. Then you beat up the yaller of an
egg with some good corn flour and mix it all up into a
paste. Then you break off pieces of the paste and bile it

in the buttermilk. But you gotta add lots of pepper and salt. You got any buttermilk in this house?"

"Yes, I'm sure they have some."

"Well, then, if you made me some sour soup I'd be powerful grateful to you, and I'd eat it and I'd even ask you to write to my mama fer me and tell her I et it. Could you do that fer me, miss?"

I picked the tray up and nodded solemnly. "I'll do it," I said. "I'll make your sour soup."

He rewarded me with a beatific smile and picked up the wad of tobacco from the table. "I'll wait," he said.

Chapter Seven

With help from Mifri I made the sour soup. And that evening the young soldier from North Carolina "et" it, spooning each mouthful with such obvious enjoyment that it made me feel, for the first time in my life, that I had really done something worthwhile.

I had done something at long last for the Cause. I had done it without Mama's help, direction or permission.

The soup had made him think of home, he'd said. "I kin close my eyes and jus' be there with one spoon of this," he had told me.

I'd had all I could do to keep the tears from my eyes, watching him. Was it possible a bowl of soup could do such wonders? And if it could, what had this strange young man been through in the last weeks to render him so vulnerable?

When he finished the soup, he looked at me. "I ain't never tol' you my name, Miss. It's Tom McPherson."

"Hello, Tom McPherson."

"I'm powerful tired now. I'd like to rest. But before I do, I wanna tell you somethin'."

"I'm listening."

"The way you wuz before, when you stood up to your mama . . . it made me proud. It made me feel . . . if there's people like that in the South, I don't mind fightin'."

I knew I wouldn't be able to speak without crying, so I kept silent.

"They say, a lot of the fellers I've been fightin' with, that this is a rich man's war, and a poor man's fight. That we're fightin' for them plantation owners with all the slaves. The fellers I'm fightin' with don't have no slaves. We scratch our own livin' out of the land. I wuz startin' to believe them fellers, sayin' that, startin' to feel real low about it too. But when I saw you standin' right up to your mama like you did, it made me feel proud. You're quality, miss. Anybody kin see that, jus' lookin' at you. And if quality people kin stand up for us like you did, then I don't mind fightin'."

He sank back on the pillows exhausted.

"Thank you," I said. "No one ever told me anything nicer."

He smiled weakly. "Now you take down the address of my mama."

I did so.

"You write to her fer me. Jus' tell her I'm tolerable, and we druv the Yanks back and the war will be over by Christmas. And I'll be home fer spring plowin'. Tell her I'm obliged to the fine folk here in Richmond fer takin' care of me. And I had some good sour soup. Jus' like hers. Made by a miss with real quality."

It was dark by the time Mifri came to tell me Wilium was at the back door waiting for me. I went home to find our house ablaze and Mama entertaining two young officers. She insisted I come in and pay my respects. They were at supper, and I hesitated walking into the dining room after the way Mama and I had parted earlier.

"This deah child of mine has been next doah at Mrs. Harrold's all afternoon helping care for some wounded boys from North Carolina," she told the officers. They got to their feet immediately upon seeing me. They were from Wade Hampton's Legion, they said. One's head was bandaged, but he was jovial and polite.

"With young women such as you have here in Richmond, the South can't possibly lose," said the other, a senior officer. His arm was in a sling, and he seemed to have difficulty standing, but he bowed gallantly.

Mama flushed with pleasure. And in an instant I saw the whole scene as in a play, the table set with Mama's finest linen, the good china and crystal and silver glowing in the candlelight, and the admiring glances of the young officers as Mama moved in her shimmering gown.

In contrast, inside my head, I saw Tom McPherson, propped weakly against his pillows, thanking me for the sour soup. This was what my mother represented best, I thought. And this was why she wanted only officers in the house. They complimented her. They used flowery language. She would have been miserable around a Tom McPherson. But what of Tom, asking for sour soup with that faraway, feverish look in his eyes? Didn't he need something too?

Why, my mama is hypocritical, I thought, standing there. Instantly, I squashed the thought. It was disloyal. But the anger stayed with me.

"Mama," I said, "I'd like to take my old white silk dancing dress to use for a flag when I go to sew with Mrs. Wigfall. May I?"

"Why, Susan, darling," she smiled tolerantly at me,

then at the young officers, who were still standing politely. "Do sit, gentlemen. My daughter has another patriotic project. She is going to be sewing some flags."

They sat, murmuring their approval.

"Susan, I think not," she said sweetly. "Why, I'd gladly let you use your old white silk. But your daddy bought you that in New York. He always loved the way you looked in it. And with him away working for the Confederacy, why, it just breaks my heart to think you'd tear it up for a flag. Especially since I'm sure Mrs. Wigfall has plenty of silk. Gentlemen," she turned to them, "am I wrong? Her deah daddy said it was always his favorite when she wore it."

"Certainly not," said the officer whose arm was in a sling. "You keep your dress, little girl. Some sacrifices are just too much to ask of our women. We aren't that destitute in the South yet."

My face fell in disappointment. I pleaded a headache, was excused and left to flee to my own room where I dreamed of Tom McPherson all night.

The next morning I dressed and crept downstairs in a house that seemed inhabited by peaceful ghosts. I had wakened to fragments of dreams about Tom McPherson and Lucien, and the torn edges of those dreams floated in my mind like the clothes on the drying line behind the house. Rhody gave me breakfast in a kitchen still blissfully cool. I sat bathed in the rose-and-gold sunrise as the light came through the windows. Our cat, Hyacinth, sipped her milk, and Rhody moved her bulky frame around, gliding quietly through morning's untroubled waters.

"First chance I got to talk to you alone, Miz Susan. It wuz good seein' Lucien again."

She set a cup of chocolate down in front of me. Its

steamy fragrance mingled with the smell of her fresh-baked biscuits. Nobody could make biscuits as light as Rhody's. I smiled up at her. "I knew you'd want to see him, Rhody."

"Your mama"—she wiped her hands on her starched white apron front—"your mama would kill us both if'n she knew he'd been around. Or that you saw him."

I nodded. "I know, Rhody. But we don't have to tell her, do we?"

She shook her head slowly. "Miz Susan, you jus' don't know how I felt seein' that boy again. It did my heart good. Made me think of my Sallie and the way they wuz always together." She wiped a tear from the corner of her eye.

"Your Sallie is doing fine, Rhody. She's happy in Philadelphia. You know she writes you that she's happy. And Lucien is doing fine, too."

She nodded. "You gonna see him agin?"

"He says no. Not unless I really need him, Rhody. But it's good to know where he is."

"Shore is. Your mama know you're goin' next door agin today?"

"No, but she brags to the officers about what I'm doing, so I'm going."

Wilium came in with an armful of wood for the stove. "You take these uniforms out and brush them off good," Rhody directed him. She heaped the uniforms of the two officers in his arms and held the door for him as he went out. Then she started gathering the makings for pie dough. I watched her work. What did she really think of the war? I wondered. She never spoke about it. Suppose, as Lucien had said, the South lost? What would happen to Rhody and Wilium? Would they leave? Where would they go?

"Rhody, do you know what Lucien said the other night?"

"I doan know, lessin' you tell me."

"He said he thinks the South is going to lose the war."

She laughed. "That boy always did have funny ideas."

"Do you think that's funny, Rhody? That the South should lose?"

"Didn't we jus' be winnin' a battle? Doan let your mama hear you talk like that."

"What would you do if the South lost, Rhody?"

She turned to look at me. "Go on makin' my pies and biscuits and roasts and keepin' this house clean and everybody in it from killin' each other."

She had not understood my question, I was sure of it. "You wouldn't leave?"

We stared at each other. The coffee, bubbling on the stove, drummed in the background. "You sure are askin' an awful lot of questions you never asked before since you met Mister Lucien."

"But would you leave, Rhody? Have you thought on it?"

She shook her head. "I got 'nuf work right here. Why would I leave? You best come back here for your noon meal today an' doan forget. They's busy enuf next door without feedin' you."

The discussion was over. I finished breakfast, and just as I was going out the back door she turned to me. "I wuz brought here by Mr. Hugh. I works fer Mr. Hugh. And I stays here till he tells me I gotta go."

Our eyes met. She was answering my question and more. She was telling me not only that she understood what I had said, but that her loyalty in this house was to my father.

* * *

Mifri and Mrs. Harrold were waiting for me when I arrived next door. Mrs. Harrold came and put her arms around me. Her face was very white and there were dark circles under her beautiful pale gray eyes. Jennie and Robert, who had been sent to stay with friends yesterday, were eating quietly at the kitchen table.

"Dear Susan, you've worked so hard," Mrs. Harrold said. "Now you'll have to be brave."

Whenever grown-ups tell you that you have to be brave, you have to be careful. I did not want to be brave. I knew by their faces that something terrible was going on. "What's wrong?" I asked.

"It's your young soldier, dear," Mrs. Harrold said.

My young soldier. He must be dying if they willed him to me.

"He's had a terrible night," she went on. "The minié ball that went through his upper arm shattered the bones, and he started bleeding again. His fever got out of hand. We're still waiting for the medical officer to come to the house, but he hasn't had time yet, with all the wounded. Imagine! I thought the other young boy who was shot in the jaw wouldn't make the night. And he's doing beautifully!"

"Is Tom McPherson dead?"

"No, but we have little hope."

"Can I see him?"

"Do you think you should?" Mrs. Harrold asked. "I'll leave it up to you."

"He won't know you," Mifri added. "He's out of his head."

"I want to see him." I had always thought it would be better to be out of your head if you were dying. Especially if you were so young.

"Then you shall see him," Mrs. Harrold said. And she led me up the stairs.

* * *

There was so much blood. I had never seen so much blood. It spread across the snow-white sheets like a red flower blooming. Quickly Mrs. Harrold and Mifri got new bandages and started to redress his wound.

"Go out of the room," Mrs. Harrold said, "you shouldn't see this."

It was a little late for them to decide that, wasn't it? "I can help," I said. They didn't argue. So I stayed, handing them things, Castile soap with which they washed him, clean bandages, scissors, even brandy, which I held to his lips. Beads of sweat stood out on his brow, but as he turned to me he recognized me through his feverish gaze.

"Hello, miss," he said.

"Hello."

A tear crept down his cheek. "Will you write to my mama? And tell her. Say how kindly I was treated. Say that I did my best, fightin'. Tell her, oh, I have no more breath, miss, I have no more . . ."

He lapsed into unconsciousness and only his labored breathing could be heard in the room. After they dressed his wound, Mrs. Harrold agreed that I could stay with him. She turned to see Jennie and Robert holding hands in the doorway, looking into the room.

"Children, children, I told you to stay downstairs. Come now, come along with Mama."

"Is the man dying?" Jennie asked.

"We hope not. But we'll pray for him. Would you like that? We'll go downstairs now and read the Bible and pray for him."

She and Mifri left and I applied cold compresses to Tom McPherson's brow. I was to call, Mrs. Harrold said, if he started bleeding again.

I stayed the whole day. I never left his side. I bathed

his face and held his hand. I sensed and heard movement in the rest of the house and once or twice Mrs. Harrold came in. She would take his pulse, which she pronounced very irregular. "You must be brave, Susan," she said again. I nodded. Then I felt her hand on my shoulder.

"Susan, perhaps this is not the time to say this, but I know how brave you have been. Not just about helping me here. But at home."

Still holding Tom McPherson's hand, I looked up at her. Her lovely pale gray eyes seemed almost blue with the desire of what she wanted to say. "I know you miss your father, Susan. And how fond you are of him. And he of you. And I am aware of your mother's . . . condition. How could I not be aware? I live next door. I hear her many times when she's having one of her spells. I say this not to embarrass you, Susan, or to make you feel disloyal to your mama. But to tell you that it's all right. I realize how confused you must be sometimes. But life does things to people, Susan. I know. I've lost my own husband. I sometimes feel that if I don't pray very hard and hold on, I'll awake some morning to find that my sanity has slipped away from me."

She smoothed the top of my head with her hand. "Be patient with her, Susan. And know that you have a friend in me. That I understand."

I nodded. Tears constricted my throat. She fussed with the coverlet on Tom McPherson. "I don't think he'll make it until dusk, dear. Would you like me to take over for you?"

"No, thank you," I said, "I'll stay. I'll be all right."

"Of course you will." She kissed me lightly on top of my head and left.

My heart was so full that I could barely breathe. All my senses were heightened. I felt a love for Mrs.

Harrold, for Tom McPherson and his mama whom I did not even know, for my daddy, for Lucien, for Kenneth, even for Connie and for everyone I knew, the whole wretched lot of us caught up in what Lucien had called the stinking Cause.

I don't know the exact moment that Tom McPherson died. I was reading the Bible while I listened to his rasping breathing, and in the next moment the room was silent. I never knew, before, what real silence meant, and it terrified me.

It meant the absence of breathing, the absence of life. In this case it meant the absence of a lank-haired young soldier from North Carolina whose greatest pleasure in the last twenty-four hours had been some sour soup that reminded him of home. I sat there, realizing he was gone and feeling the impossibility of the huge gaping silence take over the room. And me.

I felt a very real terror then for the first time in my life. I sensed the vast emptiness of death, and I wondered why this young boy had to die. And for what? The Cause? It had such a sweet ring to it when people were shouting and marching or discussing it at parties, but here in this silent room it meant nothing to me at all.

What if Lucien was right? What then? What if everyone in the South was a fool? What if the Cause did stink? What if it was corrupt and evil?

What if all the Tom McPhersons would never see their mamas again because they died for a system not worth dying for?

I shivered at the possibility. And I felt for the first time the impossible chasm that existed between the songs I played on the piano and this dead boy lying in front of me. There was no connection between them, none at all.

I felt so desolate, sitting there. I wanted to die myself. But then Mrs. Harrold came back into the room, brisk and efficient. She took Tom McPherson's pulse, then closed his eyelids and came around to where I was sitting.

"Do you know what I want you to do now, Susan?" she asked.

"No, ma'am."

"I would like it very much if you would take the children to Pizzini's for ice cream. Do you think you could do that?"

"Oh, Mrs. Harrold," and I flung myself against her, crying. She held me close. And we cried together for a moment. Then she took some money from her pocket and gave it to me. "The children are waiting," she said. "It's a lovely day outside. And you look as if you need some fresh air. Don't hurry back."

When I went home that night I gave Mama a note from Mrs. Harrold about Tom McPherson's death. Again, Mama was entertaining the two officers. "Oh, my poah, deah child," and she hugged me. "Gentlemen, the soldier Susan was nursing next doah died today."

There were murmurs of regret. "Our North Carolina boys fought well," said the officer with his arm in the sling. "They suffered heavy casualties in the battle."

I felt light-headed and possessed by an eerie sense of unreality. "I wonder if that matters now that he's dead," I said.

"Susan!" Mama chided. "You know it does! To think you would say such a thing to these two officers who are, themselves, recuperating from their battle wounds. You must apologize."

"I'm sorry," I said contritely.

"It's all right," the same officer said. "Young people say what we adults dare not even think in our hearts, ma'am. I'm sure your daughter has seen enough today

to be entitled to speak her mind, and wants to be
excused to be with her own thoughts.''

"Thank you, sir." I curtsied. He took my hand and
smiled warmly at me. His fellow officer did likewise. *Is
it possible they are on to Mama?* I wondered. But I was
too tired to think on it. Upstairs, even before I cleaned
myself up, I took my pen and wrote to Martha McPherson
in North Carolina.

The next morning I accompanied Mrs. Harrold and
the hearse to Oakwood Cemetery to help bury Tom
McPherson. I shed no tears, for I had done all my
crying. After the funeral I went directly home and to my
room where I found the white silk dress Daddy had
once bought for me in New York. I left a note for
Mama, telling her I was going to the Spotswood to meet
Mrs. Wigfall. The white silk dress was in a small carpet
bag that I carried along with me. The least I could do
was donate it to make the Stars and Bars, I decided. For
Tom McPherson, if not for myself.

Chapter Eight

I waited in the lobby of the Spotswood for Mrs. Wigfall. I busied myself watching the important people
walking across the elegant Persian carpet under the huge
chandelier. Many were Confederate officers, their uniforms looking a little worn from the recent battle.

"Mrs. Wigfall will be down in a few minutes, miss."
The nigra messenger stood over me. I thanked him,
then felt my eyes widening with horror as I spied Mrs.
Turnstable and Connie coming down the sweeping stair-

case. In a moment they were at the bottom step, had seen me and were coming in my direction. I wanted to run. How could I face them?

"Well, Susan."

I was so shocked to hear Mrs. Turnstable speak to me that I could not form a proper answer.

"And what brings you to the Spotswood? Aren't you a little bit outside your element?"

I wasn't quite sure what this meant, but I knew it couldn't be good. "I'm here to do some sewing for the army," I said.

She laughed. "Indeed. You are talking about sewing for the Confederate army, are you not?"

My cheeks were burning. Beside her Connie took a step back and lowered her eyes. *If you were truly my friend, you'd say something instead of standing there looking like a raccoon that just raided the cookie jar,* I thought.

"Yes, ma'am, I'm sewing for the Confederate army."

"I just wanted to make sure." And she laughed again. "One can never tell with you Chilmarks. After all, only a few days ago I saw your brother in this very lobby. I couldn't imagine what he was doing here when everyone else was gathering for news of the battle. He is a handsome devil, though. And impeccably dressed, although his civilian clothes made him stand out like the proverbial fox in the henhouse."

Tears came to my eyes, but I knew I couldn't defend Lucien. To do so would be an admission that I was not only close to him but that I was less than a true Confederate. "Is Kenneth all right?" I asked.

Mrs. Turnstable was fussing with her net mitts. My daddy always said that a woman who takes a long time to get her gloves on is plotting. "Kenneth survived the battle, thank the Lord. You may tell your mama that.

You may also tell her that if I see her son in this hotel again, I will not be responsible for what I say to him."

"I'm sure my mama won't mind what you say to him, Mrs. Turnstable. It's what you say to others about him and about her that hurts."

Her nostrils dilated. She raised her chin. "Come along, Constance." She gave me a final glare as she swept off. I sat there wanting to cry. It never occurred to me until later that I had defended Mama.

"My deah! Tears!"

"I'm all right."

"But tears! Heah, heah," and Charlotte Wigfall enfolded me in her arms. I allowed myself to be led through the lobby and up the stairs while she chatted about her children. Louly and Fanny were coming down from Massachusetts. "I expect them around the first of August. And I'm enrolling them in Miss Pegram's. So you can be friends."

The afternoon light filtered in a soft haze through the green draperies in the parlor of her suite. She had tea and iced cakes waiting.

"I could use some new friends," I said.

She smiled. "I wasn't quite eavesdropping, mind you," she said in her soft Texas drawl, "but I was within earshot. My deah, I am so sorry. Emily Turnstable has her concerns, with Kenneth off fighting, but between you and me I always thought she was a troublemaker."

"You may feel that way about us, too, if your boy leaves the university to enlist," I said. "And you'd have every right."

She sighed. "No one ever has the right to be cruel. Susan, I don't know your brother but I have heard of him. He is the talk of Richmond. Now you know why your mama doesn't want you out. I should have come and fetched you sooner.''

"I'm not a serving of ice cream from Pizzini's that will melt,'' I said.

"No, you aren't. You're a deah and brave little thing. And I'm sure your brother has his reasons for not enlisting. I understand he spends his days on the rivers and brings in all sorts of fish and game. The very same people who indulge in gossip about him aren't above enjoying the food he brings in.''

"You're so kind,'' I said impulsively. "I wish you were my mama.''

Her hand flew to her throat. "Well! My deah! I am flattered. But you have your own mama. I know sometimes she is unjustly harsh with you. We, my husband and I, have heard about her difficulties, Susan. Your deah father has confided in us. For his sake, and for your mama's, we are determined not to let either the cruel gossip about your brother or your mama's ... difficulties keep us from being friends. This is why I offered to teach you to sew the flags, deah. I think you need to get away from your mama a little bit. It would do you good. And at the same time it makes her happy that you are working for the Cause.''

"I still wish you were my mama,'' I said. "I can't make my own mama love me, no matter what. I could sew a hundred flags, and it wouldn't matter.''

"I'm sure she loves you, Susan.'' She got up from her chair and sat down on the settee to put her arm around me. "She just is ... not quite right in the head sometimes. Your deah daddy explained it to us. We must be patient with her. Come now, let's have our tea before it gets cold. And then we'll get to the sewing. We can be friends, you and I. Sometimes, between women, that is just as important.''

* * *

When Charlotte Wigfall's carriage dropped me off in front of our house later that day, I was surprised to see another vehicle parked there. A nigra was unloading the baggage. *More company,* I thought dismally. Would Mama never stop entertaining? Even in the middle of war? And then I saw one of my daddy's portmanteaus.

"Daddy!" I ran into the house. The foyer was empty but I heard his voice coming from the back parlor. I ran down the hall. He was standing at the window in the parlor, looking out, his hands clasped behind him. My mother sat in a nearby chair. Neither of them noticed me.

"Isn't there anyone else Anderson can send but you?" Mama asked.

"My dear, I must travel to recover the rails that were seized by Stonewall Jackson's army from the B. and O. Railroad," my father said. "We're also going to acquire old rails from the Virginia Central. I'm not the only one Anderson will have out there searching for iron for the project."

"But I need you here," Mama said. "I have wounded in the house. With the war I have all sorts of new responsibilities. And I'm having a difficult time with Susan."

"I know that, my dear. But Tredegar has contracted with the secretary of the navy to supply the iron for sheathing the vessel. It must be found as quickly as possible."

"Daddy?" I said hesitantly.

He turned, saw me and beamed. His face was bronzed, making the gray at his temples stand out more than ever. "Susan!"

I ran to him. He held me, his embrace saying everything.

"There was a battle, Daddy. And the town is full of soldiers. We have two officers right here in this house."

"I know." He smiled down at me. "I've been told of them."

"I helped Mrs. Harrold nurse some wounded. I stayed all day with one boy, reading the Bible while he was dying. I was with him when he died. He was from North Carolina."

"Susan, calm yourself," Mama ordered.

Indeed, I was shaking. Why not? The only person under God's sun who could put some sense back into my world was in it again. "Daddy, I'm so glad you're home. How is the *Virginia?* How long can you stay? Are you home for a good long visit?"

"Susan, I insist you calm yourself this minute! Your father and I were having a private conversation when you burst into the room. Susan, did you hear me? Hugh, if you indulge her, she'll be impossible. She hasn't changed a bit. She hasn't got the sense God gave a sparrow."

"I do have sense!" I whirled on her. "I've plenty! More than that stupid Mrs. Turnstable you're always trying to impress!"

She gasped.

"Susan, hush. Don't be impertinent to your mother," my father corrected me. "Susan," he chided, "you must apologize."

"I'm sorry, Mama," I said.

"Impertinent." Mama ignored my apology and stood up. "Impertinent is the least of it. How about disobedient? How about sneaky?"

"Charlotte," my father remonstrated, "I'm only home for one night. Can't we get along?"

"Home ten minutes, and you're taking her part already. All right, then, ask her what happened to the good white silk you once brought back from New York for her. I distinctly told her she could not take it to Mrs. Wigfall's. It is not in her room. Well, why don't you ask your daughter, Hugh Chilmark?''

Daddy seemed so sad. He looked down at me. ''Is it true, Susan? Did you take the dress against your mama's wishes?''

I hugged him. ''Yes, Daddy.''

''There you are, Hugh Chilmark.'' Mama seemed satisfied.

My father dislodged my arms from around his middle and, holding my hands in his own, regarded me sternly. ''Why, Susan?''

I looked up at him appealingly. ''Because we needed the silk for the flag. The dress was of no use anymore. I wanted it to be part of a flag that some regiment will carry into battle.''

''That was naughty, Susan. To disobey your mama.''

Tears brimmed in my eyes. I couldn't bear it when my daddy scolded. I nodded. ''I won't do it again,'' I promised.

He put his arms around me. ''See that you don't, Susan.''

''That's it, spoil her some more, Hugh Chilmark. I declaah, as if you haven't spoiled her enough. And tomorrow night you'll be gone, heaven knows where, and I'll be heah trying to maintain our home and raise our daughter decently. She needs a strong hand. But, of course, you didn't have that with Lucien, either. The only time you punished him was when I insisted upon it. He knew it and that's why he resented me. And in the end we lost him anyway.''

I couldn't see my father's expression, because I was busy holding him. But his voice was firm. ''That isn't why we lost Lucien, Charlotte. We both know why we lost him. And there isn't a day that goes by in my life lately that I don't regret it. But it has nothing to do with the fact that I wasn't strict enough.''

Mama was silent for a moment. ''You forget some things, Hugh.'' Her voice had a warning note in it.

''I don't forget anything, Charlotte,'' he said sadly. ''I wish to God that I could, but I can't. You can be sure of that.''

He still had his arms around me. I buried my head against him. Whatever was going on between them, I didn't know. But it was terrible. It was more than terrible. It was sinister and threatening and I couldn't bear listening.

''All I insist upon, Hugh,'' Mama said carefully, ''is that you leave the discipline of Susan up to me, since you will be going away again. It's unfair of you to come home and interfere with my authority. Is that too much to ask?''

''No. Not if you are reasonable, Charlotte.''

''Very well, then. Susan, you may take your supper in the kitchen tonight with Rhody. That is for disobeying me about the dress. Is that reasonable enough, Hugh?''

''But, Mama, Daddy's only home for one night!''

''Hush, Susan,'' Daddy ordered.

I hushed.

''Surely, Charlotte, that's a little harsh. I came home to see my family.''

''You may see Susan in the morning at breakfast,'' she said. ''You know I like to sleep late. You may visit with her then. Your daughter has gotten very out of hand lately, Hugh. I must ask you again not to undermine my authority.''

''Susan, do as your mother says,'' my father whispered. ''Go on now. Go into the kitchen with Rhody. I must meet the young officers. Your mama is planning a dinner party. I'll see you in the morning."

"Susan, your mama's condition is worsening. I'm worried about her. I know the war is making everyone's nerves frayed, but in the little while I've been home I can see that her moods are getting more pronounced and unreasonable."

"She seems just the same to me as she's always been, Daddy."

A morning breeze picked up the lace panels of the curtains in the dining room, and they rippled gently. A sound of birdsong came from outside. A horse and carriage clip-clopped by. Rhody refilled my father's coffee cup from over his shoulder. The steam rose to his face. Rhody moved around the table like some great ship prowling through a sea of troubled waters. The floor creaked under her as she went by.

My father waited until she left the room. I looked down at my cup of hot chocolate. He put his hand over mine on the table. "I knocked on your door last evening to say good night. You were asleep. I didn't want to disturb you."

"I tried to stay awake but Mama's supper party went on too long."

"I'm going away, Susan. There are things we must discuss."

I nodded. "Will you be gone very long this time?"

"I don't know. But the war is here and who knows what will transpire in our lives before we see each other again. Believe me when I tell you your mama's condition is worsening. I know her better than you do. The cruel gossip about Lucien is hurting her. She's throwing herself into her sewing because it's the only way she can fight back. She's at an age when she's feeling the hurts and losses in her life more than ever, Susan. You must be forbearing with her."

I looked down at my food. "I try to be, Daddy."

"Rhody told me about the incident when your mother turned away the soldiers and you spoke up to her and she slapped you."

"I did what I thought was right, Daddy. You were the one who told me to do that, even though it might go against someone I love."

"You did right to speak up. But with your mama you must pick and choose the right times to do so. And save the speaking up for the important occasions."

"Wasn't that important?"

"Yes, it was. And I'm sorry she hit you. Has she been doing that again?"

"No." I could lie to him, but I couldn't keep the color from rising to my face.

"You wouldn't tell me if she were. I know you love her, Susan. It breaks my heart to see what is happening to my family. I hate going away and leaving you like this, as capable as I know you are. If only I could depend on that scalawag son of mine."

"Please don't say that about Lucien, Daddy. He isn't a scalawag."

He scowled. "I sense you know something you're not telling me, Susan. What do you know of your brother? Have you heard something more than the usual gossip?"

I looked down at my breakfast. I didn't want to lie again to my father. He was going away and I wanted things to be honest between us. "I've met Lucien, Daddy."

His brown eyes were piercing, but not unkind. More aptly, they could be described as interested. "When and how?" he asked.

"At the Spotswood. I went one day to hear news of

the battle when everyone else was there. I slipped off.
Mama didn't know. I met him by mistake. I . . . bumped
into him.''

"And?"

"We got talking. He took me for a carriage ride. We
had a meal at his place. We got to know each other. It's
all right, isn't it?"

He patted his mouth with the white linen napkin, set
it down and leaned back in his chair. "You met your
brother, and you haven't told anyone about it?"

"I'm telling you, Daddy. I can't tell Mama. You
know that."

He nodded. His face went pale. "How is he?"

"He's fine, Daddy."

"Did he . . . ask for me?"

"Yes. I told him you were working on the *Virginia*."

"Did he say much else? About us?"

"He told me why he left."

He looked at me steadily, trying to assess my feelings. "How much did he tell you?"

"Well, we talked about Sallie. And the way you and
he quarreled when you found he'd taught her to read.
And how you sent her away."

He nodded. "Anything else?"

"No. I got the feeling there was more, but he refused
to talk about it beyond that."

He sighed, seeming almost relieved. "I'm not proud
of any of it, of sending Sallie away or the way I
behaved that time with Lucien. But I had to do it."

I said nothing.

"There are things you don't understand and that I
can't tell you. You must trust me. I acted badly, unwisely.
And I paid for it. I lost my son. As I told your mother
yesterday, I regret it more each day. What do you think
of him?"

I smiled. "He's a lot like you, Daddy. He's a good businessman. He owns half a gambling house, and he has a very pretty lady friend."

"Will you see him again?"

"He says only if I need him for anything. He knows he isn't acceptable in Richmond society, and he doesn't want to make things look bad for me."

He sipped his coffee and checked his pocket watch.

"What time do you have to leave, Daddy?"

"I must be at Tredegar for a meeting at eleven this morning. We have some time yet. My train leaves at three this afternoon. I'm glad you met your brother, Susan. Yes, I am." He was smiling but there were tears in his eyes. "I told you he's been on my mind more and more lately, and it isn't right you two shouldn't know each other. Now I'll be honest with you. The last I saw him was three years ago and as I told you, the meeting went badly. He hasn't forgiven me for. . . certain things. But I am aware of all his activities. My lawyer, Mr. Ratcliffe, has kept me informed about my son, at my request."

"Daddy," I chided, "that's not fair. You knew everything all along."

"Not that you two met, no." He shook his head vigorously. "I never knew that. But I am glad of it. Do you like him?"

I scowled. "Yes, I think so. He's difficult. Different from us. His ideas are so different. We argued about some things, but he's interesting. I could talk to him forever. He pretends to be very stern and uncaring. But I think, inside, he hurts a lot. He's very honest, and I like that. I think that's what puts most people off about him. His honesty. Most people don't want honesty, Daddy."

He smiled. "So you've learned that already, have you?"

"I found that out when I met Lucien. I think I could learn more from him, too. You wouldn't mind if I saw him again, would you?"

"No. The day could come when you may need him. As I said, I don't know what's going to transpire here in Richmond while I'm away. From what Mr. Ratcliffe has told me about him, he's honorable and dependable as well as being a good businessman. It takes a load off my mind knowing you have him to call on if you really need him. Certainly, if you and he have reached an understanding and can be of help to each other, I won't stand in your way."

"I knew you'd say something like that, Daddy."

He took out his pocket watch again. "Next time you see your brother, tell him I asked for him. Maybe when the war is over..." He sighed. "I'm sure there will be a reshuffling of the cards then, and we'll all take another look at things. Susan, you're growing up. You're old enough to decide some things for yourself. I trust you to know your own mind. You must stand by your mother, dutifully, in the days ahead. But at the same time you must always do what is right. That's not an easy charge I'm giving you. As I told you before, there comes a time when the two don't coincide, when doing right means going against those we love."

"How will I know what's right to do, then, Daddy?"

"You will." He put down his napkin and got up. "I must go."

"It's early yet. It isn't even nine."

"I just remembered that I must drop around to my lawyer's office and see him about something. Come, walk me to the door, will you?"

PART TWO

January 20, 1862

Chapter Nine

The organ boomed majestically in St. Paul's Episcopal Church, and outside in the bitter cold January air the bells of Richmond tolled mournfully. Wherever I looked I saw brilliant uniforms, swords, flashing spurs and bright sashes on the men. The women were all dressed in black. Richmond had turned out in full to bury the tenth president of the United States, John Tyler. Outside, on the icy streets, there were at least 150 carriages for the funeral cortege. I had seen the dark, riderless horse with the boots reversed in the stirrups that represented the dead man.

I craned my neck to see the casket up ahead in the aisle, as I stood between Mama and Mrs. Wigfall. Mrs. Wigfall had asked me for the Confederate flag I had sewed, to put on the casket. Then she had told me the cabinet had argued over whether the casket should be draped with the Stars and Stripes or the Stars and Bars.

Now I could see that there was no flag on the casket, which meant that the cabinet could not agree, and so John Tyler was to go to his grave without any flag to cover him.

I worried about the banner I had made. Would it be lost in the shuffle? I worried about my father, who had been home for only two days at Christmas and was back in Norfolk again, designing the cannon for the *Virginia*. And I worried about the Confederacy. The mood was somber today for more reasons than John Tyler's death.

The Union had secured a toehold around Charleston.
The Yankees had captured Beaufort City in South Carolina.
And Mr. Lincoln's blockade of all our ports, which kept
goods from coming into the Confederacy, made us all
miserable.

Then, as I filed down the aisle with Mama, I brightened,
for I saw my brother Lucien in the nave at the back of
the church. He saw me too and stepped forward, smiled,
then moved back into the shadows. There had been
several police raids on gambling houses in the fall. Mrs.
Wigfall had told me that the gambling house owners had
friends from the slums to the pulpit. And I wondered
how many friends Lucien had in the pulpit.

I had seen him only once in the ensuing months.
When I was walking on Franklin Street with Mama one
day last fall, he had ridden by on his handsome black
horse. He had smiled and raised his hat, and Mama had
grabbed my arm and rushed me along, refusing to
acknowledge the greeting.

At Christmas he sent a package to the house. In it had
been yards of good dark blue wool for a warm cloak for
me. Mama had been furious, not because he had obvi-
ously gotten it from a ship that had run the blockade—
plenty of people in Richmond did that—but because he
had the audacity—that was the word she had used—
to send anything to the house for me. She had wanted to
send it back, but Daddy had said no and told Rhody to
see to it that a cloak was made for me. And he
instructed me to write a thank-you note to my brother. I
wore the cloak today.

There was a package waiting for me when I got home
from the luncheon Mama and I and Mrs. Wigfall
attended after the funeral. After Mama went to her room
to nap, Rhody brought it to me. "Some man name of
Nate brung it to the door."

I opened it with trembling fingers. It was my Confederate flag! A note was with it:

Dear Susan: It was good seeing you this morning. We have lost a great man in John Tyler. He served Virginia and the Confederacy until the end even though he did what he could to prevent this awful war. I see you were wearing a cloak made from the material I sent. James Irving, the sexton's son, gave me this flag for you. I understand you made it. The fools in our cabinet let a good man go to his grave with a bare casket. James Irving thinks you are very beautiful, and I must say you looked quite the young lady today. When the weather breaks, as it will soon, I'll get a note to you, and you and I and Fanny can have a picnic on Drewry's Bluff. We can see the fortifications. Give my best to Rhody. You'll hear from me. Your brother, Lucien.

Lucien had a revolver. I saw it when he took his frock coat off on Drewry's Bluff. The brass frame of the gun gleamed in the sunlight. We sat, the three of us, on ground warmed by the sun on the side of the hills. Spring had come in the way it can only come to Richmond. Drewry's Bluff was seven miles below Richmond and overlooked a narrow place in the James River channel. We could go only so high, however. Batteries of guns were poised in formidable positions above us.

Fanny had selected the spot and spread a tablecloth, and Lucien was helping to unpack the picnic hamper.

"You have a pistol, Lucien," I said.

He looked at me. "It's my Colt. I've been using a gun since I was eleven years old, Susan, since I learned to hunt."

"John Winder declared martial law in Richmond on March first. Mama says all good citizens are surrendering their firearms. I know it's only the first week in March and everyone hasn't turned their guns over yet but . . ."

"I never claimed to be a good citizen." He smiled wryly at me. "John Winder has also forbidden liquor sales in the city. If I obeyed that edict I might as well close my gambling house down tomorrow."

"They're putting people in Castle Godwin if they suspect them of disloyalty to the Cause," I said.

He expertly popped open a bottle of champagne and filled two glasses. "Susan, I appreciate your concern and your intelligence. But it's a lovely spring day. It's been a depressing winter. The South has lost Forts Henry and Donelson in Tennessee, suffered the collapse of its line of defense in Kentucky, and Nashville has fallen. Federal armies are poised in northern Virginia, at Harpers Ferry and on the peninsula at Fortress Monroe. Both Richmond and Norfolk are threatened. Shall I go on?"

"Daddy's in Norfolk," I said.

"He'll be all right. My point is, the outlook is bleak for the South. John Winder has to do something to ward off panic so he requires hotels to deliver lists of the new arrivals to the provost marshal's office every morning. And he says no one can leave or enter the city without a military pass. And he makes some arrests. It makes the people feel better. Fanny, give her some champagne."

"I certainly won't," but she smiled and handed me a glass of lemonade, then set about cutting up the cold duck and serving biscuits and pickled eggs and potato salad and jam. "You've been accused of just about everything going, Lucien," she reminded him, "but so far you haven't been accused of corrupting the young."

"My sister isn't young. Spend half an hour with her, and you'll come to that conclusion." He grinned at me.

"You aren't a loyal Confederate," I sassed, "so how could it have been a depressing winter for you?"

"It's been depressing for all of us. I know loyal Southerners who feel bad because President Lincoln's son, Willie, died."

"Mama says it was God's punishment for old Abraham for not allowing us to live our own lives."

"God's teeth, Charlotte would say something like that. She's got the most perverted sense of logic, that woman. How did you manage to get away today?"

"I'm supposed to be sewing with Mrs. Wigfall. She'll make excuses for me if she has to."

"She's pretty high up there in Richmond society. Why would she do that, knowing you'd be with me?"

"Because she's heard of your exploits. And she thinks you're very dashing. And that I need to get out more. And because..." I hesitated.

He frowned. "Go on, I'm fascinated."

"I told Daddy I met you, Lucien. I hope you don't mind. He said he was glad we met, that there was someone I could...turn to with him away. And Mrs. Wigfall knows this, and she places great store in what Daddy says."

He sipped his champagne. Fanny paused in her eating to watch his reaction. "When did you tell him this?" he asked quietly.

"When he came home for a visit last summer."

He gazed out into the distance for a moment, saying nothing.

"Well," Fanny said, "that explains why the wool you sent at Christmas wasn't returned, Lucien. You were afraid it would be."

He nodded, leaning back, supporting himself on one

elbow, his face in the direction of the sun. Fanny and I exchanged glances, and she shrugged and shook her head, indicating that he did not want to talk about it.

"Do you think the Yankees will attack Richmond, Lucien?" I asked, wanting to change the subject.

"They've been yelling 'On to Richmond' for months now," he said.

"But the *Dispatch* said our city is so well fortified."

"Defenses only serve to gain time," he said, "and President Davis doesn't want to shut his armies inside a besieged city and watch everyone starve. Our General Johnston must strike at the Yankees' General McClellan and destroy him."

"Can he?" Fanny asked.

He laughed and sipped his champagne. "I don't know. I'm bored with it all."

"How can you be?" I demanded.

"Don't let him fool you," Fanny said. "He's anything but. He's gone and joined the Second Class Militia."

"Lucien, you haven't!" I said.

He took a bite of his food. "If it comes to defending my town, I'm ready. I'll not let the Yankees destroy what I've built up. But I won't run out on any field and fight for some Deep South slaveholders. This is my war only when my personal property is threatened."

"I think you're despicable," I teased.

He looked at me. "Then why did you come today?"

"Because I wanted to see you again, even though I think you're despicable."

He laughed.

"What I think is so remarkable about this," Fanny said, "is that you two bicker so beautifully. One would think you'd known each other for years."

"We are good at it, aren't we?" Lucien agreed. Then

he became solemn. "I've had a letter from Sallie for
Rhody. It came to me through a friend now that mails
are stopped between North and South. My friend's in
the area because he sketches for *Harper's Weekly*. I
need you to give the letter to Rhody and get her reply
back to me by the end of the month. Will you do that?"

"Of course," I said.

He took the letter out of his waistcoat pocket and
gave it to me. I looked at Fanny.

"Fanny knows," he said, "it's all right."

Fanny knew what? I wondered. That he'd once been
in love with Sallie? I didn't dare think on it. Lucien was
far too sophisticated for me. I put the letter in a book I
had brought along. Then I noticed him looking at Fanny
with something more than friendliness in his eyes as she
removed her bonnet and shook out her hair to enjoy the
sun, and I decided to leave them alone for a while.

"I think I'll take a little walk," I said.

"Don't go too far up the bluffs," Lucien cautioned.
"We don't need to attract unnecessary attention."

It was when I was a little higher on the slope that I
saw the balloon. It hung suspended, majestically, in the
blue sky upriver, hovering over Richmond. I stared at it,
as I'd done on other occasions when I'd seen it. Always
it had a strange effect upon me. It was framed against
the spring sky like a vision of hope, of possibility, of
escape. How many people in the beleaguered city of
Richmond must be seeing it and thinking the same
thing? I wondered.

One time it had hovered so close over the city that I
could hear the hissing of the gas that propelled it and
made it sound like a fire-eating dragon. I decided that I
had never seen anything so beautiful in my life. The
letters on the balloon's side facing the city spelled

CONSTITUTION. The newspapers reported that the Yankees
were using balloons regularly now to spy on our armies
in the field.

I sank to the ground, wrapped my skirts around me
and sat gazing at it. How I would love to be so far
above town, looking down. What a sight it must be! My
father had seen a balloon once at a fair when he was
North. A man had dangled from it wearing striped
tights, he'd told me.

I don't know how long I sat there, but the next thing I
knew Lucien was behind me. "Beautiful, isn't it?"

"Yes."

He sat down beside me, and we were silent for a few
minutes. "That's Professor Lowe," he said finally.
"He's sent telegraph messages to President Lincoln
from five hundred feet up. He has at least seven of
those contraptions in his balloon service. He has nine
aeronauts, too."

"What are the balloons made of, Lucien?"

"Silk."

"Like the flags I made?"

"Yes."

"Doesn't the South have a balloon?"

"Not that I know of. There were reports of a Confederate balloon last September. But no one can prove it by
me. The South just hasn't money for such luxuries."

"It makes me want to cry, it's so beautiful."

"It should make you want to cry. He's up there
taking notes of everything, that aeronaut. I bet President
Davis is crying this minute. Susan, I didn't want to give
you the impression before that the only reason I wanted
to see you today was because of Sallie's letter. That was
ungracious of me, and I'm sorry."

I met his brown eyes and waited to see what he
would say next.

"Fanny and I both enjoy your company and wanted you along on our picnic," he said.

I nodded. It was the correct apology of a Southern gentleman, with no deeper meaning behind it than that. I was foolish to think it meant anything more.

"Thank you for sending the wool at Christmas," I said. "You know, it made Mama furious."

"I have no doubt about that."

"She wanted to send it back. Daddy insisted she behave about it."

"Well, I'm glad he finally insisted she behave about something." He looked in the distance at the balloon. "So he said he's glad we met, did he?"

"Yes. He also said that maybe after the war is over you and he can take another look at things."

He grunted, still looking at the balloon.

"He told Mama, in front of me, that there isn't a day that goes by that he doesn't regret losing you. And he told me that he isn't proud of what he did, sending Sallie away."

He remained silent.

"Lucien, he knows all about you, did you know that?"

He looked at me quickly. "What do you mean?"

"He said he's kept track of your activities, through his lawyer."

"So, he's had old Ratcliffe spying on me, has he?"

"No, Lucien, it isn't that. Honestly. He sounded just as if he wanted to know how you were doing. Because he's interested."

He got to his feet and reached out to me. "We've got to get started. It's a trip back to town."

I gave him my hand, got up and smoothed my skirts. "Lucien, it's all right that I told Daddy we met, isn't it? I don't like being dishonest with him."

He shoved his hands into his pockets as we walked down the slope. "Of course it's all right, Susan," he said. "Don't be silly."

Chapter Ten

On the eleventh of March we heard the first good news that we'd had in months. The CSS *Virginia,* the ship my father had helped to create, steamed out of Norfolk Harbor under the command of Flag Officer Franklin Buchanan and, at Hampton Roads near Norfolk and Fortress Monroe, destroyed the Federal vessel *Congress,* rammed into the *Cumberland* and ran the *Minnesota* ashore. Then the *Virginia* turned around and returned to Norfolk.

"And the *Congress* had fifty guns and the *Cumberland* thirty," said elderly, elegant Mrs. George Wythe Randolph. Her husband, who was a grandson of Thomas Jefferson, had been brought in from the field, where he'd been a general, to be secretary of war for President Davis.

We were busy sewing in the basement of St. Paul's. Thirty thousand sandbags were needed for fortifications.

Mama allowed me to go out more after the news of the success of the *Virginia* was received in Richmond. Oh, the ladies could still pass remarks about Lucien, but now the edge was taken off those remarks, since everyone knew that my daddy had worked on the *Virginia*.

My job was to cut the material. I sat on a rug on the floor. There were ample amounts of tea and cakes and what passed for coffee—a mixture of sorghum seed, sweet potatoes, chickory, and chestnuts—presided over

by Louly and Fanny Wigfall. I was bursting with pride
over Daddy's work on the *Virginia*. But it was Mrs.
Wigfall who did the boasting for me.

"You all know, ladies, that this deah child's father
helped design the *Virginia*. And he was also instrumen-
tal in securing the iron for the ship."

Everyone smiled at me. I basked in the warmth of
acceptance. Across the room I saw Mrs. Turnstable give
me a haughty look. I attended to my cutting. Connie sat
beside her mother, stacking finished sandbags. I had not
spoken to her since she'd hurt me so that day at the
Spotswood. She was looking at me, so I lowered my
eyes. I may be impulsive and foolish sometimes, but I
have my pride.

"I think it's disgraceful," Mrs. Clopton was saying,
"just disgraceful." Everyone listened. If something was
disgraceful, it was worth hearing about. "Why, those
Baltimore detectives who work for General Winder
raise a little finger, and the best carriages in the city
have to turn around and go home. And those detectives
ride government horses, too. Or horses they've gotten
from some Richmond gentleman's stable. It's gone too
far! One word from them and some poor innocent
victim is sent to Castle Godwin!"

Detectives from Baltimore who were Southern sympathizers had come to Richmond to work for General
Winder. Maryland had stayed with the Union, but Baltimore was full of Southern sympathizers. On his way to
his inauguration, Abraham Lincoln had to be smuggled
through Baltimore lest there be an attempt on his life.
And last April a Baltimore mob attacked Massachusetts
troops as they traveled by train through that city.

"Those detectives may be awful, but at least we can
sleep better in our beds at night," said Mrs. Turnstable.
"General Winder's reign in this city does have its

excesses. But would you rather have the fights, knifings and shootings we had before he took over with martial law? Why, I remember late last summer seeing white men promenading with nigra women on Brooke Avenue!''

''Just the same, Winder's detectives have gone overboard,'' Mrs. Clopton insisted. ''My husband said they seized all Elijah Baker's patent medicines in their search for contraband liquor.''

Everyone laughed. It was a huge joke in town. ''Baker's Bitters,'' the medicine was called.

From across the room Connie attempted to smile at me but I would not respond.

''Let's talk about something else,'' Mrs. Wigfall suggested.

''I think it would be a wonderful idea,'' said Mrs. Vernon, ''if we ladies could raise funds to build an ironclad for the defense of Richmond. Like the *Virginia*.''

There was a chorus of ''oohs,'' and they were off on a new topic. Before the day was over they would call themselves the Ladies' Defense Association.

''My husband tells me that General Longstreet wants the South to have a balloon,'' Mrs. Wigfall said. Her husband was now lending his services as a temporary staff officer in the field. Someone laughed but was shushed.

She kept sewing. ''You all know, my deahs, that the North has balloons. We've all seen Professor Lowe's balloon hovering over Richmond, spying on us. General Longstreet dearly wants one so we can do reconnaissance over Union lines. But we don't have money for one. My husband said the general has discussed this widely in camp and someone came up with the suggestion that the South make its balloon as economically as possible. With silk.''

"And where do you propose we get this silk?" said Mrs. George Wythe Randolph.

I could have told them right off that Mrs. Randolph wouldn't go for the idea because she hadn't thought of it.

Charlotte Wigfall threaded her needle and smiled. "From dresses," she said. "We all know there isn't any silk left in the Confederacy. Except in the dresses of its womenfolk."

The room became so silent you could hear the coffee bubbling on the stove. Even the two sewing machines stopped.

"Well, I do declaah," said Mrs. George Wythe Randolph. No one else said anything.

"Give up our dresses?" Mrs. Turnstable piped up. "Why the only decent silk I have left is the one George bought me when he went to Charleston on our twentieth anniversary. He said I looked like a vision in it. And I have no intention of giving it up."

"The only silk I have I use as a mourning dress," said young Mrs. Carrington. She had lost her husband at Manassas. "I know it isn't proper to wear silk for mourning, but it was all I had when Thornton died."

"I have my pink that I wore to my sister's wedding," said Mrs. Clopton. "What a wedding that was! Both my sister and I went to the Barhamville School for young ladies in Columbia, South Carolina, you know. My sister always loved to ride. Her husband went off to war with the first cavalry company that was raised in Columbia. She gave him her favorite horse. It was killed on a Virginia battlefield."

"Do you think I'd ever part with my blue silk with the lace from France?" asked Mrs. Standard. "I intend to wear it to Mrs. Davis's next levee."

Around the room the conversation went, like a brush

fire, ignited by memory, with each lady telling about
her favorite silk dress. There were memories of balls in
Savannah, barbecues at plantations in Louisiana, trips to
Europe, parties in Washington, girlhood dances. No one
interrupted anyone, and the conversation finally died
like a bright and cheerful fire that had been put out.

Mrs. Wigfall let them finish. Then she spoke.
"Someone in this room has already given up a silk
dress. Susan, why don't you tell them?"

Everyone was looking at me. "Well," I stammered
into the sea of inquiring faces, "it didn't fit me anymore. It was my good white silk from dancing school.
Daddy bought it for me in New York. And I cut it up to
make one of the flags. Mama found out, and I was
punished."

"And rightly so," Mrs. Clopton said. "Imagine
destroying good silk like that."

"It wasn't destroyed," Mrs. Wigfall said gently. "It
went into the making of three flags. Two have already
gone into battle. The other Susan is giving to the
Washington Artillery of New Orleans."

"Well, who would make this balloon?" Mrs. Randolph
asked.

"The general said that if the dresses were donated he
would find the people to make it," Mrs. Wigfall answered.

The babble of voices rose again, like a swarm of
insects this time. The women argued, laughed, exclaimed,
doubted, criticized and scorned. My face went hot. A
balloon! Made of silk dresses donated by women of the
Confederacy! My head was spinning with fantasies. I
looked up and saw Connie watching me.

"Ladies, ladies." Mrs. Wigfall raised her hands to
quiet them. "Let's not forget our sewing. Louly, put on
another pot of coffee, please."

"I'd sooner have a hot toddy," Mrs. Randolph said.

"No reflection on your coffee, dear. You're doing the best you can with that concoction."

Everyone laughed. The room was alive with excitement. "Ladies," Mrs. Wigfall said, "I think Susan Chilmark knows a little about balloons. Don't you remember what you told me, Susan?"

"Yes," I said breathlessly. "I was told by . . . someone who knows that Professor Lowe sent messages to Mr. Lincoln from his balloon when it was five hundred feet in the air."

There were murmurs of wonder. I went on: "This same someone said that Lowe has seven balloons. And nine aeronauts. And he spies on our men in the field."

They fell silent. The idea of someone spying on their husbands, brothers and sons in the field did not sit well with them.

"Well, I'm not against the idea," said Mrs. Randolph, "and I will give up my two good silks. But who has time to go about collecting dresses? We have all we can do, sewing, nursing, and supervising our homes."

There were murmurs of approval. Mrs. Wigfall looked at me. I glanced at her, then at Connie, who was smiling at me in encouragement.

"I will," I said shakily.

They didn't hear me at first. "I will," I said a little louder. One by one they stopped talking and looked at me.

"I'll collect the dresses if you-all will give them up. Then Mrs. Wigfall can get them to the right people."

Mrs. Turnstable spoke up. "And I suppose your mama will allow you to do this, Susan?"

"Yes, ma'am," I said, meeting her eye. "There is no more staunch a Confederate lady than my mother." Of course she's a little crazy, I told myself, but that doesn't take away from her being a staunch Confederate.

"Well, she *has* to be a staunch Confederate." The words dripped like poison honey from Mrs. Turnstable's tongue. "After all, she has to make up for the doings of her son, who dallies with Richmond ladies while our menfolk fight in the field."

"Mama!" Connie said.

"Now, Emily, deah, don't be unkind," Mrs. Wigfall said. "Susan's brother has been bringing food in to Richmond's markets so that all of us may eat well. What would we do without men like him? Susan, if your mama gives permission, I will have my husband tell General Longstreet, and we will proceed. Any objections, ladies?"

There were no objections.

"Susan can't go about alone, however," Mrs. Wigfall said. "Does anyone know someone who could help her?"

"I'll help her."

I could barely believe my ears. The faces in the room swam in front of my eyes. But there was Connie standing up and offering to help.

"I'll help Susan," she said again. "After all, we've been friends for a long time."

"Connie," her mother remonstrated.

"Yes, Mama?" And she turned her round, sweet face toward her mother, smiling. "You want me to be a true daughter of the Confederacy, don't you?" she inquired sweetly.

You could almost see Mrs. Turnstable retreating inside herself. "Why, yes, of course, deah. I'd be proud to have you help Susan. I do think these two deah young girls deserve a hand, don't you, ladies?"

I faced Connie across the room while they all applauded.

Chapter Eleven

"Susan, may I see you for a moment, please?"

I had just come from Miss Pegram's and was in the kitchen hoping for a slice of Rhody's fresh-baked bread. "With honey on it, Rhody," I begged. The March weather had turned chilly again, and Rhody had a pot of water on for tea.

"Susan?"

"You better go see what your mama wants first," Rhody directed.

I picked up Hyacinth, who had been rubbing around my ankles, and walked with the cat in my arms to the back parlor. Mama was seated at her marble-topped writing desk.

"Well, come in here, Susan. Don't stand there like a ninny. I want to talk to you. And put that cat down, please. You know I don't like her hair all over the furniture in this room."

I set Hyacinth down, mentally running through my recent sins to figure out which one I was being summoned for. Mama handed me a piece of paper.

"These are the names and addresses of the women from whom you are to collect dresses for the balloon, Susan Dobson Chilmark," and she got up and came toward me, and, while I stood dumbstruck, put her hands on my shoulders and kissed me. "I want to tell you how pleased I am that you offered to collect dresses for the balloon. Mrs. Wigfall told me all about it. I

think it's a marvelous idea! And just the thing we need
to do to show all those self-sainted women that we
Chilmarks are as patriotic as the rest of them.''

"Mama, I didn't do it for that reason," I said weakly.

"Well, of course you did!" she snapped. "You've
been running around for a year trying to find something
worthwhile to do for the Cause. Don't be modest,
Susan, I won't have it.''

"I wanted to help the Cause, yes, Mama. But I never
thought about getting back at the women who made
remarks about us.''

"Ah, Susan, but if it makes them regret, for even five
minutes, the cruel things some of them have said about
us, does that hurt?''

"No, Mama, I suppose not.''

"Well, don't look so upset about it, you little goose.''
She sighed. "Susan, sometimes I think you are just
dense. But I'm too happy with you today to scold. So
take your list. I understand Connie Turnstable is helping
you. Good. I hope her mother eats all her words and
chokes on them. Now, listen. You are only to approach
the ladies on that list, do you hear? They are all the
worthwhile ladies in Richmond.''

I scanned the names on the paper quickly. They were
the socially prominent women in town. "Yes, Mama.''

"I'll not have you knocking on any strange doors.
When do you start?''

"Today.''

"Good. Wilium is to take you in the carriage. Susan,
you have made me very happy with this venture of
yours. I want you to know that.''

I had waited so long to hear Mama say such words to
me. So, why didn't I feel the glow I should have felt?
Why didn't it take the chill out of my bones? She was
only trying to be helpful. The women on this list would

have the best and the most silk dresses in town. But there was some edge taken off my happiness as I folded the paper in my hand. And I didn't know why.

"I'm staying with Mrs. Wigfall tonight, Rhody. Mama's given me permission. I'll send Wilium home with the carriage and the dresses when we're finished."

"We is goin' someplace new today," Wilium boasted.

Rhody handed him the large carpet bag with my clothes in it. "Where you goin'?" She looked at me. "You cookin' somethin' up that I doan know about?"

Yes, I was. And I could have killed Wilium for opening his mouth. "Why don't you take my bag and go tell Connie I'll be right out?" I told him.

He left. Connie was waiting for me in the carriage. Every afternoon for the past two weeks we had been collecting dresses. We had been to all the houses on Mama's list. Today was our last day to collect. Tomorrow Mrs. Wigfall was coming to our house with her nigra servants to oversee the packing of the dresses, silks of every color and description, that were piled high on the bed upstairs in Lucien's old room.

But we hadn't met our quota. There weren't enough dresses.

I hadn't said anything to anyone yet, but I was getting desperate. We were short a good dozen dresses. Oh, if only Mama had allowed us to go to houses that were not on the list! But I had complied with her orders and now what would I tell Mrs. Wigfall? What would I tell the Ladies' Defense Association, which was paying to have the dresses shipped to the armory down South, and even, for that matter, absorbing some of the cost of making the balloon?

And what about Mama? She'd been so happy about my project, so nice to me these past two weeks. We talked about the balloon every night at supper. It was the only time in my life that Mama and I had come to a real understanding about anything.

I had given the matter a lot of thought, and I knew what I had to do. To be sure, Mama would kill me if she suspected what I was planning. And the Ladies' Defense Association would be horrified. But Daddy had told me that what I thought was right would not always have the blessing of others, hadn't he?

"Where you goin'?" Rhody was demanding. "You got everybody who's decent on that list. Doan you go traipsin' through any no-count neighborhoods. You got enuf dresses. I can't walk into that room upstairs for the perfume makin' me feel faint."

"Darling Rhody," I said.

"Doan you darlin' me."

"Look," and I pulled her letter to Sallie out of my pocket. "This is where I'm going today. To deliver this to Lucien."

Her dark eyes went round in her face. "You take that child," and she motioned to the door, "to see your brother, and you don't hafta worry 'bout no Yankees gettin' to Richmond. Her mama will destroy us all. And when she gets done, your mama will finish the job. And you know your daddy ain't comin' home for a while yet. So you got nobody to stand up for you but me."

Last week Daddy's letter had said he would be awhile yet in Norfolk. He was overseeing repairs on the *Virginia*, which had gotten into a duel with the North's ironclad, the *Monitor*, the day after the *Virginia*'s recent victories.

"This letter has to be delivered before the end of the month," I reminded her.

"An' so you're jus' gonna go waltzin' into a gamblin' house with Connie Turnstable to meet the one person who's been the choice bit o' gossip for your mama's friends."

"Don't you want Sallie to get the letter?" I inquired innocently.

She looked at me. She sighed. "It's your funeral, miss. I hope you know what you're doin'. Jus' remember to be off the streets before dark."

It was a bright blue day with clouds rushing across a March sky. The wind was warm and playful. I took the list from my pocket as the carriage wound out of our neighborhood. "Connie, we don't have enough dresses," I said.

She leaned forward on the seat across from me. "You told me that. What you haven't told me is what you're planning. And I know you're cooking up something, Susan Chilmark."

"Did you know who has the best silk gowns in town?" I asked her.

"Everyone knows. Mrs. Davis, the wife of the president of the Confederacy."

"Wrong."

"Well, who, then?"

"Do you remember when you and I went by a house on Cary Street and the door was open and we saw a woman standing there wearing a real emerald necklace in the middle of the day?"

Connie covered her mouth with her hand. Her blue eyes filled with delight. "She was wearing the most beautiful silk dress I ever saw," she recalled. "Red. I shall never forget it."

"Well, then?"

"Susan Chilmark, are you saying we're going to get dresses from prostitutes?"

"I'm saying that I'm acquainted with someone who knows the right people in Richmond. The people who can give us all the silks we want."

"Who? Tell me, Susan. I won't tell a soul."

"How can I be sure?"

"Didn't I stand up to Mama in front of everyone and say I was your friend?"

"Your mama will kill you, Connie, if she finds out I took you there today. And my mama will have me locked up in Castle Godwin."

"Then it must be something deliciously naughty, and I must be a part of it."

"It's my brother, Lucien. I know where he lives and works. I've met him, Connie. And he can help us get the rest of the dresses, I'm sure of it."

She squealed in delight. "Is he as evil as my mama says?"

"Worse."

"Oh," she moaned. "And to think you've been keeping this from me. Does he own a brothel, like everyone says?"

"No. He owns half a gambling house."

"That's almost as good. My mama says there are some ministers in Richmond who go to gambling houses."

"Well, I don't know about that, but Mrs. Wigfall says gambling house owners have friends from the slums to the pulpit."

"Tell me more about Lucien."

"Well, he has a fierce temper. Although he is sweet sometimes. He may not like my bringing you around. He may even get angry if I come without being invited. I'm not supposed to bother him unless I'm desperate. You know that beautiful soft wool cloak I had this past winter? Well, he sent the material to me as a Christmas gift. Mama says it came right off a blockade-runner."

"Oh, I'm so jealous," Connie said. "Do you think he'll consider our predicament desperate enough?"

"I don't know. I think you ought to stay in the

carriage with Wilium and let me go in first. Once I get inside maybe I can sweeten him up."

"I thought he wouldn't fight for the Cause. Why would he help you get dresses for a balloon?"

"I just think he might, that's all."

She nodded. "What's he really like, Susan?"

"Oh, he's very dashing and sophisticated. He doesn't care a fig what people say about him. And he has a mistress who's very beautiful."

I thought Connie would faint right there in the carriage. "Do you think we can trust Wilium?" she asked.

"I think if we get him something to eat he won't care if we consort with the devil himself. And Lucien's place serves elegant food and drink at the house buffet. I'm sure they'll have something to keep Wilium busy for a while," I said airily.

Chapter Twelve

The young nigra woman who ushered me into Lucien's office was wearing a dusty pink dress of soft cashmere with a prim white collar and bishop sleeves.

"Mister Lucien said to make yourself comfortable. He'll be along directly."

Her diction was perfect. "What's your name?" I asked.

She set down a tray of delicate sandwiches and tea. "Sarah. I'm Nate's wife. I remember you from the day you were first brought in here. Mr. Lucien was carrying you. You had fainted dead away, he said. He was so worried."

"Was he?" Nate's wife. That meant she was a free person of color, like Nate. Richmond had about three thousand of them. Many were unemployed and suffered most of the restrictions imposed on slaves. They had to carry their papers with them, proving their freedom, wherever they went. But it didn't look as if any of this had affected Sarah. She moved about the room gracefully, setting down my light cloak, rearranging some things on Lucien's desk and adjusting the gaslight. She smiled serenely at me, and I was insanely jealous of her confidence.

"Do you work for my brother too, then?"

She nodded. "I oversee the kitchen help and purchase the food and drink for this place. I write up the orders, and Mister Lucien signs them. Fanny, of course, is the hostess."

So, she could read and write. Like Sallie. And I wondered if Lucien was making up for certain things in his past by employing Nate and Sarah. And then, as if my thoughts had summoned him, he appeared in the doorway.

"I would have enjoyed a little notice about this visit, Susan." He was scowling unhappily.

"Hello, Lucien."

He didn't respond. He crossed the room, took off his good gray broadcloth frock coat and threw it over a chair. Then he examined some papers on his desk. Next to him stood Sarah, waiting. She handed him more papers. "These are the orders for this week, Mister Lucien."

He lit a cheroot and scanned them solemnly. He was in one of his rude moods again. And it was making me nervous. I thought of Connie and Wilium, waiting outside in the carriage.

"Why are we ordering all this flour, pork and potatoes?" he asked.

"We can store it," Sarah said. "Word on the street is that General Winder is going to fix prices by the end of the month. You said if that happened the farmers and fishermen wouldn't bring any food into the city. I thought we ought to prepare for that."

"God's teeth, that man Winder will ruin all of us yet." And he leaned over and signed the orders. "No, the farmers won't bring in anything if it doesn't pay them to. Nor will the fishermen. Which includes me. Not unless I get my price. Do we have enough room to store butter and eggs and vegetables?"

"Yes."

"Then order extra. I'll leave it up to you," and he signed more papers.

Sarah smiled and went out. She was at the door when he called after her to bring some coffee because he had a splitting headache.

He sat down in his swivel chair. "I thought we had an understanding about your not coming here without being invited, Susan."

"I was in the neighborhood, Lucien. So I brought Rhody's letter. You said to have it back to you by the end of the month."

"There are six days left before the end of the month," he said distinctly. "Time enough to have given me warning. Well, let's have it."

I got up, crossed the room and gave him the letter. He looked at it. "Ah yes, thank you. That's Charlotte's carriage outside, isn't it?"

"Yes." I stood in front of his desk, waiting.

"I thought I gave you money to hire a carriage."

"You did. And I still have it. But goodness, I couldn't see the need. They're so expensive. The other day a hack driver charged a poor wounded soldier nineteen dollars to carry him six miles.''

"You'll see the need if Charlotte's carriage is recognized in this neighborhood. Do you think Wilium is adequate protection to go riding around these streets?''

Oh, he was miserable when he was in one of his moods. "I can take care of myself,'' I said defiantly.

"Can you, now? A man was killed in a duel out in front of this house awhile back. Did you know that?''

"Yes.'' I raised my chin and met his stern gaze. "That was in December. James McCullough shot and killed Washington Wortham in a fight over gambling.''

He smiled and leaned back in his chair. "Weren't you ever told that Southern women are supposed to be shy and defer to men, Susan?''

"Yes, but I don't see why, and I refuse to do it.''

He gestured that I should sit. I did so. "Now, suppose you tell me what it is that you want.''

"What makes you think I want something?''

"Hell will freeze over the day I don't know when a woman wants something from me. What is it?''

"Well, first I have a friend in the carriage. I'd like to bring her in.''

"Who?''

"Connie Turnstable.''

"Ah, the friend who explained to you what a brothel is.''

My eyes widened. "How did you remember that?''

"I've had to survive by my wits, Susan. I can't afford not to remember things.'' He went to the door and called for Sarah.

"If we could find Wilium something to eat, he won't tell I was here,'' I suggested.

He nodded and gave Sarah instructions. "It isn't bad enough,'' he said, seating himself back down, "that you come here without being invited, you've brought a friend, too. I should be as mad as a greased pig. There are reasons my wishes have to be honored, Susan.''

"I know that. If you'll let me explain..."

"I intend to." But Sarah brought his coffee then and poured it for him. A burst of laughter came from someone down the hall as she left the room, reminding me that I was taking him from his business in the middle of a Saturday. I decided to be forthright and not waste his time.

"We've been collecting dresses for the past two weeks, Connie and I. Silk dresses from all the fine ladies in Richmond. They're stored in your room."

He waited.

"The dresses are for a Confederate balloon."

Again the burst of faraway laughter. Then it died and there was total silence in the room except for the ticking of the steeple New England clock on the mantel.

"So that's what the South has come to," he breathed, "asking for silk dresses from its women for a balloon."

"It was General Longstreet's idea. Mrs. Wigfall brought it up one day when we were sewing sandbags at St. Paul's. The women in the Ladies' Defense Association didn't like the idea right away. I told them about the Federal balloons, all the things you told me. I made them understand how important it is for the South to have one."

He nodded. "Who's going to make this balloon?"

"It will be made south somewhere. By people who know how. The dresses are to be shipped out on Monday. Tomorrow we're packing them, and we still don't have enough."

I became absolutely chilled to the bone from the way he was looking at me. "How did you become involved in collecting the dresses, Susan?"

"I offered to do it."

"Why?"

"Because it's something worthwhile for the Cause, Lucien. Better, even, than making flags."

"And Charlotte is allowing Wilium to run you around the streets of Richmond, through all kinds of neighborhoods, and do this?"

"Well, yes. And no," I said.

"Which is it, Susan?"

I took a deep breath. "Mama approves of what I'm doing for the balloon, Lucien. It's the first time she's been happy with me in my life, really."

"Is that why you're doing it, Susan? To please Charlotte?"

"No," I answered firmly. "I never realized Mama would be so happy about it until after I became involved. I'm doing it for myself."

He nodded approvingly. "You said yes and no. Answer the no part, please."

"I'm only supposed to be collecting dresses from ladies on Mama's list. Which leaves me short of dresses. Which is why I'm here today."

"To get back to my original question, then, what is it that you want from me, Susan?"

A knock on the door interrupted us. Sarah stood there with a very apprehensive-looking Connie. Instantly, Lucien was on his feet.

"Lucien, this is my friend Connie," I said.

Connie curtsied, her eyes riveted to his face. I thought she would turn into a pillar of salt, like Lot's wife in the Bible, staring at him the way she was. Slowly she unbuttoned her cloak. Lucien took it from her, bowing gallantly. "Sit down." He brought forth a chair.

Connie sat, but she never took her eyes off him.

"Am I everything they're saying about me in

Richmond?'' he asked her teasingly. ''Or has my sister been adding to the legend? What have you told her, Susan? She looks frightened out of her wits.''

''You're making her uncomfortable, Lucien,'' I said.

He apologized. ''You must forgive me, Connie. I have the disposition of an ostrich sometimes. I'm annoyed with Susan for bursting in on me without notice. I have a headache that would ruin the nerves of a cast-iron lamppost, and now my sister is handing me some yarn about collecting silk dresses for a balloon. Would you like some tea?''

''Oh, yes,'' Connie said, beaming, ''that would be nice.''

Over our heads he smiled at Sarah. ''And please bring me some headache powders, Sarah. I have a feeling I'm going to need them.''

He settled back in his chair. ''All right, Susan, enough shilly-shallying. What has all this to do with me?''

''I thought you could help us get the dresses we need.''

His look was long and steady. ''And how do you propose I do that?''

''You know people, Lucien.''

''What kind of people?''

''You know''—I looked at my hands in my lap—''everyone there is to know.'' Why did I get the feeling he already sensed what I was after? Because of the evil gleam in his eyes? He was enjoying this, my coming to him, my discomfort, all of it.

''You aren't asking me, Susan, to get you dresses from women in brothels, are you?'' he asked innocently.

I blushed. ''I hate you,'' I said for lack of anything better to say.

''Do you? Then why come to me for my help?''

"You're everything they say about you in Richmond."

"I certainly hope so. Ah, here's your tea, Connie. Thank you, Sarah."

Sarah bustled about, setting the tea out for Connie. Then she gave the headache powders with a glass of water to Lucien. He waited until she left the room. "Well, the South certainly is changing when its young women decide to ask prostitutes for help with their endeavors," he said sarcastically.

"I will ask anyone I can to help so we can ship off enough dresses to make a balloon," I said distinctly.

"And will you tell the Ladies' Defense Association where you got some of those dresses?"

"No. I don't see why we have to. Connie and I talked about that. And we decided that we don't care what kind of women donate their dresses. We'll be glad to have them."

"You're an insufferable little prude, do you know that, Susan? And if I had anything to do with your upbringing, I'd shake you silly for that last remark."

I gasped. Before I could reply, however, he swiveled around in his chair, reached into a cabinet behind him and brought out a bottle of whiskey. He poured some into a glass. Then he gulped it down with the headache powders and looked at us.

"I think you are mean," I said. It sounded childish, but it was all I could think of to say.

He dismissed my statement with a wave of his hand and poured himself a fresh cup of coffee. "A Norfolk newspaper said recently that there is increased drinking amongst Confederate officers. I don't know where they're getting their liquor, but I hope it's better than the brand I've been able to get lately. I said you're an insufferable little prude. It surprises me, but I guess you've been around Charlotte too long."

I had never been so humiliated in my life. I had brought Connie along to show off my dashing brother, and all he'd done so far was insult us. I got up. "I'm sorry I bothered you. Come along, Connie, let's go."

"Sit down," he snapped, "both of you."

We both sat.

"I told you when I was angry I was like Charlotte, didn't I?"

"Yes, you did," I said evenly, "and you were more right than you imagined. Only I thought you were concerned with manners."

Our eyes met, and I knew I'd hurt him. He blinked. "Listen to me, missy," he said softly, "you come in here filled with an insane plan to collect dresses for a balloon for the Confederacy. All right, the whole war is insane, so why bicker at this stage of the game? Then you tell me you want me to get the dresses you need from women you wouldn't talk to if you bumped into them on the street. Then you say you don't care what kind of women they are, you'll accept their dresses anyway, only you won't tell your precious Ladies' Defense Association about them. Doesn't that sound just a little hypocritical to you, Susan?"

I had to admit that it did, but I wouldn't tell him that.

"Are you sure you don't want the dresses laundered first?"

I was near tears, but I still wouldn't reply.

"I'd like an answer from you, Susan. I'd really like to know what you think of what I've just said."

I raised my chin defiantly. "I'd say prayers for Mr. Lincoln before I told you that."

"We may all be praying for Mr. Lincoln before we're through. I hate hypocrisy, Susan. It's one of the things I hate most about this whole stupid war and about the South. And I saw hypocrisy of the worst kind in you a

few minutes ago. Those women you want me to get the
dresses from have far better characters than some of the
so-called ladies in Mrs. Davis's circle. I've heard about
them, popping champagne bottles while the boys they're
supposed to be caring about are dying in the fields. I
thought you were different. That's what I liked about
you."

"I wasn't aware you liked anything about me," I said
stiffly.

"Oh, come on, Susan, you know better. You're a
smart girl."

"Excuse me, sir," Connie said. We both stared at
her. "I know what you're talking about. I heard my
mama say she thought Mrs. Chestnut and Mrs. Davis
and all of that crowd were partying too much while boys
were dying in the field."

"God's teeth, the girl talks!" Lucien grinned. "Good
for you, Connie. Maybe you can make my sister
understand."

"I think she does, sir. I've been Susan's friend for a
long time, and she isn't hypocritical. You know what
else I think?"

"Go on," Lucien said, "I'm fascinated."

"I think you and Susan are just bickering, like my
brother Kenneth and I always did. We were at each
other all the time when he was home."

"Were you, now? And where is Kenneth? Or don't I
dare ask?"

"He's away fighting. I do miss him, and I'm sorry we
ever fought."

Lucien sobered. "I'm sure he knows that you love
him, Connie. And you're probably right. Susan and I
aren't in a room together for five minutes but we're at
each other. I think you've explained us very intelligently."

Connie beamed. "May I say something else, sir?"

"You may."

"Susan loves you. I happen to know that."

I wished the earth would open up and pull me in when she said that. I looked at my hands in my lap. Everyone fell silent. *I'll kill Connie for this,* I thought. I could feel Lucien's distress.

"So," his voice came out hoarsely, "the dresses are in my room, eh?"

"They're piled high on your bed," I said without looking at him. "All colors. They have laces and ribbons, and they smell of perfume. Your whole room reeks of perfume by now."

"Well, that's the closest I'll ever come to associating with the fine ladies of Richmond. You took quite a chance coming to me today, didn't you, Susan! What would Charlotte do if she found out!"

I shrugged. "She'd kill me," I said dully.

He nodded. "That lends a sort of poetic justice to it that appeals to me." He got up, reached for his expensive gray frock coat and put it on. Then he strode to the door and yelled for Nate to bring around the carriage. He called for Sarah and told her he'd be back in a couple of hours. He held Connie's cloak out and she allowed him to put it around her shoulders. Then he reached for mine and looked at me. "Susan?"

I hesitated. "I wish you were giving your help for the right reasons, Lucien."

"Reasons? And what might those reasons be?"

"I just wish," I said bravely, "that you were doing this because you believed in the South. And not because you know how angry it would make Mama." My voice trailed off. That was not what I wanted to say. He scowled deeply, and I felt so exposed, since he knew I loved him, thanks to Connie. He had been unable to say that he loved me. Instead he reached for the handiest of reasons for helping, like a gentleman reaches for a silk handkerchief.

I met his steadfast gaze. "You either want my help or you don't want it, Susan," he said. "It matters little to me whether the South has a balloon. You know that. Personally I think the South could have ten balloons made of silk hand-stitched by Far Eastern maidens, and it wouldn't help. Nashville has been taken over by Federal troops. We've lost a significant battle at Pea Ridge, in Arkansas. The threat against Savannah grows daily."

"Then why are you helping me?"

"Because I like your spirit. Because if I had that spirit when I was younger to go against Charlotte, things might be different for me now. I'm sorry, Susan, those are the best reasons I have to give."

I nodded and allowed him to put the cloak around my shoulders. But I never felt its weight so much. And I never felt so cold or alone, knowing that my brother could not say he loved me.

Chapter Thirteen

Lucien and Connie and I stood outside a tall, neatly appointed brick house on one of Richmond's better streets. Lucien had said little on the ride here. We'd left Wilium and our carriage back at the gambling house to be retrieved later.

Looking up to the top floor of the house, I saw a woman standing behind lace curtains in the mullioned transom window.

"Come along," Lucien said. He led us up the steps, then lifted the huge brass knocker on the polished oak door and in a moment it opened.

"How good to see you, Mister Lucien!"

The woman who let us in was wearing a tartan silk dress of green-and-white plaid, chastely buttoned to the neck. I was disappointed in such decorum. I had expected to see low-scooped gowns of dazzling red. Her blond curls were gathered up in a most attractive manner, however, and she made no attempt to control the fluttering of her eyelashes as she looked up at my brother.

"We haven't seen you in a while," she whispered.

Behind Lucien's back Connie and I exchanged wide-eyed glances.

"I've been busy, Ginny."

"Miss Lulie's in the back parlor."

We followed her through the front hall, which was all white. Directly in front of us was a huge archway supported by white columns with sculptured cherubs at the top. Beyond, a bright runner of red rose gracefully to a landing above. A stained-glass window was on the landing.

"Lucien." The woman in the pink-and-white-striped silk dress made soft swishing sounds as she got up from her cherry, marble-topped writing table in the back parlor to greet him. She took his hand and kissed the side of his face warmly. "It's been awhile." She held on to his hand, peering into his face. "You're working too hard. You look tired."

"I have a headache today, Lulie."

"Those headaches plaguing you again? I hear old Abraham Lincoln gets the same kind, so you're in good company." She sat down in a velvet chair and surveyed us. "Who have we here?"

"This is my sister, Susan. I've told you about her,

Lulie. And her friend Constance. Girls, this is Lulie
Ballard.''

"Of course, of course. She looks like you, Lucien.
The same high, intelligent brow and determined chin.
Sit down. What can I offer you to drink?''

"Just some coffee. Maybe some tea for the girls.''

She pulled a bell cord, and a young nigra woman
came to the door. Miss Lulie gave the order for refreshments. I looked around the room quickly, my eyes
unable to absorb everything, yet my mind registered
what I saw. The wallpaper was gold, but it did not have
a glossy finish. The draperies and settee and chairs were
done in red velvet, and there was a profusion of ferns
and polished wood and silk embroidered cushions.

My gaze slid back to Lucien, whose tall angular
frame seemed not to fit in with all this. Yet he was
comfortably ensconced in one of Miss Lulie's most
commodious chairs. And I saw the way Lulie was
looking at him. And the way he was basking under the
warmth of her gaze. "Abraham Lincoln, eh?'' he said.

"Yes. They say he gets headaches just like yours.''

"Well, he has good enough reason.'' The young
nigra woman came in with the refreshments. Lulie
poured, and Lucien raised his cup of coffee. "Here's to
old Abraham,'' he said.

We drank our tea. I avoided Connie's eyes, for she
was as stupefied as I was. Instead I took the opportunity
to pay notice to Lulie Ballard. She had chestnut-colored
hair and an ample, yet attractive, figure. Her face had
an unutterable sweetness, even an innocence that I had
never seen in Mama's Richmond ladies. She was older
than Lucien by at least ten years, but they were comfortable with each other, like good friends.

"So, how have you been, Lucien?'' she asked him.

He shrugged. "How have we all been? The war is draining everybody."

She smiled. "Business has never been better."

"Nor for me. I have to kick some of the Confederate officers out for fear their superiors will complain because they aren't reporting to duty. That's all I need for the police to shut me down."

"Are you going to tell me why you brought these two lovely young ladies to see me?"

Lucien sipped his coffee. "They need help, Lulie. My sister is collecting silk dresses for a balloon. The girls have been running themselves ragged over the past two weeks and still don't have enough dresses. I thought you could help."

She looked at me. "A balloon! Now isn't that a fine thing! I've seen Professor Lowe's balloon floating around up there, and I've said to myself—'You're seeing the future, Lulie. Men flying in the air like birds. That's the future.' And if we ever get over this silly war and stop killing each other and start acting like Americans again, why perhaps we'll set our minds to better things. Like men flying in the air. Are you telling me the South is going to make a balloon? Out of silk dresses?"

"Yes, ma'am," I said.

"And you've been selected to collect the dresses?"

"I offered."

"Why?"

"Because I feel the way you do about balloons. I think they're the most beautiful things. I think the South should have one. And the idea that women should donate their dresses . . . well, it seems to me there isn't anything more worthwhile we could do."

She nodded her head, her eyes shining. "You didn't tell me you had such a darling sister, Lucien."

"I knew you'd appreciate the whole thing, Lulie. That's why I brought her here."

"Don't you think it's a wonderful idea?" she asked him.

"You know how I feel about the war," he said. "I just want the Yankees to stay away so I can run my business."

"And they should let me run mine?" she asked.

"Of course," he said. "People should always let you run yours."

She laughed in a most undignified way and patted his knee fondly. "Lucien, Lucien, one of these days you'll look in your heart without inventing lies to protect you from what you see there."

He smiled at her. "Maybe so, Lulie. But I prefer my lies to those of other people."

"Well, at least you admit they're lies." Then she turned to me. "Did you know what kind of person I am, before your brother brought you here today?"

I cast a quick, appealing look at Lucien, but he wouldn't look back. "Lucien said you were a very nice person."

"Do you know what I do for a living?"

"Yes."

"And you'll accept my dresses if I and my girls decide to donate them?"

"I'd be most honored to accept your dresses," I said.

Lulie Ballard got up. "Then I and my girls would be most honored to donate them. I am so glad you want our dresses right up there alongside the gowns of all the fine ladies of Richmond in a balloon for the Confederacy."

Impulsively, she kissed me. Then she looked at Lucien. "I'm going upstairs now to tell my girls. We'll get the dresses together and then your sister and her friend can come and pick the ones they want. Would that be all right, Lucien?"

Connie and I looked at each other. "Oh, please, yes," Connie begged.

Lucien smiled. "I suppose it's all right. But God's teeth, if either of you tells about this escapade today, they'll run me out of Richmond on a rail. You understand that, don't you?"

We both nodded. "Have another cup of coffee, dear boy," Lulie said to him, "and stop worrying. Girls, I'll call you in a little while."

Lucien got to his feet as she left the room, poured himself another cup of coffee and meandered over to the piano. He touched first one key, then another, making discordant sounds.

"You've made her very happy," he said.

Neither of us answered. He ran his fingers lightly over the piano keys as if trying to find some chord he was looking for. "When I was down and out a few years back, Lulie Ballard took me in," he said softly. "She gave me a few good meals and staked me so I could get started in business. I was able to buy a boat for my fishing expeditions, and buy into the partnership at the gambling house. And she's never asked anything in return except friendship. I've been honored to have her as a friend."

The idea of Lucien being so unfortunate that someone had to take him in and feed him made my heart wrench. I couldn't bear thinking on it. I decided that he had more painful secrets inside him than he ever let on, and I felt my heart softening toward him.

"Susan, come here and play something for me, please," he said.

I went to the piano. He pulled out the bench. "What would you like?" I asked.

"Well, not 'The Bonnie Blue Flag,' I assure you. Play something soothing."

"I can play—'Just Before the Battle, Mother.' "

"Yes, I'd say that would be most appropriate," he answered dryly. He squeezed my shoulder and walked away. After a few minutes of playing I looked around and saw him leaning back in a chair, his eyes closed.

I played that song and two others before Lulie called us from the stairway. Connie went right to her. As I crossed the room, Lucien untangled his long frame and got out of the chair. "Susan, I'd like a word with you, please."

I waited.

"I'm having a guest at my place for supper. I'd like you to meet him. I think it might help you understand things a lot better. Can you have supper with me tonight?"

"I'm staying with Mrs. Wigfall. I suppose she'd say it was all right. Who is he?"

"My friend who sketches for *Harper's*. Timothy Tobias Collier."

"A Yankee," I hissed.

"Shh. Yes."

"Susan, are you coming?" Connie called from the hall.

"Yes, I'll be right along." I looked at my brother. "Why do you want me to meet a Yankee?"

"Because I would like you to do me the favor."

That made me angry. Did he think he could order me about, and I would do anything he wanted after he'd been so terrible to me earlier today? I promptly forgot my indulgent feelings for him. "I appreciate your bringing us here today," I said politely, "but I don't see why

I should do what you ask when you were so awful to me before."

He nodded. "I scolded you for your hypocrisy, Susan. I won't apologize for that. But I was wrong to do it in front of your friend."

Was that an apology? I waited. He smiled at me and sat down. "Go on, run along," he said.

But I stood fast, waiting. For what, I did not know.

"It's just," he shrugged, "that I told Tim about you." He did not look at me when he said it.

He'd told someone else about me! First Lulie and now this Timothy! "Do you tell all your friends about me?"

"Only the special ones. Timothy is special."

"What did you tell him?"

"How we met that day."

"Oh no! You didn't!"

He smiled. "He has a little sister. He has a whole family, as a matter of fact, and he talks about them all the time. I couldn't resist telling him about the only member of my family that I have to talk about."

I flushed with pleasure. "I'm sure that Mrs. Wigfall won't mind if I have supper with you," I said. "Although I don't know how to behave with a Yankee. I've never met one."

"Then perhaps it's time you did, Susan. I shall look forward to supper. I assure you, it won't be a waste of your time."

I ran up the stairs, my heart pounding. Why did he want me to meet a Yankee? And why, if he acted so awful to me most of the time, did he want me at his supper table, meeting his friends? Oh, I couldn't figure it all out. I paused at the top of the stairway and put it out of my mind.

"Psst, Susan, come on!"

Connie was almost jumping out of her skin, unable to contain herself. I hurried along the corridor and followed her into a room.

There were silk dresses all over the room, and for a moment I couldn't separate them from the rest of the decor. I just stood there, openmouthed.

I had heard my mama once say that certain people were using the "Turkish influence" in decorating their homes, but I could never picture what it meant.

The ceiling of this room was hung with silk draperies which seemed to be pinned up in the middle with a medallion. Silk hangings were draped on the walls, too, shimmering printed silks. The floor had Turkish carpets, and a huge, carved mahogany bed was on a platform in the middle of the room.

There were dresses all over the bed. Indeed, they were everywhere, on the chairs, on the wooden trunks, even hanging on the standing, oval mirror in the corner.

"Have you ever seen anything like it?" Connie whispered in my ear.

I certainly never had. "Come on, you two," Miss Lulie gestured, "and meet my girls."

Her "girls" were gathered in front of a huge stained-glass window, in various stages of undress. They were giggling and chattering excitedly. And they were helping each other undo buttons and bows and sashes.

"They're taking the dresses off their backs to give to you," Miss Lulie explained.

"But we don't want them to do that!" I was plainly embarrassed.

"Oh, they want to. It's a gesture. Rather a sweet one, don't you think?"

We both murmured yes, while we tried not to stare. One girl seemed prettier than the next.

"Girls, girls!" Miss Lulie clapped her hands. Instantly the chatter died, and they turned to us. Some paused, with dresses half off creamy shoulders. Others stood in pantalets and stays.

"Girls, I want you all to meet Miss Susan and Miss Connie. Little Susan here is Mister Lucien's sister."

Charlene, Iris, Ginny, Melba and Francine. They smiled tentatively, nodding their heads. They looked, for a moment, shy and bewildered. Then, after exchanging private glances with the others, a petite brunette stepped forward. "My name's Charlene," she said in a heavy Southern drawl that bespoke Louisiana or Mississippi. "And I just want to tell you-all how grateful we are that you've given us the chance to help out like this. We haven't been asked to contribute anything in this town as far as the war goes. Not nursing or money or anything."

There was a dead silence. The others nodded heads in agreement. Both Connie and I were at a loss for words, but then I gathered my wits. "We're the ones who should be thanking you," I said. "We didn't have enough dresses before you volunteered yours."

"Well, you'll have enough now," and Lulie gestured to the bed. "Just take what you need."

"All those?" I blinked. "I don't want to take all your wardrobes."

"Oh, we've got more," Charlene said.

"Anything for Lucien's sister," Ginny piped in.

I stared. "You all know my brother, then?"

"Mister Lucien?" Charlene smiled. "He's been a real friend to us. And I mean that in the best sense of the word. He always sees to it that we get the first choice of the fish and game he brings in, even before it goes to market. And whenever we need advice about dealing with banks or the civil authorities, we know we can go to him. Why, once the war started we couldn't get a doctor to treat any of us. They became scarcer than hen's teeth. One day last month Iris was real sick, and Mister Lucien sent over old Dr. Upchurch.'' She giggled, remembering. ''He's a customer at Lucien's place.''

I nodded. I was really quite speechless.

''So you just take your dresses,'' Charlene urged. ''Whichever ones you need.''

''Thank you.'' I looked at Connie, then at Lulie.

''We'll help you bundle them up and get them downstairs,'' Lulie said.

Within half an hour we had all the dresses we needed, tied into bundles. Garbed in robes, the girls worked to help us. It was awkward at first, with everyone being overly polite and walking on eggs. But by the time we were finished, some of them had tears in their eyes. There were hugs given and received before Connie and I left that strange room with the silk hangings on the ceiling and the ridiculous bed on the platform.

We left with twenty dresses, by far the prettiest we would have for the balloon.

Chapter Fourteen

Timothy Tobias Collier wiped his mouth with the white linen napkin and patted his mustache. ''I hear you're going to have prices stabilized in your city one of these days, Lucien,'' he said.

Lucien sipped his wine. ''They're bent on doing it,

Tim. It's going to ruin us, of course. But I always did say the South would destroy itself from within before the Yankees got to it."

"Well, this Yankee's gotten to you and is darned happy about it." Collier raised his own glass. "I haven't had food this good since I was last in Richmond. I'd almost forgotten what it tasted like. I'd like to steal Nate away from you and take him back North."

"You don't have to steal him. He's free to come and go as he pleases," Lucien reminded him.

"How 'bout you, Miss Susan?" Mr. Collier smiled at me. "Do you have a cook as good as Nate in your house?"

I had prayed all through the meal that he wouldn't speak to me. I didn't know how to talk to a Yankee. He wasn't anything like I imagined. He was so open, so confident, so sure of himself. He and Lucien had been friends for four years, ever since Mr. Collier first came to Richmond to do a story and some sketches when he was still in college. He had included the gambling house in that story, and he and Lucien had become instant friends.

It was an easy, close friendship. The two men did a lot of bantering and teasing, digging maliciously at each other's sore spots with obvious delight. There was such a marked difference in them that I didn't see how the friendship worked. Mr. Collier with his clipped Yankee tones, his breath-of-fresh-air assurance, and Lucien, with his faint but definite Southern accent, his languid elegance, his careful manners. But their minds were the same.

They both hated slavery and agreed on the dignity of the individual.

Lucien had told me briefly about Mr. Collier. He had gone to the University of Pennsylvania. His father was a

wealthy farmer in Salem County, New Jersey, who had
helped fleeing slaves in the Underground Railroad since
before the outset of the war. Their farm was right on the
Delaware River, across from Wilmington.

All that mattered little to me, however. What did concern me as I sat silent and listening for most of the meal
was that I had never seen such piercing blue eyes on
anyone in my life. I had never seen such graceful, yet
strong, hands and wrists on a man, and such an aura of
slender strength, not only of body, but of purpose.

What else concerned me very much was that no one
had ever looked at me quite the way he did. And that
under his gaze I both wanted to flee and stay rooted
there forever. Whenever his eyes passed over me in that
special and very provoking way, I felt childish and
frumpy in my green moiré dress with ivory lace trim,
and I hated Mama for making me wear such childish
clothes. At the same time I became painfully and
deliciously aware of the charms of my body, rendering
me totally confused and embarrassed and witless.

Mr. Collier noticed all this, of course. And he smiled
each time I flushed under his gaze. He knew what he was
doing with those furtive glances, even while he carried
on a conversation with my brother. Should I be angry
with him? Or should I be flattered? I did not know
how to act.

He himself was totally composed, of course. He wore
boots into which were stuffed his baggy trousers. He
was very clean, but in his loose jacket he looked
rumpled in comparison to Lucien. Yet it was a nice sort
of disarray, the type one expected from an artist.

I swallowed my food and took a sip of water. Did
Lucien not see what was going on between Mr. Collier
and me right under his own eyes?

"Mr. Collier is speaking to you, Susan," my brother said. "Have we forgotten our manners?" All Lucien saw was rudeness on my part.

"We haven't forgotten anything," I said sullenly, "but I'm sure if we have, you'll remind us."

Lucien's fork stopped midair, and he looked at me. "Don't be impertinent, Susan," he said quietly. "I must apologize for my sister, Tim. She thinks that sassiness is appealing. And she also thinks that Yankees eat babies."

Mr. Collier grinned, showing a fine set of white teeth. "You forget that I have a younger sister, Lucien. I'm well acquainted with sass. However, Miss Susan, I haven't eaten a baby since before Manassas. You don't honestly think that of me, do you?"

I felt tears fringe my eyes. "No, sir," I said. That ought to keep both of them happy.

"Sir?" Tim looked at me, then at Lucien. "What's this 'sir' business? What have you told her about me, Lucien?" And then to me: "Look here, Susan, I don't know what he's told you, but I'm only twenty-two years old. I'm not like this old man here." He gestured to my brother. "And I'm not a sir yet. As a matter of fact, I don't ever intend to be a sir. My father is a sir. Yes, a real dyed-in-the-wool Presbyterian sir. But not me. Nope. I'm just Tim. Do you think you can call me that?"

I nodded, wanting to disappear under the table.

"I've got an older brother who's a doctor in the Union army. Now there's a sir for you! You know how older brothers can be sometimes."

He smiled at me, warmly and sympathetically, aligning himself with me against Lucien. "Yes," I said.

"As a matter of fact," he went on, "I've met more sirs in this war than I really want to know. And that goes for both sides. I've sketched a few of them, too. I did U. S. Grant, the hero of Fort Donelson. It made the front page of the March eighth issue. But to tell the truth''—and he leaned forward confidentially—''they don't sketch well, those sirs. I'd much rather sketch the common soldier.''

''Why are you sketching the war instead of fighting it?'' I asked.

''God's teeth, Susan!'' Lucien said sharply.

''No, it's all right, Lucien,'' Mr. Collier interrupted. ''It's a normal question. Lord knows my father's asked it often enough. I'd rather sketch than kill, Susan,'' he said.

''You're like Lucien, then. You don't believe in the war.''

''Oh, I believe in it, all right. But I think it more important at this point for me to be sketching it. You see, the people up North don't know anything about the carnage and destruction of this war. I like to think my sketches bring it home to them. Does that make sense to you?''

''I don't know. I haven't seen your sketches yet.''

Lucien choked a bit on his wine. He brushed his silk cravat with his napkin. ''I'm sorry, Tim, but I never know what my sister is going to say next.''

''Your sister is most charming,'' Tim assured him. ''And I'm enjoying every moment of this. She is straight-forward, like a Yankee girl. I thought Southern belles were all chocolate-covered spiders, Lucien. Did anyone ever tell you you're like a Yankee, Susan?''

''Whenever my mama gets mad at me she calls me a Yankee brat.''

''Well, you should be flattered. Lucien,'' and he turned to his friend. ''With your permission, I'd like to do a sketch of Susan.''

''I'm not in charge of Susan,'' Lucien answered.

"My mother is. And I use the term mother loosely. May I remind you, Tim, that I had to sneak you into town tonight? You can't just go waltzing into Charlotte's house and ask to sketch her daughter. You're the enemy."

"With your permission, Lucien," he insisted. "I'd like to do it now."

"You're serious," Lucien accused.

"Very, old friend. I've been wanting to do a Southern belle. Susan is exactly what I've had in mind, not one of those flibbertigibbets we've all heard about. There's no coyness in that face. She's honest and intelligent as well as very pretty."

Lucien took a thin cheroot out of a silver case and regarded it thoughtfully. "If you keep on, she'll become impossible. She's impossible now." He looked at me. "It's all right with me if it's all right with Susan," he said.

"What do I have to do?" I asked.

Mr. Collier got up and crossed the room to rummage in his canvas bag. "Just sit there. As you are. Don't move. Don't freeze up, either. Just keep talking and stay natural."

In a minute he was back at the table, one ankle crossed over his knee, his sketch pad resting on his leg. He started sketching.

"I don't know anything about this, but isn't the light bad?" Lucien asked.

"The light?" Mr. Collier laughed. "In February when I was in Tennessee and Fort Donelson fell, I did a sketch of our army seeking its wounded by torchlight after the battle. You forget, Lucien, that I'm accustomed to working under any conditions."

"Is your work dangerous?" I asked.

"Dangerous?" He smiled. "Just before the battle in Tennessee I was met by the local Vigilance Committee.

They asked where I was going, who I was and where I came from. They asked what I was doing and whether I didn't think I needed hanging."

I waited, while he sketched.

"I answered all those questions patiently. Then they inspected my saddlebags with commendable thoroughness. They found my sketches, examined them and divided them up equally amongst themselves. And before they let me go on my way, they had me autograph them."

Lucien got up. "I can see you two are getting on without killing each other. Now, if you will excuse me, I have to make an appearance in my gambling rooms. Tim, you have an hour. I should have Susan back to Mrs. Wigfall's at nine. Susan?"

I looked up at him.

"Behave yourself." The eyes said more than the words. I nodded.

He left. For a few minutes I felt uncomfortable, alone with Mr. Collier. He continued sketching. "He's afraid you're going to offend me," he said.

"Lucien insists on manners. They're so important to him."

"He's a good man. Caught in that place where so many Southerners are caught today. Between their heads and their hearts. I'm sorry I got you in trouble with him before."

"You didn't get me in trouble," I said.

"Certainly, I did. He scolded because he thought you were being rude. I made you uncomfortable the way I was looking at you. I'm a natural flirt with women, and I shouldn't have done that to you, and I apologize."

I nodded, flustered and at a loss for words.

"You are the prettiest girl I've seen in a long time. But you are also Lucien's sister, so I should know better and behave myself. He's very fond of you."

"Did he tell you that?"

"He did," he said nonchalantly. "Why are you surprised?"

"He's never told me. Or acted as if he is. I think I'm mostly a trial to him."

"Well, of course, he can't tell you how fond he is of you." He paused in his work, cocked his head to look at me and went on sketching. "It just isn't done."

"Why not?"

"Because he's so much older than you. Older brothers have this position to maintain. They have to be standoffish and gruff and sometimes even overbearing. They must keep you at a certain distance. It all has to do with getting the respect that is their due."

"Are you like that with your sister?"

"With Mary Beth? To a certain extent, I am, but of course I'm not home that much. So when I do go home she just runs and throws her arms around me, and we have so much to catch up on. But you see, I'm not the oldest. Martin is."

"Your brother who is with the Union army?"

"Yes. Martin's thirty-two, and he always lorded it over us when we were growing up. Mary Beth and I sort of aligned ourselves against him. She's your age. Then there's Jonathan. He's twelve and a plague to us all."

"You sound like you have a wonderful family," I said wistfully.

"I do. And I miss them, being away from home so long."

"What do you really think of the war?" I asked him.

He stopped sketching for a moment to reflect. "Well, Susan," he said slowly, "I feel like this. Slavery is wrong. Black people are human beings, just like you and I. The only difference is skin tone. And what I've

seen in the South, where I've traveled . . . well, the
Southerners are good people, but they just don't think
like us. They've lost track of it all.''

"Of what?'' I asked.

He lowered his head to his sketchbook and worked in
quick, deft strokes. "Of what this country is all about,''
he said quietly. "This country is about freedom. For
everybody, Susan. Every man is entitled to dignity and
respect. The Southerners lost sight of that. They're
behaving like English lords, some of them.''

"That's what Lucien says.''

He nodded. "It isn't so difficult to see if you're
thinking clearly. The people here in the South yell about
states' rights, but this war is really about slavery. That's
what it's about, Susan. And the Northern states, well,
they just saw all this going on and said to their sister
states in the South . . . 'You have strayed too far from
the idea of what this country is about. And we must
remind you. We must bring you back into line.''

He fell silent. His sketching was the only sound in
the room.

"You know,'' he said solemnly, "the same way
Lucien just told you to behave yourself when he left the
room—don't get out of line. There are rules.''

I nodded. He believed what he said and was almost
embarrassed about voicing it. My heart went out to him.

He finished the sketch, ripped it out of the book and
handed the paper to me. There was my own face, sure
enough. And yet it wasn't my face. Certainly, I wasn't
as interesting-looking as that. Or as pretty. I gazed at
him, speechless.

"Do you like it?''

"I'm very flattered,'' I said. "What will you do with
it now?''

"Make a copy and give one to you. And sell the

original to *Harper's*. Then everyone will say, So that's what a Southern belle looks like? Well, she doesn't look so bad, after all.''

''Have you sketched many other Southern women?''

''Susan, I haven't sketched anything but wounded soldiers and dead horses and battles for so long that I wasn't even sure I could do this tonight.''

''But you've done it.''

''Yes. Does it make sense to you now that I want to sketch the war instead of fight in it?''

''Yes.''

''When we first met tonight you had a lot of hostility toward me because I'm a Yankee.''

I started to protest, but he waved me off.

''Lucien told me to expect that. It's all right. It's the way things are, and that's the shame of it. Northerners have a lot of hostility toward Southerners, too. But sometimes, after they see my sketches, they're not so hostile anymore. Would you like to see some of my other work?''

I said yes so he fished some copies of *Harper's* out of his canvas bag. The issue with General Grant on the cover had scenes of the fall of Fort Donelson and the wounded and dying, and the sketches he had done by torchlight after the battle. Another issue showed soldiers in everyday camp life.

''You're very good,'' I allowed solemnly.

''Then you think it's all right that I'm not fighting in the war?''

''Yes. You have your reasons. Just like Lucien.''

''He says you're an ardent secessionist.''

''I just want to be a good Confederate,'' I said. ''Lucien understands me and I understand him.''

''Do you think you could manage some of that understanding for me, Susan Dobson Chilmark?''

I looked at him. I felt two bright spots flame up on my face. "What are you saying, Timothy Tobias Collier?"

"That I'd like to be friends with you. I'd like to stay in touch with you by letter."

"There's no mail service between North and South since the war started."

"I can manage it. I suppose I should ask your brother for permission. I wouldn't want to take advantage of his friendship. I'll ask him tonight." He was smiling at me with that Yankee insolence of his. But the piercing blue eyes were pleading, too. I felt my heart hammering inside me.

"Do you really think I'm pretty?" I asked.

"I think you're beautiful. I've never seen such dark and luminous eyes. When you smile and your face lights up, it takes my breath away. Everything about you is just perfect."

"Mama makes me dress too childish."

His eyes went over me in a way that made my face hot and yet was most flattering. "I'd have to be blind not to see you're a very lovely young woman, Susan. And I have very good eyesight."

"Some of your sketches"—I bent over the pad—"are so awful. I mean, they're good, but sad. This one of the dead soldiers. Won't it upset the readers?"

"I hope so."

"I saw a soldier die once. In the house next door. I was nursing him. When he died I felt terrible. I couldn't help feeling that the war was so stupid. I had so many questions about it. Before that I was sure about everything. But when that soldier died I wasn't sure about anything anymore. I had only questions I couldn't answer."

"That's the way I hope my sketches will make the people at home feel, Susan."

I smiled. "I would very much like to be friends with you, Timothy Tobias Collier," I said.

Chapter Fifteen

Rain slapped in driving, dismal fingers of cold against the windows of Mrs. Wigfall's carriage. I shivered as if the devil himself were breathing down my neck, and drew my cape around me. I'd been all right as long as we had been moving, for I'd known we would be at our destination—the railroad station—within minutes. But now we were stopped. I pushed aside the curtains and tried to see out. The dark was like looking into the bottom of a well. Up ahead I saw lanterns winking through the rain.

"Who is it?" Mrs. Wigfall asked.

"I think it's those Baltimore detectives," I said.

"Oh, deah, two blocks from the station! And I neglected to get a military pass to make a shipment out of the city. In all the excitement I just forgot." Realizing her error, she was wide-eyed now with distress.

"We'll get put in Castle Godwin!" I couldn't help being so miserable. It was too early in the morning for me to be civil in the first place. And, in the second place, even though I loved Mrs. Wigfall, I was annoyed that she'd forgotten to secure a pass as General Winder had decreed should be done if someone was shipping anything out of the city.

Now our shipment of dresses could be seized by the detectives. I couldn't bear it. All yesterday afternoon, at our house, Mrs. Wigfall and her daughters and her servants and I and Rhody and Wilium had packed the dresses for shipment. We'd worked so hard. The dresses had been loaded onto two wagons, covered with canvas, and hidden in the lot behind the Spotswood Hotel, where I'd stayed again with Mrs. Wigfall. She had gone through so much trouble, even paying someone to guard the wagons overnight, and then forgotten to get the necessary papers to ship them. And they were to go this morning via the Richmond and Denville Railroad to Fayetteville, North Carolina, where the balloon would be constructed in a Confederate armory. The actual construction, we had been told, would probably take six weeks.

"What can we do?" I whispered to her now.

"We'll have to use our connections," she whispered. Then she rapped on the glass. "Shad, can you hear me?"

"Yessum."

"What's the holdup?"

"Some mens up thar askin' questions."

"Well, if they come back here, let me do the talking, you hear?"

"I hears you, ma'am."

"Don't be frightened, deah," she said to me. "I'll speak to them."

I was not as frightened as I was devastated. Under those canvases on the wagons up ahead were all the silk dresses Connie and I had collected, including those from Lulie Ballard's place. Lavender silks and silks of butterscotch yellow and the palest of blue and the most delicate of pinks and greens. Dresses trimmed with imported laces and ruffles and velvet bows. Dresses that had flirted at parties, rustled at teas, waltzed at dances, and now carried in their perfumed folds all those lovely memories of a happier South.

"Hello in there!" A rap on the door. A light pierced the window. Mrs. Wigfall opened the door a crack. "Yes?"

"I've got to check the contents of the wagons, ma'am. And see your pass from the provost marshal's office."

"Must you? There isn't time. We must make the six-thirty train."

"I'm afraid you'll have to get out, ma'am."

"Sir, I am Mrs. Charlotte Wigfall. My husband is a staff officer in the field."

"Do you have clearance to make this shipment of goods out of town?"

"Why no, I forgot. I mean I've been so busy it completely slipped my mind that I needed clearance from the provost marshal's office. But I assure you, sir, we are not carrying liquor, if that's what you're looking for."

The detective didn't care if he was talking to Mrs. Davis herself. "Ma'am, with or without your permission, my men are going to inspect the contents of those wagons. We'd like to determine for ourselves what you're carrying. And why."

Mrs. Wigfall started to get out, instructing me to stay in the carriage. I put a detaining hand on her arm. "Why don't you tell them what's in the wagons," I suggested. "Surely, if they are good Southern gentlemen, they won't stop us from shipping the dresses."

"Shh," she cautioned. "From what I hear about these detectives, they pride themselves in apprehending anyone who goes against Winder's bidding. Sometimes I think they've long since forgotten the good of the South."

She was right. These were the very Baltimore detectives the women had been discussing that day when we

sewed the sandbags. I got out of the carriage to stand
beside Mrs. Wigfall in the rain.

"Oh, please," she entreated. But the men were
moving away, walking toward our wagons. And then
something crashed out of the bushes to block their
way.

A horse and rider. "What's the problem here?" The
rider loomed over the detectives, on a massive black
horse. The voice seemed familiar, but my mind was on
other things. One of the detectives held up his lantern,
and it slashed the early morning dark with a beam of
light. The figure on the horse wore oilskins. I couldn't
believe my eyes, at first. Surely, I was imagining
things.

Lucien! Of course, I should have recognized his
horse, Merlin, but it was all too confusing.

"I said, what's the problem here!"

The detective lifted up his lantern higher. Merlin,
proud and shimmering in the rain, stood blocking his
way.

"The problem, sir," the detective bellowed, "is that
these wagons are moving something out of town at an
ungodly hour of the morning without official sanction.
Now, if you'll just move aside and stop interfering with
the law, we can get on with our business."

"I can vouch for these ladies."

"I suggest you vouch for yourself first, sir. And you
can start by giving your name."

"Tom, you old coot. You recognize me easily enough
when you're gorging yourself on the house buffet at my
place. You mean you don't know me now?" Lucien slid
from the horse. As he did, I caught the flash of the Colt
revolver at his hip under the oilskins and held my
breath, for by now the detective had a gun in his hand.

"Who is he?" Mrs. Wigfall tugged my arm. But I

was too stunned to answer. There was a moment of recognition by the man called Tom, and then they were all in a huddle up ahead. I heard laughter. Lucien's voice was low, the detective's inquiring. Then Lucien's voice again, placating, reassuring. They turned to look at us. The man named Tom apologized.

"Sorry for the inconvenience, ma'am. The gentleman here has explained. I had no idea you were shipping out the sandbags yet."

Mrs. Wigfall drew her small frame up to its full height. "We can't get them to their destination fast enough, sir."

The detective came and opened the door of her carriage and offered his hand. Mrs. Wigfall took it, hesitated and looked at Lucien. "I didn't catch your name, sir."

Lucien stepped forward. "Lucien Chilmark, ma'am, at your service."

Mrs. Wigfall's mouth formed a perfect *o*. Her eyes went wide. But a true Southern lady is never at a loss for words. "So, we finally meet," she said. "Susan has told me so much about you. I hoped to meet you the other evening when you delivered her to the Spotswood, but I was at a dinner party. I have heard much about you, Mr. Chilmark. What I have not heard about is your penchant for coming to the aid of ladies working for the Cause."

"I have an inclination to come to the aid of ladies in distress whatever their politics, ma'am," Lucien said. "And if you'll allow, I'll accompany you to the station."

"I'd be most honored, sir."

Lucien bowed, clamped his hat on his head and grinned. "The honor is mine." Then, just as I thought they might truly break into a Virginia reel right there in the rain, he turned and mounted Merlin. We got into the carriage. The door slammed shut.

"My deah," and Mrs. Wigfall held her hand to her throat, "so that is your brother Lucien."

"I told him we were shipping the dresses out early this morning," I said. I had not confided in her that some of the dresses had come from Lulie Ballard's place. A true Southern lady, after all, can stand only so much. "I never expected him to see us off to the station, though."

"My deah, just thank your stars he came along. But you didn't tell me he was so dashing!"

The train was waiting at the siding, belching forth huge clouds of steam. Lucien insisted we stay in the carriage, then he was off Merlin, overseeing the loading of the crates onto the train. The detectives had gone back to search for better game. Within half an hour all the crates were loaded, and he came to our carriage to hand us the bill of lading.

"I don't know how to thank you," Mrs. Wigfall said.

"Just don't mention around town that I've been helping the Cause," Lucien quipped. "It would ruin my reputation."

"My deah sir." Mrs. Wigfall took his hand. "I don't know about or question your politics. I only know that you are a good man. And I am indebted to you."

For once Lucien was speechless. He nodded, then looked at me. He withdrew something from a coat pocket inside his oilskins. "For you," he said.

"What is it?"

"It's from a friend," was all he would say. "He had to leave last night, but he insisted I deliver this to you. Now, you're both sopping wet. I'd suggest you get back home. It promises to be a beastly day. My sister has told me much about you, Mrs. Wigfall. I'm indebted to you for your kindness and friendship to Susan when she needs it. And I mean that.''

I saw his eyes meet Mrs. Wigfall's. And I knew that without saying it that they were acknowledging mama's ''problem,'' and that Lucien was thanking her for being a surrogate mother to me.

''Susan is a deah child,'' Mrs. Wigfall said, ''and her friendship means much to me.''

Lucien squinted up at her. Rivulets of water dripped off the brim of his hat. ''We're living in bad times,'' he said. ''The world is changing all around us. Sometimes the only thing that's recognizable is an act of human kindness.''

The train hissed in the background, the rain made rhythmic sounds on the floorboards of the platform. Lucien looked as if he were about to say something else, then changed his mind. He tugged at the brim of his hat and turned to walk to his horse in the rain.

I untied the rolled-up paper he had given me. It was a copy of the likeness of myself that Timothy had done. ''One of these days it will be in *Harper's*,'' he wrote in the accompanying note. ''And until we meet again you will be in my thoughts. I hope I will be in yours. I will be in touch. Yours, devotedly, Timothy.''

PART THREE

April 5, 1862

Chapter Sixteen

When Lucien had said that the world was changing all around us, he could have been writing an editorial for the *Richmond Dispatch*. Nothing was the same anymore. Even church, that last refuge of tradition, was not safe from the onslaught of war.

Almost every Sunday that spring a trooper clanked into our church, walked noisily up the main aisle in a filthy uniform and presented a written note to our minister while the congregation held its breath.

I had been halfheartedly listening to Dr. Hoge's announcements while fingering the last of Daddy's letters which I had folded in my hymnal.

"The Second Baptist Church of Richmond has donated its bell to be cast into cannon," his voice boomed.

I peeked into my hymnal and reread Daddy's letter:

Dear Susan: When the *Virginia* met the Federal ironclad on March 9, the Confederate gun crews had no iron bolts with which to load their rifled guns. Such projectiles could have gone through the windows of the *Monitor* and served as the only real weapons to do any damage. I hounded them about this problem beforehand, but no one would listen. I predicted that the only available cannonballs we had would bounce right off the *Monitor*'s iron plate. Now, of course, Tredegar is quickly furnish-

ing us with bolts. I hope it is not too late for the
Virginia to still prove herself.

I am completely enamored with the ship. It has
become very close to my heart. It has taken 53 tons
of new plates to repair the cracked armor.

I miss you. Word reaches me of affairs in Richmond,
and it does not make me feel any better to know
that McClellan is marshaling forces on the peninsula. But I have faith in our good generals and
soldiers. I have heard, from your mama, about
your venture collecting the dresses for the balloon.
She is very proud of you. When the repair work on
the ship is finished, I will try to make it home.

Perhaps balloons are the answer, Susan. Perhaps in
future wars, God forbid, we will fight in the air.
Regardless, I see you have found a direction for
your ambitions, and I pray it brings you peace of
mind. Stay my dear and darling girl.

Your loving father...

"Sacrifice!" Dr. Hoge was saying. "Keep that in
mind now that the Confederate Congress is about to
authorize conscription for men between eighteen and
thirty-five. Sacrifice should be familiar to us all these
days. And so, it is with both joy and sorrow that I tell
you I will soon be leaving for England to secure
religious pamphlets for our troops."

A murmur of protest went up from the congregation,
but he held up his hand. "I know, I know. Travel is
dangerous. But I intend to run the blockade."

It was then that the soldier came into our church,

shuffling, dragging one foot. He handed a note to Dr. Hoge. The silence was terrifying.

"Our services will be concluded early today," said Dr. Hoge, "so that the women and girls may go home and collect and cook what they can on such short notice and take it into the streets. Within an hour or two, troops will be passing through town. There will also be a large portion of our army at the station, for trains will have a layover in Richmond. We will now have a brief prayer and conclude services."

In no time at all, it seemed, there was a regular procession in the streets of town. It was strange and silent, not at all disorderly, yet not at all ordered. People just appeared out of their houses bearing trays and buckets and dishes and pans of food.

There were old men, and women still in Sunday clothes. There were children struggling to carry some pan of food or bucket of water or "Confederate lemonade," which was really vinegar and water. I know that Mama put a generous amount of honey into ours. Not every household was fortunate enough to have honey.

It was the first Sunday in April, and soldiers were passing through town on their way to the peninsula. More waited in trains at the station to see what the people of Richmond would bring.

One man walking next to me had a dish of bacon and cabbage. Indeed, it looked as if Sunday dinner had been taken right off the stoves and tables. Nigra servants carried enormous pitchers of buttermilk or sorghum or dishes of corn pones. All I could hear was shuffling feet as we walked in the direction of the station.

I followed Rhody, who was carrying a pan of roast pork and potatoes—our Sunday dinner. Mama was walk-

ing up ahead. When we arrived at the station there were
the trains, flatcars and freight cars and stock cars.

They were all loaded with dirty, hungry soldiers. A
great shout went up from them as they saw us approaching.
They cheered and laughed and stomped and some even
cried. The din was terrible. The depot echoed with the
sounds of their voices. Their officers kept them in some
kind of order, however, as the women set up a system
of distribution in the middle of all the confusion so the
food and drink could be passed from one person to
another all down the line of cars.

Every husband and son and brother and father had
food to eat. I was kept busy ladling out soup. When that
was gone, I handed out pieces of cake. I cried at the
sight of those men and boys, but they were in high
spirits.

One grabbed my hand and leaned out of the window
of the train and kissed my face as I handed him the
cake. Before the two hours were over I thought I would
drop from exhaustion. And then the train whistles were
screeching and there were cries and hugs from the
soldiers as they reached out from the trains, or jumped
back on. They were shouting and singing as the trains
pulled out of the station.

And then they were gone. Only the echo of their
voices remained. The women stood, dirty and empty-
handed, hair mussed, sleeves rolled up, tears streaking
down their faces. The kettles and buckets and pans and
dishes were empty.

We were all not only exhausted but drained of every
emotion we had.

"Well now," Rhody said, "leastways they won't
fight hungry."

Yes, leastways they wouldn't fight hungry.

* * *

"I'm going to bed, Rhody," Mama announced when we got home.

"There's some leftover ham and biscuits in the kitchen," Rhody offered.

"Give it to Susan." Mama waved her off and went up the stairs.

I followed Rhody into the kitchen. My head hurt and my feet ached, but I was afraid to close my eyes for fear of what echoing, clamoring and haunting scenes I would conjure up behind my eyelids.

Rhody fried up some ham bits with greens and gave me some buttermilk.

"Since that Gen'l Winder fixed prices nobody been comin' to the market with food. Only reason I had the pork and potato dinner was 'cause I knows how to sweet-talk the right people at market. Here, sit down and have what's left."

There was a knock on the front door while I was eating. Wilium went to answer it. In a moment he came back and stood staring at me. "There's a soljer askin' to see you, Miss Susan," he said.

"Whare he from? Tell him to come to the back door if he's hungry," Rhody said.

"No, ma'am. Says he gotta see Miss Susan and nobody else."

"I'll go, Rhody," I said.

April sunshine dappled the hallway, and I could see the outline of the soldier in the glass panels at the side of the door. When I opened the door he took off his hat. "Miss Susan Chilmark?"

"Yes?"

"I'm from the Washington Artillery. New Orleans, miss. It's my proud duty to ask you to be out on this heah porch at four o'clock this afternoon."

I looked at the young face, the hazy blue eyes, the freckled nose. "What for?"

"My commanding officer requests it, miss."

"But can't you tell me what for?"

He looked at me as if I were not too bright. "Why, miss, you're the one who made our flag, aren't you?"

"Yes, I am."

"Well then, we'll be marchin' out of town about that time. All I know is they're detourin' the march to come by this heah house." He turned to go, clamped his hat on his head and looked back. "I'd be heah, miss. They're goin' through a powerful lot of trouble to come by this heah house."

"Thank you. I'll be here," I said.

At a quarter of four I went to stand on the front steps of our house. The street was so still that I was beginning to think I had dreamed the episode with the orderly. Having given the last of their food to the soldiers on the trains, people were now closeted inside their houses, recovering from the awful ordeal of seeing those boys off at the station.

It was a fine day in April. Spring had come with a vengeance to Richmond, with green leaves and the bursting of the magnolia trees and the blossoming of flowers in all the front yards. But not a soul was to be seen on our street. Our house, too, was deathly silent. Mama was sleeping, and I suspected Rhody was too. Wilium was nowhere in sight.

And then, from the distance, faintly, as if I were imagining it, came the delicate sound of fifing and drumming. My heart quickened as the sound came closer.

The Washington Artillery from New Orleans came around the corner. In full sight the soldiers seemed magnificent, nothing less, with their flags and their bright music. But as they got closer, I could see that their uniforms were the worse for wear. Their trousers were mud-splattered, their gold was tarnished, and their scarlet was tattered and faded. They were on their way to the front, to Yorktown. As they filed by our house someone gave the order: "Eyes left," and they all looked in my direction. The officers saluted with their swords, and the band struck up "The Girl I Left Behind Me."

For a minute or so they paused while the sassy yet sad strains floated on the spring air. Then they proceeded on. The soldiers sitting on the caissons, the wagons that carried the ammunition, cheered. And there was my flag, dipping low as it passed.

I waved. The tears streamed down my face. How I wished someone were here to share this moment with me. My father or Rhody or Lucien—or Mama. My heart seemed to burst inside. And then, before the tears were dry on my face, they were gone, their sassy music fading, the shuffling of their feet and the sound of the caissons echoing in the deserted street.

I rubbed my face, blinking, unable to believe it had really happened. The Washington Artillery of New Orleans had found out where I lived and come by my house to salute me for making their flag.

The last I saw of them as they went around the corner was that flag, raised high in the April breeze, with the white from my old silk dancing dress a part of it, going off to war.

Chapter Seventeen

•

I was hungry. My stomach growled with the awful gnawing discomfort of hunger which I had never known in my lifetime and did not want to know now. I tossed in my bed. Was it the hunger that had awakened me? No, someone was knocking on our front door. Where was Rhody? Mama was fond of saying that the Yankees could march through Richmond, and they wouldn't wake Rhody. I got up, put on my robe and stumbled into the hallway and down the stairs. I tried to get my mind in working order. What day was this? Friday, April eleventh, that's what it must be. On the seventh of April, only four days ago, General Winder's fixed prices had gone into effect in Richmond, and, as Lucien had predicted, the city was now almost foodless.

There were no greens or potatoes or eggs or butter at the market. No fish or fowl or hogs were brought into town by farmers or fishermen. We had eaten watery potato soup and leftover raisin bread the night before. I wanted to smell bacon frying in the kitchen, but we had none left. There was scarcely enough flour for Rhody's famous light breakfast biscuits. After last Sunday, when most of Richmond's families had brought their food out to feed the troops, homes were pretty well cleared out of anything decent to eat.

I hurried down the stairs. Purple fingers of light filled the foyer, enough for me to see that the chiming clock my father had once imported from France said five of six. The house was still chilled. Normally Rhody would be up by now, working her morning magic in the kitchen, but with no food to cook, why get up?

The shadow outside the double glass front doors knocked again. "I'm coming," I whispered. I pushed aside the panels of lace curtains, as Rhody had admonished me to do. And there, in the blurry morning light, stood Nate.

I opened the door. "Nate, how are you? What is it?" And a stab of fear passed through me. "Is anything wrong with Lucien?"

Why would Nate come here like this? Something was surely wrong! I had neither seen nor heard from Lucien since that morning at the train station, two weeks ago now.

"Good morning, Miss Susan." Nate calmly removed his hat. "I've brought this." And he picked up a heavy wooden food hamper at his feet and set it inside the foyer on the floor.

"But . . . what . . ."

"Compliments of Mister Lucien, Miss Susan. He says, 'Just deliver it, Nate. Don't take no for an answer. Find out how they are and hurry back.'" He grinned, showing his pleasure at my surprise. I knelt down just inside the foyer and opened the lid of the basket.

"Food! Eggs! Butter! Fresh fish and greens! Even a bag of . . . of . . . flour, Nate!" I looked up at him. "But where . . ."

He shook his head, holding his hat in both hands in front of him. "I don't know, Miss Susan. You know Mister Lucien, he has his ways."

"Is he all right?"

"Oh, he's all right. He's been out on his boat all week, since that Gen'l Winder feller put the lid on prices. He says you're not to worry 'bout nuthin', Miss Susan, you won't go hungry."

I stood up, tears in my eyes. "Thank you, Nate. Tell

Lucien thank you. Tell him . . . I don't know how to say it, Nate."

"I know, Miss Susan, I know." And he bowed and backed off the stoop, waving before he got onto the wagon. "I'll tell him just what you said."

I closed the door and knelt down again to look at the food. I couldn't even pick up the picnic hamper, it was so heavy. But the contents had to go on ice! The day would turn hot with sunrise. "Rhody!" I yelled it, running through the foyer, down the hall and to the back of the house, where her room was, off the kitchen. "Rhody!" I dashed into the little room to shake the still-sleeping form on the bed.

She moaned. "Rhody!" I beat at her large rump impatiently with my hand. "Get up, Rhody! We have food! We're going to eat!"

Mama sat, thin and elegant and erect, across the dining room table from me. The lace curtains lifted gently in the breeze as thunder boomed distantly on the horizon. The sky was overcast, and Rhody had lighted the candles and set the table with the finest linen and silver. Now she moved around us cautiously as she set the dishes down on the table. She had stuffed the fish, and it sat in a rich butter sauce. There were garden vegetables and small browned potatoes and onions. I smiled at Mama as Rhody set the platter down in front of her.

"I'm not hungry, Rhody, thank you," Mama said.

Heat lightning flashed in the distance. "Mama," I chided, "you are. You know you are. You must eat."

She raised her chin ever so slightly. "It's too hot."

"It isn't, Mama. There's a lovely breeze. Doesn't the food look delicious?"

"Don't ask me to eat, Susan. I'll be happy with some grits and tea."

I was about to say something else, but the look on her face stopped me. We had not had a cross word in the last month, not since I had started collecting dresses for the balloon. True, the dresses had been shipped off a good two weeks ago, but her attitude toward me had definitely changed for the better. Now, however, I saw a flicker of the old anger cross her face.

"Lucien sent the food so we wouldn't be hungry, Mama. Daddy wouldn't want you not to eat and be sick."

"He's gotten himself exempt from the draft." That was what she said. That's what she was thinking about.

"He's been exempted because he brings food into the city, Mama."

"Well, I will not eat this food. I would not eat it if I were dying. You may eat, Susan. There's no reason you shouldn't."

I took a forkful of the stuffed fish and allowed it to disintegrate inside my mouth. There had been crabs in the basket, and Rhody had made crabmeat stuffing. I couldn't stop eating. If it meant I had no morals, so be it. "We can't let it go to waste," I said. "Can't we send some over to Mrs. Harrold and the children?"

"No one is to know we have this food in the house," Mama said. "I would rather feed it to hogs before I let anyone know I accepted food from Lucien."

That hurt me, and it also made me angry. I hurt for Lucien. And I was angry with myself because I did not dare speak up in his defense.

Monday, the sixth of May. Dear Daddy:

I hope this letter finds you well. For the past two days all of Richmond has been in a panic because of the appearance of Yankee gunboats on the James River. Early this morning I looked out my window

to see people loading their valuables onto wagons,
and Mama says that General Winder's passport
office is mobbed with people who suddenly want to
visit a sick aunt outside Richmond. But Mrs.
Wigfall tells us the fortifications on Drewry's Bluff
will protect the city from the Yankees.

The ladies of Richmond ended up sewing thirty
thousand sandbags for the fortification of Yorktown.
But now we hear that our army has evacuated that
town and is fighting McClellan at Williamsburg.

We hear that New Orleans has fallen. Our Mayor
Mayo told the newspapers here that before God
and heaven, if anyone wants him to surrender
Richmond, they must get some other mayor, because
he will never do it. We are all very proud of him.

Still, things have been difficult here. When General
Winder fixed prices, no food came into the city.
People started giving starvation parties. I attended
one that the Wigfall girls gave. We sat around and
sang and caught up on gossip, but of course there
was no food to speak of.

I have not seen Lucien for a while. He has been
sending baskets of food around regularly, once a
week. But Mama will eat none of it. I think she is
getting very thin. At the end of April, when General
Winder lifted his price schedules, eggs went up
to $1.00 a dozen. In two days butter went from
50¢ to $1.40 a pound. But Rhody has found ways
to make many delicious things to eat and not spend
all our money.

* * *

I miss you. Everyone here seems so frightened and uncertain about everything. I miss the way our life used to be. Sometimes I ask myself how it all could have changed so. And why I didn't appreciate it more before when it was so wonderful. But there is good news! Mrs. Wigfall received word that my balloon is finished and about to be shipped back to Richmond. Now I understand your love for the *Virginia,* Daddy. I have such a special place in my heart for that balloon. I will write you soon again. Do take care of yourself, dear Daddy. I love you.

Your affectionate daughter, Susan.

On the fifteenth of May the church bells tolled all day in Richmond. For hours we heard the sound of guns as our batteries on Drewry's Bluff met the Federal invasion on the James. But by the end of the day the Yankees had learned that they could not get by our well-posted guns on the bluff, and withdrew. The panic subsided somewhat in the city. My mother and her friends were off to oversee the cleaning of the hospitals in Richmond in preparation for returning wounded. Our army, retreating from Yorktown and Williamsburg, was camped in front of the city.

Rhody and Mama would not let me out. "They be stragglin' into the city, muddy and exhausted," Rhody said of our soldiers. "I ain't never seen such forlorn-lookin' bein's. Are these the men who are supposed to protect us from the Yankees?"

"They've done their best, Rhody!" Mama snapped. "Which is more than I can say for the Davis family!"

President Davis had sent his wife and children out of the city on the ninth. It had done little to buoy up spirits.

On the twelfth had come the most demoralizing news of all. The Confederates had blown up the *Virginia!* Daddy's ship! We were all stunned, then despairing. And first reports made no sense. I spent days in my room, moping and crying and waiting to hear from Daddy. Then on the sixteenth a letter came.

Dear Susan: I have written to your mama and now I write to you. We have blown up our own ship, my beloved *Virginia.* I am heartsick, Susan. But we had to do it. When Yorktown and Williamsburg were lost, it left Norfolk wide open. When we knew the Federals would be marching in we destroyed supplies, and machinery, but they still got a fine haul. The brave *Virginia,* which held off the Federal navy for the last few weeks, had no post from which to operate. We had to destroy her so that she would not fall into the hands of the enemy.

I am sorry to say that I personally oversaw the destruction. When you have created something that has no more reason to exist, it is up to you as the creator to destroy it.

I am now offering my services to the Confederate army as an engineer. Don't cry, Susan. I must do this. I cannot come home now. I must go on and give new direction to my energies. Stay well and brave and God bless my wonderful girl. I love you. I think of you every day. In the middle of war and destruction, you are the future.

Your loving father...

Chapter Eighteen

The thirty-first of May was scorching even before the sun came up. I sat at the kitchen table with Rhody and Wilium. It was still cool in the kitchen. We were planning our day. We were going to the hills surrounding Richmond, where everyone else in town would be, to follow the progress of the impending battle.

The Yankees' General McClellan had to cross the Chickahominy River in order to get to Richmond. Reports said that the main body of his army was on the north side, and that the river was flooded.

"McClellan split his army," Wilium said. "I heard tell, when I wuz at market yesterday. I heard some mens sayin' that a general shud never split his army. Makes it weak, they said. Now our General Johnston is gonna pounce on him. Like that!" And he slapped the table with his fist.

"I hear that President Davis hisself is tourin' the battle area," Rhody said.

Mama appeared in the doorway of the kitchen in a blue morning gown. "I couldn't sleep." She had something in her hand, but she held it behind her.

"I tol' you you been workin' too hard," Rhody admonished, getting up. For the past week Mama and the other ladies had been working at St. Paul's, preparing bedding for the hospitals.

"The War Department records were moved to the railroad depot the other night." Mama sat down at the table as Rhody and Wilium got up. "We all know what that means. The government is thinking about leaving."

"People been comin' back into town," Rhody said. "Not like the first half o' the month when everybody wuz leavin'."

"You're right about that, Rhody, they have been. Virginia's Baptists are holding their annual meeting here this week. And the Episcopalians held theirs the week before. Of course, the Episcopalians never did have a wit of sense. When are you-all going to see the battle?"

"Any time now, Miz Charlotte," Rhody said.

"You go along with Wilium, Rhody. I want Susan to stay here."

"Oh, Mama!" I protested.

"You can join them later, Susan," she said. "That battle will go on all day. I want to talk to you about something first." The way she said it, I felt something cold and heavy inside me.

Reluctantly, Rhody and Wilium left. Mama took something from her lap and tossed it on the table. "Do you know what this is?"

I felt my face go white. "It's *Harper's Weekly*," I said.

She reached out and opened it to the exact page she wanted, the page with my portrait drawn by Timothy Tobias Collier. My name was under it. A SOUTHERN BELLE, it said, SUSAN DOBSON CHILMARK. Timothy was not given credit for the sketch. *Harper's* did not disclose the names of its artists.

"Would you like to explain," my mother asked, "how your portrait got into this famous Yankee publication?"

I ran my tongue along my lips and looked at her appealingly. No words came out, but my mind raced furiously. I had been foolish to think that Mama would not see my picture in *Harper's*. Sooner or later all the Yankee publications reached Richmond, somehow.

"How could you, Susan? How could you disgrace me like this?"

"I'm sorry, Mama. I didn't mean to disgrace you."

"I was so proud of you and what you did with the balloon! And now you go and do this! And bring new shame on me. Haven't I had enough?"

"Mama, I never thought it would bring shame on you. I didn't think of it that way."

"Of course you didn't! You never think of anyone but yourself! Who did this sketch? I want to know where you met a Yankee artist!"

I couldn't tell her. I'd die first. I clamped my lips shut.

"You little Yankee brat," she hissed. "I was wrong to think you had changed, that you had any real feeling for me. Or for the Cause. Our men are assembled to fight this very minute to save Richmond! My friends and I have worked our fingers to the bone all week gathering bedding and bandages. Your father is off . . . God knows where, with General Jackson in the field. And I don't know if I'll ever see him again. And you! Oh!" She put her head in her hands. "Oh, how I rue the day I ever . . ." She lifted her head. "Do you have to let the whole world know you're a Yankee?"

"Mama, I'm not a Yankee!" I stood up. "The paper says I'm a Southern belle!"

"Don't get uppity with me, miss. Don't sass me like that! I won't have it!"

"I wasn't sassing you, Mama. I was just . . ."

"You think Mrs. Turnstable hasn't seen this already? And Mrs. Clopton? And that self-righteous Mrs. Randolph? I've been working so hard to gain the respect of people in this town and you . . . you have to get your picture in a Yankee publication!"

"Mama, if you'll just read what it says . . ."

"I know what it says!" In the next instant she was on her feet. Then she seized me by the arm and pulled me over to the kitchen door where she grabbed the switch that hung there.

"Mama, no . . . please!"

"I know what it says!" and the switch came down on my back and shoulders. I screamed and tried to pull away, but she had a grip on me like iron. "I know what it says!" I put my free hand up to ward off the blows, but it did little good. She hit me and hit me and hit me. She pushed me into the corner, and I cowered there as the switch came down again and again on my shoulders, my arms, my back, my legs, my bottom.

"Mama, please, stop!" There was no way I could get away from the blows. I sank down onto my knees, huddled in the corner, covering my head with my arms, sobbing. Finally, exhausted, she flung the switch down and stopped. She stood back, holding her hand over her heart, gasping for breath, the way she did whenever she went into one of her rages. I hurt so badly that I wanted to die from pain and humiliation and sheer terror. But the pain of seeing my mother like this, of knowing she was all I had and that she hated me so, was worse.

"Tell me," she said between gasps of breath, "where you met the Yankee artist. Was it when you were collecting the dresses for the balloon?"

I nodded yes, even while I sobbed quietly.

"When that balloon comes back, you'll not see it. I'll keep you from seeing it."

"No, Mama," I sobbed, "please."

"Yes!" She slapped the table with her hand. Then she picked up the copy of *Harper's* and threw it at me. "Go on. Get out of here. Get out of my sight. And take this with you when you watch the battle. Do you know what kind of woman allows herself to be sketched for any newspaper? Do you know what kind?''

I ran out of the house. I didn't want to hear what kind. I had heard enough.

The sound of my shoes on the pavement echoed in the deserted street. I ran and ran until I couldn't run anymore, until I thought I would die from the stitch in my side. But it was my heart that I thought would burst. I felt wild and crazy. I didn't know where to go. And then I remembered that I had some money rolled up in a handkerchief in my pocket. I had been meaning to take it along to hail a carriage to the outskirts of town if Rhody got too tired. I took it out and counted it, wondering if it was enough to take me where I wanted to go.

It took me only ten minutes to get there. The hack driver was glad to see my money, with the town deserted and no other customers. When I got out of the carriage and saw the gilded oversized number on the polished oak doors of Lucien's gambling parlor, I almost started crying again.

Then something else on the huge doors caught my eye. A sign was hung there. It said CLOSED.

Closed! How could it be! Lucien's place was never closed! The carriage had gone, and I was standing alone in the deserted street. Had everyone in the world gone to the hills to see the battle? And then I heard hammering from around the back of the house. I ran through the neat yard. There on the back porch was Nate, nailing up another sign.

I was so glad to see a familiar face. I ran to him. "Nate!"

"Why, Miz Susan, what a surprise!"

"Why is the place closed, Nate?"

"Oh," and he rolled his eyes, "they all closed. All the 'hells.' "

"Hells" was the name given to the gambling parlors of Richmond.

"Have the police shut him down?"

He laughed. "Oh, no, Miz Susan. They had a meetin', all the owners, a couple of days ago. And they decided to close."

"Lucien would never do that. Where is he, Nate?"

"He's inside, Miz Susan." He smiled and opened the door. "He's packing some things."

I ran through the deserted halls to Lucien's office, calling his name. At the doorway I stopped. He was kneeling down, locking up the safe. He was wearing boots and trousers and a shirt made out of a rough, homespun type of material.

"Lucien!"

He looked up at me. "God's teeth, you look as if you've been chased by the Yankees."

"Where are you going? Why are you closed?"

He got up and laughed. A cheroot was clenched between his teeth. "The proprietors of all the 'hells' met on the twenty-ninth and decided that we've been luring too many officers from their posts. And if we want to save Richmond, we'd better close until the crisis passes."

"I don't believe it!"

"Oh, believe it, do. We've also pledged twenty thousand dollars to purchase items for the wounded."

"Lucien, that's wonderful!"

He shrugged, then scowled, taking in my appearance. "Do I get a question now?"

I blushed. "I know... how I look, Lucien."

"Almost as good as the day we first met. Did you run all the way here?"

"I took a carriage. I had the money you gave me. It's all gone now. He charged me fifteen dollars!"

"There are those of us who still have no qualms about profiting from the war. Are you going to tell me the purpose of this visit? Not another balloon, I hope."

He was looking at me shrewdly. I sank down in a chair, realizing I was still holding the copy of *Harper's*, that I'd clenched it in my hand all the way in the carriage. I was trembling. I had all I could do to keep from crying again. He took the cheroot out of his mouth and came and sat down next to me.

"Tell me," he said.

"Oh, Lucien, I didn't know what to do. I ran and I ran, until I couldn't run anymore. Then I came here. I didn't know where else to go."

He nodded, waiting. I caught my breath and held the copy of *Harper's* out to him. He took it. It was folded open to the page with my picture. He nodded somberly. "He did a wonderful job. But you didn't come here looking like that to show this to me. You look as if you've run a gauntlet. Is it Charlotte?"

I nodded.

"Don't tell me. Let me guess. Somebody showed it to her."

I nodded. "She was furious, Lucien."

"How furious?"

"She hit me. She hit me and said awful things. She said I disgraced her by letting the whole world know I was a Yankee."

"What did she hit you with?"

But I didn't answer. I just lowered my head. He reached out and touched my shoulder and I winced.

"Answer me, Susan."

I shrugged. "She has this switch. She keeps it behind the kitchen door."

He nodded. "I feel responsible for this. I never should have allowed Timothy to do the sketch. I should have known she'd see it. But I never thought..."

"I'm glad he did it," I said. "I'm not sorry at all."

He took out his handkerchief and wiped his face. "I've locked all my brandy up, or I'd give you some. You look as if you need it."

"I'm all right," I insisted. "Really, Lucien. She didn't hit me that hard at all."

He smiled faintly. "You poor devil. I wish I could do something about the way she treats you, but I can't. I'm powerless to do anything. My hands are completely tied. You know that, Susan."

I nodded. "I know. I just had to come here for a little while. To talk to you. Mama says that when my balloon comes back she isn't going to let me see it, Lucien. That hurts worse than anything. She can't do that, can she?"

"I'm afraid she can do whatever she wants, Susan."

"Oh, I wish Daddy were here! I wish he hadn't gone and joined the army!"

He got up and began pacing the room. "It was a fool thing for him to do. Have you heard where he is?"

"Somewhere with Jackson. In the Shenandoah Valley. That's all we know. Lucien, what am I going to do?"

He stopped pacing and thought for a moment. "You're going to have to go back home, Susan," he said.

"Oh, Lucien, how can I, the way Mama treated me? She said I should get out of her sight, that she didn't want to see me anymore."

"I know, Susan. And I'm sorry. I feel bad that our father isn't here the way he should be to keep his family in order. And I feel worse that there isn't anything I can do, as your brother. But I haven't any say, Susan, any rights. So you're going to have to go home. There's an awful battle about to be fought. Johnston is fighting to save Richmond."

"Well, I know that."

"Lives will be lost. There will be thousands of wounded. They'll be brought into town. The only ones to take care of them will be Charlotte and the other ladies of Richmond. And no matter how you or I may feel about her, this is no day to take a personal stand against Charlotte. We've all got better things to do right now than think of our problems. Before today is over there may no longer be a Richmond if Johnston doesn't hold. That's all I can tell you, Susan. We all have our place to be today. Mine is on the river, to bring in more food. The wounded will need it. Yours is home with Charlotte, much as you hate her and she deserves to be hated. Your hands will be needed along with the others. So go home."

I sobbed quietly. He came to stand over me. Gently, he rested his hand on my head. "Susan, I feel so bad that I haven't anything better to tell you. But I guarantee you, before this day is over, Charlotte won't remember anything about *Harper's*. She'll have too much else on her mind. So will everyone else in town." His hand rested on my head for a minute, then slipped off.

"Why can't I go with you?" I asked. "I can put on boy's clothing. Take me with you. She'll never miss me."

"Susan, you know better than that," he said sadly. "How old are you now?"

"Fifteen."

"You're growing up. You are very beautiful, Susan. Timothy was very taken with you."

I shrugged. "What difference does that make? I'll probably never see him again."

"Oh, I think you will. This war won't last forever. Do you want to see him again?"

I blushed. "We got on all right."

"You got on more than all right from what he tells me."

"Mama says do I know what kind of women have their sketches in *Harper's?*"

He scowled. "Charlotte's crazy. Don't let her sell you that pack of lies. You know what you are, Susan. And so do I. Not a day goes by in our lives that someone doesn't try to take from us what we are . . . our accomplishments, our abilities, our personal pride. When that person is your mother . . . well, you've got to be very strong to fight against it. I think you're strong enough. So don't listen to her. She's half-mad. But she's going to need you today. They all will. So, come on, I'll get you a carriage."

He hailed a carriage on the street outside. He paid the driver and ordered him to take me directly home. "Will you be all right?" I asked him.

"I'll be fine, don't worry." He shoved some money into my hand. Gold coins, not paper money.

"Lucien, what if the Yankees get past Johnston and take Richmond?"

"The Yankees aren't savages, Susan. They're Americans. I've been telling you that. But you have Rhody, and I'd trust her with my life. Anyway, I think Johnston will hold. I don't think Richmond will fall, not yet, anyway."

Chapter Nineteen

Richmond didn't fall. But the guns that started booming around one o'clock that afternoon didn't stop for two more days. At sundown the town seemed bathed in a hot, dusty orange glow and the cannon fire became part of our lives. Rhody and Wilium came home with the other people of Richmond at sundown, and the streets were crowded with citizens of the town rushing back and forth, saying that Johnston's army had attacked and won.

I did not see Mama that night. Or the next morning. But I did receive a note from Mrs. Wigfall, asking me to come to St. Paul's and help distribute the bedding and bandages to Richmond's hospitals. When I got there I found a dozen or so young girls and women, one of whom was a tearful Connie. Her brother was with Johnston, and she was certain he was going to be killed. We worked together, loading bedding onto a wagon which was driven by a nigra boy. We delivered the bedding to Richmond's hospitals. It seemed that the town had a hospital on every corner now, thanks to women like Mrs. George Wythe Randolph, who had given her energy and resources to preparations for the wounded over the past few months. All that day, while cannon continued to boom on the outskirts of town and Connie sat next to me in the wagon, alternately jumping and crying, we delivered bedding and bandages.

The hospitals had both names and numbers. Georgia Hospital between Main and Cary; Arkansas Hospital,

between Pear and Peach streets; Louisiana Hospital near
the intersection of Grace and Lombardy. The list went
on. Where had I been these past few months that I had
never noticed all these hospitals? Here they were, right
under my nose, and I'd never paid mind to them.

The day grew hot. The dust choked us as we tore up
one street and down the next, meeting other wagons on
the same mission, barely missing nigra servants who
were darting to and fro, in and out of the same hospitals
with food. There was no time for socializing. We'd
stop, then I'd check my list and go in. I'd find the head
matron or the surgeon in chief. I'd lug bandages and
direct the young nigra boy who was helping us to where
to put the bedding. We'd accept a fresh cup of water, a
piece of fruit or a slice of buttered bread, pause for a minute
to hear the latest news or to say hello to a familiar face,
and then be on our way.

By the middle of the day, which was June first, we
heard that General Johnston had been wounded and that
General Lee had taken his place. Connie was frantic for
news of her brother, but no casualty lists had come in. I
tried to keep her spirits buoyed up, but by the end of the
day it was all like a dream. I was dirty and perspiring,
my hair was coated with dust and all I wanted to do was
have a bath and go to bed.

I dropped Connie off home at sundown. Inside my
house Rhody was like a field commander, cooking and
directing three or four nigra boys where to take her
covered trays of food. They were friends of Wilium's.

"Your mama won't be home," she said. "You come
'n' eat and then go have a hot bath."

"I don't want to eat, Rhody, I'm so tired. And I have
a headache. Won't the cannon ever stop?"

"When they stop you start to worry. Means either
they lost or we did."

I had a warm bath and was asleep, in my cotton nightgown, before my head hit the pillow. It was dusk, warm and thick with a strange, eerie light on the horizon. Rhody had brought some cold meat and biscuits and lemonade to my room. I had eaten ravenously. My head was spinning. Tomorrow I was to report back to St. Paul's again. I went to sleep with the cannon booming in my ears, tossing and turning fitfully all night.

The next day, I found Mama at Chimborazo, the largest hospital in town. It was run by the military. The word at St. Paul's that morning was that the enemy was repulsed but that our casualty list had been heavy. As Lucien had predicted, in the thousands. I was teamed up to make my deliveries with Connie and the same nigra boy again. The familiar faces at St. Paul's and at the hospitals, the faces of the ladies of Richmond, were pale but determined. Hands worked quickly, white aprons were smoothed down, orders were taken from surgeons and assistant surgeons, medicines and bandages and food were in place. Some transformation had taken place in the ladies of Richmond. They were ready for whatever came.

They were no longer belles, or even mothers or wives. They were nurses.

The wounded started coming in. Now no matter where we went to deliver bedding and bandages and medicine, the wagon with the wounded was there first. We had to step aside for stretcher-bearers carrying their grisly cargo, which arrived in vehicles of all kinds. Some men came walking in, holding a makeshift bandage against a face or head wound, gripping a bleeding arm or dragging a leg.

Now blood dripped on the floors where we walked, and we had to be careful not to slip in it. Yells and moans mingled in the air with prayers and curses. Doctors barked orders, and cots and beds were filled up. With the flies buzzing around open wounds in the heat, wounded men whined like boys, delirious boys cried for their mothers, and the plea for water was everywhere.

The hazy heat, thick with the smell of death and sulfur from the black gunpowder that drifted into town, stupefied everyone. Rumors were as thick as flies and despair alternated with hope.

We held them. We didn't hold them. Our General Longstreet attacked, but it was anticlimactic. Our Joe Johnston was dying in Richmond's Church Hill section. (It turned out later not to be true.) Their General McClellan's left flank had degenerated.

There were those who thought our General Robert E. Lee had been a failure in Western Virginia, yet most people had confidence that he would defend Richmond.

Our General Jackson, with eighteen thousand men, had outfought sixty thousand Yankees in the Shenandoah Valley. Jackson, the stern Presbyterian. My father was with him. Was my father still alive?

Was Connie's brother still alive? We didn't know but we kept going, delivering the last of our cargo and buoying each other up through the afternoon. At the hospitals, matrons and doctors treated us like grownups. They had no time for children, and we were children no longer.

Late in the afternoon, at Union Hospital at Nineteenth and Main, the head matron gave us a note asking for morphine. They had run out already and were requesting some from Chimborazo Hospital. It was just east of the city limits on a hill named for a mountain range in the Andes. We were to give the note to the matron in charge of supplies and return with the morphine as quickly as possible.

Outside the hospital we found some water buckets, filled to the brim. We were sweating and tired and so we poured the water over our heads. I never felt anything so good in my life. The water dripped down my bodice, soaking me to the skin. We laughed and threw water at each other, Connie and I, in a last stolen moment of childhood. Then we gave the horse what was left and started off for Chimborazo.

It was made up of 150 unpainted frame buildings and covered forty acres. On a nearby hill was a herd of cattle and goats. It was there, in that maze of buildings and wagons and wounded and cots and nurses and doctors, that I found my mother.

"We can spare only so much morphine," Phoebe Yates Pember said to us. "After that, they will have to start using brandy."

She was a dynamic little woman from the Deep South, and she was already part legend in Richmond. She was the chief matron at Chimborazo. She gave us the morphine, told us to guard it with our lives, then asked my name. I told her.

"We have your mother here." She smiled. "She came in the other day to inquire about our method of feeding so many men, and she impressed me so much I asked her to stay. I begged her, as a matter of fact. She's been working for two days with hardly any rest."

"Where is she?"

She directed me to the ward. I asked Connie to wait in the wagon with our driver and wound my way through rows and rows of cots. Most of the soldiers had already had their wounds dressed and were either sleeping or unconscious. The walls were whitewashed and adorned with cedar boughs so the smell was not bad here.

I saw my mother before she saw me. I stopped to

watch her, leaning over the bed of some half-awake soldier, talking to him, smoothing his brow. "I'll write the letter for you tomorrow when you feel better. Why don't you rest now?"

She looked thinner than ever and exhausted. And as she moved from one bed to another, she seemed to drag herself in weariness.

"Mama?"

The fading afternoon light coming in the window got in her eyes, and she had to shield them to look in my direction. Her shoulders sagged when she saw me, and she continued what she was doing, straightening the pillow of a soldier whose head was completely bandaged. She raised his head and gave him some water. I waited. She moved away from him and stood in the aisle, looking at me.

Why had I never noticed before how small she was, how fragile her shoulders were, how thin her wrists? "Is everything all right at home?" she asked dully.

"It's fine, Mama. I'm helping deliver bandages and bedding and supplies. I've been doing it for two days."

She shrugged wearily. "Why are you here?"

"I was sent to get some morphine for Union Hospital. They need it badly."

"Then why are you loitering? Get back with it." She started to turn away.

"Mama?" I took a step closer. She sighed and turned halfway around.

"When are you coming home?" I asked for lack of anything better to say.

She laughed bitterly. "Do you miss me? You have Rhody. It seems that's all you need."

"I just thought you looked tired. You should get some rest."

"The whole world is tired."

"Phoebe Yates Pember told me you were here. I didn't know it. I have . . . Connie and our driver waiting in the carriage. I just wanted to see if you were all right. And say hello."

"I'm all right as I can be in hell. Tell Rhody I'm fine. I'll be home when I get a chance. Tell her if Wilium is free he can bring me a change of clothes tomorrow. That would be nice."

She started to move away. A soldier was calling. "Mama?"

She turned around and looked at me. "Well?"

"I'm sorry, Mama."

"About what?"

"The sketch in *Harper's*."

For a moment she looked at me as if I were daft. "Oh, that," and she dismissed the whole idea with a wave of her hand. "It doesn't matter anymore. Nothing matters. I don't even know where my husband is. For all I know he's in some kind of hospital like this somewhere. I've seen enough in the last two days to know that the word sorry will never have any meaning again. I'm exhausted."

She sat down on a nearby chair. "And my fool husband has gone off to join Jackson. Have you had any word of him?"

"No, Mama. Nothing. But I did hear that Lucien closed his gambling house. All the gambling house owners closed. And they donated twenty thousand dollars for supplies for the wounded."

"Am I supposed to cheer over that?"

"I'm just telling you what I heard."

"Has he joined the army yet?"

"No. He's gone out on the rivers to bring in food for the wounded."

"How long have you been seeing him, Susan?"

I flushed, realizing how I'd given myself away.
"What?"

"I know you've been seeing him. I knew you were
up to something. It makes sense. The picture in *Harper's,* your defiance, everything. All behind my back.
You always did go behind my back. Just like your
father."

"I met him by accident, Mama." I was glad, actually, to have it all out in the open. "I've only seen him
once or twice."

"Don't lie to me. Not in this place. Not in the
presence of such truth."

I fell silent, ashamed.

Her voice dropped to a whisper. "That's why the
food came to the house, isn't it?"

"Yes, Mama. But you can tell by that how he means
well. He . . ."

"Don't tell me how well he means. Look around
you. His good intentions are a mockery here."

A soldier called to her. "I'm coming," she answered.
She moved to go. "I think less of you, Susan. I tried
with you, but I lost you somewhere. Maybe if your
father hadn't been away so much. I had all I could do to
keep up with my nursing. And you took advantage."

"Mama . . ."

"Go," she whispered. "Deliver the morphine. Men
are waiting for it. You want my love, yet you want to
deceive me. You can't have both."

I turned to go. Tears came to my eyes. She was right.
I heard her ministering to some man in pain, and I
realized I was outside the circle of her love. By my own
choosing. And I still wanted her love, I couldn't help it.
But a person couldn't have both. A person had to make
a choice and pay for it like all these wounded men
around me.

Now I would have to pay for mine. And I had made a choice, somehow, in having my sketch in *Harper's*, in making friends with Timothy and in seeking out Lucien. What that choice meant to me I didn't know yet. But sooner or later I would have to decide what I believed in and go in that direction.

The trouble was I didn't know what I believed in. Was that what my father had tried to tell me before he left? I was so confused! All I knew was the sense of loss that cut through me like a minié ball, because of my mother's anger. I had seen her today as I had never seen her before. At her best, nursing, sacrificing, trying to raise a daughter alone in time of war. For the first time in my life, I was able to not only see her clearly, but weigh the good and the bad in her and realize that in spite of her craziness she was still a good person.

I had found my mother just at the moment that I had lost her. And now it was too late for me to decide that I could forgive her for anything. Or hope that she would forgive me. She didn't want my forgiveness. She didn't want me.

To give myself some credit, I had grown up over the last couple of days. But was that what growing up meant? That you acquired answers to questions you never wanted to ask in the first place? What good was growing up, then, what good?

Chapter Twenty

"We'll take Fourteenth Street and go over Mayo's Bridge," Kenneth said. "They said it was on a steamboat tied up on the far side of the wharves beyond the bridge, didn't they?''

"Yes, but can you walk that far, Kenneth? We should have taken the carriage,'' I said.

"I feel as if I could walk ten miles. Come on, let's keep walking. It's a beautiful day to be out, and I'm just glad to be alive, out of the stench of that hospital. I can't wait to see this balloon you girls got the dresses for. I'm so proud of you both.''

That was Kenneth, proud of us, when he'd been wounded in the leg at the Battle of Seven Pines. Of course, it was just a flesh wound, no broken bones, but as soon as his family found him in Howard's Grove Hospital, they had taken him home and pampered and nursed him for a week. This was his first day out, a bright blue day, the eleventh of June.

My balloon was back. Mrs. Wigfall had received word yesterday.

Richmond was not out of danger yet. McClellan was still near our city, and there would probably be another battle before long. But word was that McClellan believed the tales of Southern strength that he'd heard from his spies and was now hesitant to attack. And we had Lee, who was waiting for an opportunity to strike. So, temporarily, Richmonders were not in danger. Or perhaps they were just getting used to living on the edge.

We were in gay spirits, the three of us. Connie couldn't do enough for Kenneth. Her adoration of him was so obvious. And he, in turn, was the shy hero, hobbling along in his tattered uniform, basking in the glow of admiration of two young girls.

"Look, there it is!'' We paused in the middle of Mayo's Bridge. The little steamboat was tied up on the far side of the wharves. On the dock, beside it, was the heap of colorful dresses that was my balloon.

"But I thought it would be up!" I said in disappointment.

"They're inflating it now," Kenneth said. "Listen!"

We heard the hissing sound that Kenneth explained was the gas. The men on the dock were spreading the silk out, making it smooth. You could see the bright-colored patches jumping and bubbling. The men could barely keep the ropes from tangling in the netting that covered the outside of the silk. Lying there on the dock, the crazy patchwork mass of material was like something alive. The men had all they could do to hold it down as the gas hissed in. The smell of gas was everywhere.

"Anybody lights a cheroot, it'll be good-bye all," Kenneth joked.

"Well, at least the gas will kill the perfume smell," I said.

"Come on, let's get closer, if they'll let us." Kenneth led the way, hobbling over the bridge.

We got down onto the dock. The workmen waved at us and smiled, then gestured that we stand back. One of them saluted Kenneth good-naturedly, and he grinned back. The hissing sound prohibited speech so we just stood and watched as fold by fold of the balloon took life and it rippled into a mass of shimmering, bouncing silk.

"Look," I yelled at Connie. "There's Iris's yellow! And Melba's blue!"

She screamed in delight and pointed out Francine's green, Lulie's striped pink, and the other colors we recognized from the girls at Miss Ballard's. We collapsed in fits of laughter, our arms around each other's shoulders. The workmen grinned and Kenneth just stood there, the bright June sun shining on his blond hair, smiling.

Then the men waved us back because the balloon was taking on a life of its own, swelling above our heads into a glorious maze of colors. The men had to hold the ropes because it was beginning to tug from the force of the gas. The basket had been on its side on the dock, but now it was jerking to an upright position. Kenneth and Connie and I watched in delight as the men guided the basket across the dock and onto the deck of the little steamboat. They held on to the mooring ropes and tied them securely down, anchoring the balloon to the steamboat. Then they put sandbags into the basket to weigh it down. It was fully inflated, and the sight it made, against the blue sky, was nothing less than dazzling.

"Where are you taking it?" Kenneth asked one of the workmen.

"Up the James," was all the man would tell. He clapped Kenneth on the shoulder. "You understand, son, that's all we can say. It'll attract enough attention as it is."

Kenneth nodded. "My sister and her friend here collected the dresses for it," he said.

"That so?" The man took off his hat. "Well, this here's a project, that's fer sure. But we got a balloon now to match the Yanks, thanks to you two. You kin be mighty proud. And we'll take good care of it. It's gonna make the Yanks mighty nervous, once they see it floatin' up there in the sky. Yessir, mighty nervous." He tipped his hat, winked and jumped onto the boat.

We stood watching as the distance increased between the boat and us. The balloon danced lightly on its tethers against the framework of blue sky while the steamboat paddled away. And I thought my heart would burst with the happiness and pride inside me.

I had done it! Not I alone, no, but I had played a great part in the making of this balloon. My happiness, as I watched the balloon going downriver, was almost complete.

Oh, to be sure, I was on the outs with Mama. She spoke seldom to me when we met at mealtime, which was the only time I really saw her lately. She was still busy with her nursing. Her attitude toward me was one of almost total disgust, even while she still attempted to control my actions.

She had not stopped me from going to see the balloon today. Many of the threats she made to me she never carried out. But that was all a part of her craziness. When Connie and Kenneth had come to pick me up earlier today, she could not say no. Indeed, she had acted sweet toward them, which was her way of keeping up appearances. My life was not a happy one at the moment, yet whose was these days?

I only knew that my happiness, standing with Connie and Kenneth on that dock, knew no bounds. My heart wouldn't be held down, not even with mooring ropes. Today, like the balloon, it wanted to fly.

Chapter Twenty-one

My happiness was short-lived. When we got back to my house, Mama's carriage was outside. She hadn't come home early from her nursing since the Battle of Seven Pines, in which Kenneth was wounded, a little over a week ago.

A horse with a military saddle was tied up outside the house. Kenneth briefly inspected the horse's tack and declared that the fellow riding him could be with General Jackson.

I was seized with both hope and fear. Could it be Daddy? Since late April, Richmonders had followed Jackson's campaign in the Shenandoah Valley with delight. He was the one bright hope in the South's almost continual defeat in the West. But since Daddy had joined Jackson, we had not heard from him at all.

"Oh, Kenneth," I wailed.

"Easy now," and he took my arm as we went up the steps. "Sometimes these fellows are detached from their regiments for one reason or another and stop by the house of someone they're serving with to visit. Don't go expecting the worst."

But it was the worst. I knew it in the hall even before we went into the front parlor. I knew it the minute I saw the young officer, tall and sorrowful in his dusty and worn uniform, standing next to Mama in the parlor. He turned to look at us, and I took him in all at once. The unmistakable grace about his movements, despite his shabbiness, the growth of beard, the determined set of his shoulders, the mustard-colored gloves tucked into the sash at his waist, all bespoke the war. He smiled at us, but I saw the bruised look in his eyes, and my heart fluttered.

"This is my daughter and her friends, Lieutenant Hotchkiss," Mama said.

"I'd know Susan in a minute from her father's description," he said.

Mama was seated in a chair by the window, erect and pale. She stifled a sob.

"What is it, Lieutenant?" Kenneth asked.

"Your deah daddy, who just had to go off and fight with General Jackson, has been killed," Mama said. I just stared. It couldn't be true. Why, Mama was falling back on her low country accent, the way she did when she wanted to impress people. Surely this was not true.

"It's true, Miss Susan, I'm sorry," the lieutenant drawled. "I've brought his things," and he gestured to a marble-topped table where Daddy's hat, his pistol and a daguerreotype of Mama lay. I put my hands over my mouth and screamed.

Instantly Kenneth was beside me, his arm around my shoulder. Connie supported me from the other side. I held my breath, afraid to breathe. "Are you sure, sir?" Kenneth asked. "Did you . . . see him?"

The lieutenant nodded in understanding to Kenneth, as one man who had been on a battlefield to the other. "I recovered his body myself," he said.

My shoulders shook with badly controlled sobs. Kenneth and Connie led me to the settee, where I numbly sat with them on either side of me. A wet-eyed Rhody came in with a tray of lemonade and proceeded to pour it into frosted glasses. "Ain't gonna be the same house without Mr. Hugh," she said, not caring that she hadn't been given permission to speak. "Doan care what nobody say. Jus' ain't gonna be the same house."

She handed the glasses around and left. "Sit, Lieutenant, do," Mama said.

"I've been in the saddle too long, ma'am, I'd rather stand."

"Then do tell us everything you can about my husband."

He nodded and looked around at each of us, not sure where to begin. "Since he joined us in May, Captain Chilmark was my tent mate," he said. "He was pleasant and good-natured, kind and gentle, with few faults. He was one of those fellows everyone liked, not a small-minded or mean man. He always tried to do his share of everything."

He drained his glass of lemonade and set it down. "In thirty-eight days, from April twenty-ninth to June fifth, Jackson had us march about four hundred miles. The Federals outnumbered us, but he kept them guessing. They couldn't bring him to bay. He kept reinforcements from McClellan, and his name has become symbolic on both sides."

"We have been following Jackson's campaign with interest," Mama said.

Hotchkiss nodded. "Then you know what he's done. When your husband joined us, he was welcome. We needed a good engineer. His job was to constantly inspect fortifications, to reconnoiter for routes and positions, to make maps and write reports. He rode at the head of the column on marches. In the short time he was with us, he laid out a line of defensive works for twenty miles and supervised their construction."

He paused. We waited. "It always amazed me that a man with so little prior experience in military engineering could plan and carry out his tasks as he did with so much professional knowledge and skill."

"My husband was a graduate of West Point," Mama said.

"I know that, ma'am." He drew in his breath and let it out slowly. "On the morning of June ninth, General Jackson rode out to oppose Shields's main Federal force under E. B. Tyler, north of the village of Port Republic, Virginia."

Lieutenant Hotchkiss clasped his hands behind him and seemed to study the floral pattern on the rug as he spoke. "Jackson was riding ahead of his men with his staff. Your husband was with him. So was I. I was your husband's subordinate, ma'am. I served directly under him, and I was proud to. He told us he was riding off a ways to reconnoiter for a better route. He bade me stay behind. That route took him under a volley of musketry.''

He cleared his throat. ''The enemy opened up. We were a little distance behind . . .''

I sobbed. Kenneth clutched my hand. Mama still sat, expressionless, listening.

''By the time I got to him, ma'am, to get him out of the line of fire, he was dead. He was pierced through the heart with two balls and shot through the leg. I don't think he suffered any. Death was instantaneous.''

Sun filtered through the lace panels on the windows and made crisscross patterns on the lieutenant's dusty uniform. I thought, crazily, how out of place his rough, dirty uniform was in our immaculate parlor. And the sight of it, dust-caked and dirty, the sight of him, war weary and sunburned, brought the war home to me, even more than seeing the wounded in our hospitals.

Everyone was silent. I blew my nose. ''Was . . . my father happy serving with Jackson?'' I asked.

The lieutenant gave me a sad smile. ''He was very happy. He told me once—'I would rather be a private in such an army as this than a field officer in any other army.' Of course, he was an officer and a good one.''

''Where . . . is he buried?'' I asked tremulously.

''We sent him back to Port Republic. We buried him just as the moon rose. I wept for him. He was a kind and gentle man who loved his family and spoke of you-all constantly and looked forward to rejoining you when a break came in the campaign. General Jackson selected me to bring his belongings and offer his condolences. But I'd rather spend twenty consecutive hours in the saddle than do what I had to do here today.''

''You have been most kind, Lieutenant,'' Mama said, ''and you are tired. We would be honored if you would stay and have supper with us. And if you have no more pressing duties, then certainly you must stay the night. You'll not find a room anywhere in this town to accommodate you."

"Thank you, ma'am," and he bowed and picked up his dusty hat and stood turning it around in his hands. "But I have other military calls to make in town. And then I must be getting back to the field."

Mama got up. The lieutenant hesitated. "I can show you the grave if you desire to come to Port Republic when things quiet down." He pulled a piece of paper out of his tunic pocket. "Or, if you want to make a trip there and I'm not around, here's the name and address of the people who know where it is."

Mama took the folded-over paper and said nothing. How could she be so calm, so accepting? I wanted to scream at her not to accept the paper, for to accept it was truly to acknowledge Daddy's death.

"You could have him shipped home," the lieutenant suggested, "eventually."

"Lieutenant, you have been most kind." Mama held out her hand. He kissed it and bowed. Kenneth got to his feet. "I'll see you out, Lieutenant," he said.

The lieutenant nodded and bowed again and took his leave. But I did not want him to go. He was the last connection I had with my father! I dashed out into the hallway after them. "Lieutenant . . ."

He turned and something about him struck a chord of response in me, made my heart go out to him. He was so lean and brown and worn-looking. He turned to face me and stood straight as a ramrod, wary and alert for whatever came next. He looked so forlorn and yet, at the same time, so elegant.

He was what the whole South was about at the moment, I thought as I stood there. Forlorn, yet elegant. He smiled.

"I wish you would stay so I could hear more about my father," I blurted out.

He looked at Kenneth, then me. He took a step toward me. "I'll be back someday, and we can talk. If you want."

"Yes," I said, "...did...my father ever say anything to you about how he felt about me?"

It was a bold question, but he understood. "Why, you were all he talked about, Susan," he said, quietly surprised that I should not know. "You were the joy of his heart. You were his hope for the future. He told me about your flag sewing, your balloon, everything. I probably know more about you than you know about yourself."

I looked at the floor.

He gazed at his hat in his hands. "He loved you very much," he said simply.

"Thank you, sir."

He nodded and went out the door with Kenneth. I peeked through the lace panels and watched as he mounted his horse, clamped on his hat, shook hands with Kenneth, pulled on his gloves and turned his horse's head to town. My body shook with sobs, watching him go. It was like watching my father ride down the street, away from me. And I still could not believe the message he had brought. It had all happened so fast. Why, scarcely an hour ago I was on the docks with Connie and Kenneth, my heart bursting with happiness to see my balloon dancing against the sky. And now that same blue sky had come down in pieces on my head.

Chapter Twenty-two

Sun streamed in the pleasant white-walled office of Mr. T. H. Ratcliffe, but at four in the afternoon the temperature was starting to wane and was no longer unbearable. He had a spacious office with handsome furniture and a red-and-white ingrain carpet. I squirmed, uncomfortable in my mourning dress. Mama sipped the lemonade that Mr. Ratcliffe had provided.

From outside the open window came a sudden piercing rebel yell and the galloping of horses. Dust filtered in. Mr. Ratcliffe, a white-haired cheery man of about sixty-five, got up and, smiling tolerantly, closed the window. "My, my, those cavalry boys are sure having a good time."

Jeb Stuart's cavalry had arrived in Richmond today, the fifteenth. Brigadier General James Ewell Brown Stuart had led his twelve hundred cavalrymen on an expedition that was not yet to be believed. They had ridden around the entire Yankee army on the peninsula in a four-day reconnaissance. Reports were running like a brush fire on the street. They had moved around McClellan's right flank, chased a Federal wagon train, thrown a hastily constructed bridge over the swollen Chickahominy River and enjoyed many other exploits which were now being forged into folklore on Richmond's streets, even as the people welcomed the mud-caked and weary riders, and Stuart reported to General Lee.

It was something I would have thrilled to four days ago, as I had to the sight of my balloon. But now I viewed everything as if I were underwater. Everything seemed murky and happening to someone else.

I had moved through the last four days as if in a dream. In contrast, Mama had gone right back to her nursing. Daddy's death had seemed to galvanize her into renewed action. This afternoon was my first venture out. I sat waiting. Mama tapped her foot impatiently.

"How long do we have to wait, Mr. Ratcliffe?"

The door opened and my brother stood there. I had not seen him in weeks. He was dressed in a white linen suit and he was very brown from the sun. I heard the quick intake of Mama's breath.

Lucien took off his hat. "I apologize for my tardiness, but the cavalry owns the streets out there today." He shook hands with Mr. Ratcliffe, smiled at me and nodded to Mama. "Good day, madam."

She did not answer. Lucien took a chair. "You could at least have paid a call when you heard of your father's death," she said coldly.

"I've been out on the river," Lucien said, "so I didn't know of his death until I was summoned, yesterday, to come here."

Mama's eyes narrowed. "You prosper, Lucien, when others grow shabbier every day. And you look in the best of health."

"I apologize on both counts," Lucien said.

Mr. Ratcliffe was watching, while pretending to go through some papers.

"How can you live with yourself?" Mama asked. "How do you sleep at night?"

"I'm asleep before my head hits the pillow, as is wont to happen when one spends whole days in the sun on the river," Lucien said easily.

"You're paid well for your services," she accused.

The corners of Lucien's mouth curved down in a sad

smile. "I hate to blast your illusions or ruin my reputation, but I have not accepted a cent from the Commissionary Department since I was exempted from the draft."

Mama tossed her head haughtily. Lucien smiled at me. "How are you, Susan?"

"I'm fine," I said.

"She is not fine," Mama contradicted. "And I'll thank you to stop encouraging her to sneak behind my back to see you. Your influence is not good."

"I agree she doesn't look fine," Lucien said, "but I don't think that's a result of my influence. You ought to come out on my boat with me one day, Susan. The air would do you good. What do you say?"

"I forbid it," Mama said before I could open my mouth.

Lucien took out a cheroot and lit it. "I think Susan would look better if you didn't make her wear black. I don't care for black on one so young. I'm sure Hugh Chilmark wouldn't care for it, either."

Mama's face blazed. "Mourning is only proper! And it's none of your business what Susan wears."

Lucien regarded her steadily. "I feel sorry for you, Charlotte," he said. "However, I suggest we continue our discussion later. And not bother Mr. Ratcliffe with our family quarrels."

"There is nothing more to discuss!" Mama hissed. "When we finish heah today, I do not want you to see Susan again!"

Mr. Ratcliffe cleared his throat. "I am sorry, Mrs. Chilmark," he said, "but I am afraid there is a lot more to discuss. You see, in the true tradition of Southern custom, your husband has left Mr. Lucien Dobson Chilmark, his only surviving son, head of the family and the prime beneficiary of his estate."

I thought Mama would faint from surprise. But then, Lucien was speechless too, for I was sure he had not expected this.

"It is," Mr. Ratcliffe said with quiet dignity, "in the true spirit of common law. For you see, Southern honor requires masculine headship of the family."

He explained it. Mama was to continue living in the house and be cared for, financially, as she was accustomed. I was to live with her and be her "support and companion," since, as Mr. Ratcliffe said, "your dear daddy hoped you and your mama could come closer together in this war and learn to really appreciate each other." But Mama could make no decisions regarding me without consulting Lucien. And if Lucien perceived that my "happiness, well-being or sense of security" was impaired by living with Mama, he had the obligation to see to it that the situation was "rectified by whatever means he thought best."

I felt tears gather in my eyes. Daddy had put aside his disappointment in Lucien to ensure my well-being. This was his final gesture of love and concern.

Mama recovered her voice and was livid. "I will not have it," she said. "I shall go to court and retrieve my rights. I am perfectly capable of being responsible for Susan's well-being and handling my own property."

"Apparently your husband was not of the same mind," Mr. Ratcliffe said. "By common law tradition, minor children are under the jurisdiction of the head of the household. Male protectors are indeed a requisite in our world, and I'm sure you will not deny your daughter that protection to which she is entitled. As for your property, I thought you would expect that everything goes to the eldest son. Male honor..."

"Male honor, fiddlesticks," Mama said. "My son is a ne'er-do-well and a rogue. What's more he gambles."

Mr. Ratcliffe sighed. "Mr. Chilmark was aware of all his son's activities. He determined that owning a gambling house does not make one a gambler. It only makes one a good businessman. Gambling is an old Southern custom."

"And is it also an old Southern custom to dally with women and have a mistress?" Mama asked.

Mr. Ratcliffe scowled severely. "To repress natural impulse is to defy nature itself. Your husband has deemed your son capable and honorable enough for the responsibilities he has outlined."

"But we were estranged from Lucien." Mama was almost pleading now. "We had not seen him in years. I never supposed Hugh would do this to me."

"Mrs. Chilmark," said Mr. Ratcliffe, closing a lawbook emphatically, "when it comes to wills and inheritances, one should never suppose anything."

Across the carpet Mama faced Lucien. "You know all I have now is Susan. You planned this. You want to take her away from me in revenge for . . . for . . ."

"Madam," Lucien said, "this surprises me as much as it does you. I expected nothing from my father. But I intend to carry out his wishes and assume my responsibilities. Now let's say good day to Mr. Ratcliffe and continue our discussion outside."

On the sidewalk, in front of Mama's carriage, we stood waiting while another column of Stuart's cavalry passed.

"We are not out of danger yet," Lucien said. "The city could still fall. There will be another round before Richmond is safe."

"You needn't pretend you care about the outcome of the war," Mama said.

"Madam, I care about the safety of Richmond. My business and personal interests lie here. And now my responsibilities also. My prime concern is Susan. She looks pale and I know how my father's death must have upset her. I will honor my father's wishes that she live with you, since a girl Susan's age needs the closeness of her mother. But I expect you to honor Hugh Chilmark's wishes also and concern yourself with her happiness and well-being.''

I had been petting the horse, a bit away from them, pretending I did not care. But I saw Mama raise her chin defiantly. "Are you intimating that I have not been doing that?''

"Susan, come over here please," Lucien directed. "You're old enough to hear a discussion that involves you.''

I went over to them.

"In answer to your question, madam," Lucien said, "I have reason to suspect that you have not been concerned with Susan's well-being. As I recall, you have always made a habit of taking your rages out on the person nearest to you.''

"How dare you!" Mama said. "Susan is my child!''

"She is also now my ward," Lucien said quietly. "But I will not take her away from you if you treat her decently. I also expect you to permit her to see me whenever she wishes and allow her out when I send my carriage around. Isn't that what you want too, Susan?" He looked at me.

I nodded. But I knew Mama would not give in to Lucien without a fight. And I knew I would be at the center of it.

"What's wrong, Susan?" Lucien asked. "It isn't like you to be speechless.''

He was standing up to Mama on my behalf, and I was lollygagging. Oh, I loved him for what he was doing, but didn't he know I would only suffer for his kindness? I was the one who had to go home with her.

"Susan"—his tone was sharper—"what are you afraid of?"

I started walking back to the horse. I paused, half-facing him. "I wish you would go away," I said.

Lucien scowled, but Mama smiled maliciously. "Now let's see how you are going to handle this darling child who is your ward," she said.

Lucien ignored her and came toward me. "Do you really want that, Susan? Look at me."

I looked up into his warm brown eyes. Didn't he see? McClellan, on the outskirts of Richmond, posed no greater threat to me than Mama did right now.

Lucien saw, but he had to have his answer. "If you want me to go away, I will," he said gently. "We don't have to see each other. But you must tell me now if that's the way you want it."

He was making me choose sides in front of Mama! I looked at his boots. Of course I didn't want him to go away! But if I said that, there would be the devil to pay when I got home. Couldn't he just leave it be?

Of course, he couldn't. He had waited a long time to stand up to Mama like this. But he was doing it for me! Why didn't I have the courage to back him up? And what about Daddy! He had wanted Lucien and me to be friends. He had said he was glad I had someone to turn to.

Daddy had planned it this way for me. Why, the last place he'd gone that morning, after I'd told him Lucien and I had met, was to his lawyer's office.

Thinking of Daddy cleared my head. I looked up. "I'm sorry, Lucien," I said, "I was so rude. I just don't know what got into me. I want us to see each other. Often. And I want to go out on your boat, too." I purred it in my best Southern belle voice. "I won't let you forget the invitation."

He nodded. Then he took my wrist, and we walked back to Mama. My knees were shaking as we faced her.

"We'll leave it at this for now," Lucien told her. "Except for one thing. If I ever hear of you hitting Susan again, I'll take further steps."

"Then I expect you will instruct Susan that she is to obey me," Mama said. "And not provoke me and go sneaking around."

"Susan will behave accordingly," Lucien promised.

"And what, pray, would those further steps of yours be? Would you take her from one of the finest houses in Richmond to live in Rocketts? Or perhaps to live with your mistress?"

Anger smoldered in Lucien's eyes. "Don't make light of what I say, madam, or you will indeed be sorry. I inherit the worst from you. Your temper."

Mama's face went white. "Get in the carriage, Susan, deah." Honey dripped from her tongue. I got in. Lucien had won for now. But I knew there would be another battle.

Chapter Twenty-three

It came sooner than I expected, the next battle. It came at supper.

Candles flickered in the summer breeze that lifted the curtains in the dining room. "Did you enjoy your meal, Susan?" Mama asked.

"Yes."

"Good, then let's take our dessert into the parlor so we can talk."

Through the open parlor windows we could hear sounds of celebration from down the street. Mama fanned herself with a handkerchief. "I declare, Richmond's gone crazy over Stuart and his cavalry. Well, it's been awhile since we had anything to celebrate. I know you'd much rather be out with your friends enjoying the festivities. Kenneth and Connie sent a note around while you were napping before. I took the privilege of responding that you were too tired to join them this evening at a party. Anyway, I don't think Lucien would want you out in the streets tonight. I wouldn't want to do anything that would anger him. My deah, that boy always did have a temper."

I waited. She was up to something. "What is it you want to say, Mama?"

She continued fanning. "You'll find you'll have to mind him a lot better than you minded me."

I was starting to tremble.

"Perhaps," she said in a singsongy dreamy way, "things will work out better this way. I'm so busy with my nursing. And after matters settle down heah I want to take a trip to Charleston and see my relatives. I think I deserve a trip away from all this. Charleston is still the spiritual center of the Confederacy, you know. Of course, it hasn't been the same since the fire there in December, but . . ."

"Mama, please."

"My deah, you are touchy tonight. All right, I'll get to the point. My concern in Mr. Ratcliffe's office was warranted. I don't know how to tell you this, but . . . oh, well, I'll just say it. Lucien is not your full brother."

I just stared at her.

She sipped her coffee. "You should know. You're old enough now. I just thought you should be informed of the fact."

"What . . . do . . . you . . . mean . . . by . . . that?" I said.

"Oh, deah, this is all so messy." She got up and set her cup down and began to pace, twisting her handkerchief in her hands. "I have an . . . indiscretion to confess to you, Susan. This isn't easy for me."

"What are you saying about Lucien? If he isn't my brother, who iş he?"

"Oh, he's your half brother, deah. You have the same mother, not the same father. Of course, he's still your brother, but not the way you may have thought of him before."

"You mean he has a different father?"

"No, Susan. You are being dense. You have."

The room swam in front of me. Sweat broke out on the back of my neck. My legs started shaking. "Mama, tell me what you mean."

"I mean that Hugh Chilmark was not your father! Oh!" She made a dramatic gesture of impatience and turned aside, pacing again. "I told you I had an indiscretion to confess. When we were up in Saratoga, the summer you were conceived, I met this very lovely gentleman. He was a professor, from the College of New Jersey in Princeton. He had so recently lost his wife. We . . . became quite friendly."

Someone was beating drums. For Stuart's cavalry? No, it was the sound of blood pumping in my eardrums. "You mean," I said dully, "you had an affair and . . . behind Daddy's back?"

Mama laughed. "Oh, deah, that is funny. After what Hugh Chilmark did to me? Why, he went behind my back with that . . . that nigra woman in my own house!"

I couldn't stop my legs from trembling. They seemed to have a life of their own under my dress. "What are you saying now, Mama?" I was ready to believe anything.

"Lettie, that's who I'm talking about. You remember

her? No, you don't, you weren't born yet, what am I thinking? She ran off right after her child was born. Right after she gave birth to Hugh Chilmark's daughter."

"You mean..." My mind raced. "Sallie? You mean Sallie was my father's child?"

"My deah, he wasn't your father. I told you that," she said icily.

I couldn't keep it straight. I didn't want to. But it was there, in front of me, as straight as any figure of sums I'd learned in school. And it all added up, too. Perfectly.

"Oh, I know, I know. The true Southern woman is not supposed to let such things bother her. We are supposed to look the other way. We are supposed to ignore masculine indiscretion as part of nature. When I was home, growing up on the plantation, it happened all the time. We had more little mulatto babies running around, and my deah mother pretended not to notice. Where did she think they came from?"

She looked at me. I said nothing. I was too dazed to speak, too wrapped in horrible fascination.

"I was determined it would never happen in my household. But it did. Our marriage was never the same when I found out. I found out when Lucien was eleven and the girl, Sallie, was nine. After Isabel died, I couldn't bear having Sallie around anymore. They had been playmates, and every time I saw the child it reminded me of Isabel. I begged Hugh to sell her off but he wouldn't. He said Rhody loved her as her own. We had many arguments about that. I never could figure out why Hugh didn't get her out of the house, knowing her presence hurt me so. And then one day I came across some of Lettie's old things in a box in the attic. In it was a letter from your deah father to Lettie, urging her to stay after she had their child, that he would always provide for it."

She paused. I held my breath. "I confronted Hugh with the letter, and he admitted everything to me. That summer we went to Saratoga where we usually summered. And I met . . . your father. I was foolish. I let myself get carried away, to get back at my husband. The result was you."

She looked at me. My throat was dry, my temples throbbing, my legs shaking and my palms wet. On the horizon, thunder rolled and summer lightning lit up the sky.

"Rain," she said, fanning herself. "Thank heaven. We need it."

"Did Daddy know?" I croaked.

"Hugh Chilmark did not know. I never told him."

"Then all these years he was trying to make up to you for what . . . he did. It all makes sense now. Lucien said he was trying to make things up to you. But he never told me what. And that's why you hate Lucien. Because he loved Sallie."

"He made me sick." She made an impatient gesture with her handkerchief. "Always defending Sallie. I told Hugh we had to get that girl out of the house, once again, after she grew up. She had eyes for Lucien. Hugh only laughed. He finally sent her North when he found out Lucien had been teaching her to read. He realized how close they'd become and knew he had to send her away. He eventually had to tell that hotheaded brother of yours that Sallie was his half sister. That was a night I don't like to remember. That was when your deah brother decided that we were corrupt and wanted nothing more to do with us."

So that was the quarrel Lucien had had with Daddy that caused him to leave. I clenched my hands in my lap. I felt dirty and corrupt and evil, just hearing this from Mama. She was smiling at me.

But did that mean that Daddy was corrupt and evil? Oh, I couldn't think. Why did she have to tell me this when all I had left of Daddy was his love?

"Daddy's dead," I said dully. "Why are you telling me this now?"

"Everyone's had their say today. Your father in his will. Mr. Ratcliffe. Lucien. I wanted to have mine. You made your choice today between me and Lucien. I thought you ought to know all the facts."

I got up, suppressing a sob. Lucien! I wanted to see him! "Does he . . . does Lucien know?"

"No, he doesn't. I saw no need to tell him as I saw no need to tell Hugh."

"Why didn't you tell Mr. Ratcliffe today? You could have used it as an argument in your favor!"

"Tell that old goat? He hates me. He always has! And it wouldn't have worked in my favor. Masculine supremacy is still the order of things."

"You didn't tell them today because it isn't true," I said. "You made it up! To hurt me."

"Susan! How could you?"

"No one can prove you are wrong. You made it up to hurt me because you're angry with Lucien and with me. And you can't hit me because Lucien has forbidden it. So you decided to hurt me this way!"

"Susan, I'm ashamed that you think so little of your mama."

"Think little of you?" I whirled on her. "I hate you!"

"Susan, come heah! Where are you going?"

"I'm going to ask Wilium to get the carriage. I want to see Lucien."

"You're going nowheah! I forbid it! Those streets are filled with cavalry officers and soldiers. You may see Lucien tomorrow. Susan, you are to obey me! I have

Lucien's promise on that. If you do otherwise, he'll heah from me!''

I stopped at the door. She was right. Lucien had made her a promise. And I had to honor it. I was trapped. I started to sob.

"Now, Susan, it's just been too much of a day for you. Go to your room. I'll have Rhody bring you some warm milk." She came and put her arms around me. I stiffened, resisting. "You always were the inquisitive one. I thought you had a right to know," she purred. "I wanted you to realize what you're dealing with in Lucien. Now go to bed and think it over. Things will look better in the morning."

I lay on my bed in the dark listening to the rumblings of thunder on the horizon and the faint music from down the street. My head was pounding, I felt feverish, and I was lonely and heartsick and confused. Mama's words spun around in my head. How could it be? Daddy not my Daddy? It hurt so bad when I thought of it I wanted to die.

Rhody came in. "I got some warm milk for you, honey."

I sat up. She set it down and was about to leave. "Rhody, please stay."

She cast a fearful glance at me. "Tell me if it's true about my daddy and Lettie," I said.

"Lawd, honey, you loved your daddy so. And he loved you. Let it be."

"Let it be? How can I? Tell me, Rhody!"

She rocked back and forth in the chair. "It's true, honey. Doan cry, now. That sister of mine, she wuz a bad one. Always makin' eyes at Mr. Hugh. I knew what she wuz up to with him. Man had to be a saint not to be tempted by her. She wuz so pretty. I tol' her time after time that she'd make trouble, and we'd lose our good home. I blame her, child, I doan blame your daddy.''

I stared at her in amazement. Good home? She didn't blame Daddy? ''How could he do it, Rhody! He was married to my mama!''

''Oh, honey.'' She shook her head. ''It happens with the best of men. It ain't nuthin'. And your daddy wuz the best.''

It ain't nuthin'? I wanted to scream at her. Didn't she see? Hot tears came down my face. I felt a blinding sense of disbelief and shock and fury at Rhody. How could she accept such behavior? ''What . . . Mama says about me,'' I managed to get out. ''Is it true I have a Yankee father?''

''Nobody tol' old Rhody nuthin' 'bout that. But your mama wasn't never happy after she lost Isabel, honey. I was in Charleston with her when it happened. Then, when she found out about Lettie and your daddy, she was plain miserable. She wuz never that happy in Richmond to begin with. She missed her family. That's why she wuz always wantin' to run down to Charleston. Course, down there they never really liked your daddy. That's why she went alone or with one of her children most o' the time. That's why she went that time when Isabel got the fever. She wuz just achin' to see her family. Here in Richmond, all she really had wuz your daddy, till she found out she didn't have him no more. So if she say it happened . . . I guess it did . . .'' She stopped. ''Drink the milk, honey. Go to sleep.''

She left. Within fifteen minutes I had on Lucien's old clothes and was out on the street.

Wind was kicking up, making little miniature tornadoes of dust, and on the horizon, heat lightning and rumblings of thunder were more frequent. The sky was heavy with dark clouds. I walked very fast, past all the elegant houses with gaslight glowing softly inside and the sound of laughter and music drifting out the windows. Everyone was celebrating Stuart's ride. I didn't know where I was going, and I didn't care. A storm was coming, and I felt as disturbed as the weather. I passed a group of cavalry officers, walking toward one of the houses, and envied their laughter and companionship. I was plunged into loneliness, and a fresh grief for my father welled in my chest. It was like losing him all over again after what Mama had told me.

I don't know how long I walked. Rain started to fall in cold slashes against my face. It felt good. I wished I could take off my boy's hat. I was out of our neighborhood by now, heading toward Lucien's gambling house. I was soon soaked to the skin but I kept walking, head down. Eventually I was across the street from Lucien's establishment.

I stood there in the downpour, gazing at the lights that seemed to glow with such a dazzling effect through the ceiling-to-floor windows at the front of the house. I could see forms moving about behind closed curtains. Gaslights outside the establishment lighted the wet sidewalk for patrons who constantly disembarked in carriages. The gambling houses were all mobbed now that they'd reopened. I longed to go in, but of course I couldn't, not even in the back way. I couldn't face Lucien now. How would I explain leaving Mama's house against her wishes? "Sneaking around," she would call it. And Lucien had promised her I would not do that.

So I was in trouble with Lucien before I even started, let alone that I should even consider telling him that I was only his half sister. How could I tell him that? Oh, the shame of it! He would want nothing to do with me anymore, I was sure of it. Oh, I couldn't think! I didn't

want to go home, but I couldn't go to Lucien. I just
wanted to stay where I was and perhaps get a glimpse of
him when the huge polished front door opened. Sometimes he saw special customers out and bade them good
night.

A gang of tough-looking boys was coming up the
street. Probably the notorious Hill Cats. Boys' gangs
were a plague to everyone in Richmond, constantly
fighting. And this one looked particularly vicious. I
started to cross the street, just as a carriage came
dashing around the corner, and narrowly avoided being
run down. The driver yelled. I slipped and fell in the
mud. Now I was really a mess. Well, the rain would
wash it off. I knew I couldn't stand in front of the
gambling parlor where I now found myself, so I slipped
through the side gate, into the yard.

Just beyond the back porch there was a little arbor,
and I crouched under its scant protection. There were
roses growing around it. They had prickly thorns, and I
scratched my hand. It started to bleed. I was very cold
now. How could rain be cold in June? Oh, I was so
miserable. What did I expect to accomplish here?

I closed my eyes. I was exhausted, my head was
spinning and hot, but I didn't care if I died. I wanted to
die. What good was being alive when everything was so
awful?

I was starting to doze when the back door opened, and
a light pierced the dark. "Here, Kitty, Kitty. Oh, you
ornery cat. Where are you? You'll catch your death in
this rain."

It sounded like Sarah. The cat was purring around
my feet. I brushed it off but it wouldn't go away. The
light was coming closer.

"Kitty, wait till I get you, I'll skin you alive. Don't

you want your nice supper? Fish. Kitty, you come here now...Eehhh!''

I put my hand up to shield my face. ''Who are you, hiding there! Get on your feet, boy. You heard me.''

I got up. The lantern swung in front of me. Sarah had a shawl flung over her head. ''What do you want, boy? You out here waiting for a chance to break in after the place closes? I'll call out Mr. Lucien and you'll get a fine thrashing. You'll be sorry you ever drew breath.''

''No,'' I appealed, ''please. I'll go.'' I started to move away. A scowl of recognition crossed Sarah's face. ''I know you.''

''No. I just wandered in the yard. I just...''

She came closer, peered into my face, and her eyes went wide in astonishment. She pulled the hat from my head and my hair tumbled loose. ''My God!'' she said.

''Please, Sarah, don't tell.''

''You're Mister Lucien's sister. And you're in some kind of trouble. I've got to tell him...''

''No, no, please.'' I grabbed at her wrist and started to cry. She put her hand on my forehead.

''You're burning up. What are you, crazy? He told me you were a lively little minx, but I didn't think you were *this* crazy. What kind of trouble are you in that you don't want him to know? Come on, you tell me. I don't fancy standing here getting soaked in the rain.''

''I...ran away from home.''

She nodded. ''You live with his mama. He told me. Even though he's responsible for you now. Why are you wearing those clothes again?''

''It's easier getting around in the streets.''

She nodded. ''The first time he brought you here, you were dressed like that. He wasn't too happy about it. Come onto the porch, out of this rain.'' She put her shawl around me.

On the porch she looked at me. "You're shaking. Why did you run away from home?"

"I . . . can't tell."

"Hhmph. Don't expect your brother to take that for an answer when he asks. Well, it's none of my business, anyway. You ever seen your brother mad, girl?"

"Yes," I said meekly.

She shook her head. "There isn't a better man in the world, in my estimation. Except when he's mad. Then you want to stay clear of him. I expect that if I went and fetched him right now, we'd both have to stay clear of him." She stopped and sighed. "I liked you when we first met. And it goes without saying, I like him. So I'm going to help you both. I'm going inside, but I'll be out directly. You run away, and I'll tell him you were here in those clothes. And then you'll know what trouble is. So you just wait for me, you hear?"

I grabbed her arm. "You sure you won't fetch him?"

"Honey, I told you. I don't want to see him mad. Now you wait."

She went inside and was back in five minutes, dressed for the weather. She threw a blanket around me and within five more minutes had a buggy hitched up. I moved as if in a dream, obeying her orders. I didn't ask where we were going. It didn't matter.

I knew we were near the wharves because I could smell the water. The house she led me to was attractive and neat with high ceilings and carved woodwork. There was a center hall and a graceful but modest stairway. The furniture was plain but good. As she took the blanket from me in the hall and ordered me to take off my boots, I noticed through my feverish gaze that the front parlor had a lovely carpet and that a secretary and a chest of drawers flanked the fireplace. Everything

was done in simple but classic taste. The rooms were
not as large as ours, by any means, but it was cozy and
cheerful.

"Whose house is this?"

"Your brother's."

I gasped. "But I don't want to see him. You don't
understand..."

"Honey, I understand more than you think I do. If
you didn't want to see him, why were you hovering
around his yard?" She was turning up all the gaslights.
"Seems to me you're going to be seeing him whether
you want to or not. The way he tells it to me, he was
left in charge of everything since your daddy died,
wasn't he?"

"Yes," I admitted.

"Well then, you'll be seeing him. You better face up
to that. What did you intend? To run loose in town all
night?"

"I don't know." I shrugged.

"You don't know," she repeated dully. Then she
shook her head. "Well, I know something. I wouldn't
want to answer to Mr. Lucien if I permitted that to
happen. So you calm down now. We're going to get you
in a hot bath and out of those clothes. You go on
upstairs. It's the last room on the right."

"Can't I go home with you?"

"We live here, me and Nate. We keep this place for
Mr. Lucien. Go on, go."

I was at her mercy. Upstairs, she lit a fire and heated
some water. I sat, wrapped in a blanket, having taken
off my clothes as she had ordered. I huddled in the
blanket and looked around. It was a small but attractive
room done in blue and white. When she had gotten all
the water in the tub, she looked at me.

"You come on and get in, now. And scrub good. You're filthy."

I slipped into the tub while she was turning down the crewel bedcover. The floors in the room gleamed under the glow of gaslight. Soft curtains framed the windows. There was a bookcase in the corner and even a small desk. The hot water felt good. I started to wash. She left the room and came back in ten minutes with a hot lemon toddy.

"Mr. Lucien would be mortified if he knew you were so dirty." And so saying she proceeded to wash my hair, pouring warm water over it. I was giddy-headed and shaking when she was done. "If there's one thing Mr. Lucien can't stand it's somebody who doesn't take care of their personal appearance," she told me. "Especially if that person is female. You want to make him mad, you let him know you were running around in these clothes again."

She gathered the muddy clothes and ordered me out of the tub.

"Don't take them away," I begged.

"I'll see they're washed and returned to you since you're so fond of them. Look, it's your business, but I don't think we ought to let him know you were wearing them."

"All right," I agreed gratefully.

"You're a little shorter than I am. Otherwise we're almost the same size. I can fit you in a nightgown."

She dried my hair while I sipped my toddy in front of the fire. In a very short while I was in bed. She put another blanket on me. Gradually I stopped shaking and became warm and went to sleep.

I slept as if sleep would claim me forever. My bones and head and back hurt. I slept and dreamed. I heard voices, felt people walking around me. I felt Sarah's gentle hands putting cold compresses on my head. I slept some more.

"Susan."

I heard Lucien's voice from very far away and pulled myself out of sleep. I felt as if I were coming back from a long journey. My lips were parched and when I opened my eyes they hurt.

He was standing over me, wearing his white linen suit. "Lucien."

He leaned down. "What is it Susan? Tell me."

"I'm sorry. I couldn't."

"Couldn't what?"

Didn't he understand? Oh, why didn't he understand? "I couldn't stay there with her. I couldn't keep your promise."

"Tell me what happened, Susan? Why did you leave?" He pulled a chair up to next to the bed.

"She told me."

"Told you what?"

"About Daddy. And Lettie."

"God's teeth." He was silent for a minute. "I'm sorry you had to hear that. Is that why you left?"

"No." Tears ran down the corners of my eyes. I felt his hand, cool on my face, brushing them away.

"Don't cry, Susan. Tell me why you left. I'm not going to scold."

"You won't want anything to do with me if I tell you."

"What?" He leaned closer. "Why won't I want anything to do with you?"

"Because . . . I'm . . . not your sister."

"What nonsense! Of course you are. Did she tell you that?"

"She told me . . . oh, Lucien, I'm so ashamed!"

"Of what? You have nothing to be ashamed of. What did she tell you?"

I told him. He said nothing for a moment. Then, "I should have taken you out of there immediately. I should have known this couldn't have worked."

"Is it true, Lucien? That I have another father?"

He shook his head. "I don't know. I never heard anything like that. But it doesn't matter. Not to me. You're just as much my sister as before. It doesn't matter if we had different fathers. You're my sister, and I love you dearly, Susan."

Tears crowded my eyes so I couldn't see. "Do you mean that, Lucien?" I could bear anything if he meant it.

"I don't say things I don't mean, Susan Dobson Chilmark. You ought to know that by now. Hugh Chilmark loved you, too. He was your father as far as I'm concerned. You and I have a lot in common. We've got a very bitter and confused mother, for one thing. She's tried to hurt us both, and we've got to help each other repair the damage she's done. Now you get better, you hear me?"

I heard. And it was all I ever wanted to hear. All I needed.

PART FOUR

June 20, 1862

Chapter Twenty-four

Lucien's directive to get better was not that easy to obey. If I didn't have pneumonia, Dr. Upchurch said, I had the nearest thing to it. I was so sick I didn't care what name they gave to it. I thought I would cough my lungs out, and every time I coughed, my head hurt. Before it was over, stomach muscles I never knew I had were causing me misery.

Sarah nursed me. She forced soft eggs and soup and tea into my mouth. She washed me and got me out of bed so I could use the chamber pot. She combed my hair and gave up most of her other duties to do all this. I couldn't keep track of the time, I slept so much. But I knew when each day had passed, because around dusk Lucien came in to see me. Sometimes he still had on the clothes he wore on the river. Sometimes he was dressed to go out. He'd stay about fifteen minutes, and we'd talk.

Lee was in command, he told me, getting ready to strike at McClellan. I shouldn't worry. Richmonders were confident all would be well. He'd been to see Mama, to inform her that I would be staying with him from now on. He'd asked to have all my things sent, so Rhody had brought them over. Sarah had told him I'd refused to see Rhody. Was that true?

But I wouldn't answer.

"You shouldn't take it out on Rhody," he said gently.

"I can't help it. She doesn't think that what Daddy did with Lettie was wrong."

"It isn't her fault that she doesn't know. That's part of the corruption I was telling you about."

"I just don't want to see anyone from...home anymore, Lucien. I can't. I hate Mama now. Maybe I always did."

"I don't think that's true, Susan. I think you just ought to give yourself a chance to let it all sink in before you burn any bridges."

I looked at him. "Don't you hate her?"

"No, Susan. I'm angry with her. There's a difference."

"I thought I loved her," I said. "And I kept trying to make her love me. But she wouldn't. Now I don't care anymore, Lucien. You can't make somebody love you if they don't want to, can you?"

"No." He got up. "I'm sorry you had to learn that so soon. And at the same time, I'm sorry it took you so long. Just get well, Susan. You don't have to see anyone for a while if you don't want to."

Into the second week I started getting up a little each day. Fanny had sent over a lovely white cotton wrap with lace trim, and I sat in the chair reading *A Tale of Two Cities*, the latest book by Dickens, which Lucien had given me. It was Sunday. Richmond's church bells were ringing, and I felt a sense of peace. The windows in my room were open and cool breezes drifted in from the docks at the end of the street. I watched some sea gulls making circles in the blue sky. Sarah came in. "You have visitors. Constance Turnstable and her brother."

I recoiled inside myself. "Oh, Sarah, I couldn't. Please, I'm too tired."

She nodded and went out. Five minutes later there were footsteps in the hall, a brief knock and Lucien came in. "We have guests for breakfast, Susan. I'd like you to come down."

"I can't. I'm not strong enough."

He pulled a chair up next to me. "You have to face people sooner or later."

"How can I? Everyone knows about me."

He took the book from my hands, looked at the cover for a minute. "You've done nothing to be ashamed of. Now, I'm being patient with you, because you've been sick, Susan. But I'm not going to put up with this self-pity of yours much longer. You have spirit and brains and that's what I've always admired about you. I can't have you languishing up here like a social leper. No one outside the family knows about Charlotte's insane story and those in the family who do know, don't care."

"I don't think it's very nice of you to scold when I'm so sick," I sniffled.

"Good. Give me an argument. That's what I want. I'd rather have you sass me than whimper about how ashamed you are. I want to see some of that spirit I saw the day we first met. And the day you asked me to take you to the brothel for dresses. And speaking of that, Mrs. Wigfall paid a call. Your balloon is being used for reconnaissance now on the peninsula. She has a letter from General Longstreet, thanking the girls who collected the dresses for it. Now tell me you don't care about that."

I smiled weakly. "Well, of course I care."

"Then come downstairs and greet your friends."

"Lucien, I'd never make it back up the stairs again, I'm so weak."

"I'll carry you back up if you can't do it on your own."

"Oh, Lucien, don't be a bear. Make my excuses, won't you?"

He got to his feet and stood over me, scowling. "Don't give me that Southern belle act, Susan. That isn't you. And it isn't going to work with me, anyway. That boy downstairs is going back to his regiment. He's come to say good-bye. There's going to be a big battle within a few days, and he'll be part of it. He's been a friend to you. I won't have you treating him shabbily."

"Well, of course, I don't want to," I said petulantly.

He set the book down, went to my closet, opened it and paused. Instantly he spotted what he was after, the two dresses he had bought me last week. He had purchased them in a shop that sold goods straight off blockade-runners. . One was a pink organdie and the other a flowered muslin. I had been thrilled with them when he brought them home, for although I hadn't tried them on yet I knew they were the kind of dresses I should have been wearing all along, in the style and cut to flatter my figure. Fanny had helped him pick them out, he'd said.

He selected the flowered muslin and set it down on the chair. I looked up at him pleadingly, but he would not relent. "I've been patient with you, Susan," he said gently, "but I must insist you get dressed and come down and do what is right."

I nodded. "I should wear my black for Daddy," I said.

"No black. Your daddy wouldn't want it. And neither do I. Now I'll send Sarah up to help." He paused at the door. "For the last few years I've been the talk of Richmond, Susan. I never let them make me feel ashamed of what I was. I knew who I was. I expect you to know who you are, too."

"Who am I, Lucien?"

"You're Susan Dobson Chilmark," he said. "Your daddy died for the Confederacy. And you're my sister. Now get into that pretty dress I bought for you. And come down and greet your friends."

Seeing Connie and saying good-bye to Kenneth wore me out, and I took to my bed again for two days. Lucien didn't bother me. He was satisfied, but old friends made me ache for the life I'd had before. Yet, that other life had never been real in the first place. What was real, I didn't know. I still had to find out. I felt as if I were walking on ice and at any moment, whatever it was that was holding me up would break, and I'd plunge into the cold and darkness.

Twice when I was sleeping, I thought I heard guns. Then one morning I awoke to the booming of cannon. I got up, put on my robe and went to find Sarah.

"Sarah," I called over the banister, "what's happening?"

"The battle's started. Soldiers are on the Mechanicsville Turnpike. General Jackson is joining forces with Lee."

"Where's my brother?"

"He's out on his boat. He says the striped bass and blueback herring are running good. They've closed the gambling houses again. Everybody in town has gone to the hills to see and hear what they can."

"What day is this, Sarah?"

"The twenty-sixth of June. Your brother won't be back until nightfall. When this battle is over there will be scores of wounded to feed."

All day the sound of guns echoed in the distance. I wandered listlessly around the house. I ventured downstairs to Lucien's back parlor, which he used as an office. I took comfort from the books and maps, the papers on his desk, although I didn't pry or touch anything. Then I wandered out back to where Sarah and Nate kept a lovely little kitchen garden and sat in the shade under a tree. By late afternoon Sarah gave me supper and said people were coming back from the hills but no one seemed to know anything.

I heard Lucien come in very late that night. In the morning he was gone again. A terrible heat hung over everything, and the town was so quiet, except for the booming guns, that I couldn't stand it. Very late Friday night the guns woke me, and I got up. Peering over the banister I saw a light from the kitchen and went downstairs.

Lucien was at the kitchen table, eating alone. His clothes were dirty, and the kitchen smelled of fish. He looked up and smiled as he bit into a chicken leg. "How are you?"

"Have you brought a lot of food in?"

"Yes. Striped bass, smallmouthed bass, American shad, even three enormous turtles. The battle is moving toward the James River. I hear there was poor coordination by the Southern commanders, and Jackson was delayed. But they're saying that Hood's Texas Brigade and Pickett's troops broke through the Federal line. Are you feeling better? I hear from Sarah that you've been up and around."

"Yes. I even went outside today. You have the loveliest garden in back. And it's cool there. I don't see why Mama criticized where you live."

"Most of these houses are owned by merchants who find it convenient to have offices next to the docks. One or two even live here. But don't get too fond of it. You can't stay forever."

I looked at him in dismay. "Why not?"

"By the end of the summer, I'm sending you away to school," he said quietly.

A shot of fear ran through me. "Don't look like

that." He smiled at me. "I'm not packing you off to get rid of you. You're bright, and you need good schooling. Fanny knows some excellent girls' academies outside Richmond."

"Why can't I stay at Miss Pegram's and live with you?"

"Because you'd be socially ostracized living here with me."

"Well, I don't care about that. I'm happy here. I'd rather be socially ostracized and stay with you." I leaned my forehead against the doorjamb, near tears.

He sipped his coffee. "Thank you, Susan. But it's my responsibility to see that you're brought up in proper surroundings."

"They were proper before," I argued, "and just look at what happened. Why do I have to go to a silly school at all? I could learn from Sarah. She knows as much as any teacher."

"You have to be educated to take your place in the world, Susan." His voice was kind but firm. "I'll not have you hiding away here afraid to face it. Hugh Chilmark trusted me to bring up his daughter right, and I'm going to do it. You'll enjoy school, with girls your own age. And we can still see each other frequently."

"I am not Hugh Chilmark's daughter," I enunciated clearly.

"Stop it, Susan! I don't want to hear that kind of talk out of you again!"

He was angry. Guns boomed in the distance, reverberating in my bones. I slithered into the kitchen in my bare feet and moved around, touching things, out of the circle of his anger. I cast him furtive glances but he went on eating impassively, not looking at me. "You're nothing but an old Southern gentleman, is what you are," I said in my best Southern belle voice. "You can say what you want about not believing in Daddy's traditions."

"You may have something there," he said dryly. "I'm only twenty-seven, but I feel old tonight. However, I think these fish-smelling clothes disqualify me from being a gentleman. Now I'll tell you something nice. I'll bet Timothy is in the area."

I turned from fussing with Sarah's utensils. "Oh, do you think so?"

"Well"—he grinned—"it's good seeing your interest perked again."

The color rose to my face. "Do you think he'll come see us?"

"I'm sure he will. Once the fighting is over. I've something else to tell you, too. I saw your balloon out there today, overlooking Federal lines."

"Was it pretty?"

"It was beautiful. You ought to be proud of it."

"Well, I don't feel proud." Saying it made me realize I meant it.

"Oh," he asked lightly, "why not?"

"I don't know. It all seems so stupid now. Those guns never stop. And I don't know what they're for."

"You're in good company. Many other people don't, either."

"Lucien, I've been thinking, and I've decided you're right."

"Well, that's nice to hear. Why don't you come sit and tell me about what."

I accepted his invitation and sat down. "You were right about the Cause being corrupt and evil. What Daddy did with Lettie . . . that was corrupt. Oh, I love Daddy, Lucien, but it was! And Mama . . . she said she couldn't look the other way. Southern women are supposed to. Did you know that?"

"Yes," he said quietly.

"I've decided that I don't care if Mama loves me or not, anymore, Lucien. But I can't blame her for feeling that way. I wouldn't look the other way if my husband did such a thing."

"You shouldn't be expected to."

"Lucien, can I ask you something?"

"Ask away."

"The night you had the row with Daddy and left our house, that was when he told you Sallie was his child, wasn't it?"

Silence. The spoon stirring his coffee was the only sound. "Yes," he said, "what of it?"

I just looked at him.

"Do you know what you're asking?" he whispered hoarsely.

"Yes."

His jaw muscle twitched. "Well, I've encouraged you in this line of thinking, so you deserve an answer. I didn't know Sallie was his child before then. If I had, I would not have allowed myself to become so attached to her. But what Sallie and I had together was . . . on the finest level, Susan. There was never anything between us to be ashamed of. Is that the answer you're looking for?"

"Yes, Lucien," I said primly. "Thank you. I wonder, if Daddy hadn't done what he did, would Mama be the way she is? She told me she committed her act of indiscretion . . . that's what she calls it, Lucien . . . her act of indiscretion, just to get back at him. It's just so awful. Like . . . like . . ."

"Like a house of cards," he suggested, "and it's going down. Oh, not yet. Our brave boys are out there trying to save it. But it will collapse eventually. I get angry at the waste of lives."

Nate came in the back door. He looked as dirty as Lucien. He nodded to me. "Evenin', Miss Susan. Mr. Lucien, the boat's secured for the night."

"Thank you, Nate."

"I hear people are on the roofs of the hotels in town, to see the fireworks."

"Some fireworks," Lucien said dryly.

"I hear McClellan's retreating," Nate said.

"I'd heard that earlier, Nate. Let's hope it's true."

"I'll get the water for your bath," Nate said, going out again.

Lucien pushed his chair back and stretched his long legs out under the table. He lit a cheroot.

"Lucien, do you think other Southern families are as bad as ours?"

In the distance guns boomed. "Half the children in the South have half brothers or sisters who are nigra," he said.

We fell silent. He smoked. I shivered. Nate came back in and put some water on the stove to heat. "Go to bed," Lucien said to me. "There's a chill in the night air. You'll take cold."

I got up and started for the door. Turning to see him slumped in his chair, I realized how tired he was, how spent. He worked hard, that was the truth of it. "They don't pay you for bringing food in, Lucien, why do you do it?"

Nate gave a smile and went out to get more water. "It's the only way I can get out of the draft," Lucien said.

"Don't tease."

He grinned. "I'm not teasing."

"You mean otherwise you'd charge to feed the wounded?"

"You're really calling me to account tonight, aren't

you? No, I don't think so. We all have a sense of honor that can be appealed to. Even me.''

I went to him, impulsively, and put my arms around his shoulders and kissed his face. "You shouldn't," he said hoarsely. "I'm filthy."

"I don't care. Lucien, I love you. I don't care what the rest of Richmond says about you. And I'm glad things turned out this way, and I'm here with you."

He raised his eyebrows quizzically. "Even if I send you away to school?"

"Don't tease! Do you know what? The way I feel about the Cause now, I'd destroy my balloon if I could. Like Daddy destroyed the *Virginia*."

He looked at me with a bemused expression. "It isn't yours to destroy, Susan. Don't even think such a thing. Now go to bed."

Chapter Twenty-five

But I did think such a thing. I thought of it several times over the next four days while those incessant guns made the very floors of the house tremble, and the wounded started coming into the city.

Ambulances went by the house, since General Hospital number 23 was just three blocks down on Peach Street and about a block beyond that, behind the York River Railroad depot, was General Hospital number 21. By the last day in June, Sarah said that every hospital in the city was overflowing.

Before it was all over we knew that thousands of Confederate soldiers had been killed and thousands more wounded. We knew that Lee had tried, but could not cut McClellan's line in two at Malvern Hill. However a Southern victory of major proportions had been won. Richmond was saved.

Sarah was everywhere at once, cooking, running to the nearby hospital and caring for us. The creak of wagons was endless outside our windows, day and night. Once I saw a wagonload of dead. A man's still arm was raised to the heavens, as if in vengeance.

Lucien and Nate were gone most of the day to get more food. Evenings they came in from the boat and went right out to the surrounding battle areas with a wagon to bring in wounded. Sarah brought home reports from the hospital that the city was filled with wounded and dying. Because of my feelings of hatred for the system of the South, I felt guilty and confused. I decided I needed something to do. So when I heard Lucien come in late the night of June thirtieth, I caught up with him in the back parlor.

"Lucien, I want to help at the hospital down the street."

"No," he said distractedly. His back was to me. He looked very dirty. He was going over a map on his desk.

"But I'm fifteen and capable. I helped last time."

"You're not well enough yet. You're still pale."

"Lucien, I'm all right," I argued. "Don't be like Mama."

He turned. There were bloodstains all over the front of his clothes. And his look was murderous. "Explain that, please."

I gasped, seeing his bloodstained clothes. His red-rimmed eyes looked haunted, he had two days' worth of beard, and he looked as if he hadn't slept in a week.

"I . . . didn't mean that, Lucien, I'm sorry."

He nodded and turned back to his map. I went to him. "Lucien, where have you been?"

"Out picking up wounded after Lee's latest attempt to cut the Union army in two. Hearing the pitiful cries of the wounded and the dying. Stepping over fragments of bodies and limbs that are strewn in every direction. What they're doing out there is murder, not war. They're all crazy."

"Oh, Lucien, I feel so guilty because I said such terrible things about the South. And men are dying. And I thought . . ."

"You thought that if you could help, you could believe again in what they're dying for. Is that it?"

He turned to look at me. "Yes," I said.

"Well, you can't. Any more than I can. So accept that, Susan, and let the past go. It's dying. Let it be."

"But *you're* helping."

He folded the map up, shoved it in his coat pocket. "It's my job. Now there are more wounded to bring in. Nate and I could work all night and not get them all."

"But you look so tired."

"I may never be able to sleep again after some of the sights I've seen out there."

"Lucien, please let me help at the hospital."

"I said no, Susan! In your condition you'll pick up anything in the hospital. Stay and help Sarah." He strode past me to the door. "There's blood running in Richmond's streets. I don't need you sick again in the middle of all this." He slammed the door and went out.

The next day I helped Sarah cook for the hospital. I cut and rolled household linen into bandages. Lucien was right. It exhausted me. I was resting in the parlor when Mrs. Wigfall came by. She had been working for days in the hospital, she said, and was ready to lose her mind.

"Come, let's go for a ride." She kissed me. "You do look pale. Where is everyone?"

"Sarah's at the hospital, and Lucien is on his boat. He wouldn't let me help at the hospital," I pouted.

"He's right, my deah. The stoutest of heart faint attending our dying boys. Now, I have bad news for you. You must be brave. Your friend's brother has been killed."

"Not Kenneth!"

She nodded, and I burst into a torrent of tears. "Where?"

"At Savage's Station, two days ago."

She held me while I cried. Then she told me to get my bonnet, that we were going for a ride. "I'll take you to see Connie. Kenneth has been buried already, but she'll be glad to see you. First, however, I know where your balloon is. It's on a gunboat on the James. We'll go see it. Leave a note for your brother."

I sat numbly in the carriage with Mrs. Wigfall, watching my balloon dancing on its tethers on the gunboat *Teaser*, which was anchored in a protective cove in the river. Confederate pickets were guarding the shore.

"Aren't you proud of it?" Mrs. Wigfall asked. "Oh, deah, you're crying."

I could not believe that dear, sweet, gallant Kenneth was gone. He had been a brother to me before I'd met Lucien. And after. "I'll be all right," I said.

"Well, you just stay heah. I want to speak to one of the guards."

I recognized each silk dress in the bright patchwork of colors in front of me. But the balloon filled me with unhappy feelings. Another girl had run around Richmond collecting those dresses, an innocent girl who believed in the Cause. She was gone, yet she still haunted me. And I was caught between her and the girl I had become. I was so confused it was making me sick inside.

Kenneth was dead. Daddy was dead. Tom McPherson was dead. Lucien, the last time I had seen him, had been wearing the blood of how many others? And for what? To defend a system that had allowed Daddy to have a child with his nigra slave? A system that tore families apart?

The balloon danced brightly before my eyes in the bright sun. It mocked my questions, even my heartache.

Mrs. Wigfall came back, breathless. "It's going to be heah at least over the Fourth of July. Isn't that lovely? We can come back and see it. Would you like that?"

What I would like, I thought as we drove away, is to come back in the middle of the night with a knife and cut it loose and let it fly away. If I could do that, I knew I could cut myself loose from the past. I could be rid of the old Susan who used to be. Let the past go, Lucien had said. Let it go.

The more I thought of the idea, the more I liked it. I was a different person now than I had been before my sickness, before meeting Timothy, before Daddy's death and before Mama's revelations to me about my family. That new person was struggling daily to emerge from my confusion and pain. The only way to help her come fully into being, I knew, was to get rid of the balloon. The balloon that had been the focal point of the old Susan's life. How, I didn't know. But I would find a way.

Connie and I sat on a filigreed wrought-iron bench under the great magnolia tree in her garden. We had finished our crying and were now catching up. "Do you like living with Lucien?" she asked.

"Yes. We're friends and we help each other a lot. Of course, he runs things, and I don't always agree. Then we argue and he growls like an old bear and makes decrees, and I have to listen. But five minutes later we're friends again. He's very sweet sometimes. You saw one of the dresses he bought me. For the first time I look grown up when I wear them."

"Why didn't you wear the other one today so I could see it?"

"I didn't think it would be right, with you in mourning."

She nodded. "Before you didn't have a brother and I did. And now..." She shrugged.

"I'll share Lucien with you, just like you used to share Kenneth with me," I said.

She smiled weakly. "Susan, did you ever think it would turn out this way? When we collected the dresses for the balloon, I mean. I thought it was a lark. I never dreamed it was all about...killing."

"Neither did I. But that's what it's about. I saw the balloon, Connie. It's on a gunboat on the James."

"How does it look?"

"I hate it."

She nodded. "I can understand that. I don't think I could bear seeing it now. It brings back too many memories that I can't remember without crying."

I touched her hand on the bench next to me. "Connie, I want to let it go."

She looked at me, not comprehending at first. So I told her how I felt. "It's your balloon, too," I said, "so I wanted to know what you think."

"But how would you be able to let it go, Susan?"

"I don't know. I'll find a way. I wanted to ask you, first."

She thought for a moment. "It's more yours than mine. Do you think it would be right?"

"Probably not," I said, "but I don't care. I'm angry. I'm angry at the South for all the death and waste. We never should have fought this war. Lucien told me that, and I never believed him. He was right. He was right about other things, too."

"What other things?" Her eyes were wide and still innocent.

"I'll tell you, Connie, but you must keep it a secret. I'm half Yankee."

She gasped.

"It's true. Mama told me. She committed an act of indiscretion with a Yankee up North years ago. But she only did it because my daddy was being adulterous with a nigra right in our own house." I told her the rest of it in halting tones, my face burning.

"Oh, Susan, how awful for you!"

"Awful for the South is what it is. That's what we're fighting this war for, Connie. That's what Kenneth died for. And my daddy. Lucien told me it was all corrupt, and I didn't believe him. Now I do."

"Do you really, Susan?"

"Yes. Only it hurts, having to believe it. I hate the South, and yet I love everybody here and cry for our dying boys. I want to believe again in what they all died for. But Lucien said I should accept that I can't and let the past go. When I saw the balloon out there today, I knew the only way I could do that is to set the balloon free. I have to find a way to do it, Connie. I think, right now, it's the only way I can make things right inside me again."

She nodded solemnly. "You can't do it yourself. You need help."

"With help it would be easy," I agreed. "It sits right on that boat on a sandbar. You could practically walk to it when the tide is out. Connie, I'd give it to the Yankees if I could."

She gasped again. "You don't mean it."

"Oh, yes, I do mean it. Let the fool Yankees have it. They seem to have the right answers for everything. Only there's no way I can do that, of course. I just wanted to let you know what I'm thinking. In case I find a way. Do you think I'm awful?"

"Oh, I don't know, Susan. I'm so confused about everything. Kenneth died for the South, but somehow his dying seems so stupid now. Such a waste! If I thought that our collecting those dresses for the balloon was all about war and killing I'd never have collected them in the first place. I don't care about the old balloon anymore. Do what you think is best."

"I've told you things here today that I haven't told anyone, Connie. If you tell about the balloon, I'll end up in Castle Godwin."

She hugged me. "Do what you have to do, Susan. Just be happy and at peace with yourself. One of us might as well be."

I stayed up half the night trying to figure a way to cut that balloon loose. It wasn't until Lucien's clock in the downstairs hall struck three that I fell asleep. I woke late to the tantalizing smell of coffee and bacon. I got up, crept into the hall and leaned over the banister to hear male voices below. I heard Lucien's laughter. "Sarah," I whispered. She was passing by the foot of the stairs.

She looked up. "We have company. Your brother

says where is his lazy sister. Go get her down, he says. I was just coming up."

"Who is it?"

"His friend. The one that sketches for *Harper's*. That Yankee."

Chapter Twenty-six

As "that Yankee" stood in our front parlor between me and Lucien he was making me tremble with the look in his eyes.

"Do you have to go, Lucien?" I asked. I wanted my brother to leave and yet I wanted him to stay, for all through breakfast I'd been aware of the way Timothy was stealing glances at me. I was wearing my new flowered muslin that flattered my figure, outlining my bosom and my narrow waist. In the middle of flushing under one of Tim's glances, as a matter of fact, I knew that I was going to ask him to help me get rid of the balloon.

As my eyes met his across the table and I smiled at him, I knew, too, that he would help me. I sensed it. Which is why I was trembling as the three of us stood in our front parlor. Not because I was afraid of being left alone with Timothy. But because I was afraid of what I had just discovered about myself.

Inside, I knew I had crossed over some line. That having discovered the power I had, I was going to use it. And I was excited and afraid all at the same time. Was it wrong to use that power to get what you wanted from a man? Especially when you really liked him? I didn't know. But I supposed I would very soon find out.

"I have to make my reports out in the commissary's office, even though I'm not taking the boat today," Lucien answered. He was wearing his oilskins. It had been raining when I woke and now there was a downpour. "I'm sure you two have a lot to talk about anyway," he continued. Then he looked from me to Tim and tweaked my hair. "These doors," he said with mock severity, "are to remain open."

I blushed, but Timothy only grinned. "I was planning on sending Sarah out to get me some tobacco," he teased.

"You can smoke my cheroots," Lucien said, going out the front door.

He left and we were alone. We looked at each other, embarrassed. "That's Lucien," Tim said. "He's been out picking up bodies for how many nights now? And he still insists on Southern decorum. Do you suppose he noticed the way I was eyeing you at breakfast?"

"My brother doesn't miss anything." I looked down at the floor.

"Do you?"

"No. I'm a lot like he is."

"Then I have to apologize, once again, for being a flirt. But I couldn't help it. I tried to remember, all the time I was gone, what you looked like. And I thought I had. And here I come back and you're prettier than I even remembered. You look so..." He hesitated.

I glanced at him coyly. "So what?"

He seemed, momentarily, to suffer an attack of shyness. "You look so different from the last time. In that dress."

"Different?" I pretended ignorance, making him explain.

He explained. "Grown up."

"Lucien bought this dress for me. From a blockade-runner. I suppose I shouldn't be wearing it when everyone in town is so shabby. But I wanted to wear it. For you."

"Lucien has good taste," he said.

"Do you think it's awful of me to wear it, though?"

"I think . . ." He stumbled over his words and had to start again. "I think you are the most refreshing and sane sight I've seen in weeks. And I've seen some sights. I'm very honored that you wore the dress for me today. Am I embarrassing you?"

"I suppose as a good Southern girl I should say yes," I conceded.

He grinned. "But you never really liked playing that role, did you, Susan?"

Oh, it was so wonderful to see him, with his teasing blue eyes and his Yankee voice! There was something sane and impudent about him in the middle of our confusion and sorrow. I lowered my eyelids decorously. "Would you like more coffee?" I asked. "Sarah's left us some. Come and sit down."

"Coffee, yes," Tim agreed. "Especially when it's real. That's one thing about Lucien. He doesn't go for any of these poor excuses for coffee you Southerners have been drinking."

"He gets the coffee from the blockade-runners, too." I sat and poured, feeling very sophisticated under Tim's gaze. I could hear Sarah moving around upstairs, doing her morning chores. We sipped coffee. It was pleasant in the parlor. Nate had made a low fire in the grate to ward off the rain's chill, and the gaslight flickered charmingly. I could feel my heart hammering under the flattering bodice of my new dress. There was no doubt about it. It was very heady and tantalizing to be looked at the way Tim was regarding me.

"What did you think when you came to see Lucien and heard I was here?" I asked.

He shook his head in disbelief. "I couldn't believe my good luck." He leaned back in the chair. "Old Lucien, head of a family. That's something I never thought I'd see. I wonder, though, how different it will make things for me."

"Why should it?"

He shrugged. "Lucien is my friend. And you're his sister."

"I was always his sister, Timothy." I knew what he was getting at, but I pretended innocence.

"I know, but"—he shrugged, again looking sheepish—"you know what I mean. If I wanted to ask permission to court you, well, it's different. He's the boss now, and if he said no it would get in the way of our friendship."

"What makes you think I would want you to court me?" I asked saucily. "Providing that you *could* court me, which you can't because you're a Yankee and have to sneak in and out of town."

"Wouldn't you?" His blue eyes were burning holes into me.

"You asked his permission to write to me," I said evasively, "and he said yes. And you never even did that."

He blushed. "I've been in the middle of a war, Susan. I've been on the run. Don't be hard on me. I thought of you every minute."

He looked so dismal, I took pity on him. "How was it out there? Tell me, Timothy."

He shook his head. "You don't want to know."

"Yes, I do. Lucien told me some of it. He had blood

all over him the other night, even on his boots. He said they were committing murder.''

"That describes it very aptly, I'd say.''

"Where were you?''

"With McClellan all through the seven days. Right up to Malvern Hill. I've never seen such artillery fire or hideous shrieking of shells and musketry as I saw there. I thought I was in hell.''

I nodded. "The brother of my best friend was killed at Savage's Station.''

"I'm sorry about that, Susan. Lucien told me.''

"Did you get good sketches?''

"If that description can be applied, yes. I sent them North by courier. I don't know why Lee attacked at Malvern Hill. McClellan would have withdrawn during the night, whether he attacked or not. All Lee did was lose five thousand men. We lost about three thousand. The field was crawling with dead and dying men when it was over.''

We fell silent. The fire crackled. It occurred to me, watching him, that he could have been killed. I looked at him sitting there, browned and slender, emanating artistic grace and manliness in his movements all at the same time, and I knew in one rushing, overpowering instant that I loved him. I felt such a surge of tenderness for him, thinking that he could have been killed, that I wanted to die. Why, I had been in love with him all along, I realized. And I hadn't even known it! How was that possible? Is that how love happened? Of course, he had been in the back of my mind over the last few weeks through all the horrible things that had happened to me. Whenever I'd thought of him, there had been a warm feeling of sanity inside me. How could I have been so stupid?

"What's the matter, Susan?''

I flushed, feeling exposed to him. "Nothing. It occurred to me that you could have been killed out there. Just like Kenneth."

His eyes sparkled impudently. "Would you have cared?"

"Don't be silly," I said angrily. I looked at my coffee cup, but he wouldn't leave it be. He set his cup down and came to sit next to me on the settee.

"You wouldn't say you'd let me court you if your brother gave his permission. And yet you're all upset, realizing I could have been killed. Now what am I supposed to think, Susan?"

"You can think whatever you wish," I said haughtily.

He smiled. "I think you are a handful. Like your brother tells me."

"Oh, is that what he tells you?"

"Yes. Of course the responsibility is very appealing to him. He's flattered that your father left him in charge. Don't let him know I told you this but I think he loves every minute of it. I also think that you've discovered a few things about yourself, seeing me again, and that you're trying to sort it all out."

"You have an awfully high opinion of yourself, Timothy Tobias Collier."

He moved closer to me on the settee. "We're going to have to be serious for a moment, Susan."

He was so close that I began to tremble. "About what?"

He reached into his jacket pocket and took out a letter. "I like this verbal jousting with you. We're having a good time, and it's all normal and innocent fun. But now I have an unpleasant task. Your brother assigned it to me because he thought I could handle it. I must give this to you."

I looked down at the letter he held in his hand. "What is it?"

"This came to me at *Harper's*. I've carried it through battle after battle for you. Do you remember the sketch I did of you?"

"How could I forget? Mama was furious when she saw it."

"Lucien told me. I thought this made no sense at first, but when I showed it to your brother he said no, it made perfect sense." He turned the letter over in his hands and looked at me carefully. "It's from a man who is a professor at the College of New Jersey in Princeton."

The fire spit on the hearth. The clock in the hall chimed the half hour. "What"—I ran my tongue over my lips—"does he want?"

"He wants to get in touch with you. He says he's your father."

Tears welled in my eyes. "My brother told you."

"Only because I showed the letter to him. We talked, and he said I should tell you about it and let you make your own mind up about whether you wanted to respond to it."

"Lucien said that?"

"Yes. He said that whatever you decide to do is all right with him."

Tears rolled unchecked down my face. Timothy produced a handkerchief. "I know how difficult this must be for you," he said.

He let me cry. He put his arm around me and the next thing I knew, I was sobbing against his chest. He held me, chastely, as Lucien would have done, while I cried. "I just can't get used to having a Yankee father," I said.

"You're talking to a Yankee, Susan," he reminded me. "A Yankee has his arm around you."

"I know that." I straightened up and looked at him. "Still, I can't think of anybody being my father but my own daddy who died. What am I supposed to do? Write to this man and call him Daddy?"

"You're supposed to do whatever you feel like doing," he said softly. "Lucien didn't want to keep this from you. He wanted you to make your own decision."

"What does he . . . say in the letter?"

"That he'd like to correspond with you. And meet you when the war is over."

"I couldn't do that." I shook my head vigorously. "I couldn't do that to Lucien. He's the one I look to now for everything. No, Tim, I don't want the letter."

He put it back in his pocket. "I'll leave it with your brother in case you ever want to read it. I can see how terrible this must be for you."

"Terrible? Tim, I'm half daft trying to figure it all out. One minute I hate the South and my own daddy for what he did. I suppose you know about that, too, don't you?"

"Lucien told me."

"And the next minute I'm crying because Daddy's dead. I want things to be the way they were before the war. But I know the way things were then wasn't right, either. When I think of what Daddy did . . . and my mama . . . and how they treated Lucien, I hate the South. It's all evil and corrupt, as my brother says. And then I think of poor dear Kenneth and others like him and oh, Tim, I don't know what I am or what I want anymore."

I was aware, even while I was saying all this, even though I meant every word of it intensely, that I was making my appeal to Timothy so he would help me get rid of the balloon. For a few moments I had forgotten about it, but seeing the tender look in his eyes, I knew once again the headiness of a woman who held a man in the palm of her hand.

"You'll make yourself sick again if you don't stop with that line of thinking," Tim admonished. "Lucien told me how sick you were. The best statesmen haven't been able to figure it out, Susan."

"I don't care," I said passionately. "They're all fools, the statesmen. Lucien once told me this war started because the South had too many long-winded orators. I've got to figure it out for myself."

"Give yourself time, Susan. You'll make peace with yourself inside."

"I don't have time." I looked at him from beneath lowered lids.

"What do you mean, Susan?"

"I've found a way to make peace with myself. I know what I want to do. But I need help. And I only have a couple of days to do it."

He scowled. "Susan, I don't like the way this sounds. Tell me what you're thinking, please."

"Oh, Timothy." I turned to him. "How much do you really like me?"

He blushed. "I tried to tell you that before, Susan. Only you gave me a difficult time. You acted like a Southern belle, teasing me."

I looked at him beseechingly. "Did I do that?"

"Yes. You did a good job of it, too. I've a mind to tell your brother what a little coquette you are. I'm sure he'd love to hear it."

I moved closer to him on the settee. "You wouldn't do that, would you, Timothy?"

His eyes twinkled. "I haven't decided yet whether I want him to know what a shameful flirt his little sister is. He might not let us see each other again."

"Would that bother you awfully, Timothy?"

He smiled, enjoying himself. "What do you want from me, Susan?"

"Don't say it that way. You sound just like Lucien."

"I don't feel very brotherly toward you right now, miss. I'm warning you."

For a moment we gazed into each other's eyes. I felt myself trembling, on the brink, as if I were about to leap into a chasm and destroy myself. But I wanted nothing more than to leap. "What do you feel like?" I whispered.

He put his hands on my upper arms, gently, and my head went spinning from his touch. And then, in the next moment, he kissed me.

I had been kissed once before, by Kenneth, in an innocent fashion. But properly enough to make me eligible to join in the whispered conferences of the girls at Miss Pegram's when they giggled about boys and kisses. Yet as Timothy's arms encircled me and I yielded to the gentle demands of his mouth upon mine and felt the pressure of his hands on my shoulders and back, I knew this was nothing to giggle over or even whisper about. I knew, too, that it was wrong, of course. A properly brought up young woman did not allow a young man to kiss her. Not unless they were betrothed to marry.

But I did not care about any of that. I did not feel very proper in Timothy's arms. I didn't want to be proper. I wanted to be, in one terrifying moment, anything he wanted me to be. Timothy made it all seem perfectly natural. Even right. So right that if he had made any other demands on me I knew that I would have had a difficult time denying him what he wanted.

But he made no other demands. Finished with the kiss, he pulled away. I folded my hands demurely in my lap next to him on the settee, my whole being shaken.

"Well." He ran a hand through his curly hair. He looked quite miserable.

"I suppose that was naughty of me, wasn't it?" I asked.

He smiled weakly. "That's one word you could use to describe what just happened."

"Lucien would be upset with us."

"That's putting it mildly." He grinned. "Old Lucien'd kill us."

"I just wanted to know how much you really like me."

"And do you know now?"

"Yes," I said solemnly. "I think you like me enough, Timothy Tobias Collier, for me to ask you what I want to ask you."

So I told him about my idea to let the balloon go. And how it had to be acted upon swiftly, for the balloon would be on the gunboat *Teaser* only until the Fourth.

"What do you think?" I asked.

"I think you see this balloon as something that meant a whole lot to you because of your love for the Cause. And now it's your way of showing that you don't love the Cause anymore. It makes sense."

"Then you'll help me?"

He got up and began pacing. "You say it's on a gunboat, well guarded. I couldn't reach it, Susan, even if it's on a sandbar. The only ones who could are Yankees."

"Good. I've been thinking more and more about giving it to the Yankees anyway. Is that very awful?"

"No. But listen to yourself. Are you sure you just want to get rid of the past? Or are you committing yourself to the other side for the future?"

The fire crackled. If he didn't stop looking at me with

those blue eyes, I felt I would faint. "Whatever do you mean?" I asked.

"Your heart is with the Union, Susan. Somewhere along the line you made a hundred-eighty-degree turn. Your heart is with the Union."

I caught my breath. "My daddy's heart was with the Union. He told me that before he went to Norfolk."

"It's a fine place for a heart to be, Susan. Don't be ashamed of it. If he were honest with himself, your brother would find he feels the same way. Only he hasn't gotten beyond hating the stupidity of the South."

"Lucien is a dyed-in-the-wool Southern gentleman," I said.

"And they don't come any better," Tim said fervently. "He's worked hard for the South, even though it's failed him. He has loyalty and honor. So how are we going to tell him what we want to do?"

I stared at him. "Then you will help me?"

He grinned. "How else can I prove how I feel about you, Susan? How else can I make you feel the same way about me?"

I blushed. "Heavens, would I have allowed you to kiss me the way you did if I didn't . . ."

"I don't know, Susan. Would you?"

"Why, whatever do you mean, Timothy Tobias Collier?"

"I mean I'm not entirely convinced you're still not being the coquette. To get what you want from me. But it doesn't matter. If I have to prove how I feel about you, I will. And when I've finished you can decide whether you meant that kiss or not, Susan. Now, how are we going to tell your brother what we want to do?"

"I hadn't thought about it," I said.

"I know you haven't. But we don't do anything unless we tell him first. I'm under his roof, Susan, a guest in his house. He's my dear friend. And I'm charmed, if a bit unsettled, over his sister. You Southerners aren't the only ones with honor."

I nodded, agreeing. "We'll tell him at supper," I said. "Now let's make our plans."

Chapter Twenty-seven

Lucien sipped his wine and put the glass down. He stared first at Timothy then at me, at the supper table. "It's insane," he said. "I won't permit it."

Timothy and I looked at each other. "Why?" Tim asked.

"It's too risky in the first place. The balloon is guarded. These rebels aren't stupid. They didn't drive McClellan away from Richmond by being stupid. I can't have Susan involved in anything like this."

"Susan doesn't have to be involved," Timothy said.

"And in the second place," Lucien went on, "it's treason."

"Not for me," Timothy reminded him. "I'm a Yankee."

Lucien cut his meat and took a bite, thinking.

"I could tip the Yankees off about the whereabouts of the balloon. The way Susan describes it, the Rebs have the *Teaser* hidden in a cove on a sandbar. The information doesn't even have to come from Susan," Timothy said.

Lucien took another sip of wine. I hadn't touched my food yet. "The James is a tidal river, remember. You'd have to know the time of the tides."

Timothy smiled. "You could tell me that, Lucien."

"Then I would be involved."

"Not necessarily. We talk about fishing all the time."

Lucien buttered a piece of bread. "Eat your food, Susan."

I put a forkful of meat in my mouth. "Why," Lucien asked, "do you want to get involved in something like this?"

"Susan wants to do this," Timothy said carefully. "She has her heart set on it. I want to do it for her. The way she tells it, it makes sense."

"Then tell it to me, Susan," Lucien ordered quietly. I could see he was getting angry.

I explained to him how I felt. He listened impassively without interrupting. "You told me to let the past go, Lucien," I finished.

He chewed his food and swallowed. He looked at me. "Can't you get your heart set on some other act of rebellion?"

Color rose to my face. "You make it sound like a childish prank."

"Tell me what else it is," he said softly.

"It's more than that, Lucien," I protested.

"It's nothing more. Timothy, I thought you had sense. I'm disappointed in you."

"It was my idea, Lucien," I said.

"Then I'm disappointed in you also."

Timothy and I exchanged looks across the table. "You don't understand, Lucien," I said.

"It's simply a childish act of rebellion," he insisted.

His dismissing it that way made me angry. "Well, you were the one who wanted me to know the South was wrong. Now I'm convinced of it."

"Fine. You're convinced. That's a long way from treason."

"Why do I have to be loyal to something I no longer believe in? Why do I have to have this... this stupid patriotism... when I know it's for the wrong cause?"

"Because you live here. Because you're a Southerner. Are you planning on going somewhere else to live?" He looked at me, and I realized he was asking if I wanted to get in touch with my Northern father.

I met his look. "No, Lucien, I'm staying right here."

"Well, then?"

"No one would know if Timothy told the Yankees about the balloon."

"I would. And so would you. There is honor to consider. I'm hoping we both still have it. And I don't see how either of us can still have it if I agree to let you commit this act of treason."

I looked down at my plate. "At least I'd be committing something," I murmured.

"What was that?" Lucien asked. "Would you care to repeat that, please?"

Timothy kicked me under the table, but I didn't care. I had to say it. "It means I'm committing myself to something and not just sitting around mouthing off about how bad the South is. I want to do something about it."

Anger suffused my brother's face. "I see," he said. "Because I won't go charging off committing treason you think I don't stand behind my words, is that it?"

I didn't answer. Timothy set his glass down carefully.

"You would rather I delivered my fish and game to the Yankees every day and let the wounded in Richmond starve? Is that what you're saying?"

"I didn't say that, Lucien."

"Then what, precisely, did you say?"

I looked at him, tears in my eyes. "I can't be like you. I have to do something, or I think I'll go crazy."

"We're embarrassing our guest," he said. "We'll take this up later."

"Timothy is a part of this, Lucien. He isn't embarrassed."

"Well, I am! And I said later! I'll hear no more of it! Now, if you can't remember your manners, you may be excused!"

I fell silent, pouting for the rest of the meal. Lucien and Timothy started talking about the gambling house.

After supper, which I thought would never end, they got up to go to the parlor to smoke and have brandy. As the sliding doors closed behind them, Timothy turned and winked at me from across the hall. I crept into the hall and stood just outside the doors. Nate and Sarah were in the kitchen. I stood listening.

"You're being dictatorial, old friend," Timothy said after some preliminary words about the excellent supper. "Don't you think?"

"I'll thank you to allow me to handle my sister as I see fit."

"Oh, come on, Lucien. I couldn't believe that was you in there. You had the poor child in tears."

"She's not a child. She's old enough to have more sense. And manners."

"You were the one who wanted her to meet me, as I recall, because you wanted her to understand the other side of things."

"I wanted her to see the other side of things. Not commit treason."

"I told you, it isn't treason if I do it. I'm a Yankee."

Silence.

"I'm your friend, Lucien. But in the past I've always told you when you were being bullheaded. And you're being bullheaded now. I should think you'd be proud of the way Susan has come round in her thinking.''

"And I should be proud of the way she sassed me, I suppose?''

"She didn't mean it. She worships you. Do you know what she said when I told her her father wants to see her after the war? 'I couldn't do that to Lucien,' she said. 'He's the one I look to now for everything.' She's thinking clearly. And it took courage for her to stand up to you like that, in there. You told me you admired her spirit. Well, you can't sit on it when it doesn't please you.''

"I can still expect a certain amount of manners and deference to my authority.''

"My God!'' Timothy laughed. "I don't believe you! You sound like the lord and master of a plantation in South Carolina! I can hear the darkies singing in the background. Don't you think it's about time all that was put aside? You saw the results of it out there on the battlefield.''

More silence.

Timothy went on. "Susan is hurting, Lucien. When I gave her the note from her father, she cried. She's been through a lot, and she's hurting.''

"We're all hurting,'' Lucien said. "Everyone in Richmond.''

"Then it's time to start the healing. And Susan has found her way. Why, you just allowed her to make her own decision about her father! I admired you for that. But how can you allow her such leverage in that and then turn around and tell her to stop thinking.''

"Because she has stopped thinking. She's behaving like a silly little girl, and I can't allow it. Can't you see that?''

"You said she wasn't a child a moment ago. You

can't have her grown up one minute and a child the next, just to suit your moods."

"But that's the way she is, Tim. One moment she's as old as Methuselah and the next she's under my heels driving me to distraction."

"You know you enjoy it."

"I may. But I'm the one who's commissioned to keep the sense around here. Do you know what would happen if Susan were caught in such a scheme? We still have martial law in Richmond."

"I told you, she doesn't have to be involved. I told you I would do it for her."

"Why, Tim, when up to now you've stayed out of this war. I have to ask you that again."

"And I'll tell you again. For Susan. It's important to her. That balloon represents everything she wants to forget right now. Everything she's got stored up inside her. And everything that's making her look wan and pale."

"A balloon?" Lucien scoffed. "Don't be ridiculous. How can it?"

"It can," Timothy said, "if Susan sees it that way. Her spirit will heal all the faster if I get rid of it for her."

"Her spirit, is it?" Lucien said dryly. "You're trying to tell me it's her spirit you're interested in, Timothy Tobias Collier?"

Tim's answer didn't come right away. I held my breath. "I won't lie to you, Lucien. Because you're my friend. I'm very taken with Susan. One moment she's a charming and bewitching child and the next she's a very sweet and solemn and thoughtful woman. She's been hurt, and I don't want to see her hurt any more. So right now, yes, that's what I'm telling you. It's her spirit I'm interested in. And I'll do anything I can to help her."

Lucien grunted. "So you'll go against my wishes and undermine my authority with Susan."

"Good heavens, man, why do you think I'm arguing with you? If I wanted to undermine your authority with Susan, we wouldn't have told you about it, would we?"

"How can I agree to this, Tim, and resolve it inside myself?"

"Easily," Tim said. "Why don't you try remembering Sallie."

The silence stretched out very long. Then, "I walked off on my family because I thought they were narrow-minded and corrupt, Tim. And it was the wrong thing to do. Look what happened to them. I should have stayed and tried to put them back on course. The South is being narrow-minded and corrupt right now. But I won't walk off on it. Not yet. I want to stay and be one of the right-thinking men to put the South back on its feet when the time comes. Perhaps I should have emphasized that more with Susan. The way I feel now I can't give you, or her, a yes on this. I'm sorry."

"Will you at least think on it?" Timothy asked. "Sleep on it?"

"There's no sense. I've made my mind up. My answer is no. In the future I may decide the South is just hopeless for me to want to stay with it any longer. But that time hasn't come yet."

"It will, Lucien." I heard the sadness in Tim's voice. "I know you. And it will. You just don't see it, and I'm sorry. But you'll have your breaking point."

"I hope you're not going to do this thing anyway, Tim. I wouldn't want that."

"I haven't decided yet."

"I'm asking you not to."

Silence. Then, "I won't involve Susan," Tim said, "I promise."

"She's already involved. You wouldn't know about the balloon if not for her. She told you where the Confederates have it hidden and how it will probably be moved after the Fourth. So, as far as I'm concerned, she's already involved."

Tim cleared his throat. "I don't know. I think I'll sleep on it."

"Good. I'm sure you'll come to your senses in the morning. My sister has turned your head. I had no idea she was such a vixen. And I'm going to have a word with her about this. Now, can we talk about something else? Tell me about your family."

Chapter Twenty-eight

I crouched low in the underbrush on the bank of the James River. I could hear my own heart hammering. The sound of it was like a drum in my ears, broken only by the sound of my rasping breath. I had run along the ridge while the picket was walking away from me. Now he turned and came back in my direction. I could barely make out his face in the gathering dusk.

It was eight-thirty in the evening on the Fourth of July.

The sun that had scorched Richmond all day had dipped out of sight, leaving a few remaining fingers of pink and purple across the sky. The lines of the gunboat *Teaser* were silhouetted against the flaming sunset. The tide was out, and the *Teaser* was high and dry on a sandbar, even closer to shore than when I'd last seen it. If I could have gotten past the pickets, I could have walked out to the boat myself. It would be easy. All the Yankees had to do was come down the James in a small boat from the Union ship *Maratanza* and steal the balloon.

A Confederate flag fluttered bravely from the *Teaser*'s deck, where my balloon danced, held tightly by ropes. I could see some men walking around beneath it. They wouldn't have that balloon if it wasn't for me! They were going to use it now to spy on the Yankees at Harrison's Landing, ten miles from Richmond. That's what Lucien had heard.

I fingered the note from Timothy in my pocket. It explained the plan. I took it out and read it again. "Tonight at nine," it said, "all will be well. I'm going along for the ride. In my heart, when I think of you, it is like fireworks on the Fourth."

My heart pounded. The note had come to me through Connie, as Tim and I had planned yesterday morning when he bade me good-bye. We'd stood in Lucien's yard when Tim was saddling his horse in the cool quiet and spoken in whispers. Lucien was inside, finishing his breakfast. He had begrudgingly given us ten minutes to say good-bye. I knew he wasn't happy with me. He'd said that when I came back inside he wanted a "word" with me.

I shall never forget the look on Timothy's face as he tightened the cinch on his saddle. "He didn't say anything to me about the balloon when we said good-bye. He didn't ask me if I was going to do it. He trusts me."

"Oh, Tim!"

"It's all right." He smiled. "Old Lucien will be madder than a wet porcupine when he finds out, but he'll get over it."

My eyes moistened as I looked up at him. I loved

him so much! And I knew what it meant for him to go
against Lucien. "I don't want to come between you," I
said.

"Well, that can't be avoided, apparently. So it might
as well be for a good cause."

"I don't want to hurt Lucien, either," I said. "He's
been so good to me. But my daddy told me that
sometimes you have to do what's right, even if you hurt
someone you love. If Daddy had gone against Mama
when she wanted Sallie sent away, Lucien wouldn't
have left our house."

He bent to adjust his stirrups. "Your daddy should
have done what was right on one other occasion, too,
from what Lucien told me."

"You mean Lettie. I know that, Timothy. My daddy
made a lot of mistakes. But I still love him. And I'll
always remember what he told me that day at Tredegar."

"Well, you try explaining it to your brother. That
little word he wants with you isn't going to be a lullaby.
He's angry because he said you turned my head."

I nodded. "I know. He's going to scold. I'm ready
for it."

He looked down at me, his blue eyes shining. "You
have turned my head, you know. It's true and Lucien
knows it."

I blushed. Then he told me he would see the Yankees
about the balloon and get a note back to me. We
decided on Connie as the intermediary. I would fore-
warn her. And then, in the quiet dewy morning, he
kissed me good-bye.

Lucien was waiting for me in his office. When he
summoned me he told me, quietly, to close the sliding
doors.

Then he stood, his hands clasped behind him, in front

of his desk and lashed out at me about loyalty and
honor. From there he went on to how I had embarrassed
him at supper the night before. And what had I done to
Timothy to make him so enamored? Why, his old friend
was behaving like a schoolboy! He and Timothy had
always gotten on. They had never argued. And now he
had almost gone and done a fool thing because some
silly girl had asked him to.

His ire rained down on me. I couldn't possibly absorb
everything he said, of course. But it had a lot to do with
him never wanting to hear another word about that
balloon. And it had to do with my behaving myself, in
the future, with Timothy. He did not want to hear that
his sister was a flirtatious little tease with a man. Ever.
Was that what I had done? Well, was it?

No, Lucien, of course not.

From flirtatious little tease he went right into treason.
Did I comprehend the difference between his anger with
the South and outright treason? Well, did I? Hadn't I
heard him speaking about rebuilding the South after the
war?

I responded with the right answers at the right time. I
stood and listened. I trembled because his words hurt
me as much as the blows from Mama's switch. No
lullaby, Tim had said. I felt a wrench inside me,
thinking of Tim riding away to tell the Yankees about
my balloon. Tears came to my eyes. Then Lucien
stopped. He looked at me. Tears were coming down my
face. All right, he said, and his voice was suddenly
gentle. That's all I have to say. You may go.

The note came from Connie at noontime of the
Fourth. By supper I was in a state of frenzy knowing
that Tim was going along on the expedition. I was
almost feverish. I couldn't eat.

Lucien eyed me across the table. "Are you all right, Susan?"

"Yes, I'm fine."

"Perhaps I overdid it yesterday when I scolded. You've been so quiet. But I just wanted you to understand a few things."

I nodded. His being nice to me now was worse than anything, because I was betraying him. It was easier to contemplate betrayal when he was angry.

And what about Timothy? I was having second thoughts on the whole matter. Suppose Timothy got shot tonight? The men on that gunboat weren't complete ninnies. I tried to eat some food. I would be responsible if Timothy got shot. The whole thing was my fault! Oh, why had I asked him to do it? And then it occurred to me that I wouldn't know the results of the venture until tomorrow when we heard about it in the street.

How could I wait until then?

"I would appreciate a little conversation at this table, Susan," Lucien said, "even if it's forced on your part."

I nodded and smiled. I would go to the bank of the James tonight, I decided, to the spot where Mrs. Wigfall and I had stood. And I would watch. If I dressed in boy's clothing I would be all right. I still had Lucien's old clothes. Sarah had laundered and returned them to me.

I glanced at my brother for an instant and felt an ache inside me, as if I had just crossed over some line that put him on one side and me on the other. And there was no going back. I didn't want to hurt Lucien. I loved him dearly, in spite of the way he had scolded me yesterday. But it was too late for self-recrimination. The thing had to be done. I had made the commitment with myself and with Timothy. He was gambling a lot for me. His friendship with Lucien, for one thing. And perhaps even his life. There was no going back.

I smiled at my brother. "I'm sorry for not talking. I've been rude. Sarah isn't feeling well. Did you know that? She has a fierce headache. I told her to go and lie down, that I would clear things from the table."

"That was good of you, Susan." He leaned back in his chair, relaxing. "I'll be leaving directly for the gambling house. Look in on her later, would you?"

I thought I saw the outline of a small boat on the water. It must be the Yankees! It looked only the size of a rowboat. It was getting dark. I had sneaked out of the house in my boy's clothing about seven-fifteen. I stood up to see better.

And then the moon came out from behind some shredded pieces of dark clouds, almost a full moon. The surface of the James shone, and I could see everything. I saw the men running from the boat across the sandbar, four of them. One had to be Timothy! *Oh, please don't let them be spotted by the guards on the deck of the* Teaser, I prayed. But the guards were conveniently turned the other way. In another moment the moon was obscured again by clouds, and I hoped the Yankees and Tim would use the temporary darkness to board.

But I couldn't see what was going on! And then I heard shots from the boat, and I let out a loud moan. Unthinkingly, I started to move closer so I could see.

"Who are you?" I heard the words in the dark, and I froze. I leaped into the depths of the underbrush, trembling. The picket had spotted me!

A shot was fired, not on the river, but on the shore! A ball whistled over my head. A picket was shooting at me! I heard him run toward me, and I muffled a sob. But he ran right past, up the slope. I lifted my head to look. Should I get up and run or wait? If I waited he might come back in my direction. The moon was still obscured. I got up and started to run.

"Halt!"

But I kept running along the slope, back in the direction of home. He had spotted me and was coming after me. I ran faster. The ground was uneven, and I couldn't see. I stumbled and fell twice, but I got up and kept running. While all this was going on I was aware of activity on the sandbar, of shouting and shots, but I didn't dare look. The other shore pickets had probably run out to help the attacked *Teaser,* but this one was concentrating on me. I could hear his rasping breath getting louder behind me. I felt a burning stitch in my side. Then I fell again.

The ground came up and hit hard, taking the breath out of me. I had to keep moving! But the man was beside me. And then I heard another sound.

Hoofbeats. Someone was coming on a horse now, too!

I whimpered and tried to get to my feet. Rough hands grabbed me, pulled me upright and whirled me around. And I was looking down the barrel of a Confederate musket.

"Jus' you hold steady theah, boah, that's it. Who are you?"

I backed off, but he kept coming. "Talk, boah, or a'll beat the stuffin's outta you."

I kept going backward, lost my balance and fell. My hat flew off. He threw down his musket and pulled me up, his arm drawn back to hit me. And then his eyes widened and a leering look came over his face. "Why, you're a girl!"

"Let me go," I demanded, but his grasp on my arm was firm.

"A'll let you go, missy, after I see how much of a girl

you are." And his hands were on my shirtfront, on Lucien's shirt, roughly grasping the material, about to pull it open.

I screamed and kicked. He laughed, but he never got the shirt open. A shot rang out, and I saw his eyes bulge, felt his grip slacken. He slumped to the ground in front of me. "Oh, my gawd," I heard him moan.

I stood stunned. Horse's hooves were coming closer, so I turned and started to run again. I ran, crying, seeing the man's leering face in front of me. My sobs came with every breath as I stumbled along. The horse was gaining on me. Dear God, I didn't have the strength to fight off anyone else.

I heard the horse's snorting breath and then it was beside me, reined in for just a second as someone reached down and pulled me up, kicking and yelling. "Let me goo . . . ooo. Damn you!" I used the swear word I had heard most frequently from Wilium.

I was lifted onto the horse in front of him. "Quiet," the voice ordered, "and hold on. And stop your swearing."

I grasped the horse's mane and held on while Lucien's arm encircled my waist, and we galloped on Merlin up the slope.

Down the road a ways he slowed Merlin to a walk. I was gulping sobs. "It serves you right. You deserve the scare you got. Are you all right?" The words tumbled over my shoulder.

"Yeeess."

"Then quiet down. We can't be seen or heard coming into town. You hear?"

I heard. I smothered my sobs, and he galloped Merlin on, never saying another word. Through my misery I saw that he was taking back streets in town, going through dark alleys. Merlin picked his way fastidiously

over barrels of trash. Finally we arrived at the back of
the gambling house. Nate was waiting. Lucien slid off
the horse and lifted me down.

"Is Sarah here?" he asked Nate.

"Yes. In my office."

"Good." He took my arm and led me, pulled me was
more the word for it, through the back door. I could not
imagine what was going on. The sudden light in his
office hurt my eyes, and I shielded them with my hand.
Through my fingers I saw Sarah and Fanny waiting.

"Have I been missed?" he asked.

"No. You were gone forty-five minutes," Fanny
said. "I've been in here all the time. Is everything..."

"I've shot someone."

She gave a low cry. "Is he dead?"

"I don't know." He took off the rough jacket he was
wearing over his good shirt and waistcoat. "Get out of
those clothes," he said to me without even glancing in
my direction.

"But, Lucien, I have nothing else to put on."

"Do as I say!" He whirled on me, and I saw murder
in his eyes. He flung his jacket down on a chair. "Sarah
has brought clothes for you! You dare argue with me
now! You have defied me! You have gone behind my
back! You have caused trouble for everyone and
endangered your life. And you dare argue with me!"

"No, Lucien." I sat down and started to remove my
boots. He strode over to a small mirror across the room,
straightened his silk cravat, ran a brush through his
curly hair and put on his good frock coat. "Take her
home when she's dressed," he told Sarah. "Have Nate
burn those clothes. Fanny, you'd better come out in five
minutes looking very pleased with yourself and hang on
my arm the rest of the night."

He did not look at me as he went out.

* * *

I sat on the edge of my bed in my long cotton batiste nightgown while Sarah brushed my hair until it stood out. "You've been a bad girl tonight," she said quietly.

"I know, Sarah. But why did you tell on me?"

She shook her head and regarded me with her hands on her hips, one hand holding my silver-backed hairbrush. "Honey, I knew you were up to no good when I saw you leave in those boy's clothes. I had to tell Mr. Lucien. I asked Nate to follow you a little ways. When he came back and told me what direction you were going in, I went right to the gambling house to tell your brother."

"I was worried about Timothy," I said. "Have you heard anything? Do you know if anything happened to him?"

She shook her head no. "And if I were you I wouldn't go mouthing off about Mr. Collier in front of your brother. Your brother's about to take a buggy whip to him. And to you."

"Did he say that?"

"You come on and get into bed now. He said lots of things. And I imagine he'll be saying more. I wouldn't be in any rush to hear it if I were you."

I needed no urging to get into bed. I fell asleep crying for Timothy, hearing the gunfire out on the sandbar and seeing the Confederate picket's evil face. I awoke with a start as the clock downstairs struck two. I had been dreaming of Timothy, and hot tears came. Then I heard footsteps coming up the stairs and down the hall. The doorknob turned and someone came in. Lucien! I closed my eyes, pretending to be asleep.

He came to the side of the bed and I felt him standing over me. Was he going to drag me out of bed and beat me? I trembled and clenched my fists under the covers.

Then I felt his hand on my face, tracing my jawline
down to my chin, gently touching the tears. "Open
your eyes, Susan," he said. "I know you're awake.
You have to face me sooner or later."

I opened my eyes. The moonlight coming in the
window fell across his face. The jaw was set in a firm
line, the eyes were hard. "Get up, Susan. I want you to
see what nice fireworks you made for the Fourth of
July."

I stared at him, not comprehending. Impatiently, he
snatched the covers and flung them off. "I said get up.
Don't make me have to say it again." And he turned
and walked across my room to the window that gave a
view of the river up the street.

I sat frozen for a minute, my legs dangling over the
side of the bed. I pushed my long tousled hair off my
face. What was he doing, staring out the window? What
was he looking at? His back was to me. His broad
shoulders were outlined against the light, an unusual
light coming in the window for two in the morning.

He turned to me. "I want you over here," he said.

I crossed the room, still in a daze, rubbing the sleep
out of my eyes. Before I got to him he reached out and
grabbed my wrist and pulled me to stand in front of him
at the window. "Do you see that?" His voice came
close to my ear from behind. His hands were on my
shoulders.

I looked. In the distance a fiery glow lit up the sky in
the direction of the gunboat *Teaser*.

"Well?" His hands tightened on my shoulders. "Do
you see it?"

"Yes, Lucien."

"Do you know what it is?"

I knew. With a sickening sensation that made my
knees buckle, I knew. I stood there in my long night-

dress, shivering. Under my feet the floorboards were warm, but I was cold.

He shook me. "Answer me," he said.

I burst into tears. "It's . . . the *Teaser*." I lowered my head, sobbing.

He dropped his hands and came to stand beside me. Then he put one hand under my chin and forced me to face him. "I want you to look at it, Susan. The *Teaser* was used by the Confederate navy to lay mines in the James to assist Lee's Army of Northern Virginia. And now it's burning. A shell from the Union ship *Maratanza* blew up its boiler. The crew had to abandon it, after some Yankees boarded her and took the balloon. A reporter from the *Dispatch* was at one of my gaming tables tonight. Everyone was talking about it."

He dropped his hand and I stood crying. "How do you think I felt, hearing them all talking about it, knowing my sister was the cause of it all?"

I didn't answer. I wiped my face with my hand, gulping sobs.

"Not only my sister," he growled, "my dear friend."

I wanted to ask if Tim had been killed. I was sure he had. But I didn't dare ask. And I couldn't have gotten the words out for crying, anyway.

"Answer me!" he snapped. "How do you think I feel? And look at me. The least you can do is look at me!"

I raised my eyes fearfully. His face was terrible to see. His eyes burned with an awesome anger that seared me and made me cower in fear.

"Treason, Susan. That was treason," he whispered.

I shook my head no.

"Yes!" He stepped forward, grabbed me by the shoulders and shook me roughly. "God's teeth, are you such a little fool you don't see it?'' His grip on me was like a steel trap.

I sobbed. "Lucien, you're hurting me."

He shook me free. "I'd like to take a switch to you. Now's the time you deserve it." He surveyed me disgustedly. "Stop that fool crying."

I wiped my tears with my hands. We stood facing each other.

"A fine sister and friend I have, going behind my back and defying me. The only two people in the world, besides Fanny, that I really cared about."

"Lucien," I pleaded.

"Don't, Susan. Please. Spare me the sweet-little-girl appeals. Don't tell me what a wonderful brother I am. I was too good to you, that's what I was. And him . . ." He waved off the thought of Timothy. "You'll not see him again in this house. Good riddance to him."

"Lucien, what are you saying? Is Timothy dead?" I felt the blood draining from my face.

"Dead?" He grunted. "No, he isn't dead. That's what you're worried about, is it? Timothy."

"Well, of course, aren't you?"

"Worried about Timothy?" He gave a short, bitter laugh. "He steps in this house again and I'll get out my old dueling pistols. No, my dear sister, put your mind at ease. The reporter from the *Dispatch* said nobody was killed. Your precious Timothy is safe. For all the good it will do you." He walked toward the door. I ran after him. I grabbed his arm. "Lucien, please," I said.

He looked at me coldly. "Please what?"

"Please try to understand why we did it. Please let me explain."

"Explain what? Deceit and treachery? I know what they are. I don't have to have them explained to me."

"Lucien!" I hugged him. I put my arms around his

middle and buried my head against his white linen coat. "We've always talked before. About everything."

Like my father had done once a very long time ago, in what now seemed another lifetime, he dislodged my arms from around his middle. Gently, he pushed me away. "We'll talk," he said, "when I'm ready to talk. And when I decide what to do with you."

He went out. I stood in the middle of the moon-dappled room, crying. Lucien had been my whole world since Daddy died. He had been good to me. But now it was over. He was disgusted with me. I couldn't bear the thought of it. My love for him welled inside me until I thought I would burst. I had wronged him! Oh, I had done the right thing with the balloon, I knew that. But I had hurt Lucien. Like Daddy had said, doing right even though it might hurt someone you love is the most difficult thing in the world.

And what about Timothy? The three of us had gotten on so wonderfully. Now I was never to see him again. And Lucien was talking about getting out his dueling pistols if Tim ever came around!

I cried with a torrent of renewed grief.

The door opened. Startled, I looked up. Lucien stood there eyeing me contemptuously.

"You will stop these hysterics," he ordered coldly. "Right now. It won't work with me, Susan. Grow up and stop feeling sorry for yourself. If you insist on acting like a child, I will treat you like a child, which means I shall be forced to deal with you the way I did in the carriage the day we first met."

I stifled a sob.

"Do we understand each other?"

I nodded. With a final warning look, he went out. I flung myself down on the bed and buried my face in the pillow so he would not hear my sobbing.

Chapter Twenty-nine

I awoke the next morning to the sound of voices raised in argument downstairs. For a moment I lay there, stunned and unable to piece together the fragments that my life had become. And then the fragments became a huge ball of understanding that crashed down on me. My mouth was dry, my eyes felt swollen from crying and my head hurt.

Sarah came in with a tray of breakfast and set it down, then bustled about, getting my clothes.

"Why are you bringing me breakfast, Sarah? I'm not sick."

"Your brother says you're to eat and get dressed and come down when he sends for you and not before."

I got out of bed and stood in the middle of my room. "So I'm being punished by having to take my meals up here. Well, I won't eat it," I said.

She turned to me and sighed. "Are you going to make trouble? Don't we have enough?"

She was right. "No, I'm not going to make trouble. But I'm not going to eat, either. Who's downstairs? Who is Lucien arguing with?"

"Some business acquaintance," she said.

Something in the way she avoided my eyes made me run to the door.

"You come back here!" she snapped.

I turned, closing the door. "It's Timothy! I know his voice! That's why Lucien doesn't want me downstairs!"

I started getting dressed, reaching wildly for clothes. I pulled my pantalets on under my nightgown.

"I'd advise you not to go down there," Sarah said.

"I thank you for your advice, Sarah. Now, are you going to help me with my dress? Because, if you don't, I'll do it myself."

They were in the front parlor. I know I should have knocked, but if I hesitated one moment I would have lost courage. I slid the doors open and went in. Lucien was standing in front of the fireplace. Timothy was slumped in a chair. Lucien turned, startled, and immediately Timothy jumped to his feet.

"Susan!" I met Tim halfway across the room, and we stood a foot or so apart, not daring to do or say anything.

"Susan, leave this room immediately," Lucien ordered.

I barely heard him. I was looking up into Tim's blue eyes in which there were so many questions. And answers. His face was very white.

"Are you all right?" I asked.

He grinned, and it almost broke my heart. "Sure."

"Lucien said he'd get out his old dueling pistols if you came around again. And it's all my fault!"

His grin widened. "Well, then, he'll have to shoot me. Because I'm not dueling with my old friend. I came around to make sure you're all right, and that you don't get punished on my account. I heard about the girl in boy's clothing on the riverbank last night, and figured it was you."

"I said out, Susan." Lucien stepped forward and grabbed my wrist and pulled me to the door. "It seems you could have knocked, miss, before bursting into a room where a private conversation is going on. You're not only disobedient, you're absolutely without manners. And I'll deal with you later on all counts." He slid open the door and was about to push me out. His face was white with anger.

"No!" I threw myself at him. I hugged him around his middle. "Lucien, please! I don't care how you punish me. I've got to see Tim. Please!" I held on to him desperately. He tried to pull away. I felt him resisting. And then a thought struck me, and I looked up. "Don't you remember how it was when Daddy sent Sallie away?"

"How can you refuse a plea like that, Lucien?" Tim's voice came over my shoulder, tinged with amusement.

I saw a moment of hesitation in my brother's face. The muscle in his jaw twitched. I saw something in his eyes, too, a flicker of understanding, before he dropped his lids.

"Go and wait in the dining room," he said quietly.

"Will you let me see Tim?" I looked up at him hopefully.

He scowled. His face was set and cold. "Do as I say," he said sharply, "if you want any consideration out of me at all."

It seemed like an eternity before those doors opened again. In that eternity I heard raised voices that made me tremble. Then it got quiet and finally the two men came out. I ran into the hall.

"I'd like a word with Susan before I go," Timothy said.

"I'd rather you just went," Lucien said.

"Lucien! You promised!" I flung the accusation at him. I know he hadn't really promised, but he hadn't said no, either. And I was going to hold him to even a hint of a promise because I knew how much store he put in his word.

He turned to level a long and sad gaze at me. "It seems I did, after a fashion, doesn't it? And a Southern gentleman always keeps his promise. A Southern gentleman is always true to his word. That's part of what the South is all about, isn't it, Susan?" he reminded me sarcastically.

I stood trembling, but gave no answer.

"Very well. You may say good-bye. You have five minutes."

I followed Timothy through the hall which went from the front door to the back. In the yard his horse was waiting under the tree.

"Five minutes!" I said desperately.

"It's all right, I'm coming back," Tim said.

"When?"

"When he cools down."

"Did he say you could?"

"No. He said I couldn't. Ever."

"Oh, Tim! He won't let you! You don't know Lucien. He has a fierce temper. And he's so angry with me. He's not ever going to forgive us."

We were standing close enough to touch. The look in his eyes was so intense it became the center of my world. Everything else fell away. "I shouldn't have asked you to do it," I said. "Now your old friend is angry with you. And everything is ruined."

"Did you want to give the balloon to the Yankees, Susan? Or were you just testing me?"

"Why, of course! You know I did!"

"Then don't be sorry. Stick to what you think was right. I've known Lucien longer than you have. And he'll get over it. Everything isn't ruined. It's only different. Do you love me, Susan?''

"Oh, Tim! You have to ask?''

He smiled down at me. And there was a confidence and serenity about him that made him seem older than his years. "Yes, I have to ask.''

"All right, then, Timothy Tobias Collier. I love you. Why do you think I went to the James last night? Because I like being chased by Southern pickets?''

He shook his head. His horse nuzzled him, and he patted its nose. "You shouldn't have done that,'' he said sadly. "That's part of why he's so angry with you. And I can't say as I blame him, either. I hear he had to shoot that picket last night to save you from being attacked.''

I nodded.

"If you were my sister...''

I moved a step closer to him. "What would you do?''

"I know what my father would do. I imagine old Lucien isn't at a loss for ideas, either. He certainly wasn't at a loss for words with me in there.''

"Well, I'm not your sister. And I've told you I love you. And I haven't heard you say it to me yet.''

His eyes widened. "God's teeth, Susan, as your brother would say, why do you think I did what I did last night?''

We stood silent, eyes locked. And I didn't care about anything then. The war, the balloon, Lucien's anger, none of it mattered. Only the look in Timothy's eyes. And the ache in my heart. "I don't want you to go.'' I started to cry.

"I must.'' He took my hands in his.

"I can't bear it.''

"You have to. So do I. Until he comes round.''

"Will he ever?''

"I think so. If you behave and mind for a while. And don't give him any more reason to run off in the middle of the night shooting people for you. What you said to him before about Sallie had its effect, I think. You might try working on him in that direction. Old Lucien isn't mean. But he's hurting. He feels we both turned on him. And we did."

"Did we do wrong?"

"No." He touched my chin, and I shivered. "The balloon is gone, Susan. You didn't do it to hurt Lucien. You did it because you felt it was right. Along the way you stood up to him and told him where your heart is, concerning the war, for the future. You had a right to do that. It was your balloon. And your past. And it's your future."

"The future scares me, Tim. All I am is scared."

"That's a sure sign you're growing up, then." He grinned at me. "Don't look now, but I just heard someone come out of the house. Am I right?"

"Yes." Lucien was standing on the porch, leaning against one of its columns, smoking a cheroot.

"Then I guess I better go. Don't want to provoke him any further. It'll only make it worse for you."

"Oh, Tim!" He was about to mount his horse, but I was in his way.

"I want to kiss you, Susan," he said, "more than I want to live right now. But it would be like slapping him in the face. You understand?"

"Yes," I said.

He squeezed my hand. "Be patient with him. Be contrite. And be a good little sister. He needs that. He thinks I'm taking you away from him. Don't let him feel that way." He mounted his horse. I looked up at him, tears streaming down my face. He winked and grinned. "I'll be back, Susan, I promise."

He put his heels into his horse's flanks, and as he trotted past Lucien he saluted smartly. Lucien just stood leaning indolently against the porch column, smoking. When Tim was gone he threw the cheroot down and looked across the yard at me.

"Come on in here," he said.

Chapter Thirty

A white, vaporous heat hung over everything. I lay on my bed watching the occasional breeze from the river lift the curtains in my room. Next to me on a table was my morning tray of food.

I looked at the food, carefully prepared by Sarah, and I knew I would not eat it. There was no real reason to, just as there was no real reason to get dressed. I lay in my pantalets and stays. Sarah would be angry when she came back for the tray and saw I hadn't eaten and wasn't dressed yet. But I didn't care.

After Timothy left, Lucien had announced, firmly and quietly, that I was to stay in my room until he decided to let me out. And so I had lived like this for the past three days, sipping only an occasional cup of tea and nibbling enough to keep me alive. Most of the time I lay on my bed, in a stupor of unhappiness, trying to figure everything out, crying, thinking of Timothy and listening to the sounds in the rest of the house.

I heard Lucien come and go, in and out of his own room down the hall. But he never even stopped outside my door. I existed alone, wrapped in my silence and pain, brokenhearted and abandoned, sealed off from the world and cut off from my brother's affections. And that was the worst punishment Lucien could have inflicted. His cold disregard of me stung worse than any blows Mama had ever delivered.

I wanted to die. If not for Sarah's admonitions to eat and get dressed, to be good, I probably would have.

"If you don't eat tomorrow I'll have to tell him," she had said last night.

"I don't care, Sarah."

She came in to get the tray and gave me a resigned look. "I'm going to have to tell him," she said.

I told her I didn't care much if she did.

"Susan!"

The knock on my door came five minutes later. Lucien! I flew off my bed and grabbed my dress which Sarah had laid out for me. I was pulling it over my head when he came in. Behind him Sarah stood with the same tray of food. She set it down and helped me with the dress, straightening it and buttoning it up the back for me.

I stood, flushed with apprehension, facing my brother. But I was surprised to see lines around his mouth and hollows under his eyes as if he hadn't slept, as if he, too, were going through some kind of private torture. Even under his sunburn he looked wan. He was dressed to go out on his boat. A copy of the *Richmond Dispatch* was under his arm.

"Sarah tells me you haven't been eating."

I said nothing.

"Are you attempting to try my patience?"

I felt a stab of fear. "I... haven't been hungry, Lucien."

He nodded, his eyes raking over me, taking in my

disheveled state with one glance. I knew how I looked in the hastily adjusted dress with my hair still uncombed.

"She also tells me you've been neglecting your appearance. That you lie around half dressed. Is that true?"

"It's been hot," I said. "And I saw no need to dress up since I wouldn't be going anywhere."

He gave me a contemptuous look and pulled out a chair next to the table. "Come over here and eat," he said.

"Lucien, I'm not hungry. I . . ." His look stopped me. I sat. He motioned for Sarah to leave, telling her he would be down for his own breakfast shortly.

I stared at the food. "It's always nice to know you have friends you can trust," I said to Sarah's back as she went out the door.

Lucien stood over me. "Yes, it is, isn't it?"

I flushed, realizing I'd walked into a trap of my own words.

"You will apologize to Sarah for that remark when you next see her," he directed. "She had been a friend to you. A good one. Now, however, you will eat. I'm late this morning. But I will sit here if I have to until you do."

He took a chair next to the window and opened up his newspaper. I looked at the food, wanting to cry, convinced that if I ate I would be sick to my stomach. But I knew that he was watching me from behind his paper.

"Suppose I don't eat," I challenged, "what then?"

"Don't make me address that question, Susan," he said quietly.

I took a bite and tried to chew. I thought of that last breakfast I'd had with Daddy so long ago, before he left for Norfolk, and I wanted to die. What had happened to us all? Daddy was dead, Mama never even inquired about me, and Lucien and I were locked in a battle of wills over a tray of food. Lucien, whom I'd so admired and loved, treating me with a cold and detached hatred. Hot tears rolled down my face. "Daddy didn't want it like this," I said.

"Nobody does, Susan." He continued reading.

"If Daddy had known how you would treat me he wouldn't have made you head of the family."

He shook out his paper. "How am I treating you?"

"Like I'm a prisoner in Castle Godwin."

"If you read the newspaper accounts of the way the balloon was stolen you might realize that perhaps that's where you deserve to be."

Oh, the cruelty! I wiped my face with my hand. "What are they saying?"

"I'll leave the paper for you to read, when you've finished eating."

"Well, I don't care what they say. Even Mama would never lock me in my room like this."

Now he looked at me. "You are behaving like a tiresome child. I don't think you realize the implications of what you have done. So I shall keep you in your room until you do. And if you continue acting like a tiresome child, I shall send you back to Charlotte, since you seem to prefer her to me."

"I didn't say . . ."

"However," he interrupted, "if you wish to continue living with me, you will obey me. And show at least an outward appearance of manners and respect. And be sufficiently contrite for the trouble you have caused everyone."

I glared at him. I knew I should be contrite, as Tim had said. But Lucien was being so pompous. Why, it would kill me to be submissive and not say what I felt when he acted like that. "I never knew you were such a grumpy old goat," I said. "If a meek little ninny is what you want for a sister, maybe you don't want me!"

For half a second he was speechless. His face went white with rage. He stood up. "I have taken just about enough from you, miss." Then, just as he was about to lose control, Sarah came in.

"Mr. Lucien."

He refocused his gaze upon her. "Yes, Sarah."

"There's a Baltimore detective downstairs. Something about the other night on the riverbank. He says the man who was shot died. And they know that the boy he was chasing was a girl. And they have reason to think it was your sister."

Lucien set the newspaper down carefully, calming himself as he absorbed the news. "I heard, three days ago, that the man died, Sarah. Invite the detective for breakfast. I'll be right down."

I stood up, shaking. No wonder he looked so terrible! He'd killed someone! On my account! He'd killed a Southerner! "Oh, Lucien"—I knocked over my chair as I ran to him—"you killed someone for me! And I've been behaving like a spoiled child!"

He walked past me to pick up the chair. "That you have," he said. "I'm glad you finally realize it. I was about to take a hand to you when Sarah came in. Eat your breakfast, Susan." The eyes that I saw when he straightened up and looked at me were so swimming with dark anguish that I trembled. But he remained calm.

"And make yourself presentable. You may be summoned downstairs. So put on a prettier dress and fix your hair. If I do have to call you down, remember, you were here the other night. At home, with a headache. Sarah nursed you. Do you understand?"

"Yes, Lucien."

"Be polite, but lie your head off. No one can prove it was you. And act as if we're getting along. The way it was ... before all this."

That broke my heart, but I nodded bravely. "I can act," I said. "I learned drama at Miss Pegram's."

He nodded. "Good. You'll need it. Especially when it comes to the part about us getting along. Now eat your breakfast."

"But what about you! If the man is dead..."

He turned at the door. "Are you worried about me, Susan?" he asked wryly.

"Of course!" I gulped a sob.

"Well, that's sweet," he said sarcastically. "Such affection. I never would have known it by your actions. You needn't worry about me, little sister. I have a habit of always landing on my feet."

Thank heaven for Miss Pegram's. I bounced into the dining room, dressed in the flowered frock Lucien had bought me. I knew the dress was his favorite. I made straight for my brother. The two men got to their feet. I stood on tiptoe and kissed Lucien. "Good morning, brother deah. I was naughty and slept late. Do forgive me."

I gave special emphasis to the last words as I kissed his face, looking coyly into his eyes.

He nodded, and I caught the amusement in those eyes at my pronounced Southern belle accent and gushing affection.

"How are you feeling this morning, Susan?" he asked.

"Oh, I'm fine, thank you."

"Good. This is Detective Tom Simkins. He wants to ask you some questions."

I smiled sweetly at the detective and recognized him

instantly as the one who had stopped Mrs. Wigfall and me when we were taking the dresses to the train station. "Heavens, what for?"

"It's about the other night, miss. The night of the Fourth." He looked shorter than he had that morning. And without his hat, I saw that his head was bald. "There was a girl in boy's clothing running around the bank of the James the night the *Teaser* was attacked. She was apprehended by one of our pickets. The poor fellow was shot in all the action and died on the morning of the fifth, but he definitely told us the boy he was chasing turned out to be a girl."

I put my hand to my throat. "Oh, how awful! But why are you questioning me, suh?" I sat down. Sarah set breakfast in front of me. I would have to eat again! I looked, appealingly, at Lucien, but he only smiled and sipped his coffee. Sarah refilled Simkins's cup and went out.

"By now you've heard that the Confederate balloon on the gunboat *Teaser* was stolen, haven't you? Everyone in town is talking about it."

"I have. And I was devastated over it! That was my balloon, suh. I collected the dresses for it. Didn't my brother tell you?"

Simkins looked at Lucien, who smiled again. "I told you that, Tom, didn't I?"

"People tell me things all the time, Lucien. Good people. People I like. It doesn't make my job any easier. We think the girl on the shore was creating a diversion so the guards couldn't focus on what was happening on the river. And we know, for a fact, that your sister has been running around in the past in boy's clothing. It's our job to know things like that. We just put it down to a childish prank."

I swallowed my coffee. "Mr. Simkins, it was a

childish prank," I said contritely. "But that was all in the past when I lived with my mama. I was always doing naughty things like that. My daddy was away so much, working for the Confederacy. And I wasn't happy with Mama. And so I used to dress in boy's clothing and run around the street. I'm happy with Lucien and so I don't do such things anymore."

Over Simkins's shoulder I saw Lucien watching me.

I leaned forward to Simkins and lowered my voice to a conspiratorial whisper. "You know, Lucien has forbidden me to ever do it again. And, while he is a deah sweet old thing, he does have a ferocious temper. Why, I do believe he'd take a buggy whip to me if I ever put on boy's clothing again."

Now Lucien raised his eyes to the heavens.

Mr. Simkins nodded. "Where were you on the night of the Fourth, miss?"

"Right heah in this house. I had a terrible headache. I retired early and deah Sarah gave me headache powders and brown paper soaked in vinegar for my forehead. The headache lasted two days."

"I see."

I fluttered my eyelashes. "I haven't been out much lately. Lucien wouldn't even allow me to help at the hospital. He was an absolute beah about that. But then, I have been quite sick ever since my deah daddy was killed fighting in the Shenandoah Valley for the Confederacy." I looked as if I were about to cry.

He cleared his throat. "Yes. You have my condolences for that, miss. Thank you for your time." He got up.

"I'll see you out, Tom." Lucien got to his feet also.

Mr. Simkins gave me a little bow. "That's a very pretty dress you're wearing there, Miss Chilmark. Very pretty, indeed."

"Why, thank you, suh. How gracious of you to

notice. My brother bought it for me. He does spoil me
so." I went to Lucien and kissed him again and held
on to his arm. "And I'm afraid I don't deserve it." I said
it with just the right amount of humility.

"Nevertheless, we Southern men do like to spoil our
women. Looks like the dress came from a blockade-
runner. Am I right, Lucien?"

My brother smiled. "I buy them for Fanny all the
time. I can give you the name of the shop that sells
them, if you're thinking of sending some home to your
daughters, Tom."

"Wonderful!" he said enthusiastically.

They went out. I sat finishing my coffee. After about
five minutes Lucien came back in. He poured himself
another cup of coffee, stirred in the sugar and took a
sip. I waited, afraid to say anything.

"So, I'd take a buggy whip to you, would I?" He
eyed me across the table.

"Well, heavens, Lucien, I used everything I learned at
Miss Pegram's. Tell me, please, what did he say?"

"He doesn't believe a word of it. He says you're a
bewitching, pretty little thing, but he doesn't envy me
the responsibility."

"Why, whatever does he . . ."

"He advised me to keep a firmer hand on you." He
sighed. "It's a good thing I hold a lot of promissory
notes for gambling debts from Tom Simkins, all duly
registered at the county clerk's office. The man I shot
never told them he tried to take advantage of you. He
said he ran out to the sandbar to help the other pickets.
Then he was shot and came back and, with his last
ounce of strength, chased a girl wearing boy's clothing."

"Well, at least they don't think you shot him."

"No. Tom was in my gambling rooms running up yet
another debt when Fanny seductively lured me from the

room because Sarah was waiting to tell me you'd slipped off. Since I was back in forty-five minutes, all anyone thinks is that I had a romantic liaison with Fanny in my office. It hurts my sensibilities, but it saves my neck.'' He stared into his coffee, brooding.

I looked at him. ''I never thanked you for what you did for me that night, Lucien,'' I said. ''We . . . were too busy fighting.''

He raised his eyes. ''Do you know what I did that night, Susan?''

''Yes. You . . .''

''I saved your honor? Perhaps your life?'' He sipped his coffee and set his cup down carefully. ''I could tell Tom that and never be held accountable, except that I can't admit you were there. But that isn't what I did.''

Something was bothering him. Something terrible was eating away at his insides, uprooting his soul so that it was all exposed in his eyes.

''I could have stopped that man by jumping off Merlin and knocking him senseless, with little effort. But I chose to shoot him instead. It seems I've finally made that commitment you accused me of not making, haven't I?''

Yes, he had. And I saw how it was tearing him apart.

He shook his head. ''I saw in that picket the corruption of the whole South. And I wanted to destroy him. Like you wanted to destroy your balloon. So I did. I shot a man without thinking of the consequences.''

He fell silent. ''Killing,'' he said. ''And treason. We're a fine pair, aren't we? Did we have a right to do what we did? To think only of our own selfish motives and not of the long-range results? I'd like to know your thoughts on the matter, Susan.''

''We . . .'' I hesitated and looked down at my hands in my lap.

''Look at me, please, when I talk to you.''

I did so with great effort. "We did what we thought was right. Daddy told me that sometimes you have to do what's right, even though it may hurt others. Even though . . ." My voice trailed off.

"Go on," he insisted.

"Even though it may hurt someone you love."

"He told you that, did he? Is that the reasoning you applied to the giving away of your balloon?"

"Yes."

"And I'm the person you knew would be hurt. Is that it?"

I could barely get my answer out. "Yes."

"Then how do you live with the person afterward? Did he elaborate on that little detail?"

"No, Lucien."

"And what about the fact that if a lot of people hadn't been alert, you might have been raped. Or killed. Did the consequences figure into Hugh Chilmark's lofty theory?"

"Don't." I was ready to cry. "He said that because he knew he was wrong not to go against Mama for you."

He looked into his coffee. "I see. And I can understand why he tried to take the mistakes from his life and translate them into commandments for you. But you took his principle too far. I'm sure he wanted you to consider the consequences. There are always consequences. That's what I wanted to teach you."

He poured himself another cup of coffee. "It may interest you to know that these past few days I've been as miserable as you. I've got myself locked in a room of my own making. And I'll be there until I can figure out where it leaves me because I shot that man! If it takes me the rest of my life."

"But . . ."

He smiled sadly. "But what? I didn't come down on the side of the Union when I killed him, Susan. I came down against the corruption of the South. I'm still a Southerner. My choices aren't as clear-cut as yours. And speaking of choices, what about you? Do you still believe you did right giving away the balloon?"

"I was wrong to go to the riverbank," I said carefully. "I caused you too much trouble. And I wish you could forgive me, Lucien. But I still think I did right with the balloon."

He sighed wearily. "That buggy whip you told Tom I would use on you . . ."

"Lucien, I was just . . ."

"Be quiet and let me finish, please. That mythical buggy whip you invented in my name. If I thought that by using it I could prevent you from causing yourself and others heartache in the future—God's teeth, I would use it, Susan. However, I can't prevent that. Only you can. By learning responsibility."

He looked at me, hesitated a moment and went on carefully. "Your balloon is gone, Susan. I believe you did it out of the conviction that it was right. But now you must find out what I meant by living with the consequences."

My face went white. "What do you mean?"

"Tom and I are old friends. He isn't going to pursue this thing about the girl in boy's clothing. But his colleagues will. They've had too many Federal spies in Richmond to deal with. He suggests that I get you out of town within the week."

Everything seemed to drop inside me. The world came to a standstill.

He cleared his throat. "I'm afraid I'm going to have to send you away, Susan."

I burst into tears. I covered my face with my hands.

"Susan, don't cry like that. Stop, please."

But I couldn't. The world was all wrong, had been for too long now. And I was sure it would never be right again.

"Susan, I'm ashamed of you." His voice was sharp and raspy.

"I don't care."

"Come here, then." He pushed his chair away from the table.

I went to him, sobbing. "Don't send me away, Lucien, please. I want to stay here with you."

"God's teeth, child." He pulled me onto his lap. "You can still say that after the way I've treated you these last few days?"

I buried my face in his shirtfront. "Yes."

He hugged me. There was forgiveness in that hug, no words were needed. He held me on his knee and talked to me in solemn, quiet tones. He didn't want to send me away, he said. He had left home when he was only a little older than I was now. And he knew how terrible it was. But everyone in town was talking about the balloon. It was the subject of editorials in all the papers. So I had to be sent away. At least until things died down.

"Where?" I asked tremulously.

"I don't know, Susan. But it will be a proper place with good people."

"And can I come back and live with you when things die down?"

He smiled with that downward curve to his mouth that was so familiar to me by now. "Yes. I'm going to buy a larger house in a good section of town. But you must consider, Susan, that I will probably never be socially acceptable in Richmond, regardless of who wins or loses the war. Even if I have the money to help rebuild the South afterward."

"Why?"

"Because I haven't fought for the Confederacy," he said quietly.

"I don't care about that, Lucien. If you'll have me I

want to come back and live with you in your large new house in Richmond."

He nodded. And then he spoke of Timothy. He was miserable, he said, because he had sent his dear friend away. "I did to you just what our father did to me, Susan. I knew it was wrong and stupid, but I did it anyway."

Sitting on his knee, my eyes were level with his. "Perhaps Tim can be persuaded to come back," I said carefully.

"No," he said, "no. I threw him out, Susan. Yankees have their pride, too, you know."

"But, Lucien, if Tim knew about our trouble he might want to help."

He only looked more dejected then. "No, no, Susan. This is my problem to resolve. Besides, I couldn't ask."

"Lucien."

He looked at me. He saw the expression on my face and he understood. He sighed. "All right, Susan," he asked patiently, "what did he say to you?"

So I told him. "He said he would come back. When you cooled down."

He grunted. "Oh, he did, did he?"

Chapter Thirty-one

"North," Timothy said. "North!"

We sat at the kitchen table, Timothy and Lucien and me, and we spoke in whispered tones that fitted the occasion. We used candlelight instead of gaslight. It was after midnight of that same day. Lucien had sent Nate with a note to find Timothy and Tim had slipped into town in the dark and gone to the gambling house. I was in bed when Lucien brought him home. I sat in the kitchen wearing my robe over my modest cotton nightgown.

Lucien did not like the idea of North. Lines appeared in his forehead where lines had not been this morning. Deep circles were under his eyes. He looked haunted.

"No," he said. He reached for a piece of ham, then buttered some bread. "That's impossible. I can't send Susan North."

"Why not?" Tim asked casually.

We had not had a chance to be alone. When Lucien summoned me down I'd just stood in our kitchen marveling at Tim's presence. He took off his hat and grinned at me shyly. "Hello, Susan Dobson Chilmark. I hear you've got yourself a parcel of trouble."

"Hello, Timothy Tobias Collier. I hear you've come to help us out." I probably would have stood there staring at him the whole night if Lucien hadn't scowled and told me, sharply, to get Tim something to eat. I felt Tim watching me while I got the ham and biscuits and marmalade from the pantry and made some coffee. And I was painfully conscious of my every move.

The two men smoked and drank brandy while Lucien laid out some of his maps. There was a strain between them. The old easiness, the old teasing with the undercurrent of fondness, was gone. It was different now. Not ruined, as I thought it would be. But different, as Tim had predicted. I felt a sharp pang. Something was lost forever in their friendship.

It had not been easy for Lucien to send that note with Nate summoning Tim back. And Tim knew it. Now they were settling in, eyeing each other, getting a new footing, carrying on a careful minuet, being overly polite one minute and purposely gruff the next. I was so nervous I thought I would scream.

"Because," Lucien answered Tim's question, "it's North, that's why not. I told Susan, and I'll tell you. I may have shot a Confederate, but I'm still a Southerner. I don't want either you or her to think any different."

Tim nodded.

"So I don't like the idea of North, at all."

"Where will you send her, then?" Tim asked.

Lucien bit his white teeth savagely into the bread and ham. "To Charleston, if I have to, with my mother. She's making a trip to see her family."

"Lucien, no!" I turned from the stove where I was watching the bubbling coffeepot. "I don't want to go with Mama!"

Lucien spoke quietly. "I don't remember asking you."

My face flamed, and I turned away. He was re-establishing his authority with me for Timothy's sake. I knew that. We had settled our differences and had no quarrel with each other anymore. But I knew enough not to challenge him.

"Charleston could still fall," Tim reminded him carefully. "Do you want Susan there if that happens?"

Lucien didn't answer. He chewed and swallowed.

Tim winked at me. "Salem County, New Jersey," he said.

Lucien raised his eyes.

"My family," Tim elaborated. "They're proper people, Lucien. You said you wanted her with proper people. They'd love to have Susan stay with them. It would be a fine place for her. It's cool there summers, on my parents' farm. And there are plenty of good things to eat."

The coffee was finished. I took the pot to the table and poured three cups. Was Timothy insane? Lucien would never agree to it! My hand trembled, just thinking on it myself. Tim's family! Could I go there? Would they want me? Would Lucien allow it? I stole a look at him as I sat down with my own cup of coffee. He sipped the hot dark brew, holding the cup close to his face. I could tell he was hurting. Something was bothering him.

"I wanted Susan to go to a decent school," he said.

"My sister attends a fine girls' academy across the river in Philadelphia," Timothy said. "She comes home often on weekends. And I'm never home, Lucien, if that's what you're worried about."

My heart went out to Tim. How dear he was! How considerate of his friend's concerns and feelings.

"And even if I did get home, well, my father is so strict . . ." Tim shrugged and grinned engagingly, blushing. "All you have to do is tell them what you want for Susan and my parents would carry out your instructions."

I held my breath. What was wrong with Lucien? Tim was giving so much ground, pacifying him so. If Lucien didn't start to meet him halfway, the friendship would be lost forever!

"It isn't that," Lucien said finally.

"What is it, then?" Timothy asked cautiously. I could tell he was hurt.

Lucien could barely get the words out. "I'd . . . lose Susan if she went North."

"Lose her? How?"

Lucien didn't answer. But I knew. This was the most difficult part for my brother, the Southern gentleman, to agree to send me North.

"Well, if you don't beat all!" Tim said indignantly. "You're afraid she'll become a Yankee! Well, you have just offended your guest, suh," he said in a mock Southern accent, "and ah will not have it."

Lucien smiled in spite of himself. I relaxed a bit. We all did.

"You're not going to lose Susan," Tim said fervently.

"Don't you know yet how she feels about you?" He looked at me. "Tell him, Susan," he said.

What could I say? How could I manage the right words that would mend what was broken between these two fine people who meant more to me than anybody else in the world? I searched my mind desperately. I had to find the right words! I sensed that only I, the one who had come between them, could make things right again.

"He knows how I feel, Tim," I said. "I was . . . I was a silly little girl, dying to do something for the Cause when we met. You taught me so much, Lucien. You made me see things like I'd never seen them before. Why, when we met it was like . . . like . . ."

"Like two trains colliding," Lucien finished for me.

"Yes." I looked at him gratefully. "And you gave me a home. And you . . . were always there when I got into trouble. Why you . . . even killed for me. I know what that's done to you."

He nodded. "I wanted to give you a proper home, Susan. And now I have to send you away."

"You did your best," I said fervently. "I gave you a terrible time. When I came to you from Mama, I was confused. I'm not confused anymore. Because you helped me. Daddy told me to do what I thought was right, Lucien, but you're the one who made me strong enough to do it."

Nobody looked at anybody for a moment. Lucien sipped his coffee and set his cup down carefully. "So you want to go to Tim's family, then?"

"I don't want to go anywhere," I said firmly. "But you said I have to. So I might as well go there, if it's all right with you."

He looked at Tim gloomily. "There isn't even any mail service."

"No regular mail service," Tim agreed. "But you

know there are people who act as letter carriers and
profit on the war. Sure, they charge a dollar or two a
letter, but they have special passports and the mail gets
through. And I'd sneak you through the lines to visit.
You said it might not even be for a year."

Lucien let out his breath slowly. "How would we get
there?"

Tim was jubilant. "You mean you'll agree to it?"

"I was going to send Susan away to school anyway.
This is just farther away, that's all."

Tim mapped out the route. "Well, all the ports are
blockaded, so that leaves out the water. There is an
open area, right now, just north of Richmond and
southeast of Washington, between Pope's and McClellan's
armies, where contraband can slip through. We'd have
to go on horseback."

"We?" Lucien asked.

"Of course," Timothy said. "I know the route so I
can . . ." He stopped himself, blushing.

Lucien met his eyes. "Not unless I go along, you
don't take her, you cocky, impudent Yankee."

It was all right again! It was going to be all right!
Lucien had started insulting him! I breathed a sigh of
relief.

"Glad to have you along, old friend," Tim said. "All
right, then, we go on horseback, moving north to the
Potomac. I can get Susan a horse from the Yankees if
you want. Then we get a ferry across the Potomac. I
know a ferryboat captain who is sympathetic to the
South. We'd sidestep Baltimore, since it's secessionist,
and ride through Maryland, into Delaware. We can go
through Wilmington and take the ferry across the Delaware right into Salem County."

He finished. He looked at Lucien. There was silence.

"It would be a trip, but I'll get you there safely," he promised.

Lucien nodded. "Do you think you can make the trip, Susan?"

"Yes."

"Perhaps you'd better take Merlin out riding for the next few days to get accustomed to being in the saddle."

"All right," I agreed.

"It would be better if Susan traveled in boy's clothing," Tim suggested.

"Well," Lucien said dryly, "she's an expert at that."

Chapter Thirty-two

I looked up from where I was sitting on the floor in the middle of my room, surrounded with all my earthly possessions, to see my brother standing in the doorway.

"How are you managing, Susan?"

I was not managing. I was exhausted and upset from the sad and draining task of packing. I was physically hurting from riding Merlin two hours every day for the last four days as Lucien had directed. And as I looked around me at the neat and attractive blue-and-white room, the horrible realization was settling over me that I was leaving.

It was an hour after breakfast. We were leaving tomorrow. I was surprised to see Lucien still in the house, for he was dressed to go out to his gambling establishment. He came into the room and looked down at me.

"What, may I ask, is all this?" He stood surveying

the two bulging carpetbags that were filled to the brim with possessions.

I looked up at him. "They're my things, Lucien."

"What *things?*" he enunciated clearly.

"Why, everything I'm taking with me."

"Susan . . ." He looked around him again. He shook his head wordlessly. "I told you that you can't take a lot, didn't I?"

"Yes."

"Then what *is* all this?"

"This isn't a lot, Lucien. Why it's the bare necessities."

"The bare necessities, is it?" He bent over and picked up the two overflowing carpetbags. He tested their weight in his hands. "God's teeth, the horse won't get one mile carrying this once you add your eating utensils and blanket for sleeping." He handed one of the bags to me. "Empty it out so I can see what's in it," he directed.

I sat there stubbornly, near tears, looking up at him.

"Very well, I will, then." He strode over to the bed, set one carpetbag down and started to take the contents out of the other. I scrambled to my feet and ran over to him.

"Lucien, I need all that. You can't not allow me to take it."

"I can't, can't I?" Lingerie, my good cotton night-gown, my extra set of boy's clothing, two dresses and two petticoats came out of one. He reached for the other bag.

"Lucien!"

He continued unpacking, throwing the stuff on the bed. Out came my toilette items, my two towels, the lavender for my clothing, the daguerreotype of my parents and the one of him that Fanny had given me. Out came my silver-backed hairbrush, some precious writing paper and my favorite books.

He finished. The contents of the carpetbags were all over my bed.

We looked at each other. He was scowling and I was starting to cry, my chin quivering. "I need all that," I protested.

"You may need it," he said quietly, "but you cannot have it. This is not a picnic, Susan. This is serious business. We're contraband, traveling through enemy lines. I don't mean to frighten you, but common sense should tell you that we have to travel as lightly as possible so as not to burden the horses."

"But how can I leave my things? It isn't"—my voice broke—"fair."

He looked at me levelly. "I told you there would be consequences, Susan. This is part of them. I'm sorry." He handed me the carpetbag. "Now you may put in it what I tell you to take," he said gently.

He allowed me to fill one bag. Into it went a change of boy's clothing, some underclothes and my hairbrush.

I looked at him beseechingly. "There's room left."

He handed me one towel. Then some soap.

I looked longingly at the two dresses he had bought me, which were rolled up on the bed. Then at the daguerreotypes of my parents and the one of him, each in a silver frame.

"Take your pick," he said, "either one dress or the pictures."

I felt the last reserve of control give way inside me. A tear rolled down my face. He was watching me. "I'll take the pictures," I whispered.

He nodded. "A good choice. If we're stopped and searched no one should know from the contents of the bag that you're a girl." He picked up the daguerreotypes, took them out of the silver frames and handed them to me. "I'll give you money when we get to the

Colliers' to go to Philadelphia with Tim's mother and buy clothes," he said soothingly. "Now we have another matter to discuss. Put that carpetbag down and pay attention to me."

I did so.

He walked across the room to the window and looked out. "Your mother wants to see you before we leave. I promised her I would take you over this evening."

A dozen arguments rose in my throat even while my skin crawled and I felt the panic rising in my chest. "Why?"

"Because"—he turned, half-facing me—"I want you to see her."

"I don't want to."

He turned, fully, to look at me. "Are you giving me an argument?"

With the harsh light of morning directly on his face, I saw how tired he was. He hadn't looked anything but tired, I realized, since that morning in this room when Sarah had announced that the detective was downstairs. He was worried, I knew, about the impending trip, about leaving me with Tim's family, about everything. An argument now was the last thing he needed. He knew it and he knew that I knew it.

"No, I'm not giving you an argument, Lucien."

"Good. Then we go this evening. I saw Charlotte the other day and I told her I was sending you to school in Virginia. That is the story I am telling everyone. Charlottesville, Virginia. There is a good girls' school there and it's where Fanny's married sister lives with her husband and children. He's a lawyer. Respectable people. When Charlotte heard you were leaving she asked to see you. As your mother, she has that right."

I nodded.

He started for the door. "Put these things away," he said.

"Can I see Connie before I go?"

He hesitated. "No, Susan. I'd rather you didn't."

"But I must say good-bye! She's my friend!"

"You may write to her after forwarding your letters to Fanny's sister in Charlottesville."

"You mean, I can't even tell Connie where I'm going?"

"That's exactly what I mean, Susan. She is your friend. The detectives may be questioning her. It is your duty to protect her as well as yourself. You must lie to Connie and pretend you are in Charlottesville."

"I've already invited her over this afternoon," I blurted out.

He turned. "Then send a note and uninvite her."

"No!"

He took out his pocket watch and checked the time, then raised his eyes to look at me. "I beg your pardon?" he said quietly.

"Please, Lucien. Anyway, Connie knows."

"Knows *what?*"

I held my breath. "She knows I was going to give away the balloon. I told her before I did it."

"You told her?" He leveled a scowling glance at me.

"Yes, I thought you knew that."   •

"Since you didn't do me the honor of divulging your plans about the balloon to me, Susan, how would I?" He sighed. "You didn't tell her where you are going, I hope?"

"No."

"Thank heavens for small favors. Very well, she may come this afternoon for a brief visit. I have to have a meeting with my business partner this morning. He's just back from England. He'll be keeping an eye on my interests while I'm gone, allegedly to take my sister

away to school. I don't want you alone too long with
Connie. Bring her into my office. I'll want a word with
her myself, now that you've told me she knows about
the balloon."

"All right, Lucien. Thank you. But what if Mr.
Simkins looks for me in Charlottesville and I'm not there?"

"Tom Simkins owes me a lot of money, Susan." He
turned halfway out the door and smiled. "I'm not
pressing for payment. He's in charge of the investigation which he has to go through the motions of conducting
to keep the newspapers and the citizens of Richmond
happy. A lot of people donated dresses for that balloon.
And, as I recall, the Ladies' Defense Association helped
pay for it. Tom will say in his reports that he is keeping
an eye on you in Charlottesville. No one will doubt his
word. I have his promise that he won't allow his people
to devote their lives to pursuing this investigation.
Fortunately they have other things to keep them busy."

The look he gave me was kindly now. "Tom never
asked me where I was really sending you, Susan. The
man likes to gamble. Thank whatever gods you know
that he has a weakness for it."

"I'll miss you so," Connie said. "I do think it's
mean of old Lucien to send you away." She sniffled as
we sat on the edge of my bed.

"He doesn't want to. He has to. Everyone is awfully
put out about the balloon, Connie. And my brother is
miffed that I told you about it. We haven't much time,
and he wants me to bring you downstairs so he can talk
to you about it."

"I'll never tell! I'll keep your secret until my death!
I'll promise old Lucien that, too. But I'm glad the thing
is gone. Only now you'll be gone, too." Tears came to
her eyes.

I fell silent.

"But, oh, I forgot, I've brought you something."
She ran to fetch the book she'd brought along. She took
something out of it and put it in my hands.

"Connie!" I gasped. It was the handkerchief from
the Prince of Wales. "But it's your most precious
possession!"

"I want you to have it. Take it as a pledge that I will
never tell anyone about the balloon. I want you to show
it to Lucien, too."

I nodded, and we hugged each other and cried. I
promised to write to her, feeling terrible about lying to
her about my destination. Would she ever forgive me
for lying when the truth came out someday? I was
starting to understand those consequences Lucien had
spoken of. I hoped that being forced to leave my
precious possessions behind and lying to Connie would
be the worst part. But somehow I knew better.

Lucien sent me upstairs twice to fix myself over
before we left for Mama's that evening. First it was my
dress that didn't suit him. I was wearing an old green.

"Where's the pretty flowered one I gave you, the one
that so enamored Tom Simkins? The one that so bewitched
Timothy?"

I blushed. "My new dresses are crushed because I
was packing them to take," I said.

"I saw Sarah ironing them earlier. Come, Susan,
what's the real reason you won't wear one? Are you
still afraid of displeasing Charlotte?"

When I didn't answer he sipped his coffee. We had
just finished supper. "Go and put one of them on," he
ordered quietly.

I went upstairs and put on the pink organdie dress.

When I came down again he cast an expert eye over me
"That's better, but what have you done to your hair?"

I had parted it in the middle and taken it up in a sma
bun in back in an attempt to show Mama how I ha
matured.

"Go and take it down, Susan. Wear it loose, the wa
you usually do. I don't understand you. You don't wan
to look your age in your attire but you want to look like
a spinster with your hair. Now what is it?"

"Mama . . . is going to be dressed in genteel povert
if I know her," I stammered.

He looked at me over his newspaper. "Let her be
She's patriotic. Neither of us is. Why pretend? Now g
and take your hair down, please."

"But I'll look so childish!"

"Do it, Susan."

I turned to go. "Oh, Susan," he called after me
"how many petticoats do you have on?"

I couldn't believe the question! But I answered. "Two."

"Put on another one. I like skirts that"—he gesture
with his hand—"billow."

Billow! So now I had to billow! I ran up the stairs
not daring to speculate on how he knew so much abou
what women wore.

On the front steps of Mama's house my courag
deserted me and I got pale and my legs went weak
Lucien noticed. We were at the door, waiting for it t
open. He smiled. "She can't hurt you anymore," he said

The door opened and Rhody stood there. "Lawd
child. Hello, Mr. Lucien, come on in."

Lucien was wrong. It hurt me just to step into th
foyer. I had forgotten how large and elegant it was
Memories overwhelmed me. I felt attacked by the past

Then Rhody enfolded me in her arms, old Rhody who could see no harm in what my daddy had done.

"Oh, Miz Susan, it's so good to see you again!"

How different she was from the confident, dignified Sarah! My face flamed. I didn't want her to hug me. I was finished with all this, couldn't she see? If she held me like that I'd go back, slipping into a hole. I pulled away. She took Lucien's hat and escorted us to the front parlor.

She left us there. I sat, fidgeting. My heart hammered inside me, my palms sweated. Lucien leaned back in his chair and crossed his legs nonchalantly.

"This is her way of telling us we don't belong," I whispered. "The front parlor is for people who don't stay."

"That suits me fine," he said.

"I won't stay one damn minute if she's mean."

"Stop fidgeting. And where did you get that language? From Wilium, I suppose."

I nodded. "It slipped out."

"Well, kindly see that it doesn't slip out again."

"Do I have to kiss her?"

"You don't have to do anything you don't want to do, except be respectful and remember your manners. She is still your mother."

"You don't know what being here is doing to me. I expect to see Daddy walk through that door any minute."

"I half wish he would. I'd give you back to him with my compliments."

I made a face at him, but before he could respond Mama was in the doorway. Lucien got to his feet. Mama was taken aback for only a second, seeing us. "Well, I do declaa-ah, you are heah, aren't you?"

The familiar voice grated on my nerves, bringing back a hundred memories.

"Lucien?" She gave him an icy smile.

"Good evening, madam," Lucien said. He gave a little bow.

"You do look well. But then you always do. Susan?"

I had gotten up, too. She pecked my cheek and went to sit down. She was wearing her old blue percale and looked as ravishing as ever in it. Her hair was getting white around the temples but that only added to her beauty.

"Deah, it has been a scorcher today. Rhody will bring some lemonade presently. How are you, Susan?"

"I'm fine, Mama."

Her eyes went over me from head to toe. "I was so busy at the hospital I couldn't get to see you when you were ill. But then I knew you were in good hands. That dress is lovely. Where did you get it?"

"Lucien bought it for me."

"Of course, it must have come from a blockade-runner. Am I correct?" She turned a cold gaze on Lucien.

He met it, nodded and smiled. She turned back to me. "Come heah, Susan. It's been a long time since I've seen anything new. I must see how it's made."

I cast Lucien a pleading glance, but he gestured toward her ever so slightly with his head. I went and stood in front of her obligingly while she examined the pink organdie dress with the lace inserts on the yoke and the rose-colored ribbons on the skirt.

"Well, it's in very good taste. You are to be complimented, Lucien."

He nodded at her.

"Now," she patted the settee, "come and sit next to me. Ah, heah's the lemonade."

The ice-cold glass felt good in my hands. I drank the sweet liquid greedily. The business with the dress had unnerved me. I felt like a pawn between Mama and

Lucien. And I realized that my brother had known it would be this way, all along.

"Have you been practicing your piano?" she asked.

I shook my head no.

"Why evah not? Is Lucien spoiling you so?"

"I don't have a piano," Lucien explained. "I realize that part of Susan's education has been neglected. However, I've sent for one from England. My business partner just ordered one when he was there. It will be in my new house when Susan returns from school in the spring."

I couldn't stand this much more. I was near tears.

"Well, I miss you around heah, Susan," she said. "No one has played our piano since you left. You look surprised. Are you?"

I lowered my eyes and nodded.

"Answer properly, Susan," Lucien ordered quietly.

I gulped and did so. "Yes," I said.

She smiled at Lucien, then at me. "Well, I see you've learned to mind, haven't you, Susan? I suppose things turned out for the best, didn't they? I still miss you, though. I know you find that hard to believe. I know you think I hate you and have done horrible things to you."

She sipped her lemonade and fanned herself. "I do not hate you, Susan. I nevah have. When you grow up and have children of your own, you'll realize how difficult it is. And then, you weren't that easy to handle. I dare say, you don't try half the things with Lucien that you tried with me."

She leaned back on the settee. "We've all done horrible things to each other in this family. Oh, deah, I am getting sentimental. And that's nevah good. I know I'm not perfect. I don't pretend to be. But you are my child, Susan, and you are a beautiful child. Isn't she beautiful, Lucien?''

He nodded. ''She is getting more beautiful every day,'' he said indulgently.

''You'll be having your troubles soon with the boys, Lucien.''

''I've had a fair taste of it already, Charlotte.''

''Really?'' she gasped. ''Have you a beau, Susan?''

I shrugged. ''I suppose you could say that.''

''Who is he?'' she inquired innocently.

I glanced quickly at Lucien.

''He's away with the army,'' Lucien said.

''My, you must be so proud of him,'' Mama cooed.

I didn't know what to say. I sat, tongue-tied. Lucien sipped his lemonade. The ice clinking in his glass was the only sound in the room.

''And now you are going away,'' she breathed. ''Lucien says it's a fine family you'll be staying with in Charlottesville. I offered to take you to Charleston if he wanted you in a good school. Did your brother tell you?''

''No, he didn't, Mama.''

''But he said no. He thinks Charleston is in danger. And I do suppose he is right. Oh, the whole world's gone mad. I've seen so much sickness and dying in the hospital, nothing makes sense anymoah.'' She took out her handkerchief and sniffed. ''Well, I am so glad you could come by this evening, Susan. I did so want to see you before you left.'' She got up and walked across the room, touching things.

''I have an engagement this evening and I must be leaving soon. So why don't you come and kiss me good-bye, Susan.''

It was so abrupt I didn't know what to do. Lucien nodded at me. I got up and went to her.

She took my hands in her own. ''Be good, Susan.

You always were a Yankee at heart, you know. Don't do anything to get in trouble in Charlottesville.''

The color rose to my face. Her old words, coming at me now, did not hurt anymore. When she spoke of Yankees now I thought of Timothy.

"Well"—she looked at my hands—"mind your brother. You always did have such slender hands. So fragile. It isn't easy being a woman, Susan. It's all fragile. All of it. Make the best of it. But don't go giving your heart to just anyone.''

She hesitated, looking down at my hands, which she held in her own. "I loved Hugh Chilmark when I married him. I want you to know that.''

I nodded.

"And I love you.''

The words were like a thunderclap in my ears. I was not sure that I heard right. But the look on her face told me I had.

"Oh, Mama.'' I looked at her and I felt that the expression on my face was like that of a wounded deer. I felt naked and bleeding. I felt as if I needed a place to hide and there was no place in the whole world.

She took me in her arms. Her slender, fragile arms held me so tight I thought I would die. I should say something, I knew. But I could not get the words out. This was unfair to me! That was all I could think of. It was unfair of her to wait till now to tell me she loved me.

In the next instant she released me and moved away. "Well, I must go upstairs and get dressed for my engagement. Lucien?''

He got to his feet.

"Thank you for bringing Susan. Do let me know that you have arrived in Charlottesville safely and everything is all right.''

"I will, Charlotte, of course.''

"You must write to me occasionally, Susan," she said. "Rhody will see you out."

And she was gone. I stood dazed. I hugged my arms in front of me, closed my eyes and bent over as if in pain. Then I felt Lucien beside me.

"Are you all right?"

"Oh, Lucien!"

"Come on." He put his arm around me, and without waiting for Rhody, he guided me through the elegant foyer, out of our mother's house.

Chapter Thirty-three

So I was going.

I stood in my boy's clothing in my room in Lucien's house and looked around at the familiar things, my things, that I could not take with me, my childhood toys and dolls that were on my bed and in the corner, the rest of my books and clothing, all the old familiar possessions that had made up my life until now. It was dark outside. Downstairs Timothy was in the parlor with Lucien having a brandy.

"You behave yourself now," Sarah said to me.

I nodded mutely.

"You mind Mr. Lucien on this trip. And when you get there, mind those people you'll be living with. You'll be back before you know it. And when you get back we'll be in Mr. Lucien's new house. And you won't have to be ashamed of where you're living."

I looked at her. Had she never understood? "I've

never been ashamed of living here,'' I said. ''This has been more home to me than anywhere.''

She nodded, satisfied. ''Been nice having you. Now I'll kiss you good-bye. You have a long ride tonight. You better get started.'' She came forward and kissed me, held me, smiled and patted my hands, then turned and walked out.

I was free to go. Sarah had brought me to this house and now I had her blessing to leave. I looked around the room again, the room that had become so dear to me, and I knew that I would cry for it many a night in New Jersey.

And for Lucien. I didn't even want to contemplate the moment when I would have to say good-bye to him. He and Tim were planning on spending some time with Tim's family after we got there. But the inevitable moment would come when I would have to put my arms around my brother and say good-bye. How would I bear it? How would he? And what about saying good-bye to Tim?

I went over to my dressing table and touched some things. I smoothed the bed. There was a knock on the door and it opened.

''Susan?'' It was my brother. He was dressed in his rough working clothes and boots, and he held his slouch hat in his hands. ''It's time,'' he said.

Under the jacket I saw that he was wearing his Colt pistol. And I knew that a musket was strapped onto his horse. I had seen it in the yard. Timothy had a musket too.

''I'll be right down,'' I said.

He nodded and left.

I took one last look around, then I turned off the gaslight.

My fears enveloped me like the dark. I was going away from all I knew, to a strange country. North.

Yankee land. For a moment all the old Southern hatred and fears rose in my throat. Yankees had killed my daddy. They had killed Kenneth. I was leaving the South, my home. I had known good people here. Daddy and Rhody and Wilium. Mrs. Harrold who took in privates. Tom McPherson for whom I had made the sour soup. Connie, who had given me her handkerchief from the Prince of Wales and who had thrown her arms around my brother and sworn she would keep my secret to the death. Kenneth, who had been my only brother until Lucien came along and who was now buried under a tree in Richmond's Hollywood Cemetery. Sarah, who had taken me in. Nate. Fanny, who had supported Lucien in everything he wanted to do for me. The girls at Lulie Ballard's.

And Lucien, in whose arms I had sobbed in the carriage on the way home from Mama's house. Lucien, who had hushed me while I stained his shirtfront and silk cravat with my tears. Who picked up the pieces every time I made a mess of things.

I would take some of each of them North, where the snow piled high in winter, Tim had told me. North, where people had said to their sister states, "We will not allow this to go on. You have strayed too far from the idea of what this country is about. We must bring you back into line."

I was going North to find out what it meant to be a Yankee brat.

Could I live with the consequences of my actions? I didn't know. But I would find out.

I went out of the room and started down the stairway. Outside a horse whinnied. Probably my horse, the Yankee horse of spotted gray with the huge wondering eyes that Lucien had bought for me.

Halfway down the stairs I saw them waiting for me.

Lucien was in front of Tim, scowling up, his hat in his hand, the expression on his face impatient, about to say something about my lollygagging. And behind him was Timothy, grinning his impudent Yankee grin, looking at me, too, his eyes shining.

I stopped. "What do you think? How do I look? I like those old clothes of yours that I used to wear better, Lucien. I wish you hadn't made Nate burn them."

"Put on your hat," he said.

I put it on and pushed my hair under it as it had been the first day we met. He was watching me carefully and I saw in his eyes that he was remembering, too. Those eyes went over me. His face went soft. "Come on, let's go," he directed. His voice was gentle.

Over his head Tim winked at me. I scampered down the rest of the stairs, filled with the warmth of Timothy's wink and the promise in his shining eyes as I followed them out into the dark.

Bibliography

Much has been written about the American Civil War, a time period of our history that captivates the imagination of almost everyone. I could not have begun to approach this vast and overwhelming subject without extensive research and reading. The books and periodicals I found most helpful for the time period of my novel (1861–1862) are listed below with many thanks to the authors who so painstakingly did the original research.

Alfriend, Edward M. "Social Life in Richmond During the War." *Cosmopolitan*, 1891. Courtesy of the Library of Virginia, Richmond.

Botkin, B. A. *A Civil War Treasury of Tales, Legends and Folklore*. New York: Random House, 1960.

Catton, Bruce. *The Civil War*. New York: American Heritage Press, 1960, 1971.

Commager, Henry Steele, ed. *The Blue and the Gray*. Vol. 1. New York: New American Library, 1950, 1973.

Confederate Museum. *Illustrated Guide to Richmond, the Confederate Capital*. Richmond, Va.: The William Byrd Press, 1960.

Crouch, Tom D. *The Eagle Aloft, Two Centuries of the Balloon in America*. Washington, D.C.: Smithsonian Institution Press, 1983.

Cullen, Joseph P. "The Battle of Malvern Hill." *Civil War Times Illustrated* 5, no. 2 (May 1966).

Dew, Charles B. *Ironmaker to the Confederacy, Joseph R. Anderson and the Tredegar Iron Works*. New Haven, Conn.: Yale University Press, 1966.

The Dictionary of American Fighting Ships. U.S. Navy Department Series. 1970.

Garrett, Elisabeth Donaghy. *The Antiques Book of Victorian Interiors*. New York: Crown Publishers, 1974.

Griess, Thomas E., ed. *The American Civil War*. The West Point Military History Series. Wayne, N.J.: Avery Publishing Group, 1987.

Harper's Weekly. Reprints: vol. 5, no. 253, November 2, 1861; vol. 5, no. 261, December 28, 1861; vol. 6, no. 262, January 4, 1862; vol. 6, no. 271, March 8, 1862.

Jones, Katharine M., ed. *Heroines of Dixie: Spring of High Hopes*. St. Simons Island, Ga.: Mockingbird Books, 1955.

———. *Ladies of Richmond, Confederate Capital*. New York: Bobbs-Merrill.

Ketchum, Richard M., ed. *The American Heritage Picture Dictionary of the Civil War*. New York: American Heritage, 1960.

Long, E. B., with Long, Barbara. *The Civil War Day by Day: An Almanac, 1861–1865*. New York: Da Capo Press, 1971.

Mitchell, Adele. "James Keith Boswell: Jackson's Engineer." *Civil War Times Illustrated* 7, no. 3 (June 1968).

Pember, Phoebe Yates. *A Southern Woman's Story, Life in Confederate Richmond*. Edited by Bell I. Wiley. St. Simons Island, Ga.: Mockingbird Books, 1982.

Ray, Frederic. "As the Civil War Artist Saw Himself." *Civil War Times Illustrated* 6, no. 5 (August 1967).

Shaara, Michael. *The Killer Angels*. New York: Ballantine Books, 1980.

Thomas, Emory M. *The Confederate Nation: 1861–1865*. New York: Harper & Row, Harper Torchbooks, 1979.

————. *The Confederate State of Richmond, A Biography of the Capital*. Austin: University of Texas Press.

Acknowledgments

A historical novel is not a lone undertaking. In doing research one must seek the help of librarians, historical societies, scholarly writers, museum curators and sometimes local history buffs and reenactors. These people all act behind the scenes, preserving the papers, writing the factual books, documenting the evidence, guarding the records and serving as guides as we pick our way through the past. They are the "keepers of the flame" of history. Here are some of the ones who contributed their guidance, interest and patience to my book.

For their eager assistance, the staff of the Virginia Historical Society in Richmond, Virginia. In appreciation for sharing their treasures, thanks to the staff of the Museum of the Confederacy and the Valentine Museum, also in Richmond.

For his interest and encouragement, Daniel P. George, fire chief at Fire Headquarters on Perry Street in Trenton, New Jersey, where the Meredith Havens Fire/Civil War Museum is housed. Thanks to Chief George, also, for lending me his phonograph records on which were priceless interviews with Civil War veterans.

For sharing his knowledge with me, a special thanks goes to Edward McQuinn of Port Reading, New Jersey, a member of the 7th Regiment, Virginia Cavalry Reenactment Group.

For the use of his extensive library on U.S. military history, I thank my son Ron, to whom I owe a special debt for "turning me on" to American history in the first place. My appreciation goes to Ron also for researching certain facts in the way that only a military historian can. I am indebted to him, too, for finding those special books for me at the Firestone Library in Princeton, New Jersey.

For my husband, Ron, and my daughter, Marcella, I am grateful for patience and understanding, especially during those times when I was so engrossed in the book I couldn't look up when they came into the room. No writer can complete a manuscript without the support of his or her family.

For his enthusiasm, interest and invaluable assistance, I owe a heap of thanks to Dr. William C. Wright of Trenton, author of *The Secession Movement in the Middle Atlantic States*. Dr. Wright was never too busy to answer a question, share his expertise on the Civil War era, offer suggestions, encourage me to think things through or just listen when I needed to talk. He was the one who, when I got stuck, mapped out the route that Susan and Lucien and Timothy would take North. He served as historical consultant for the book and, because of him, I do not have the Confederate general Joe Johnston leading the right wing of the army instead of the left.

My eternal appreciation, of course, goes to my editor, Margery Cuyler of Holiday House, Inc., who encouraged me to write this book, with a note of thanks for her indulgence with the finished manuscript. Special thanks also goes to her boss, John Briggs, owner of Holiday House, who, for some strange reason, continues to publish me.

Finally, all through the writing, from cold winter nights next to the wood stove to midsummer sessions on my screened-in porch, I had one faithful companion and source of support sitting by my typewriter. I'd like to offer my wholehearted appreciation to Tabitha the cat.

Ann Rinaldi
August 15, 1987

ABOUT THE AUTHOR

ANN RINALDI is an award-winning columnist for *The Trentonian*, a New Jersey-based newspaper, as well as the author of several highly praised young adult novels, including *But in the Fall I'm Leaving*, *The Good Side of My Heart*, and *Time Enough for Drums*, an ALA Best Book for Young Adults.

Ann Rinaldi lives in New Jersey with her husband. They have two grown children.